I0578454

QUANTUM RIDGE

DAVID VALSORDA

This first edition published in Australia in 2019 by:

Prahran Publishing
P.O. Box 2041, Prahran, Victoria, 3181

© Copyright David Valsorda 2019

David Valsorda has asserted his legal and moral right under the Copyright Act 1968 to be identified as the author of this work.

Published by arrangement with Prahran Publishing, Australia.

All rights reserved.

No part of this publication may be reproduced, stored in a retrieval system or transmitted, in any form or by any other means, without the publisher's prior permission in writing.

This book is sold subject to the condition that it shall not, by way of trade or otherwise, be lent, resold, hired out or otherwise circulated without the publisher's prior consent in any form of binding or cover other than that in which it is published and without similar condition, including this condition, being imposed on the subsequent purchaser.

Every reasonable effort has been made to trace copyright holders of material reproduced in this book, but if any have been inadvertently overlooked the publishers would be glad to hear from them. The story, all names, characters, and incidents portrayed in this book are fictitious. No identification with actual persons past or present, places, buildings, and products is intended or should be inferred.

ISBN 978-1-922-2632-0-9 Paperback
ISBN 978-1-922-2632-1-6 Hardcover
ISBN 978-1-922-2632-2-3 eBook

Cover Photography Daniel Sortino
Illustrations Getty Images & Adobe Stock

A catalogue record for this book is available from the National Library of Australia

Quantum Ridge

by

David Valsorda

For my boy. Never be afraid to try.

We'll break out the popcorn in 15 or so years.

Acknowledgements

First and foremost, Dad, thank you for your laptop. When undertaking this endeavour it took about three weeks to realise my handwriting delusions were just plain ridiculous. When I did, you did not hesitate a second to hand over your Mac *(I hope you know it's gone for good now, sorry)*. To Blair, Lucie, and Carol, for giving the very definition of useful and constructive criticism. To Aaron, for reading every draft in about three days, then clearing your schedule for lunch. To Inez, for your differing *(but often on-point)* perspective. To Chappas, for your initial enthusiasm whilst I spewed ideas all over the whiteboard at 10 station. To Jim, Theo, and Ange for not laughing at my very first words. To Schmidty, for the German help. To Sorts, for the cover art. To Matthew, for making reading fun when it mattered. And last but not least, to my gorgeous wife Georgie, for your unwavering support and encouragement for me to take on whatever harebrained idea I think of next.

Hell, this book-writing thing was harder than I thought.

Prologue

Location: .... 39.1138° N, 76.7268° W
Present day name: .... Fort Meade, Maryland,
.... United States
IDTF Classification: . Ridge
Date: .... April 16th 2017

NSA Junior-Analyst Rebecca Cain sunk her head into her palms. Rubbing her blood-shot eyes, she used an elbow to sweep yet another manila folder off the boardroom table. Landing on a pile of at least 20 others it slid down to the floor next to a pair of flats she had kicked off earlier. Fighting to restrain a yawn she tilted her head back to view the flip-down clock behind her.

That couldn't be the time.

In tune with the detention-era timepiece she could feel both her will, and her eyelids dropping, flap-by-flap, blink-by-blink.

To describe tonight as just another long night in the office was the kind of shit she was comfortable letting her 1am-self shovel. Now, with the sun due to rise somewhere beyond her four walls, she was well into the realm of hallucinatory despair. The clock flipped over to 06:00:00, its six black paddles falling not quite in unison. *Goddamn, it was going to be an even longer morning.*

Cain's body rocked forward, her neck dragging behind like a slingshot. Elbows to timber veneer, she caught her chin, and took a second to survey the basement meeting room in which she sat. The air smelled stale, like dry saliva. There were no windows, and the one door opposite her was painted the same beige colour as the walls. It was locked, she knew, she had tried it earlier. Fluorescents burned white overhead, playing a cruel game of 'see what we can wilt first' – her soul, or the single, sorry-looking indoor-plant to her left. Ahead, columns of paper were stacked so high she could barely see her other colleagues. There were six of them in total, necks craned down, buried in books.

All of them had been sequestered for this supposedly high-priority, time-critical task. Those columns, the ones blocking her vision, were made up of hundreds of historically themed academic papers – journals, reports and theses written by some of the most respected professors alive today.

Cain had few details of why she was reading, but there had been gossip among the group. Apparently the late night readathon was somehow connected to the drama transpiring in Israel. 'Dr Susan Ashbury's dig', 'a bombing', 'assets down'... that was about the extent of the murmurings that had permeated through to them on the back of the mobile coffee cart.

What little Cain did know was that someone within the government was looking to fill positions and fill them fast. Her group was tasked with finding, vetting and recommending a new historical consultant for someone high on up the food chain.

The brief though was bizarre. While the government was searching for someone who could recite documented events and dates verbatim, they had also requested someone with ideas on 'past potentialities' as well as known actualities.

"Strange..." she spoke more to herself than anyone in particular. "Why would anyone need advice on events that never happened?"

A pimply-faced colleague opposite her looked up at the interruption, his eyes just visible over a stack. "Who cares?"

Cain rolled her own. *Idiot.* She picked up her next journal. Curiously, this one had been stamped with a large red 'PRIORITY' across its front. She looked at her wrist-watch; the Mickey Mouse hands on it had stopped at 3.25. She sighed and flicked open the first page... *priority my ass.*

The 'Life without Leaders' series.
Volume 4 – Adolf Hitler: A Counterfactual Hypothesis of Post WWI Europe.
Authored by Associate Professor Jacob Atlas Roy, Oxford University.

Cain scanned the first page. Immediately the paper felt different.

Page 1 Table of Contents.
I.   Somme 1916, or Ypres 1918 – The Allies kill Hitler in WWI.
II...

She pushed herself upright. This could be promising.

Chapter 1

Location: . . . . 48.1351 N, 11.5820 E
Present day name: . . . . Munich, Germany
IDTF Classification: . Tear Four
Date: . . . . Unknown
Time probability: 4% 1515–1565, 6% 1800–1850,
. . . . 53% 1898–1948, 24% 1949–1999,
. . . . 7% 2000–present

Shadows bled into black, spilling from a sea of pine.

Mason sucked in a breath. The forest, it was a stark contrast to the neon glow of modern day Munich. Darkness ran like ink down his throat, cooling his chest. The temperature had dropped 20 degrees in an instant. The air too tasted different; it felt sharper, crisper, than the city smog, smacking on his black lips with a farmland bite.

Emergence, no amount of preparation could prepare the mind for the split-second jolt. Through a Tear, sight, sound, atmosphere... the feel of the world; it was all instantly different. Mason bristled; a familiar tingle tickled his spine. It was his fourth 'visit', yet the tingle remained as his body's way of pinching itself.

'Visit', it was a simple enough term, one he reflected on as he waited for his pupils to dilate. History, sure it may ultimately judge them harshly for the work they were doing, but now, for the sake of his conscience, that was how he would classify tonight.

Unlike his team's first three visits, this fourth Tear was unique. There was an extra level of anxiety in the unknown, an extra level of danger beyond the darkness... this was the first Tear thus far through which the team was fully expecting a hostile reception.

Support technicians back in the 'Ridge' had run the numbers and predicted with more certainty than ever an approximate time destination. A 50-year window that had included two world wars meant that it was entirely possible the Tear could lead them straight into the middle of a firefight. Secretly Mason welcomed the potential. He was a Captain, a Ranger, forged in the fire of the 75th. In what was a prestigious regiment he was considered an anomaly. Men his age weren't supposed to be kicking in doors, or heads.

He crouched low, a cushion of undergrowth felt soft under foot, padding a single bent knee. His rifle was pressed firmly against his shoulder as he scanned the shadows. Slowly, as his eyes adjusted, an ominous-looking woodland materialised. Tall spindly trunks reached up into the night, their leafless lower branches like widowed fingers clutching for anyone stupid enough to stray. The canopy above hid most of the stars, but the light of an almost full moon filtered down through the branches, illuminating sections of the brush like macabre spotlights.

The forest looked clear... for now.

In among the trees the remainder of his team awaited his orders. They were an odd bunch, thrown together on the fly – like some sort of international A-Team. Mason snapped from left to right, a silent upheld fist broke into commands. He watched his team fan out among the trees like panthers through the night, their black body armour glistening with streaks of reflected white-blue light. He ran a hand through his beard and took a moment to think.

Before all else – namely the 'search and destroy' – he needed to secure the scene of emergence for the arrival of Bravo team, his academic ball and chain. Their absence at this early stage meant that the next required task, of identifying 'when' the hell his team was, was also now on him to figure out.

Fuck this. He was grumpy about this one. Time destinations and choice ramifications, it was specifically the shit that Dr Ashbury got paid for.

Aside from the 53 percent probability window, Support back in the Ridge had worked the due diligence on a number of plausible options to help him. They had provided information on the Franco Prussian war, Luther's Reformation, those crazy Anabaptists at Münster and Napoleon at Waterloo.

Mason could appreciate the prep, but in his mind he needed biographies, not event overviews. With each Tear it was becoming clearer that these visits were about men, not events.

Munich, Germany. There was only one name that dominated his conscience. *They may as well have locked in 100 percent for '89 to '45. One man's 56-year legacy of terror.*

His team were in agreement. They were all so sure of why they had been sent through this fourth Tear that they didn't even gamble among themselves as usual. If someone was willing to leave it all behind, life as they knew it, there was no way they were wasting their one chance at travel on a left field option.

Mason was sure of it... *It had to be 'him'.*

He and his team were standing in a forest outside of Munich all because someone, at sometime, somehow, had seen fit to write their own universe... and they were going to use history's public enemy number one to do it.

Chapter 2

Location: .... 51.5074° N, 0.1278° W
Present day name: .... London, England
IDTF Classification: . Ridge
Time: .... April 17th 2017

"Sir, if you could travel back to any place or event in time, which would you choose?"

It was junk time at the end of the lecture, and Professor Jacob Roy knew most of his students were taking philosophy also, so the question didn't surprise him. Still he'd play dumb. "Last time I checked Mr Peterson, time travel wasn't possible, something about needing a flux capacitor?"

Hardly a single look of recognition greeted him from among the lecture theatre crowd. "OK, you're all a bit young for that one. How about that issue of killing your grandfather. Isn't that what's holding us back?"

A few front row faces dropped.

"Hypothetically sir, come on throw us a bone. I have a little bet going on." The student named Peterson pressed.

Roy relented. "OK, give me a second." Leaning on his lectern, assuming an overly theatrical thinking pose, he rested one hand on his chin. The wooden dais creaked under his tall but slim frame. He looked up into the darkened crowd, squinting his smoky green-blue eyes into the glare of the theatre spotlights. Those eyes, staunch yet inviting, were his most prominent feature. Even now, half-closed, and flanked by the first signs of crow's feet, they pierced the room.

The overly dramatic pause had some purpose. He needed time to think of a more appropriate, more scholastic response, rather than what, or who, was currently occupying his mind. He had known his personal answer as soon as the question was asked, but he couldn't give it to these kids. To answer that he would travel back to meet his wife again for the first time would only elicit a bunch of groans.

Hey guys, I'd really like to meet my wife again... *Tragic.*

No, he needed another, more vanilla response. These first-years had a special ability to make anyone in front of a lectern feel extraordinarily old; he didn't need to be giving them any more ammunition. They had already had more than enough fun with one running joke this semester, something about a patch of salt that was springing up above his sideburns. 'Outback Ash' they called him — apparently it was a 'Just for Men' colour... *Cheeky shits.*

"Mr Peterson, considering this semester was completely geared toward powerful individuals, and their influence on the course of history, it would be remiss of me to not put my money where my mouth is, and travel to visit one of them." Roy tapped at his chin. "It's a hard choice though... The potential for a nice sit-down meal would be good. You know, hard stool, dry bread, vinegar wine..." A sly smile now, he could see some of his brighter students clicking. "Yep. I think I would go back and grab myself a seat at the last big feed. Break bread with the mystery man, and answer some of the biggest questions the world never got to ask, like 'who's your daddy?' And 'can I have a carpentry apprenticeship?'" It was a fun but also semi-serious answer. Roy would love to have known if there was something otherworldly about the man, rather than him being just a nice guy with 12 close friends. "Or…" he held up a finger. "Maybe I'd go back to last night, have another three pints and call in sick today."

The room broke out into a murmur of discussion. Both answers sounded equally topical, half the room it seemed was hung-over. Roy gave them a second. "All right, all right. Quiet down. Mr Peterson, I'm assuming you only asked me though, so that then I would reciprocate, so please, if you would, regale us with your thoughts."

Peterson looked around to make sure he had the room's attention. Roy realised he was right; the initial question had indeed been a ruse. He cocked a knowing eyebrow; the kid was a rower, not one who would be troubling the scorers at Mensa, this should be fun.

"Well, personally sir, I have felt this semester you may have focused the material a little too heavily on these…" Peterson threw up some air quotations, "…'make-believe' religious guys. How do we know that if you travelled back they would even be there?"

Really? Jesus… It was fitting blasphemy, but not at all religiously affiliated, just a by-product of an Irish family. … *Would they even be there?* Clearly Peterson had not been listening all year, because his class actually had little to do with the mythical attributes of said men, just whether or not they existed and were indeed influential.

Peterson was still talking though. "…Surely the single most influential man in history that affects our world today is big Adolf? If we could travel back, don't we have an obligation to do something about him? Imagine what the world would be like if he had never existed?" Peterson looked around seemingly chuffed with his own response and cliffhanger question.

Roy let the 'big Adolf' comment slide. Unbeknown to Mr Peterson, he certainly had imagined a history without Hitler. He had in fact written many a paper on just that type of hypothetical world war possibility.

"What would the world be like if he had won?" Roy countered.

"Hmm..." Peterson was nodding to himself as he hummed. "I suppose we'd all be fucked."

The class laughed, half with Peterson, half at Peterson. *Yep, some fantastic insight there.*

"Astute observation Mr Peterson. Very astute," Roy said with a smile of resignation, he was in both camps also. He couldn't be too hard on the lad; at least he didn't say he would travel back and invest in Facebook like one peanut did last year.

The 'Religion versus Hitler' observation was a classic first year conundrum. In his defence, Peterson couldn't know that second semester was completely about the big players in WWI and II. Roy looked forward to teaching his class about some of the underappreciated moments, and other, just as important men, who determined the course of Europe. It was the one of main reasons he had been given the job here at Oxford; he was considered an expert on the subject.

With that fact in mind, even though it may not have warranted it, Roy gave Peterson's answer consideration. "A desire for knowledge, and an obligation to right human-ity's wrongs are two very different reasons for travel. And one is certainly more complicated than the other..." He looked at Peterson directly, feigning seriousness. The boy retreated into his seat. "Who are we to decide if an event should or should not occur? If even the most gifted among us cannot completely grasp all the ramifications of even the tiniest change in leadership..." Roy paused at his self-reference. His seriousness hadn't lasted long. He got nothing but silence from Peterson, so he tried again. "I said, even the most gifted... you know the ones who write books on the topic... the topic of say, a life without leaders..." Nope, Peterson was lost. "People like... me. You know, writing... books you were supposed to have read this semester." Roy threw his hands in the air. "Come on, seriously, I know they were boring, but mate..." His accent twanged with the use of the Australian vernacular. It was a bit of a dick move he knew, referencing a small line of books he had written himself, but he did so self-deprecatingly, *so that was OK, right?* Either way it seemed Peterson obviously didn't read and row. "Anyway what I am trying to say is... I have learned, that the ramifications of any changes may seem manageable to begin with, but they can ripple out exponentially, having any infinite number of unforeseen consequences. Even if my books may lead you to believe that I know otherwise, there are so many consequences that, in fact, it would be impossible for anyone to anticipate them all. Therefore, I believe that if I, we or you, can only speculate on what effects our actions will have, then surely we have an obligation to not touch anything."

Peterson motioned to speak, but Roy cut in before he could. "But..." he took an exaggerated breath. "...I think that all of this is something to take back to Philosophy, Mr Peterson. Ms Kawolski loves the 'action versus observation' debate. She can tell you whether it is right, wrong or even possible at all, to do something about it." He thrust his fist from his shirt sleeve, exposing a stupidly large Seiko 'Tuna' that never left his wrist. "So, if you guys have no more questions..." A number of eager hands shot up. "Sweet. None. OK, class dismissed."

Roy was rearranging his slides as the class filed down to the front, split like a T, and exited out of the lower lecture theatre doors. He fussed away, completely oblivious to the caucus of giggling and line of elongated stares directed his way. At 35, his naivety concerning the small amount of allure he possessed – with the more academically minded females of the species – bordered on adolescent. Compounding the endearing dimness, Roy had checked himself out of the game long ago.

Georgina.

His eyes dipped down as memories flooded in, something they did hourly. He paused his paper shuffling ever so briefly to look down as he took a breath.

Closing his antique alligator skin briefcase, he looked up to see a collection of students had resisted the call of the bar, and were instead milling in front of his desk. He reached for the back of his chair and threw on his green corduroy sports jacket. As he did he felt his phone buzzing away in an inside pocket. *That's right.* All lecture the thing had been going, a periodic distraction vibrating incessantly behind him. *Who wasn't taking the hint he was busy?*

Addressing the waiting crowd as a collective – there were maybe 10 of them – he pulled out his mobile. "You guys got somewhere to be?" It was more a suggestion than question. No, they all seemed to gesture with just blank faces. "OK, give me one second, sorry."

What the hell? The ladder of notifications ran deeper than Roy was used to. He had seven missed calls and one text message, all from the same unknown number. He opened the text. It was only four words... actually two words and two pictures. The words 'call me' were followed by an apple and snake emoji. He caught on quickly. It had to be his younger brother, the 'God's first gardener' was a self-given sign-off he used to finish all his messages.

But why the unknown number?

Roy couldn't say. The reason for the call though was less puzzling, or at least he assumed it was. They shared something, an event that bonded them more than blood and a love of nineties video games ever could. Roy made a mental note to call his brother back as soon as he was out.

Looking up, he turned his phone off silent and pocketed it again. "All right, who's first?"

The crowd turned to one another. Apparently no one. After a second of over-courteousness it became clear they were looking for someone to speak, not first, but for all of them. "Professor…" A pretty brunette whose name Roy could not recall finally spoke up, "…we just wanted to ask you if the rumours were true?"

"Rumours?" Roy cocked back. He didn't like it when his name and the word 'rumour' were used in the same sentence, especially by students.

"Of you becoming head of faculty?" she clarified.

Roy's shoulders dropped, and he even managed a chuckle. "I didn't even apply for the position."

The group looked among themselves again, but no one looked surprised, as if they already knew this. Bernadette. Yes, that was her name, she spoke again, she seemed almost sad. "The rumour is Cholet offered it to you."

Roy bristled at the mention of Cholet's name; she was the University's current Vice-Chancellor. A draconian woman in looks and demeanour, she was as severe as the strap-lashing era from whence she came. "Well hell, guys, I'm flattered you think I'm even a contender, but I can tell you that this, right now, is the first I am hearing of anything."

The group let out a collective sigh. It was a bit over-done, but that was kids these days. "That's good to hear…" Bernadette started, and then caught how it sounded. "Not that we don't want… It's just we know that if you took the position you wouldn't lecture anymore, at least not to us."

Roy smiled, genuinely. *Did these kids really care?* "Guys, I'm touched, I really am, but trust me, I'm not going anywhere in a hurry. I promise I will be here next semester to put you to sleep just the same as I did this one."

Some in the group high-fived each other. *Did one kid actually fist pump in the back?* Roy had a flashback to his school days; he was just the same as these kids. They were kindred spirits… nerds. Studying the group, he made a mental note to bump them all up half a grade.

"OK, one more thing…" the group behind Bernadette looked more excited about this question. "A few of us, well actually most of us history majors, are going on a crawl to celebrate the end of semester." She was shyer now, back to a typical student, he could see she was trying hard not to say 'like'. "We were wondering if you, like…" *almost* "…wanted to come."

Roy felt an easy smile forming, but caught it before it could lead the group on. "Absolutely… not." He chuckled. "Thank you very much for the offer, but trust me, you don't want some crusty old professor crashing your party. And there's the little fact that my wife would probably kill me." A lie, but he wanted to bring them down gently. "You guys go and have yourself a blast, you've earned it."

Before the group could protest, a polyphonic rendition of Earth, Wind and Fire's 'September' interjected loudly. Roy motioned apologetically with a soft palm. The group took it as a cue the discussion was over. He retrieved his phone expecting to see his brother's unknown number for an eighth time, but was surprised to see an actual name flash across the screen.

Shit. He gulped.

It was Vice-Chancellor Cholet.

Chapter 3

Location: .... 51.5074° N, 0.1278° W
Present day name: .... London, England
IDTF Classification: . Ridge
Time: .... April 17th 2017

Roy's shoes screeched as he scurried down the second floor corridor. He was huffing like a pregnant lady, trying to remain calm. His gait, neither walk nor jog, was more an awkward shuffle.

Reminiscent of Wayne Manor on the outside, the Faculty of History Building's early century grandeur unfortunately failed to extend to its interior. Down the length of the hall standing suits of armour had given way to student noticeboards that convexed outward like vertical speed-humps.

The building did have some redeeming features though. Under his sliding feet, a patchwork of red tessellated tiles – polished by years of soft-bellied loafer traffic – glistened like a mirror. On his left, white subway tiles blurred together into one long surface. The floor and walls absorbed lovingly an afternoon sun that streamed through leadlight windows on his right. The abundance of refracted light caused the whole hallway to glow with warmth. Roy felt it; his plaid shirt was already soaked. *Of course his office was at the end.* His focus narrowed on his door. It was a half-timber, half slumped-glass kind, one that should have had a gold 'Private Eye' embossed across it.

Roy was almost at the end of the corridor when he heard a door open to his left. From his periphery a figure flashed forth from the black. Roy flinched backward quick as a trap, limbo style, but was still nowhere near quick enough. An object homed in on his face like a rocket.

"Ahhh, I got you!" A fist stopped short, poised inches from his nose. "Got be quicker than that, if you ever want to beat me boy."

Roy's heart was in his mouth. "Jesus Johnny, you scared the hell out of me."

John Abigail, or 'John the Swan' as he called himself when they sparred, was rocking on his haunches, quite pleased with himself. He was older than Roy, shorter and thicker, with a head like a cinderblock. "Here I was thinking we were making progress."

The boxing was all John's idea. *'Can't have a friend o' mine bitch slapping blokes, can I?'* Roy had no idea how he could have taken it any other way than as an insult, but he had obliged anyway. The Swan was both obnoxious and lovable like that. "Johnny, you can't just spring out of nowhere throwing punches like that. What if I was...?"

John let out a higher-pitched chuckle than anyone would have guessed could come from a head like his. "Ah sha' up boy. Knew it was you, recognise the screech of them loafers anywhere."

Roy looked down, his toes were pointed slightly towards each other. "What's wrong with them?"

"I know you're gen-Y fella, but seriously they are horrible."

Roy's tan Air Max 90s were not exactly standard professor attire, but then again he wasn't a standard professor. The fact that they were leather passed them for professional in his mind.

"We still on for later today?" John was back onto boxing. "You can try and get some revenge."

"Possibly, though I've just had a spanner thrown at me. Cholet is waiting in my office right now."

John rocked back again and let out a whistle. "Oh right, promotion, promotion, promotion."

"What? No... Wait... How am I the last one to hear about this?" This was the second time now in the space of an hour.

"Who are you kidding boy? You have your head in the sand like one of them Aussie emus half the day. Apparently the board is forcing her hand, account'a your meteoric rise and all."

Roy didn't know what to say, he couldn't help but look down at his feet again. He knew John would have been in line for the job, he'd been at Oxford a lot longer than himself.

John broke the short silence with another slower jab up to Roy's chin, there was no envy in his voice at all. "All right then..." Roy looked up, just a proud set of crooked English teeth greeted him. "Off with you, best not keep the snooty bitch waiting... knock her dead."

When Roy finally reached his office door, he paused, one hand on the handle, unsure if he should maybe knock. It felt strange, but softly he rapped his knuckles against the timber and turned the handle.

To say his office was a shoebox was an injustice to the luxury of a shoebox. Stepping in he had to dance an awkward jig just to avoid hitting his thighs on the front of his desk. Not helping the situation, a layer of ankle deep rubbish littered the floor – the crumpled draft of his next masterpiece was lost down there somewhere, shot through the paper-ball sized basketball ring on the back of his door. As Roy closed the door, he tilted his head to avoid a row of head-height bookshelves that lined the walls. As he did, a bunch of reprints clamped together on either side by a set of original elemental stones – a present to himself from the set of his favourite movie *The Fifth Element* – momentarily shielded his view of the room.

He allowed himself a second to dream, *a promotion?* Maybe it would bring a corner office, on the 100th floor, one where he could look over his minions, stroke a white cat and plan world domination... or maybe a broom closet? Hell, he'd take anything.

"Ahem." Emilia Cholet, Oxford University's Vice-Chancellor, was sitting at his desk, three feet in front of him, staring at his absent face. It was an intimidating power-play, but could easily have been because she had nowhere else to sit. This was because she wasn't alone in his office, there were three others crammed in behind the arc of the door he had just opened and shut.

Students, the Board?

Cholet spoke before Roy could properly focus. "Professor Roy, so nice of you to join us..." Her bony face was stamped with a frown. The aged skin on her skull was pulled taut over her snivelling nose. Half-moon glasses on a gold neck chain would have topped her look, but unfortunately they weren't needed. "You have visitors..." She raised one hand in a completely unnecessary gesture, the trio were right next to him. "From the government."

For the first time since his last transatlantic flight Roy felt a wave of sweat-inducing claustrophobia. *Did she say government!?* He turned, gave an awkwardly compressed wave, and squeaked out a "hi". If it were even appropriate, there was no room for either party to extend into handshakes.

Gauging the group, Roy realised just how far off his initial assumptions had been. The trio stood out from the usual university crowd, well out. One man, roughly his age, stood at the front. He had an Indian complexion and was in a suit. The other two were Caucasian, a woman slightly younger, and a man significantly older. Curiously, the last two were wearing army fatigues.

Cholet cut back in, before Roy could say something dumb. "They have come here to Oxford seeking assistance. They asked for the best..." She fell silent with a look of staged thought. "That is why 'I' asked you here today."

Roy suppressed a smile. Emphasising the 'I', posturing herself, bluffing her importance... he could see that Cholet didn't know squat, she was waiting for details just as he was.

"So..." she turned expectantly to the trio.

Yep, he was right.

The trio glanced at each other, specifically the two in army fatigues looked down on the man who wasn't, relaying their wishes with just a curt nod. The Indian man shuffled on the spot, he was sweating almost as much as Roy was. Something about him was different; standing in front of the others as he was, he disappeared still into their burliness. He was clearly a chaperone, like Cholet. She for that matter had nestled into his chair, and was watching now with much enthusiasm.

The Indian man cleared his throat and faced Roy. "Professor, my name is Danish Parrera. As Ms Cholet mentioned, I am here on behalf of the British Government." He turned to face his compatriots. "May I introduce to you Major Lane Clarke, and Colonel Frank Richards of the United States Army."

Jesus... The uniforms should have given it away, but still Roy's jaw dropped... *Americans*. He searched his brain for an appropriate reply. The beginnings of words fumbled from his throat. "I... I... guess... you guys aren't here because you have time travel questions like the rest of my class." *Really? Good God...* it was the first thing that popped in. As soon as he said it he wanted to palm his forehead.

There was silence in the room. Roy felt Cholet's glare burning his back like a blowtorch. "Well actually, Professor..." Parrera started, but before he could continue Major Clarke coughed loudly, purposefully, the implied subtlety of the act paid no heed. Parrera's head snapped around like a frightened child, eyes wide. Clarke remained silent though, her face impassive, she simply nodded to the left, toward Cholet.

"Right..." Parrera clapped his hands together and turned to face Cholet. "Excuse me Ms Cholet, if you wouldn't mind, could we please have a word alone with Professor Roy?"

For Roy, the look on Cholet's face was worth whatever was to come. "But, but, shouldn't there be a representative from the school present? I would think it appropriate that Professor Roy have an agent here for support." She was trying hard.

Parrera turned to Roy who was fighting the urge to smile. "Professor do you feel you need a representative of the school..."

"No, I do not." Roy was a little quick on the gun; Cholet glared at him.

All eyes turned to her.

"Right..." On the opposite side of the desk she rose in silence and straightened her jacket, deliberately unhurried. "Well, I shall be waiting in my office then."

What followed was an embarrassingly close face-to-face as Cholet and Roy traded positions, both parties at pains not to physically touch each other on the pass. Forgetting almost that he wasn't alone, Roy assumed his chair and rocked back. As Cholet exited with one final huff, he was so pleased he failed to see that any supposed promotion was exiting with her. Lounging back, locking his fingers behind his head, it was a long second before he realised how cocky he looked. He almost fell backward straightening up. "Um, so what exactly is this about? Am I in some sort of trouble?"

Parrera put his palms up. "No, no, definitely not." He looked to Major Clarke, the younger soldier; she returned a 'go ahead' nod, so he pulled a manila envelope from behind him. Extracting a sheet, Parrera took a deep breath. "Professor Jacob Atlas Roy..." he stopped and looked up. "Interesting middle name..."

Roy nodded. He wasn't the first and wouldn't be the last.

"...Born January 12th 1982, Melbourne Australia. Attended University of Melbourne, double degree in History and Law. Graduated 2001, two years ahead of schedule. Immediately offered a position..."

"Are you really going to do that?" Army Clarke, that's what Roy was calling her, cut in. Hearing her American accent for the first time was jarring.

"What?"

"You're going to read him his own résumé?"

"No?"

"No." She shook her head.

"But, I put a lot of time into this." He waved the folder. "All morning."

"We don't have time for it."

Parrera deflated. He let the file fall into the lost sea of manuscripts swishing at his socks. "OK Professor, allow me then to get straight to the point. What we intend to discuss today is classified to the highest levels of both the British and American Governments. Before we start I am obliged to tell you that repeating any of it is a violation of national security. Even mentioning to another person that you had this discussion will be considered a crime against your country punishable by imprisonment." Parrera recited the seemingly pre-prepared monologue with a deadpan expression.

Warning bells were sounding in Roy's head, MI6 kind of bells. "Ahhh..." he didn't know how exactly to answer, *Do you want me to sign something or just promise?* "... OK."

"Professor..." It was Army Clarke's turn now, but Roy cut in before she could start. "Please, can we drop the formalities, everyone just calls me Roy."

"OK... Roy." It obviously didn't sit well with her military sensibilities. "I am looking for the services of a historian to advise on a multinational operation currently taking place in Germany. You in particular have come to our attention because of the certain line of papers you wrote. 'A Life Without Leaders', am I correct in saying you wrote those?"

"Ah... yes I did." Roy fumbled. "But you do know they were just hypothetical think pieces? They were purely my own opinions on how history may have played out sans some of its biggest players." He coughed out a self-deprecating laugh. "I'm not sure more than a handful of people actually read them, definitely none outside of my academic field."

"Well, those papers came to the attention of the NSA approximately eighteen hours ago Professor, and they are why I am here." Clarke was clearly in some type of hurry, the 'hypothetical' aspect didn't seem to register, let alone bother her. She changed tack. "Were you aware that there was a bombing in Jerusalem thirty-six hours ago?"

Roy was struggling to keep up. Maybe that was her aim. "Ah, vaguely, I'm not sure of details, but was it something about Hamas destroying an archaeological site?" He was sheepish, he should have known more, but weirdly the first he had heard of the supposed discovery was once it had been destroyed.

"Are you familiar with Dr Susan Ashbury?" Another tack from Clarke.

"Of course." Roy answered. "Every historian is, she is our Sagan. You need a ticket for even her most mundane lecture. She has been quiet lately though." His mind was spinning with the cryptic lack of detail, he couldn't even guess how his experimental paper, a site in Israel and Dr Ashbury tied together.

"Dr Ashbury is dead, Professor. She was shot and killed at the site in Israel... she had been helping us for the last four months."

Roy gulped. *Wow, that was cold.*

Clarke continued on with military-style precision. "Dr Ashbury was part of a specialist civilian team tasked with providing immediate, on-site, mission-critical advice to military personnel. Israel was her third mission. While all so far have ended quite successfully, her overall task is not yet complete. To be frank with you Professor, we need your help to step in and replace her..." She continued before Roy could get a question in because they both knew what he was about to say. *Ended successfully? You said she was dead!* "Now, I know what you may be thinking, but I can assure you that her unfortunate passing was not connected at all with her requirements in our missions. They in themselves are extremely safe."

The cogs in Roy's head were failing to align. How a bombing, shooting and murdered Ashbury could be considered within 'extremely safe' mission parameters was beyond him. The waft of bullshit was thick on this Clarke woman, but he was still far too dumbfounded with the entire conversation to say.

Clarke eyed him and his scepticism. "As you can see, you were not initially our number one, but by all accounts you are a gifted historian." She smoothed the slight with a compliment. "Professor, I am not overstating this mission's importance when I say it has global ramifications. This will be a field mission requiring a very open mind. You may be required to venture into uncharted territory, and possibly place yourself out of your comfort zone. We anticipate you will be required for approximately two months. All the necessary arrangements have already been made with your employer, and your government will provide a lump sum as incentive."

Roy almost fell off his chair; he hadn't noticed how he'd been sliding forward. A million questions sprang to mind, but they were creating a logjam at his mouth.

Clarke continued. "This opportunity is unprecedented, even in military circles. I will be able to divulge more to you on the plane, once you agree to travel with us."

There was a pause, Roy waited for more, but realised quickly that that was it, her spiel was over. "And that's it?" he squeaked, unable to hide his incredulity.

"Yes."

"Major Clarke," he swallowed, finding his voice. "To be fair, in among that very ambiguous spiel, you have provided hardly any actual information. How can you expect me to pack up my life and commit to a plane ride with a bunch of strangers...? And, for that matter, specifically what kind of uncharted territory is there in Germany?" Roy added a shaky laugh. "It's a first world country."

No one else saw any humour in the conversation.

Clarke's eyes cut through him. "From what we hear, there should be little to pack."

Oh, that stung.

"I'm afraid that's all I can offer Professor, but I am not exaggerating when I say this mission has the potential to affect the safety of billions of people. We have had a significant setback that must be rectified as soon as possible. Assets on the ground need immediate advice and back-up. You have been identified as the most suitable person for the job, your knowledge, age, health..." Clarke's eyes darted to a picture frame on the edge of his desk. "...and marital status, all make you the perfect candidate."

Any remaining positivity evaporated from Roy's face. His eyes followed Clarke's to the picture frame. It held a shot of the two kids on the beach in Portugal. Roy had met his wife there twelve years ago while travelling on a gap year between university degrees and adulthood. His eyes lingered on the sun-soaked Lagos beachscape. How different was life back then, you could practically see the optimism shining from their smiles.

"Thanks." Roy suppressed a familiar stab at his chest. He reached out and lowered the frame down onto its face, a swell of defiance suddenly rearing inside. "So, how many others have said no to you before me?"

But before Clarke could answer Colonel Richards intervened; he had been silent so far throughout the entire conversation. Standing behind Clarke and Parrera, he had little room, but he somehow owned the space. He looked like the kind of man who was rarely uncomfortable. His deep baritone was as heavy as the plethora of medals that hung from his chest. "Major, enough with the bullshit." The whiskers of his white moustache blew out with the force of his breath. "Give the man what he fucking needs to get him on the plane."

There was silence in the room as Clarke contemplated the overruling command.

"Fine." She pouted. "Professor, we want to send you back in time."

Chapter 4

Location: . . . . 40.7831° N, 73.9712° W
Present day name: . . . . Manhattan, New York
IDTF Classification: . Ridge
Date: . . . . February 1st 1992

Magnus Thorn sat at his expansive mahogany desk, eyes closed, pupils lost in a roll towards the back of his skull. His sledgehammer sized fists lay clenched on the emerald green leather inlay. Not a single muscle moved that didn't have to. A metronome counted his breath, his ocean-diving lungs skirting the precipice of consciousness.

Thorn was forty. Swedish, his features were classically Nordic. Lost in thought, he pictured the morning, the corners of his mouth curled ever so slightly from within a braided blonde beard.

The time for visualisation was over.

As he opened his eyes, an office materialised. A high-backed chesterfield flowed like a blood-red cape over his shoulders. The chair, positioned millimetre perfect, was the centrepiece of a floor-to-ceiling window that looked out over Central Park. It was early February, the park was lush with a blanket of white, fresh from the night's fall.

Thorn couldn't have cared less for his penthouse view. Nor for half the shit surrounding him. *Fucking ostentatious, the lot of it.*

He had purposely had the office fitted with nauseatingly generic powerplay items. Rich timbers adorned the walls, a whisky cart sat in the corner, and a chandelier hung inconveniently low over two leather sofas in the middle. A library full of first editions ran down one wall, while a stuffed peregrine falcon was mounted on the other. He'd asked for something endangered, but there was a wait on Javan rhinoceros heads.

In London as of last month, the stateside set-up had happened in a hurry. Nothing about this place was his style, but it was necessary, for now. He needed to create some semblance of history for himself.

Across the desk from Thorn now sat his first ever clients. They were two Jewish brothers, both nearly at death's door. Each, he suspected, was well over 80 years old. *Statler and Waldorf,* the resemblance was uncanny. Behind them, sitting silently on one of his low-backed couches, was their driver, or bodyguard, or manservant, Thorn wasn't sure. Either way he was doing as instructed, waiting patiently.

The two brothers were American capitalism personified. Founders of the Liebestein Property Group, they, unbeknown to most New Yorkers, owned about nine percent of all Manhattan real estate. Each were millionaires many times over, Thorn was certain, surely even billionaires, *if that indeed was a thing here in '92?*

Their money though was inconsequential. If he was in the game for cash, then there were other ways, far easier than this.

No, control was his vice, control over technology, control over events and control over men. These Liebesteins had come to him with a desire, a hope, a dream that what they had heard whispers of might be true... and now they were going to provide him with something money could not buy.

"Gentlemen, I can confirm that what you seek is in fact attainable, but please, allow me to explain my service in a little more detail." A thin smile split Thorn's lips. "What I am offering gentlemen, is a double-edged sword. Time travel... It is not only a trip to 'when', but also 'where'."

"First, before I start, it is important that I give you both an idea of what I cannot do while explaining what I can." This brought him two curious looks, but he persisted. It was important, regardless of his enthusiasm, to dumb things down. Diving headfirst into his 'machine' was a bad idea; he doubted the geriatrics opposite him had even heard of computers yet? *If his memory served him, Windows 3.1 was due out this year.*

"To do this I must first begin with a theory... or three." Thorn leaned back on his chair while the Liebesteins inched forward on theirs.

"It is generally accepted that there are three theories of time travel credible enough for open debate and speculation. One, is the classic *Back to the Future* model. You guys seen it?"

He received only a set of blank stares.

"No? Really? Michael J Fox? 1985? It's a great movie, you got to see it..." He clicked his fingers and pointed as if making a mental note. "...I'll get you copy on VHS... Anyway, it advocates that if you travel back in time and change anything, your actions will have a direct effect on the present from which you came. Just like Arnie in *Terminator*, if inclined, you could travel back, wreak havoc, travel home and reap the rewards of changes made."

Thorn paused to let the brothers catch up. *Slowly, slowly.* "This is the scenario that most humans fantasise about, it plays on our innate selfishness, on our desires to correct mistakes and realise missed opportunities, all for reward." He saw a flash of knowing in the elder looking brother. The man dabbed his moistening lips with a handkerchief.

It was an opportune moment to bring him back to Earth a little. "Now, have you guys ever heard of the grandfather paradox? I'll assume no. Well, in this free-for-all type scenario, if you choose, don't ask me why you would, but should you choose, you could in theory kill your grandfather. The only problem would be, as soon as you did... Boom!" Thorn clapped his catchers' mitts together. "You would vanish into thin air. You see the paradox? If you never existed then how could you travel back to kill him? This conundrum is called an endless paradox loop." Thorn's pace was quickening, his brow pushing up, exposing the ice behind his eyes. He was getting swept up, having fun. Sure, most of it was flying over the Liebesteins' heads, but whatever. "Now physics doesn't like this *Back to the Future* cum *Terminator* theory, because according to the science of materialisation, and Einstein's theory of mass-energy equivalence, it has been proven that objects cannot just appear and disappear into thin air with no consequence. So... basically I'm sorry to tell you, it's bullshit."

Even though disproven, the first theory was still relevant. It was what most of the population thought of time travel, therefore he felt compelled to explain its flaws.

He pressed on. He was up to his favourite part. "So then... some nerds just theorised that, sure, you can travel back, but 'hey! We, they, the universe, Jesus, Madonna or whoever, just won't let you fuck around with anything'. These sadistic bastards want to tease you with the ability to time travel, but profess that something will ultimately stop you should you try and change anything. They call it the Novikov self-consistency principle. Basically gentlemen... what has happened, will happen and has to happen." Thorn shook a tsk-tsk finger in time with his metronome. "This theory is not much fun at all, and completely useless for both us, and our business together... Although I do like to imagine that just as you are about to shoot your grandfather, a piano falls from nowhere to crush you, like an anvil on top of the coyote." He let out a chuckle, *fucking sadistic that 'kids' cartoon'*. "It gets worse too... in case you had a hope that your reason for travel would not upset some universal balance, the Chaos Theory states that even the most innocuous event can start a chain reaction of circumstances that end in huge change. This means anything and everything, from shooting your grandfather, down to jerking your dick at six o'clock instead of seven, might ultimately cause a paradox... Imagine it, a world of raining pianos, mid-load, all so the universe can keep the peace. It's not going to work."

While Thorn was entertaining himself, the two killjoys opposite and their robot butler behind were proving a tougher crowd. Thorn's smile faded as he leant forward. "This conveniently, leads me to the third and, might I add, only proven theory of time travel." Propping both elbows on the desk he cupped a fist and peered over the ball of knuckles. "What I am offering you, gentlemen, is not just an opportunity to travel back in time, but the door to a another universe... your own parallel universe back in time."

Ta da, Thorn waited for a reaction, but he got nothing. One brother, the one with the handkerchief, obliged him a shuffle. *Hang on... maybe...* Nope, he simply exhaled a small cough into the fabric.

Thorn could restrain himself no longer. "Guys? You got anything for me? Ideas, questions? I feel like I'm monologuing here, and you guys are leering like my old drama teacher." He was conscious enough to leave out the eventual paedophile part of Mr Stratford's bio.

The cough of the eldest turned into the hack of a lung coming loose. He paused between dying just long enough to regard Thorn, his English broken. "Businessman, you are, physicist, maybe, but comedian, you are not, Magnus... continue."

"All right then." Thorn nodded. "So it's a technicality, but I will not actually be sending you back into your time per se, I will be sending you to a parallel universe at the specified time you desire." He withdrew a notepad from his desk. "Imagine time as a line that has two points, A – is where we are now, and B – is where you guys want to go, for example 1980." He drew a straight line with A on the right and B on the left signifying the past. "Now when you travel with me, from A to B, you do not travel back along your own line, but instead you travel *off* your line onto another new one." He drew a second parallel line underneath the first, with a B positioned underneath the original A. He labelled the top original line 'Universe 1' and the new, lower line, 'Universe 2'.

B (e.g. 1980)__________A (present)   >>>>   Universe 1

____________B________________   >>>>   Universe 2

"The act of travel has created a second parallel universe specifically for you, the traveller. Imagine that all you're doing is dropping from the top line straight down to the bottom line."

Thorn paused. The next part was tricky. "Now, 'Universe 2' is an exact carbon copy of the world as it was at 'time B, 1980', in our original 'Universe 1'. At that time you will be the only variation, you become an anomaly of that universe. Your present day self will no longer exist in 'Universe 1' at all, but your past '1980-self' exists at point B in both universes. In 'Universe 1' your specific past is the past, and can never be altered, so you have to continue along the path you have previously lived until you get to this exact point, that is a non-negotiable. Conversely, your 'Universe 2' younger self will do exactly the same, eventually arriving at this specific point, unless you intervene or unknowingly cause him not to, which I might add you are certainly more than welcome to do."

Thorn gave his suitors another second. "'Universe 2' is a whole new world, gentlemen. You have carte blanche to do as you please. Feel free to kill your grandfather, your father or even the past version of yourself. It will have no bearing back here in 'Universe 1'. The new world is your playground. The possibilities will only be limited by your imagination." He leant back in his chair and let out a deep breath. "...And that gentlemen, is about as simple as I can make it."

The brothers turned to each other. "So..." Finally, Mr Emphysema was going to offer something profound? "... The new world. It is fake?"

Thorn took an accentuated breath. *Fuck*. It seemed so simple in his head, but he had to remember both where and when he was. *God help me if I have to get the colour pencils out*. "No gentlemen, it is not a fake. Try not to get stuck on the semantics of whether the past is your own, or a parallel copy of your own. Just trust me when I say it is all the same once you're there."

"How does it work?" The same brother again. The pair had never introduced themselves, but Thorn recalled his name was, maybe, Eli.

"Well..." Thorn rolled his eyes. "That is the 100 million-dollar question, literally. Mr Liebestein, can I call you Eli? Sure I can. I'm sure you can understand I wouldn't be in business for long if I gave up my secrets that easily. Now, I cannot claim that I am the only person to theorise this multiverse scenario, but I am the only one who has made a device to prove it. Remember gentlemen it is you who sought me out. I couldn't care less if you believe me or not." His power, and five-minute attention span were boiling his temper.

The two men looked to each other again. Something was simmering between them. "We want to kill Hitler!" Eli spat out his words and saliva in equal measure.

Boom! It was the reveal Thorn was waiting for.

All right. Thorn waited for some elaboration, nodding, a look of eagerness slapped on his face. But the brothers just sat then, staring forward. It seemed they were in agreement of their goal and that the rest was obvious.

Fuck. How do these guys get anything done?

"OK... and which one of you spring chickens wants to carry that out?"

"Enough with the patronising, Magnus." It was the other, younger brother's turn to speak. So far it had been Eli doing the very limited talking, but Thorn now studied the one called... Fritz. He could sense in him a spark that age had yet to weary. "We are old, but we are not stupid." He was surprisingly calm compared to his brother, his words measured, his accent barely noticeable. "We have listened to your condescending lecture, and we under-stand your machine." He turned his head and said some-thing in Yiddish to their manservant seated behind them. Thorn had almost forgotten he was there. The driver rose from the sofa.

"You guys leaving, so soon?"

Fritz ignored the comment. "Meet... Abner. He is an associate of ours who will travel for us. He is someone who specialises in 'conflict resolution'. He will intercept at the time of birth to nullify this man's future atrocities."

Thorn regarded the new, suddenly more important, man in the room. "Right... OK, now we are getting somewhere." He tried to lock eyes with Abner, but the man was aggressively impassive, staring ahead like a soldier.

He was Jewish all right – like he belonged instead in Borough Park selling jewellery – tight curls on his head led down to doe brown eyes and a pronounced nose. He had a five o'clock shadow that looked shaver proof; it covered the remnants of a deep laceration on his chin.

Thorn broke his gaze away from the pissing contest in which Abner was refusing to participate. He turned to Fritz, impressed. "I was wondering why you would seek out travel at your age. It's nice to know old Ab-nuts over there is more than just your nurse. We're on the right track."

"OK gentlemen, full disclosure here, I see two problems that myself in forty years is obliging me to ask..." Thorn reached out and caught the metronome needle with his fingers. A window of silence opened for a greedy smile, "...because you know I wasn't always like this."

He looked at Abner, the statue. "No offence... but what if your man fails? Could you live with the fact you will have created a whole new universe that must endure the wrath of Hitler?" The question surprised the older Eli; he looked too consumed with anger to have properly taken all possibilities into account. Fritz, though, again answered for the both of them. "Our man will not fail. It is impossible. He will have the foresight of God himself."

"OK then, I have one last point, probably my most important. As I mentioned earlier, what I am offering is a dual-edged sword. This trip comes with a strictly one-way ticket. You will be deposited at your desired time with all that you can fit into the pod, but not with the pod itself. So unless you are travelling to a time as recently as when I created this device, the technology will not exist. I should add, to further spin your brain, that even if you did have another pod you will just create another secondary universe branching off from your own. Your 'Universe 2' will now serve as 'Universe 1' to a new 'Universe 2'." Thorn scratched his head. This shit even scrambled his brain sometimes. "Gentlemen, basically this is a 'start again, leave it all behind' kind of deal. On arrival, you are on your own, at the mercy of your time period. This is usually a positive for most travellers, it means they can act with impunity..." Thorn paused, the next part was important. "But with your proposal, gentlemen, your specialist over there will do the travelling and thus create his own universe that you will have no contact with. Whether he succeeds or fails, you will be none the wiser, it will have no impact in this universe whatsoever, only in his new one." As the words spilled from him, even Thorn could hear the sounds of a deal breaker.

But he was wrong.

Eli stood, his eyes red, his teeth gritted. He rolled up his sleeve to reveal a set of faded blue numbers tattooed on his inner forearm.

Fritz spoke for him. "Magnus, we are old men with more money than God. If he is alive anywhere, in any fucking universe, we want him dead. We do not care how it happens, just make it happen... I will die peacefully knowing that somewhere that 'Mamzer' is dead by our will."

Chapter 5

Location: .... In transit
Present day name: .... Above the English Channel
IDTF Classification: . Ridge
Date: .... April 17th 2017

Roy's focus drew down to his right. Over his chest harness, beyond a twitching knee, and to the side of his canvas bench seat, the slightest hint of movement had piqued his curiosity. His eyes fell upon one particular vibrating rivet. A surge of anxiety shot up his spine and into his skull like a carnival bell. His shoulders tensed, his breath quickened and his palms – even as they rubbed two streaks of heat into his thighs – felt instantly moist. His vision compressed down, like a zoom, onto the single metallic fastener, its circular, green painted head, rotating slowly in a clockwise motion. Consumed entirely, the hive of activity that was his metallic cocoon faded into a fog, like the extremities of a daydream. It was an amazing feat considering where he was. The thrum of four turbo-prop engines – Jesus, they had been loud on take-off – were now just a soft rhythmic hum. The movements of soldiers, darting among the crates of cargo, blurred into his periphery. *Of all the things... this tiny rivet, it was going to be the death of him. Flying. It had to be the worst invention ever.*

"Um, is that supposed to be shaking like that?" Roy looked up, talking to no one in particular, his eyes burned from minutes without a blink. His world was suddenly loud again. Like a lost child, he said louder, almost shouting, "Um... anybody?"

Major Lane Clarke was sitting directly across from him in the cargo hold. She looked up. Roy made a face, *hello?* He would have waved, but his hands had moved to his chest and were clutching his harness like a lifeline. Clarke regarded him with a frown, then motioned to the headset that was hanging on the webbing to his left. She had a similar one on her lap.

Roy's reach, out over the one-foot abyss, was exhausting. As he scraped the earmuffs over his head, one ear folded down. "Um, I have a bit of a situation here." His tongue caught in his dehydrated mouth.

Clarke looked at him, her black eyes rolling. "The microphone." Her voice was delayed a second through his earmuffs. "Pull it down... Professor."

"Oh." Roy felt his cheeks redden. He found the extendable arm. Focusing on it, he went cross-eyed as it passed over his nose. "Um, I have a bit of a situation here... There's a rivet down here..." He pointed with a shaky finger. "It's coming loose."

Clarke regarded him again, this time as if he were speaking a different language, then... she laughed.

"What?" Roy did a double take. "I'm serious."

But Clarke didn't even bother to respond, she just took her headset off and returned it to her lap, shaking her head.

Roy felt the walls of an anxiety bubble forming. "This plane is hardly held together as it is." At least it seemed that way to his novice, wide-eyed blues.

The interior of the plane was completely stripped back. Structural beams, no thicker than his arm, ran the length of the cargo bay, and were joined only occasionally by triangular metal trusses. The floor, where both Roy's bench seat was bolted and supply pallets were stored, was a jigsaw of grating and rolling tumblers. The bench was raised off the plane's curved underbelly and he could see straight under it. There was nothing fancy there, nothing special ensuring their survival, it was just more vibrating fuselage. The whole thing was merely a skeleton, wrapped in an inadequate windbreaker, hurtling through the sky at 900 kilometres an hour... waiting for the first sign of turbulence to tear it apart.

Turbulence, oh God.

"This baby's a C-130J Super Hercules..." A voice came from Roy's left. Two soldiers checking inventory on a pallet were also wearing headsets. "...Premier military cargo plane in the world." The one with a clipboard was doing the talking. "This one weighs in at thirty-four tonnes, she can hold another thirty-three on top of that. It'll take more than a rivet to sink us... I hope." He turned to his compatriot and slapped him on the arm.

"Yeah, don't worry 'Professor'." The second one started, he had a thick Italian-American New Jersey-type accent. "We got a parachute for most of us. I just hope you can swim but, it's dark out, we might be floating in the channel 'til morning." Both of them looked at Roy and started laughing.

Now he felt stupid. "Thanks guys, really."

"Hey, no sweat boss, happy to help." Jersey's tone stung with sarcasm. "You know we love nothing more than flying around on fucking one-man taxi missions, collecting precious..."

"Gianinni! Collins! Are you getting smart with my passenger?" Clarke's voice cut in over the mic; neither Roy nor the men had noticed her putting her headset back on. The two soldiers almost hit the roof. Roy would have too if he hadn't been strapped down like the cargo he obviously was.

"I...I..." Jersey spun around stammering.

"I. I. I..." Clarke wobbled her head like a bobble head doll. "I'll have you both outside this fucking plane mid-flight with a rivet gun if you don't shut the fuck up. Is that understood?"

The soldiers stiffened. "Yes Ma'am!"

Her transformation was as sudden as it was brutal. She looked at Roy, her face frozen in an icy glare. He could see her mind ticking over, but still she offered him nothing. He didn't need her to; it was clear she wasn't defending him.

Roy had spent the last three hours in transit chaperoned like a parent by Major Lane Clarke. Via helicopter – that was another story – and now Hercules, she had never left his side. Sitting across from her with little interaction, and no in-flight, he had spent a lot of time trying not to stare. Unfortunately, fear, flying and vacant staring all went hand in hand for him.

His best guess was that Clarke was probably late twenties, early thirties. Tall, but slender, the obvious power in her was spread well across her frame, like she ran track, not deadlifted. Her sharp facial features were not exactly all-American – peace-prize worthy diplomacy – but she was still quite attractive in ways he couldn't quite put a finger on. She seemed colder, darker, like a bartender sick of some shit he hadn't even given her yet. Her eyebrows especially, razor-thin and constantly furrowed, fostered some level of intrigue... *or, had you fucking right off.* Either way, Roy imagined she was comfortable with both.

Both of them sat, staring, in a moment of turbo prop silence. It was only when Clarke made to remove her headset once again that Roy found his voice. Conveniently distracted by the two cargo goons, his mind had taken a momentary step back from the ledge and, as such, a flood of questions were re-entering it. First and foremost was: *what the hell am I doing here?*

"Major?"

Clarke paused, her hands on her earmuffs.

"Any chance we could get to some of those specifics you promised?"

She lent back, inhaling slowly. "Are you sure you want to do this now? Because you know, you don't look so good."

"I'm OK," Roy squeaked, his veneer thin.

"Really? You look like shit."

"No." He gulped, "I'm fine." He was telling himself as much as her, though her hard truth had him cracking.

"Nervous, aren't you?"

"Nope."

She considered him, well aware he was. "Have you seen *Sliders*?" she asked then from left field.

"Huh?" Roy's eyes lulled a little.

"It was a crummy TV series from twenty years ago," she said, as if that was what he was confused about.

"Yeah I get it. I was a teenager in the nineties. Every kid with a curiosity for science fiction watched it. Jerry O'Connell as Quinn Mallory, Maximillian Arturo, Rembrandt Brown."

"Good, that's a start, because I haven't."

The throb in Roy's head was starting to return. "I don't understand, what does Sliders have to do with history, or Germany, or... whatever it is you need from me?"

The plane rocked slightly. Roy heard from nowhere a lashing of rain on the fuselage. *Oh God, we are entering a storm*. He felt a familiar pit open up inside his belly.

"Well, Dr Zhu says it is exactly like that."

Her cryptic crossword clues weren't helping anyone. "What...? How...? And who is Dr Zhu?"

"Dr Zhu is the lead physicist of our scientific team. He and Stan-Lakely are pretty much the only ones who have any idea about... where you'll be going."

"Going? You mean like Germany or..." Roy's breath quickened "...the other place?" he couldn't even say it, the notion was so ridiculous. He felt a rush of pins and needles in his feet. Maybe she was right, maybe this conversation wasn't such a good idea a thousand metres off the ground.

The plane rocked again, a little more violently this time. Then it dropped. It was only a couple of metres, but the weightlessness was enough to send Roy's heart into his mouth. He tasted a slick of bile running the wrong way up his throat.

Clarke, it seemed, hadn't even noticed the turbulence. "Yeah, the other place, about that..." she started, but stopped. "You sure you're OK? You're looking pale."

Roy's mind had jettisoned all thought of the questions he was asking. "Yeah. I just need a second... it's the flying..." His voice was softer. "I'm not so good with..."

The plane rocked again, its most severe movement yet. The sound of shuddering metal filled his ears. The lights of the cabin flickered once, twice, then completely off before a red beacon flared inside the cargo hold, bathing the space like a photographic dark room. He closed his eyes; he could feel the hum of the plane slipping away from him. He felt himself pulled, dragged into the blackness of his mind's eye. A soothing warmth washed over his arms, creeping up toward his head. He felt his body float first, then dip away from him, as if he were in the third person watching himself descend into an imaginary pool.

"Professor Roy?" Clarke was calling, but her voice laboured through water.

"Yeah..." but he was only in his mind now.

Hang on...

Roy had one final thought before he fainted, one final moment of clarity. He tried to open his eyes, but it was no use.

...In Sliders *they don't travel back in time, they travel... to other dimensions.*

Then... he was out.

***

"Princess."

Roy heard a voice in the blackness.

"Ey princess, rise and shine."

His eyes fluttered open to see the face of Jersey Gianinni inches from his own. His Bobby Cannavale-style head was wobbling so close Roy could see the blackheads on his nose. A Cheshire cat smile exposed his excessively whitened teeth.

"Yo, get your shit, we're here."

Chapter 6

Location: . . . . 48.1351 N, 11.5820 E
Present day name: . . . . Munich, Germany
IDTF Classification: . Ridge
Date: . . . . April 18th 2017

Perlacher Forest: a 13.36-square kilometre community recreation zone south-east of Munich.

Roy had landed at Flughafen München – Munich International Airport – only twenty minutes ago. Now, already, skimming low over the forest in a Black Hawk, he was nearing his final destination. It was his second chopper ride in one day, and the third time he had had his feet off the ground, *enough for a lifetime.*

"We are coming up on the LZ, sir." The voice of the pilot, not intended for him, crackled through his earmuffs.

Only as the chopper slowed could Roy peel his eyes from between his knees, and his conscience from the 'joys' of flight. The forest below, or sudden lack of, was a sight to behold. Beneath the craft's hovering underbelly a significant section of the birch woodland had been crudely levelled, creating a clearing roughly the size of a football pitch. In among the mulched dirt, uprooted tufts of semi-buried grass lay scattered like seeds for a bird, and around the clearing perimeter, the shredded springtime canopy had been bulldozed into a huge pile.

An off-world colony was what it looked like to Roy. In the middle of the field an assortment of white portable structures were positioned in a ring around two, large, white plastic domes. The more he focused the more he could see how hastily the site must have been thrown together; between exposed supply crates and half finished walkways, cables zigzagged from dome to dome like snakes through a disaster relief zone.

As the chopper started its descent, Roy could also see that the site was cordoned off well past its perimeter. What looked to be German military troops were stationed well back, creating a massive, uninterrupted ring of camouflage around the park.

Whatever this site was... it was safe to reason that Perlacher Forest was very much closed to the public right now.

Crouching low, buffeted by rotor wash, Roy fumbled behind Clarke as she led him away from the chopper. With her glare fixed dead ahead, Clarke strode upright, defying the rotors to even try and take her head off. Towards the middle of the camp they marched, Roy's feet failing still to coordinate properly with his brain. At a door marked 'debrief hut 1' Clarke stood aside and motioned with a straight palm for Roy to enter. It was not a discussion.

Inside, the hut was empty save for a whiteboard, table and twelve chairs. Everything, including the walls and floor – which was made from a hard plastic, inter-lockable grating – was white. Three steps in, and a waft of pine disinfectant burnt high up in his sinuses. The table looked slick with the stuff, like a surgical prep board.

"Sit. I'll get Zhu and the others," Clarke said from outside before she slammed the door shut.

Roy, lost in the blizzard-like whiteout, was half-expecting to hear her lock him in, but she either didn't, or did so quietly. Was he in trouble? He felt like he was. His little episode on the plane had yet to be mentioned by either of them. Like a cloud of shame, his embarrassment hung over him.

Pulling up a chair, he placed his hands on the table, and let out what felt like his first full breath since the beginning of this surreal adventure. Listening to nothing but his body, his mind centred itself within the triangle of his flattened palms, forefinger to forefinger, thumb to thumb. There was so much he hadn't had time to properly process, so much flying past him.

Most pertinent, obviously, was his distinct inability to annunciate the single word *NO*, or *UM... NO*, two words, or, *I'M AFRAID NOT*, three words. His eyes, watering from a stare into nothing, could almost see the letters appearing, N then O, like a magic eye from within the Exxon-Valdez-esque oil-slick on the table. *Hindsight, what was it again, something-something twenty-twenty.*

He thought on the meeting in his office, not more than six hours ago. *Time travel...? Really...?* He didn't believe it, or more so couldn't believe it.

Yet here he was.

What had made him say 'yes'? He couldn't say.

Maybe it didn't matter.

Maybe what mattered most, he realised, as he blinked away the illusion... was that he really didn't have a reason to say 'no'.

After the bizarre end to his afternoon, it had been a surprise to see how easily he could get his affairs in order. If he were honest, it was actually a little depressing to realise that he hadn't had to organise much, nor inform many people of his potential extended absence. The only real plans he had had to cancel had been with his...

Damn it...! In the whirlwind of proceedings he had completely forgotten about his brother.

Roy pulled his mobile phone from his pocket; of course he had zero reception. He opened his text application anyway. Hopefully at some time or another his phone would find a roaming tower and send a pending message through. He typed quickly, he didn't want to endure Clarke's wrath should she find him doing so.

Mate, sorry for the missed calls and late reply, been called away for work. Next week... I'm sorry I can't. Can't explain now, you wouldn't believe me anyway. Hope you're well, I'll call you asap.

Roy hoped it sounded sincere, and not like he was blowing the birthday – Henry's, his nephew's, third as an eight-year-old – off. He didn't know what else to say, he himself had no idea what lay in store for him. Lying wasn't an option, it never was; it didn't come naturally. The 'supposed' truth wouldn't suffice either. *Mate, just heading back in time, see you soon with a souvenir. I'll try and grab a Germanic tribal axe, or Henry one of those snow globes he collects, does he have one with a plague scene?*

***

Twenty minutes later Roy heard a key in the lock of the debrief room door. He wished he hadn't, but he'd been right about the lock. Clarke entered with five people in tow. Four of them were new faces. One was a woman, looking as bewildered as he was. Two were scientists, dressed in laughably long shoulder-to-toe lab coats, and the last was a young buck, definitely Army. The fifth, whom he recognised as Jersey, refrained from entering and took up a position as sentry as Clarke shut the door behind her.

"Everyone, please take a seat," Clarke began. Next to her one of the scientists remained standing. Asian in appearance, he had a face that was somehow familiar. Roy assumed he must be Dr Zhu.

"May I introduce you all to your fellow members of 'Team Bravo'... of the United Nations Joint Interdimensional Task-Force, or the IDTF for short."

All at the table managed a hesitant glance side to side. It was comforting to think they were all in the same boat.

Clarke proceeded around the room. "Joining us from Italy we have Professor Loretta Panatoli, linguistic expert." She pointed to the lost looking lady. "Next is Professor Jacob Roy, lead historian." Roy offered a meek wave. "Dr Brian Heathcote, our travelling physicist." He was the other man in a lab coat. He looked settled, as if he had been here for some time. "And..." she pointed next to the only other person in Army fatigues. "Sergeant Stanley Doran..."

"Huh hum..." The sergeant cut her off with a cough and exaggerated smile. He leant forward to face the group. "Everybody done call me Spike."

The room was quiet as 'Spike's' chair rocked back, squeaking for a full three seconds. On account of the sharp blonde hair that looked concreted in place, his name at least made some sense. Thin, young and wiry, he looked like one of those southern catfish wranglers. Drumming at the air in front of him, Roy guessed a roadrunner tattoo on the inside of his rolled sleeve had more to do with his energy levels than a love of Warner Brothers.

Whether Clarke was irritated by the Kentucky Fried interruption Roy couldn't tell, but the lack of any explosion from her was not what he was expecting.

"Sergeant Doran... and I are your designated Army chaperones. We will be responsible for your safety once inside the Tear." Clarke gestured to the man to her left.

"Lastly up here we have Dr Ronald Zhu. Head physicist for this mission, Dr Zhu will not be travelling with us initially, but will instead follow us through at a later stage." She took a step to the side. "Doctor, if you would."

"Right." Zhu assumed the floor. A tiny man, he looked fragile, like a sparrow. Dressed in a comically large lab coat, his heavily tanned face was besieged by row upon row of wrinkles that started at the back of his bald scalp and rolled forward to a pair of thick-framed tortoiseshell spectacles. The glasses, far too large to sit properly on his flat nose, had a gold chain that looped behind his ears and around his neck, as if he were Blanche from *The Golden Girls*.

"Good evening ladies and gentlemen..." he began, his excitable words pausing ever so slightly courtesy of a thick Korean accent. "I believe you have been informed of the seemingly miraculous phenomenon central to this mission. I will assume you have parked your initial disbelief, so I can get straight to the facts of what we know."

Roy's jaw dropped a little. *What?* He hadn't even found a car spot, let alone parked anything.

Zhu continued, "Approximately six months ago a 'H.E.A.D.E', High Energy Atmospheric Distortion Event, was discovered in an abandoned warehouse in Washington DC. Two weeks later another was found in Brooklyn, New York. The events were intermittent and unpredictable at best, appearing and then disappearing at what seemed to be random intervals and for unpredictable lengths of time."

HEADE? How did I never hear about this?

"The US Government immediately quarantined both sites and orchestrated an entire media blackout of events," Zhu clarified, as if reading his mind. "Analysis revealed that the 'HEADES'..." He pronounced 'HEADES' like 'Hades' the Greek god "...were in fact localised distortions to the fabric of space and time. Think of them as mini controlled black holes. Now I know what I just said, but fear not, these are not traditional black holes. Unlike their deep space counterparts, they do not 'yet' have the huge gravitational forces capable of sucking you, light and everything else known to man, into the nether. The HEADES are, or were, in fact rather tame, one could even say, user-friendly versions." Zhu looked across the room nodding eagerly. He pushed his large glasses back up the bridge of his nose. "Now while it may be hard to imagine visually, instead of a black circle whirlpool, they resemble rather a rip through a two-dimensional piece of paper. Hence the name 'Tears' quickly took off, replacing the HEADE acronym. The assimilation of a black hole into the unknown, and the god of the underworld was something we were also happy to avoid." When Zhu smiled, his eyes disappeared almost completely.

"Yeah, and whose genius idea was it to send us through?" Spike interjected. Leaning back on his chair with his hands on his head Roy could tell he really wanted to put his feet on the table.

"Exploration into the Tear was unfortunately a necessity more than anything else... Spike. It was discovered that even though the Tears were initially sporadic, they were changing significantly. They began to open with accelerated frequency and for longer periods. This caused them to have new and untold effects on their immediate surrounds. Of major concern to us was the fact that the Tears began to syphon energy, electromagnetic radiation energy to be precise. It was small amounts at first, but that was increasing as time went on. Projections were calculated by my assistant Tee, sorry, Ms Stan-Lakely, and it was found that the Tears were on track to grow exponentially in size, duration and... thirst."

Zhu was still smiling, making it hard for Roy to properly process the implication of his words.

"We have theorised that, after starting with electromagnetic radiation, the Tears will begin to search for and draw thermal, chemical and ultimately gravitation energy. It is the unchecked thirst for gravitational energy that could potentially convert them into the black holes we observe in space. If this did occur, it could ultimately lead to the destruction of the world as we know it."

Roy's hand slipped off his chin. *Jesus, did he just say the destruction of the world?*

Zhu's comment hung in the air, allowing Clarke to chime in. "A decision was made to involve the Army. Colonel Frank Richards was placed in charge to oversee an expedition. Answers were needed."

"Hmm, hmm, yes." Zhu nodded and readjusted his glasses again. "It often seems the default reaction of power is to welcome the unknown down the sights of a rifle." His comment had all the subtlety of a church bell, but was delivered with another smile. He turned again to the group, wresting back control of his presentation. "The initial Tear in Washington became one big learning experience for all involved. Even now we are still processing the implications that travel has on the established theories of physics we once assumed sound. I'm happy to go through the finer scientific details..." Zhu turned to the whiteboard behind him.

Roy watched on as around the room, eyelids, like dominoes, began to drop one after another. Zhu had trailed off into a theoretical scientific wonderland. Talk of quarks, Higgs boson and dark matter shot like the subatomic particles they were straight over the group's head. Unable to hold himself back any longer, Roy put up a hand. "Doctor, what did they find on the other side?"

"Huh?" Zhu spun around, marker in hand, lid between teeth, all manner of Venn diagrams intersecting like rainbows in the whiteboard.

"The other side doctor, what did they find?" Roy repeated.

"Oh, sorry. Right." He tried to spit the red lid into his hand, but it sailed straight through his pigeon claw. "Well Mr Roy, I suppose that is the million-dollar question. The first team through the Tear..." Zhu raised a wispy eyebrow above his glasses. "...Discovered a portal into the past. In the case of Washington, they found themselves exactly four years, sixty-five days, thirteen hours, and fifty-six minutes into the past. New York, similarly, was relevantly recent, with the Tear leading back only to the mid 2000s. It was only after Israel did we realise the Tears could potentially lead *anywhere* in time."

Roy's mind started to spin. *Time travel!?*

"Now, importantly, it is imperative we acknowledge the ambiguity of the term 'time travel' and the multitude of hypothetical definitions it is attributed to. This has become especially relevant to us because, after some initial confusion, we observed that our destinations, which we originally thought of as the past, were in fact not an exact copy of previous events in our world. Some things were slightly... different."

"Different? How, exactly?" Roy had found his voice.

"Well, for instance in Washington Professor, we had a completely different President."

Clarke stepped forward again. "It happened to be a wealthy senator from Vermont named Broadford, Wilson Broadford. Apparently, he usurped Obama as the Democratic candidate early on in the primaries. At this stage we're not sure how."

"Yes, yes." Zhu agreed. "This fact leads us to believe the Tears do not lead back in time, but instead to a parallel universe running at some predetermined time behind our own."

The news was a kick to anyone's sensibilities. Roy scrunched his face. He looked around the room, Panatoli and Spike looked as dumbfounded as he felt.

Zhu continued. "The new universe is feeding off our own, using it to sustain its own lagging time period." He was on a roll now, smiling again, dropping bombshell after bombshell with joyous abandon. "Now, most importantly, these slight differences that I mentioned, between our world and those beyond the Tears were all tied in some form or another to a specific anomaly. We discovered that in each world the differences revolved around someone who did not belong there... a measurable, tangible, unique... human singularity."

Boom! There was a pause in the room.

"Are you saying Doctor... that someone has travelled through the Tears before us?" Roy was connecting dots.

"Was it this Broadford?" Professor Panatoli, the Italian, was doing the same.

"Broadford was unique to the first Tear Professors; each Tear since has revolved around a new anomaly," Zhu answered. "Not only do we think that someone has travelled before us each time, we think that that person is the only reason the universe exists in the first place. Each anomaly forms an integral part of the link between our worlds. This link cannot be severed without their express 'cooperation'."

Cooperation? Whatever that meant, Roy felt a picture forming, albeit one with massive holes. "So Broadford has some universe traversing device? Why can't we just ask him? Why can't we ask any of the anomalies, I mean? Surely they can fill in the blanks."

"I wish we could Professor. Unfortunately there have been some issues on the tactical side of..."

"It is easier said than done, Roy," Clarke cut in, talking straight over Zhu. "There have been some complications while trying to attain the 'cooperation' of the anomalies." Again, with the same vague emphasis on cooperation, she stepped back into the centre of the room. "All right, so is everyone up to speed?"

"Um, no, I'm certainly fucking not." Spike looked like a five-year-old who had just had calculus explained to him. He smacked his hands on the table and snapped his head around, looking for support. "So let me just get this straight. Are these time travel thingos and the Tear thingos... not the same thingos?"

"No." Clarke's jaw was clenched. "One occurs as a result of the other. Travel first, Tear later."

It was a surprisingly astute observation. Roy had not considered the 'chicken and egg' conundrum of the 'anomaly and the Tear'. *So the initial traveller has his own means of travel. Tears happen later.*

"So am I right to say then..." Spike held up two hands like counterbalance scales. "...Time travel, good? Tears, bad?"

Zhu took his chance to cut back in. "Almost Spike, except they are both bad. It's because of the initial time travel that we have Tears. The time travel is a one-way-trip that creates a universe. The Tears are a two-way-corridor that opens once the universe can no longer be supported and starts searching for juice."

Spike looked more confused now. He shook his head. "I'm sorry Doc, I'm gon' need that again."

"That's OK. Try it this way. Travel..." Zhu paused for a second. "...Creates an isolated world... Imminent collapse of that world... creates a Tear for us to get there."

"And the imannnnen... part"

"The imminent collapse?"

"Yeah. So it's gonna take us both down?"

"Correct. Imagine an electrical powerboard. Our universe is that powerboard. Each time travel occurrence plugs a new universe into our powerboard. We now are under the strain of too many piggybacking universes. To put it simply, eventually, instead of a fuse blowing, the overload of power is going to burn down our house."

"OK, why didn't you say so?" Spike dropped both hands and thumbed his chest. "Got three weeks electrical apprenticeship under me. All over it... And you're sayin' the link cannot be severed while this anomaly fella is alive on the other side?"

Zhu gave Clarke a nervous glance.

Jesus. So that was what they meant by 'cooperation'.

"Correct again Spike, the link cannot be severed if the original anomaly is there to keep re-initiating it.

"All right?" Clarke had clearly had enough. "We done?" It was not an invitation. "Remember, first and foremost, you are all here because we need your help to locate the anomaly inside this German Tear. Only once we have identified him or her, can we save our world."

"No Major." Another voice interrupted her. It was Panatoli this time. "We're only here because your initial academic team were all murdered in Israel." Her accented Rs rolled off her tongue adding to her already sassy Italian bite.

Roy liked Pantoli's gusto. Watching her from across the table, he noted her hazel eyes sparkled with an immediately recognisable astuteness. She sat bolt upright, hands crossed over her tightly gripped knees.

Clarke stiffened, her porcelain skin turning a deeper shade of red. "That is unfortunately correct Professor Panatoli, but doesn't change what you are here to do. The fact remains that we have a Tear on the precipice of disaster, and we have no idea what to expect on the other side. Each of you has a specific skill set that will prove vital when information is at a premium and conversations with Support back here may be limited to a six-day turnaround. So, if you don't mind... the next opening is in roughly twenty-four hours, and you all have a lot of training to do."

Chapter 7

He had all the necessary details. He knew where he needed to be and when. Salzburger Vorstadt 15. 6:30pm was zero hour.

Following his emergence, the trip south had been curious... testing, but curious. *Same same but...*

From Munich through lower Bavaria, the trek had been more into-forest than cross-country, but the journey had served its purpose. An unaccommodating guard at the border had broken his duck and settled the nerves. Death it seemed, at least the mechanics of the act, was the same everywhere. Stepping over the body and into Austria-Hungary, it had been only thirty kilometres before he found himself on the edge of town.

For two days Abner had watched, waited and studied. From the shadows, folds and creases of Braunau he had had numerous opportunities to complete his assignment, but with each opportunity came a conscious decision to resist.

The girl was twenty-three. Pregnancy did not befit her frame. Fat like a spring duck she had plod around town, waiting to spew forth the devil inside her. Over the sidewalk bluestone she struggled, cart ahead of her, whining like an old mule, begging to be put down. It would have been merciful almost, an act of kindness, a relief he had afforded many an over-ripened watermelon down the range of his farm, to split her open in a spray of pink mist. One silenced bullet, maybe two to be sure, would have ended both of them, quickly and painlessly. But no, he was under strict instructions. *The boy, he must be born, he must be alive in order to die.* The Liebesteins had obsessed over this one stipulation.

Abner understood. It was their way of retaining some semblance of control. The only way the Liebesteins could garner satisfaction from this mission was to dream of how it would unfold, so he would follow the plan as they imagined it. They had put their faith in him, and he would repay it, as he always did. *Wait until the birth* they had said... *then proceed at will.*

Waiting until the birth, or just after, did offer him at least one ancillary benefit – it would assemble all of his targets into one location. The youngest Liebestein, Fritzal, had been explicit. In a torrent of gob-spatter he had demanded, *EVERYONE!* There was to be no possibility of history somehow repeating, leading another child or Hitler descendant to power. Adolf, Alois, Klara... and even Adolf's stepsiblings Alois Jnr and Angela were all on his list. Whether he agreed or not, it was to be so... for the crimes of Adolf, the entire family must pay.

The three-storey building was like any other in the street, pretty, but nondescript by European standards. Semi-detached on the left and flanked by a lane on the right, its rendered façade was painted a soft yellow and punctuated by three rows of arched windows set upon large bluestone sills. A sturdy wooden barn door at ground level on the left seemed the obvious entrance.

Abner had been excellently briefed. Blueprints of every floor and all potential incursion opportunities had seared themselves into his memory like a gunpowder Etch-A-Sketch. The building was home to three separate families, one per floor. The Hitlers currently resided on the middle floor. It was a complication, but nothing he could not manage. Tonight, at 2030 hours, he would utilise the twilight for cover. Along the street, a sparsely set of gas powered lamps left the mouth of the laneway in relative darkness. He would enter from the rear through the kitchen of the lower dwelling... the boy would be two hours old.

***

Frederick Joseph Biegel was the first to die, for the sole reason that he was the poor soul living on the ground floor. Abner felt a tinge of sorrow; he had studied Biegel and his wife almost as intently as the Hitlers themselves. He was a good man, as good as possible.

"Ja, das ist der arzt." – "Yes, this is the doctor."

Biegel pulled the door wide without hesitation, chuckling to himself, spouting a line of German Abner could not quite understand – something about forgotten tools. Beneath chubby cheeks his smiled dropped though when it was greeted with the extended barrel of a '92 silenced Glock 9mm pistol.

THWACK. Abner fired point blank right between his eyes. Biegel's knees buckled as blood splattered across the adjacent cupboard wall.

The mission... it was now well and truly alive.

Abner stepped over the body and into the kitchen, methodically clearing the room. He swung his weapon from side to side, almost brushing the walls with his muzzle in the tiny space. A haze of smoke, puffing from a cast-iron stove in the corner, clouded the light of a flickering candle. Burning timber crackled away, popping red, glowing, unattended embers now onto the slate tile floor.

Abner moved quickly. Silenced weapons, from the future or not, were not as silent as the movies led people to believe. In the confines of the Biegel home his shot had surely travelled. He moved his back against the cupboard and teetered into the hall.

"Frederick?" A woman's voice called out to her husband.

"Frederick? Was war das?" – "What was that?" It was Sofia.

Abner had crammed in as much German as possible, but the time for trickery was over, the shadows would be his from now on.

The house was a rabbit warren, but that suited him. A multitude of pokey rooms abutted each other, connected by multiple doors. Abner slipped left, away from the hall, and through a small boot and storage room. He took another door and surfaced further down, at the end of the central corridor.

Footsteps.

Sofia was up and moving.

Exiting her sewing room, she headed for the kitchen entrance. Turning right into the hall she did not notice Abner crouched in the dark to her left.

"Freder..."

THWACK THWACK. Abner double tapped two bullets into her upper back, one through the heart and another just millimetres higher. Sofia was dead before she hit the floor. She fell facedown onto the rough hardwood floor, her wrist bouncing and cracking on a linen-covered sideboard. The corridor walls flickered with a dance of shadows. A solitary candle, skewered left on a triple pronged candelabra, rolled as if in a whirlpool. From one knee, Abner somersaulted forward, catching the ornament as it tipped. Holding the flame aloft he breathed into the shadows, the yellowy glow, up close now, served only to make the rest of the hall three shades darker. Using his foot he nudged Sofia's body an inch. Blood, black as the night outside was leaking from her, slowly soaking into and between the unpolished boards. Abner brought the candelabra down and snuffed the flame... killing by candlelight... the mechanics of death had indeed changed.

It took his eyes only a second to adjust to the dark as he moved on. The Biegels had an adult son somewhere he needed to find. Through the lounge, sewing room and bedrooms he strafed, one sideways step in front of the other, stalking the night.

But the boy was nowhere to be found.

Re-emerging into the hall, he had come full circle again to Sofia. Her body was resting at the base of the only door he was yet to open. Abner ran a hand across the deep indentation in his chin. The missing son was a variable, variables created uncertainty, uncertainty created...

Damn it.

He stepped carefully over Sofia's body and lifted the solid wooden door as he pushed, quietening the iron hinges to just a squeak.

Beyond lay the internal stairs that rose to level two.

The stairwell had the cold sweat of a cellar. It was solid timber, floor to ceiling. Thick exposed beams hung overhead, so low Abner could touch them. Underfoot, knotted Baltic treads did their best to hinder his approach. With each step, a pulse, like a drum, thumped away at his forehead. Over the barrel of his pistol, his peripheral vision drew in, his focus locked on a slither of light cutting the darkness at the peak of the stairs. His ears burned, searching. A new set of sounds greeted him. Music, a duet of strings and horns, and beneath them the cries of a newborn baby. He isolated the swelling orchestra, leaving nothing but the baby's cries and the soothing sounds of young Klara's voice. At the top of the stairs he took a moment, visualising where in the house they resided. He checked his weapon; it was unnecessary, but it allowed him one final breath before he reached for the handle.

Never before had the Liebesteins asked him to complete a task so complex... with so much death.

Abner found the eldest Hitler in the living room. Peeking from the hallway, he watched as Adolf's father, Alois, fussed over a gramophone with his back turned. The room was warm, inviting. Two armchairs faced a fireplace, next to which the record player sat. There was an odour of tobacco, oak and cherry. A pipe rested on the arm of the furthest chair, the red velvet of which looked thin and its cushion sunk low with fatigue.

Abner watched as Alois lifted the stylus short on a soft longing cord. Even from behind it was obvious that he was a burly man. He huffed, spluttered and hacked phlegm from his thickset neck while he re-sleeved the record and reached for another.

In Abner's unvarnished, compressed lessons, history decreed Alois an obstinate beast. Harnessing an unwavering chauvinism – a respected trait for the time – he had surpassed expectation and class to rise from bastard farmhand to the post of inspector of customs, a lucrative position in the gateway town of Braunau.

Even now, at night, Alois was still dressed in his regal customs uniform. Abner had read reports that he was rarely seen without it. Watching, waiting, he indulged Alois his last peaceful act of preparing a new album. The music would serve as cover sure, but the precision of Alois' routine made for absorbing viewing.

A crackling filled the room, followed by a calming horn.

...Bach.

Alois savoured the first few opening chords, his eyes to the ceiling, his head tilted slightly. He rotated on a dime and began a march across the floor. At the foot of his chair he stopped, straightened his jacket and aligned himself for descent.

In doing so he unwittingly opened himself completely.

It was almost too easy.

Without hesitation, Abner fired twice into Alois' chest. The sudden unexpected impact of two bullets jolted the man backward down into the chair. The first bullet hit dead centre, right in the breastplate. The second, though, caught Alois higher than Abner would have liked, more in the neck than chest. Blood splattered up and over Alois' white handlebar moustache as his eyes shot wide.

Abner listened as, as if on cue, a quartet of graceful strings were introduced to the room. Beauty and pain, the contrast was vexing. A piano commenced next, its minor keys soaring to major as Alois' thickset face grasped for, and then choked on, its final breath.

The first Hitler was dead.

Abner hoped the Liebesteins could somehow feel it.

Stalking the length of the corridor, Abner paused next at the children's bedroom. Through a crack he could just make out the silhouette of six-year-old Angela asleep in her bed. Alois Jnr, he assumed, would be similarly asleep on the other side.

He lifted his pistol, forcing the timber ajar with the end of his barrel. Watching the rise and fall of Angela's blanket, his finger paused on the trigger. Her breath, it was soft as she turned toward him, toward the light. His body tensed… but her eyes remained closed. For how long he watched he didn't know, the seconds felt like minutes, it could have been either. The dream she was having, he could read it across her face… it was intoxicating.

He felt a fissure slice through his conviction.

Children... how had he deluded himself it would be so easy? Shaking away his empty stare he lowered his weapon... that bridge, he would cross it later.

At the end of the corridor the baby and mother were both quiet now, the entire house was silent save for Bach's concerto.

His head heavy, Abner's entrance into the master bedroom lacked his earlier patience. More breach than stealth he rolled in, right to the foot of the bed, into the wake of a silk sheath hanging from the four-poster bed.

Focusing through his confusion, Abner vaulted to his feet...

The bed, it was empty.

"Wer bist du!?" – "Who are you!?" He heard from the window.

He spun around, gun up at the ready, but hesitated. Klara was leaning into a daybed connected to the window-sill. The baby was cinched to her chest in a wrap. She looked different now after birth. A moonlit glow soaked her porcelain face. She looked calm, radiant... innocent.

Abner stood, completely exposed in the middle of the room. Mesmerised in that instant, he could not bring himself to shoot.

"Was machst du hier?" – "What are you doing here?" Klara was more curious than concerned... until she noticed Abner's gun. Her face contorted as she began to scream for her husband. "Alois? Alois!"

She was going to ruin everything.

Abner's finger compressed without him really thinking. His first shot sliced into the window architrave, but his second – albeit misplaced – found its mark. As it entered the upper left side of her forehead, Klara snapped backward against the windowpane, what remained of her face locked in a half-finished call for help.

Abner stood in disbelief, his trigger finger numb.

A woman... a baby.

He had no time to dwell on the thought, because right then, as if her newfound fate were not punishment enough, Klara began to slide out of the open window.

Jolted into action by reflex, Abner dived forward.

As her body tipped completely through the opening, Klara's ankles rapped on the timber and her slippers flung skyward.

Abner stretched with all he had. He threw one hand out into space as his other latched onto the window frame. With his body half out in the street and at the extremity of its reach, his fingers found purchase on something soft. His grip tightened, fighting with the knotted wrap of fabric.

Not a moment later, gravity seized Klara in its talons. Dragging her down to an asphalt end, it left him dangling, his chest heaving, with a newborn baby in his grip.

As he hauled himself up, curling his weight with just one arm, shock seized his joints, paralysing his body. The mission had taken a sudden drastic turn. Klara had fallen two storeys into the middle of the street below. Landing with a thud, she had crumpled into a heap, one leg at right angles to her body... Exposure for him was now a mere matter of time.

Abner stared down at the baby that was now in his arms. Miraculously, it was unharmed. The death of its mother and her subsequent slide had roused it from sleep, but it was strangely calm.

He was mesmerised. Never before had he held a baby. Back in the real world he had had no family at all, let alone children of his own. The child looked up at him, its blue eyes wide, its mouth a circle of lips, its arms waving as if clutching just for him. The delicacy of the thing struck him. Its helplessness, its innocence, it resonated within him like a bell reverberating from the tips of his fingers to his toes. He could feel his heart smashing at its confines within his chest. His stomach churned with sickness. His body was clearly rebelling against what his brain was telling him to do. This thing, it was just a child, a beautiful child who had yet to make a single mistake in life. How could such innocence be punished for crimes not yet committed, or crimes it now may never commit?

BAM!

What sounded like a cannonball thundered into the timber joist above his head.

"What...!" Abner moved on instinct. He dived for the floor, well and truly yanked back to the moment.

Standing at the doorway to the bedroom, holding his father's ceremonial Liege Model handgun, was Alois Hitler Jnr. The boy was only eight years old, and he was shaking.

An eternity passed as both boy and man counted their breath. Alois Jnr shifted his eyes up, not at the stranger now flat on the floor, but instead to the bullet hole in the ceiling. His hands quivered; it was as if he had mustered all he could to fire the shot and now the weight of the weapon was too much to bear. He dropped the handgun, but his hands remained outstretched.

Abner slowly rose to his feet still clutching the infant, his heart only now beginning to beat again. *How could I be so stupid?*

He heard a commotion upstairs. Half the block must have heard the blast.

A scream now... from across the street. Someone had noticed the body of Klara outside.

The precariousness of his predicament was compounding fast. The mission was over surely, but something was still salvageable. He needed to snap himself out of his pitiful state... it was time to survive.

Abner made for the door. As he brushed past the frozen boy, his hand reached for but resisted the boy's shoulder. He had a sorry respect for the child who had almost ended his life. From this day forth, whether he was prepared or not, Alois Jnr would be thrust into manhood. That was penance enough.

Retreating down the stairs, it was once again at the body of Sophia Biegel that he heard pounding on the front door. Neighbours, they were calling for both Frederick and Alois.

Ignoring the pleas, Abner sliced through the ground floor maze, making his way to the rear lane. He pressed the baby tightly to his chest to muffle its cries. Through the kitchen and out the rear exit, he was just metres from the safety of the dark alley when...

Crash! He was almost bowled over by a young man rounding the corner of the building simultaneously.

It was the Biegels' boy, Deryk. Face-to-face Abner could smell the liquor on his breath.

Taught with tension, Abner's body was primed for contact. In one fluid motion he spun left to protect his cargo while smashing his pistol butt into the boy's temple. The spin was all reflex and, though the strike was not his crispest, the Biegel boy stiffened and fell like a pin.

He would be out for long enough.

Abner stood in darkness on the edge of the laneway and surveyed the Hitler residence one last time.

He had failed, but all was not lost.

He tucked the whimpering infant under his jacket and fled into the night.

Chapter 8

Location: ....48.1351 N, 11.5820 E
Present day name: ....Perlacher Forest, Munich, Germany
IDTF Classification: .Ridge
Date: ....April 18th 2017

"Yo princess..." Jersey spoke like he was running a pizza shop. "...Just put your religion down as Jedi and quit your whining, you're holding up the line."

Roy bit down hard on his lip. Funeral arrangements, they were a formality he was far too familiar with. Through the 'next-of-kin section' of the form in front of him he cut a slash with his biro all the way to the carbon. *No reason to say no*, the mantra played over in his head.

Moving down the line like he was running a tray along some imaginary buffet, Roy was next comforted somewhat by a relatively painless medical. The site medic, Dr Purvis, a cheery man with a dust-brush for a moustache, reassured him with a pat on the balls and short cough that he was in good shape. "All going well..." he said. "You shouldn't be needing those funeral plans for some time."

All going well... what does that even mean?

It wasn't until his third station, a uniform fitting, that Roy had a chance to properly introduce himself to his fellow team members, Brian Heathcote and Loretta Panatoli.

From the makeshift change-room, Panatoli moved inside of his awkwardly extended hand and planted two kisses either side of his cheeks. Holding him by the shoulders, she looked him up and down. "Honey, you looka like a puppy..." The front on her quickly gave way to a slyly curled lip. "...Cute, but lost."

Roy caught her smile, only just. "I'm sorry, I didn't realise we had to be across our parallel-multiverse theories."

"You didn't do the pre-reading on the plane?"

"I've seen *Donnie Darko*... I didn't get it, but I've seen it. Surely that counts?"

It was a corny line, but somehow it extracted a laugh from her. Roy's whole body relaxed. He sensed her smile had that effect on people.

"So, what were you doing today?"

"Huh?" He was slow across her subject jump.

"Today? I'm-a guessing they found you somewhere? What were you doing?"

"Oh. Teaching. I'd just finished a first-year lecture."

"You're at Oxford right?"

"Yeah. How...?"

"I've heard your name before, you're impressing people."

Roy laughed off a blush. "Hardly... It's funny actually. When I got the call, people were trying to tell me I was walking into a promotion." He looked around the tent. "This is a step up from my office, so maybe they were right."

He snuck a distracted glance behind a modesty curtain, hoping to God it was empty. "How about you, Ms Panatoli? What were you doing when the SWAT team kicked in your door?"

With a classic mean-girl shrug she flicked a lock of her auburn hair. "Only my lawyer calls me Ms Panatoli. Call me Loretta."

"Right, sorry."

"Well, the old one, with the moustache, he and three of his goons found me on the promenade. Interrupted my macchiato... so I made him sweat for a bit."

Roy didn't doubt that she did.

Looking around the room, Loretta's attention settled on a trunk overflowing with garments. She let out a gasp. "I'm-a not wearing that camou... flage." For a linguistics expert, she struggled with some of the trickier English. "...I seen what it does to a woman's body; that Clarke, she looks like a weight... lifter."

Roy knelt down next to the box. "I'm sure there will be something." He started handing items up for Panatoli to hold against her body. "You have a colour preference, jungle green or sandblast beige?"

Loretta's face hid none of her disgust as she flung garments aside. "Skinny bitch, skinny bitch, skinny bitch. I thought Americans were supposed to be fat?"

Overstating her dimensions somewhat, she was not at all large. Voluptuous maybe, but even that, Roy figured, was a stretch. As she stood over him, dressed in her own classic, Italian, 'just off to the shops' style, Roy actually found himself a little tongue-tied. Beneath a black pencil-skirt and white silk blouse, she had on those black stilettoes with the red underneath.

He looked down sheepishly, *shit*. The only parts of his outfit that didn't look crinkled were the stiff camel-coloured patches stitched on the elbows of his jacket. He did have leather shoes on at least... kind of.

A khaki jumpsuit landed over his head, shrouding him in shade. "Right then, I'm done, your turn."

Underneath his camouflage veil Roy marvelled, but then smiled... he might come to regret it, but he figured he may have made his first friend.

As comforting as his introduction to Loretta Panatoli had been, Roy's first interaction with Doctor Brian Heathcote was, unfortunately, an altogether different story. Apparent almost immediately, was the fact that he instead... was a dick.

"Out of my way." Heathcote grabbed at a two-person-tent-sized-shirt that was surely infinity-XL. "I am needed back at Support, I don't have time for dress-ups."

His elitism reeked worse than his body odour, but both were so bad Loretta actually recoiled. She turned to Roy, not even bothering to whisper. "Is there some sort academic hierarchy we were not told about?"

"Get used to it, honey." Heathcote's smile was smugger than a slap on the ass. His wrinkles, bony nose and chicken lips all snivelled down, as if scrunched into a funnel. As he spoke he opened his shirt to his navel. "You get your head around the quantum technicalities of these Tears and then maybe we can talk."

"Ew..." Loretta's shudder was the harshest comeback possible.

"Ugh," Heathcote scoffed, as he held his shirt to his chest. Muttering to himself he moved into a change room cubicle.

Roy turned to Loretta. "I think I'm good, we should probably sit this out in the debrief tent. Give him some space."

Loretta scooped up her handbag and extracted a menthol cigarette. "Am I too much?"

"No..." Roy's voice pitched up with his lie. "...Not, at, all."

For their second briefing the rest of Bravo Team eventually regrouped in the original debrief hut.

"Could everyone please open the folios in front of you and observe the three profiles." Major Clarke stood at the head of the table. 'Strategic Intelligence' was scribbled on the whiteboard behind her.

Roy opened his folio to see a face staring back at him. It was an A4 headshot of a man in a blue suit and solid red tie. The whole ensemble, the outfit, the cheesy grin, the orange tan, it all screamed campaign shot.

Beneath Mr 'Make-America-Great-Again' there were more photos, of different men. Clarke spoke while Roy began to flick through them.

"Retired Senator Wilson Broadford. American. Listed missing twelve years. Whereabouts unknown." She was reading from a clipboard, pacing slowly in front of the whiteboard. "Harley Vincent. American. Listed missing six years eleven months. Whereabouts unknown. Francesco Girobaldi. Italian. Listed missing three years three months. Whereabouts unknown." Clarke looked up from her board. "Ladies and gentlemen... let me introduce to you the first three interdimensional Time Tear Travellers."

"Goddangit." Spike straightened from his recline. He pulled his finger from his nose and snatched up his previously unopened folio, like he only now realised it was important.

Clarke continued. "On the top of the pile there is Senator Broadford."

"He was the new President?" Roy confirmed.

"Correct Professor. We were quite fortunate to find Senator Broadford in such an obviously different situation inside Tear One. It provided clues we didn't even know we were looking for. He saved us a whole lot of needle-in-the-haystack type work, because, before him, we didn't even know we were looking for an anomaly."

"Could he have been a innocent by-product of someone else's actions? A butterfly effect maybe?"

"Potentially yes. But upon discovering the significance of the initial human traveller – that basically the new world was created just for them – Senator Broadford seemed our first obvious lead. The plan was simple: while we were over there trying to differentiate him from the other 'Ectypes', Support back here in the 'Ridge' set about investigating his current disposition." Clarke allowed them all a second for processing lag.

The pause was welcome, 'Ridge' was a term that Roy was still getting used to; it was short for o'rig'inal universe. 'Ectype' though he had never heard before.

She continued. "His status as a missing person back in the Ridge gave us the confidence to make him a person of 'level-one' interest inside the Tear and, as such, aggressively pursue his cooperation. Once cooperation was attained and confirmation received that he was indeed the anomaly, we knew we were potentially onto something with the missing persons angle."

"How exactly did you confirm he was any different to whatever it was you just called an ordinary person?" Roy asked.

"Ordinary people? We call them Ectypes, Professor."

"Ectypes...?" Roy's memory of the word's literal meaning jogged. "...Right."

"Yes, it's how we refer to the rest of the population inside the Tear." She turned to Spike, answering his question before he could ask it. "It's a fancy word for imitation. A copy, replica, duplicate."

For his part Spike just poked his tongue out.

"And..." Clarke cleared her throat. "...As for the confirmation component Professor... we leave that up to the tactical team." Her answers were morphing now from purposefully vague to overtly menacing. "Using Broadford as test case 101, the idea was then born to collate a list of all wealthy or significant missing persons and investigate them as potential travellers. Currently we have a list of seventeen missing persons. We think we can narrow that down further depending on certain scenarios and time-frames we find inside the Tears. The list has provided us with a starting group to look into if changes like a new President are not immediately obvious."

"So someone here is selling trips back to those who can afford it?" Roy asked.

"That is what we believe, Professor. The three men all have a unique thing in common: they have, or more so 'had', a net wealth well in excess of 100 million dollars before vanishing from the face of the Earth. We believe people are purchasing trips, and then becoming anomalies once on the other side."

"For any reason?" Roy pressed.

"The currently accepted proposal is that people might travel for two... one is to greatly enhance their own imme-diate situations via selfish manipulations. We found exam-ples in Tears One and Two. The second is to greatly affect the course of history for all mankind by manipulating a world event. An example like we found in Tear Three."

"Someone actually travelled for reasons other than money?" Loretta pulled her chair in.

"Yes, Professor Panatoli." Clarke turned back to Roy. "It is in this such scenario that your expertise will be needed Professor Roy, to identify subtle, and potentially not so subtle, world changing events." Clarke looked around. No one said anything. "Please everyone turn your attention to the background information packs in your folio. It will all make sense."

A new, even more literal, Clarke began again. "Harley Vincent was found in Tear Two using the list of missing wealthy persons. He was found to be the head of a multi-national conglomerate that supposedly owned nearly all of the internet's most famous software. Google, Facebook,

Twitter and YouTube were all invented or purchased by him just prior to them exploding in popularity. He was not happy with his 100 million, he travelled to turn it into 100 billion."

The boyish face staring at Roy from the second photo looked right at home behind a keyboard.

"Francesco Girobaldi in Tear Three was the first we think to travel for more utilitarian reasons. Spike, that means not for financial or personal gain," said Clarke.

Spike made to throw a paper he had been scrunching, but thought better of the idea.

"Unselfishly, for a greater good? Maybe it was because he wasn't American?" Loretta offered.

Clarke ignored the jibe. "Being a devout Christian, we speculate Girobaldi travelled to meet his messiah in Israel, maybe to become a disciple, or get his own chapter in the King James. Unfortunately, we cannot confirm this theory because no anomaly was detected in Tear Three. We assume he met a premature end, captured and murdered or possibly sold into slavery to die at the end of a Roman whip."

Israel, Romans, Messiah? Roy's mind was refusing to connect the obvious dots.

Clarke continued before anyone could throw a question into the information void left exposed. "The expertise of your predecessor, Dr Ashbury, was integral to a Tear Three outcome, Roy. Once the time destination was confirmed she provided invaluable insight as to where to look for..." Clarke stopped, and scanned the room as she shuffled on the spot. "...excuse me ...Jesus Christ."

Roy's mind blew up. "Major Clarke, are you saying that you have had contact with..." Roy himself paused, aware of how ludicrous the question would seem in any other situation. "The... Jesus Christ?"

He could see the cogs turning in Clarke's head, searching for a diplomatic response, when...

BANG! BANG! BANG! – The door to the room hammered inward. "Major Clarke Major Clarke!" a voice, short on breath, yelled from the other side.

Clarke opened the door to expose the keeled over figure of Jersey behind.

The man looked up from his kneeling position and pointed down the row of huts. "Major... You gotta see this."

Clarke leant out, holding both sides of the frame. From his spot inside Roy couldn't see what exactly was happening, but in Clarke's face he saw all that he couldn't outside.

Her eyes were wide.

"Major... The Tear... it's opening." Jersey was staring, as she was, to the right.

Speechless still, Clarke's eyes were glued on whatever it was that was beyond Roy's scope of vision.

"Major. The room, Support, the whole tent, it's all gone dark."

"Yeah, I can fucking see that, Gianinni!" The concern in her voice was something new. "Zhu get over here!"

And that was when Roy felt it... the rumbling.

Everyone in the room did too. Roy grabbed for the table. Those standing split-step, their fingers splaying wide. All eyes shot together to the cup in the middle of the table, which was where the first clatter started. Jumping like popcorn, first a black and then a red biro leapt over the lip. The shaking, expanding as if from an epicentre, spread next to the table, then Roy's chair, the floor, the walls and the lights above him too.

"Doctor...!" Clarke's voice was shaking like she was jackhammering.

"Yes." Zhu was already at the door. "Oh my... that's... not good."

They were both staring right, Roy remembered now, it was toward the Tear Tent.

"Zhu what's happening? Why is the Tent blacked out?"

"Um... I'm not sure... but something tells me it's not good."

"Is it collapsing?"

Zhu's silence was damning.

"Doctor... is it collapsing?"

"I... I don't know?"

Unable to contain their curiosity, Heathcote, Spike and Loretta were up and out of their seats.

Roy looked about the now empty table "Um... is there something we should be doing?"

"Yeah." Clarke stuck her head back in. "Bravo! Get your shit together. We've got to move!"

Chapter 9

The dock was thick with the clatter of applause. A sea of people rolled as one, up and down like the waves chopping at the water's edge, smiling, cheering, waving to strangers they didn't even know. Across from them, on the other side of the expanse, hundreds packed shoulder-to-shoulder against the balustrade, blowing down kisses. An unbridled excitement gripped all aboard, while below envy flooded the dock.

Hidden in among the outpouring of emotion it was easy to miss the figures of two men who stood stoically still. With their necks craned skyward, the two could not share in the joy, not with the knowledge they possessed...

The RMS Titanic was a sight to behold. The tales – of a Kingdom ship touted as the largest to ever set sail – were no lie. The ship was indeed a marvel of 'this' time. From up close on the Southampton dock the older man could see the ship dwarfed every structure around it, both on land and at sea. Its plate-black steel rose up before him, to a row of portholes, before disappearing white into the crisp sky above.

The Titanic's four gigantic smokestacks bellowed. A deafening air-horn sounded.

It was noon, departure time.

The older man had seen all he needed.

"David..." Abner turned to his boy. "...It's time."

Stepping off, it was only he who moved early, before the ship set sail. Because it was only he that knew already, that for most of the 1500 souls on-board, in five days' time, neither tale, nor size... would count for anything at all.

At twenty-three, the boy trailing Abner through the crowd was now well and truly a man. His appearance, genetically predetermined, was developing slowly, day-by-day like a lifelong Polaroid, rather than growing into its own. He had a bowl of dead-straight black hair and bulging eyes that looked black more often than blue.

His reminiscent looks, though, were where the similarities with his comparable double ended. In the place of that man – who was in Vienna about now, getting rejected from art school not once, but twice – was a farmer and soon to be soldier, with a strength that many underestimated. Abner could see it now beyond the shoulders of his dusty brown vest; his muscles, thin and wiry, ran like sinewy tendons over his shoulders.

At the end of the dock Abner paused. "Take one last look, this ship is not long for the sea."

David eyed the wall of black steel, end to end. He had learned better than to question. "Shame, I suppose."

Abner pushed off through the throng, but David paused, his next words only for himself, "...so many," he smiled, "...so ignorant."

The pair cut through Southampton with not another word spoken, across cobble, between bluestone.

The time had come for Abner to set his master plan into motion. His goal – albeit two years away – would require some work; some manipulations he had thus far been careful to avoid. This venture into town would serve a purpose, as every action served a purpose.

He did not intend to be caught short... not before the world went to war.

Providence Estate was a farm a half-day's travel from Southampton. Walking beneath the wrought iron arch, Abner and David trudged the dirt drive in the shadow of a rising sun. Through muddied puddles, they were led by a waist-high wall of stacked stone to a cottage in the valley recess.

The property, not just in name, was Abner's offer of atonement: self-flagellation on the end of a plough, a constant reminder of the seriousness of his decision, of the ramifications should his dedication slip. *It was the simple who suffered.*

Twenty-three years ago he had been sent back with more gold bullion than his escape could handle, plenty enough to drop some along the way and still have a life-time supply. From Austria the convenience of English had led him quickly to the United Kingdom. Southampton, chosen simply as the first place he had landed, was where he had settled without much ado, a widowed father of one, looking to hide himself away from the world.

As much as travelling, settling and establishing a life with a newborn child had necessitated sacrifice, the isola-tion of the estate had proved exactly his idea of happiness... for the first two decades at least.

Providence Estate... how fitting the name was.

"Up slightly and to the right." Abner crouched beside his boy with a pair of binoculars.

The two were propped upon a rise, beneath the blackened husk of a lone elm tree. Overlooking the property, they were close to a sky that had turned a threatening shade of grey.

David was lying prone on the sodden grass, his feet splayed out, toes dug into the mud. A '92 model, American-made, Barrett M90 .50-calibre sniper rifle was nestled against his right shoulder.

The rifle was a leap for the boy, but he had already mastered his 1880 Lee-Metford bolt-action, and Abner had no other weapon to bridge the 110-year technology gap.

"Let it float in your hands."

Without a word the boy shuffled on his stomach. Cupping the scope he clicked the zoom two stiff turns left.

"Exhale, hold and then fire. Ready..."

A boom split the sky like thunder.

The shot almost put David's shoulder out – Abner could tell – but a slight wince was all the boy allowed himself. Lesson learned, he released a shallow breath before reeling off a second and then third shot. Through his binoculars Abner watched plumes of dirt kick up two paddocks over, drawing in each time on a red dot he had painted on an old plough.

PANG!

The plough was blown onto its side.

Abner lowered his binoculars and studied the boy's back, his shoulder blades were cocked close, but his chest was deathly still, completely empty. He did not move a muscle.

Abner paused, for only a moment. The silence, it was all that would pass between them, it was all that was required. His boy, he knew...

Abner raised the binoculars once more. "Again..."

PANG! The plough rolled again, a hole like a fist punched straight through it.

"Again..."

PANG!

"Again..."

Abner felt something within him stir. His son was good, unnaturally so, better even than he was at the same age. He closed his eyes and envisaged his plan... Just maybe, the events in Braunau were no failure. Just maybe, some good could rise from the ashes of evil. Just maybe, the devil of one world could redeem himself in the next.

"Sir... By the dam."

Abner looked up to see that David had shifted silently to the left. Still he had one eye peeled down the length of his sights.

Raising his binoculars again, Abner twisted both grips to focus in on the farm's main dam, this time four paddocks over. So far was it across the property, even the slightest movement shook his vision above and below the horizon.

He settled himself on the pool of brown.

David's meaning was immediately plain. A great stag was stuck up to its knees in the mud surrounding the dam.

Unheard at such a distance, it was obvious still that the thing was in distress. Its mouth cried up to the sky, its eyelids drooped, heavy with exhaustion. Completely helpless, the animal could not even collapse and drown itself in the low-lying water, so entrenched in the mud it was.

"Should I?" David was already clicking his scope.

"That's almost a thousand metres."

Neither man looked at the other when they spoke.

"I can do it."

"Just because you can doesn't mean you should. If you miss..."

"I won't miss."

"If you do you'll be digging him out on your own... alive."

There was only silence from David as he seemed to contemplate the risk versus reward, the effort versus the hit to his pride.

"...But should you hit, I will bury him myself."

It was the kicker David didn't need. He was already settling himself.

Abner also prepared a weapon. Reaching behind his back he pulled his pistol free from his pants and pointed it into the air.

David's breath left him.

As his trigger finger pulled close, so did Abner's.

CRACK BOOM!!! Two shots rang out across the farm, one with purpose before the other.

David's sailed wide, hitting the water like a supersonic anvil. He snapped to his father, his eyes burning in a moment of instinctual anger... but he said nothing... the lesson was clear.

Abner was looking out still. "Shovel is in the shed."

David pushed up from his elbows. "Yes sir."

As he walked behind, Abner lowered his binoculars. "David..."

The boy turned.

"Get two... We're in this together from now on."

Chapter 10

Location: ....48.1351 N, 11.5820 E
Present day name: ....Perlacher Forest, Munich, Germany
IDTF Classification: .Ridge
Date: ....April 18th 2017

Roy was standing in what looked to be a decontamination corridor. Hot like a greenhouse; above him, a series of nozzles protruded from the roof, while below, a metal grating flexed underfoot.

In front, Loretta, Heathcote, Spike and Clarke stood in single file, in that order. Like they were in an elevator, no one had said a word since they had filed in.

Roy shuffled on the spot trying to disguise a not-so-subtle rearrangement of his jocks. Whether it was the condensation or the sweat from his back drenching them, they were well and truly soaked. *Goddamn, why'd we settle on the beige pants*, he could only imagine the sweat-soaked butterfly-splodge he must have had on his arse.

To go with the pants, his Under Armour long-sleeve, hiking boots and webbed carry vest with enough pockets to lose things in, had him – quite uncomfortably – feeling like a '90s South African safari ranger.

The outfit – thrown on in double time – was only temporary he knew, because travelling with them was an entire crate dedicated solely to 'apparel'. It was bizarre, but made complete sense when he thought about it. They had no idea how far they were heading back, so preparations were necessary to fit in with the local population. They had wardrobe variations ranging from that of a 1600s aristocratic noble, with ruffs, tights and heels, up until an assortment of 1970s and 80s velvet tracksuits, bedazzled denim jackets, and skintight jeans.

If only the German Hasselhoff-era was what he had been brought up on, Roy thought.

"All right everyone, two minutes," Clarke yelled to no one in particular. "Crates are through, we're next." She was looking into the 'Tear Tent' through a thick porthole in the door.

The 'Tear Tent' was what Roy had taken to calling the room at the end of their bottleneck; it did have a more technical designation, but at least Tear Tent was better than 'The Big-Top Motherfucker' Spike was rolling with.

From Clarke, down the line of Bravo, Roy could feel the tension inside the corridor. It shot from person to person, hunched shoulder to hunched shoulder, like they were all actually ionised, electrifying the person behind.

The anxiety between them had been building now exponentially for the last fifteen minutes. The exact reason their run for the Tear had been delayed now was something no one felt pertinent enough to explain. The blackout, some apparent radiation... *the giant sphere of blackness that had extended into the sky above the Tear Tent!* Fuck, it had all happened so fast he felt he was just bobbing askew on the crest of a we-don't-know-but-let's-go-anyway wave.

"What does your wife think of you doing this?"

So lost was he, down his rabbit hole of trepidation, Roy didn't notice Loretta turn to him and whisper. She was motioning down with her eyes to where Roy's hands were fidgeting with his crotch. She had clearly noticed he was wearing his wedding ring.

"Oh, um... she... doesn't really know," Roy stammered. "I mean actually, it's..."

"...Complicated," Loretta finished for him. "I'm sorry, I didn't mean to pry. I was just thinking she must be some woman to let you on this adventure."

A familiar lie logjammed in Roy's throat. He wanted to tell her the truth, to unburden himself, but right now – inside this twenty-metre long industrial shower – was not the time to be opening up.

Loretta sensed his apprehension and saved him. "If I were still married, there is no way my husband would have been happy about this. He would have huffed and puffed like the macho idiot he was and I would have come along just to spite him." Her red lips split into a grin. How she still had lipstick on he didn't know. "That's probably why we're not married anymore."

"Oh...?" Roy started. "You're divorced...?" *Fucking duh.*

She laughed. "Two times and looking for a third my love."

Loretta's warmth was making a habit of putting him at ease, making him feel less stupid than he should. Desperate to change the subject, she gave him the confidence to pluck at a piece of subconscious garbage his mind was contemplating.

"Do you think they will have Wi-Fi where we are headed?" Roy blurted.

What... Hang on! He wanted to catch the words as they spilled from his mouth. Why did he always say dumb things when he was nervous?

"Why?"

Oh fuck... he'd started now. "So I can maybe start us up a messenger group..." He swallowed hard. "...I was thinking of calling it 'Bravo Bravo'."

She turned to him, her face blank. "I don't understand?"

I knew it. You idiot. Just do the world a favour and punch yourself.

Roy shuffled. "Um... Bravo... doesn't it mean 'good' in Italian? I thought, you know, we are Bravo Team and..." He stopped, was he actually going to explain it? "...Never mind."

He was looked down at his feet when he heard her laugh.

"Dio... Roy." She pushed him. "...You're too easy."

"Oh..." He almost fainted from relief, like a balloon with the air let out. "You..."

Her eyebrows shot up. "Bitch, eh?"

"Wow, no, I was going to say '...got me'." He smiled, "...but hey, now that you mention it."

She smiled too. "Be careful Professor, you're beginning to sound like a future husband of mine."

As they both laughed, neither realised that Heathcote's ears had pricked.

Turning to them, his rat face compressed into a snigger. "You people are about to travel through to another dimension and here you are concerned with the frivolities of this one. It's embarrassing." He turned then, away from them, pushing his way forward.

"Shuddup, why don't you?" Loretta called after him, her waving hand shaking at the air.

Spike turned into Heathcote's void and offered Roy a wink. "Don't worry Professor I got it. If there is Wi-Fi Bud, I'll join your group, maybe even hook myself up some interdimensional swipe-right action."

Roy appreciated the support, but Spike joining in on his joke probably proved just how bad it was.

Spike took a quick survey left and right, a giddy look in his eyes. "How about this one then: how far back we got to travel in time until we get to a place where being big is a sign that you are... you know... big."

"Ah..." Roy did a double take, not really following.

Spike though was already smiling. "...Because whenever it is, that fat motherfucker would be made *king* for sure."

Roy couldn't help but cough out a laugh. Loretta too.

Spike kept at it. "It's not just me, right? He *is* hard to deal with?"

"He's not the warmest fella." Roy was trying to be diplomatic.

"Please Roy," Loretta scoffed. "He's an A-grade asshole. I bet you when he sits in an exit row, he still reclines his seat all the way."

"Oooh nice." Spike was nodding. "He done try the same with me earlier, quizzing me on my credentials like he was hiring a personal fucking bodyguard. He should realise with his big fucking brain and all, that it's not a good idea to talk down to the men with the guns." The sergeant began bouncing up and down on his heels. "Anyway... Onto the bigger issues, what are we expecting inside, what's the bet? A hole into hell, a portal through the wall, a beam-me-up type arrangement? What are we thinking? Blue, green, invisible even?"

Roy's mouth opened, ready to spill some more unconscious thoughts, but before he could, a pneumatic hiss from the front of the room interrupted him. *Stargate, the '94 Kurt Russell classic...* was he really about to say it?

"Eyes up!" Clarke's voice cut in again.

Roy looked up to see the pair of automatic doors had slid open. A curtain of steam was falling from the top of the opening.

Like golden flakes the vapour sparkled in mid-air.

A hush fell over the team as the fog cleared.

Good God. Roy gulped.

Beyond lay the Tear... in all its glory.

Roy felt his bottom lip actually drop an inch, an intake of breath stalled in his chest, burning his lungs. His eyes were charged in their sockets, never before had a sight gripped him so ferociously, so instantly.

"Oh Dio..." Loretta breathed.

"Well, I'll be..." Spike managed.

Roy couldn't agree more, but all eloquence had abandoned him. Beautiful... magnificent... dazzling... nothing could capture the sight he was seeing.

Tear... the name garnered a tangible relevance now. Dr Zhu had been spot on with his description; the room, it indeed looked 'torn'.

Roughly three metres high, the Tear was thinner at the top and bottom, compared to the middle, which was like a jagged slit. Inside – where the room that had been theoretically ripped – an endless seam of gold shimmered as if backlit. Tiny waves danced across the surface, as they would in a glass dancing to heavy bass. The vibrating surface provided the Tear's only sense of depth. Everything else about it looked somehow cut and pasted, two-dimensional almost. From the front it was fully visible, but Roy could see that by just taking a step to the side he would be reducing its surface visibility.

Could it be completely invisible from a right angle?

Only as he moved to the side did his other senses begin to drip-feed him information. His face prickled, popping with electricity. All sound had evacuated the room, to the extent that he could hear his own breath and the beginnings of a pulse returning to his heart. *Deafening silence, negative decibels... no way.* He had read of the phenomenon, but never believed it possible.

Drawn to the atmosphere immediately surrounding the Tear, Roy could see that something about the space was definitely off. In the same way a room distorted when he pressed a finger on the side of his eyeball, his eyes strained to nail down one spot on the static. He tried to refocus, yet black spots still darted across the Tear's periphery. *Was the air itself, quaking?*

As the team filed forward, like bugs drawn to the light, a grated gangplank greeted them. The walkway rose up on an angle to roughly two feet by the time it reached the mouth of the Tear. Following it, Roy only noticed then that the Tear was floating.

Dr Zhu was standing on the plank. Behind him Roy could see through a transparent section of wall, a viewing room was looking back at him, full of Army brass and Support technicians.

"Doctor, is that normal?" Roy pointed to the distorted atmosphere around the Tear.

"Ah, keen observation Professor." Zhu's shrug slid his glasses down his nose. "I wish I could say, but unfortunately this is the first time we have witnessed the phenomenon. It might have to do with some advanced cycle, or advanced energy drain, kind of like the blackout occurrence we witnessed when it first appeared. Either way, I dare say this Tear may be older than we first anticipated."

Zhu was much more forthcoming with his ideas now he didn't have Clarke to pull his leash. She was further ahead at the mouth of the Tear.

Roy took his chance. "Is it possible that this Tear could have remained hidden for longer in the depths of this forest, that it could indeed be closer to collapse?"

"Of course Professor, this Tear could be thirty years old for all we know. It could be older than any of the previous three. The order in which we named them relates to when we found them, not the sequence in which they were created."

"What if it is, or was… first?"

"It would mean then, yes, it is surely closest to collapsing." Zhu's smile wrinkled his nose; he was enjoying this way too much. "If it is, you had better get a wriggle on then, before it collapses and takes us all with it." Roy gulped as Zhu slapped him on the shoulder. "I'll be sure to fill you in in greater detail when I see you on the other side with the Detachment-Array. We can discuss it at length then while we are shutting the world down."

Hang on… Roy flinched as Zhu moved past him. *What did he just say? What are we shutting down?* "Excuse me, doctor…" he tried. But before he could complete the question, Clarke's voice cut in from the mouth of the Tear.

"Come on people, let's move! Beware though, all that glitters ain't gold. This may not feel good for you first-timers." She chuckled then as she stepped through the pool.

Wow wow wow. Watching her vanish completely, Roy's brain popped a vessel.

He hadn't noticed, but Spike had moved to the rear of the line. "All right, all right, you heard the lady."

Heathcote and Loretta were next up to the plate. Neither of them so much as flinched when it came time to immerse themselves.

As Roy's turn came he paused. *Hang on, can we talk about this a second?*

"Royston, stop fucking around, through you go." Why Spike was calling him Royston was anyone's guess.

Roy's face was inches away from the Tear; the golden glow filled his entire vision. He could feel a thermal drag ever so slightly pulling him closer, as if the room had dropped temperature and the Tear was inviting him with warmth. He was unsure if he should step or jump through; he had an irrational fear of being stretched beyond the possibility of reconstruction.

Jump, definitely jump...

It hardly mattered though, because the last thing he felt of his world was a stiff push in the back.

Fucking Spike... he had shoved him head first into the abyss.

Chapter 11

Location: .... 48.5442° N, 12.1469° E
Present day name: .... Landshut, Germany
IDTF Classification: . Tear Four
Date: .... June 22nd 1914

Abner and David sat in a familiar silence, shoulder to shoulder, staring at a water-coloured landscape. Above the unoccupied seat opposite them, the rich forest-scape was hand-painted, not wallpaper – a nice touch, lost to commuters back home.

For the start of summer, it was unusually hot. Even with the shades drawn the late morning sun had thickened the atmosphere in the cabin. Both men were formally dressed, first class dictated it so. Their matching three-piece suit and top hat ensembles were fitted tight, in a manner to which only Abner was accustomed.

A screech of brakes, metal on metal, signalled the imminent end to their journey. The pair rocked gently forward as the Royal Bavarian jostled side-to-side on its long deceleration into Landshut's new railway station.

"Happy?" David's voice was flat.

Abner replied with only a nod.

On the bench seat opposite David had assembled, checked and deconstructed their two rifles. Leaning forward, he hid them again in their respective briefcases, below a hard flap that held clothes above.

As David closed the second case, a knock at the door broke the silence. Before either man could answer, a man in uniform snuck his head through.

"Papiere?"

Abner held up his papers fanning them out like a winning hand.

"Arbeit oder vergnügen?" – "Business or pleasure?" The man exaggerated the strokes of his pen on a clipboard.

Abner produced a pamphlet from his inner jacket pocket. "Importe."

In 1914, Germany, through BASF and Bayer, held a ninety percent trade monopoly over the global chemicals market. A father/son business was their guise, if it went that far.

The man hardly looked up, "danke," and a second later was gone.

David leant back, releasing a slow breath. Abner returned his gaze to the painting, but he could feel the boy's eyes on him.

"That was close."

Abner's shrug was slow. "You would have done what was required."

Seeming to think on it, David rolled his neck, "I'm done sitting on a train."

"We're only halfway."

From Southampton to Le Havre, then east through Paris, Strasbourg, Stuttgart and Munich, their journey had been majority rail. Landshut, their two-hour detour north-east of Munich, would be their first chance to stretch out.

The silence broken, David continued, "Abner, is it possible this endeavour of yours will place our final objective at risk?"

"Maybe..." Abner ignored the undertone of the boy's 'of yours'. Turning to the window he peeled back a slit in the veil. "Remember that in this line of work, junctures in the road will present. The ability to remain flexible and grasp opportunity is vital. Detours, digression and even failings, they can lead to outcomes you will find yourself amazed you did not foresee in the first place." This specific fact he knew all too well. He turned. Any other father would have placed a comforting hand on a shoulder. "This endeavour, David, is one such experience. But a folly of mine it is not... a final test of yours it shall be."

Overseen by Trausnitz Castle and dissected by the river Isar, Landshut was a quaint town, noteworthy enough maybe to justify an over-65's daytrip. Seven-hundred years' worth of brochure facts aside, it was one particular, soon-to-be infamous Landshut resident, that had piqued Abner's interest, and necessitated their own version of an excursion.

Abner looked down at a thick manila folder on his lap. It had been there from Southampton to Munich, nearly the entire way. The dossier was his bible, under-read but over-quoted. Its seam was worn and its corners dog-eared. Across the top of the folder the letters 'P.F.E' were barely visible in calligraphy. The term stood for 'Potential Future Exploitations' – a Liebestein-coined travel designation.

How had Fritz surmised it? *"Like our business maxim boy... 'Investment, Invention and Human avenues for change' ...Keep it safe, use it wisely, shape the world how you see it needed."*

Abner opened the folder. Staring up at him was the face, crisp and flat, like the day it was printed. So buried the photo had been under a mountain of financial advice it was a wonder he had even come across the gem. Abner looked down at the smiling headshot, through the man's circular frameless spectacles.

"Here," he handed David the photo. "It's all you need."

"Who is he?"

"That doesn't matter."

Oh, but how it did, because the man in the photo was a Nazi general of the most despicable degree... his name was Heinrich Himmler.

As David studied the photo, Abner read the man's bio.

...Often grouped with the likes of Goering, Goebbels and Heydrich, as mere Hitler underlings, Heinrich Himmler is instead a man who stands peerless as the second most powerful man in Germany during WWII. Conceivable even to many will be the notion that he should share the very pedestal of infamy as Hitler himself... because for where Hitler controls the war, Himmler controls the genocide.

A staunch anti-Semite, Himmler – using the SS and the Gestapo – will position himself as the architect of the most notorious Nazi endeavour... the 'final solution'. Though it will be undoubtedly Hitler who authorises it, it will be Himmler's intellect and cunning that makes the Holocaust a reality. His disturbing legacy – one of operational efficiency – is a well-oiled extermination machine that includes numerous extermination camps and hundreds of concentration camps. Places where, thanks to him, more than six million European men, women and children will be systematically sent to die.

"No problem..." David handed the photo back. "...I don't need to know."

He looked away then, as he knew to, while Abner replaced it once more in the folder. Only once before had David attempted to peek inside. Abner had caught him, on his seventh birthday, stealing a glance. It was his first and last attempt.

As Abner closed the folder, his eyes fell upon an inscription on Himmler's photo. Carved into the negative, scratched into the bottom corner, was the number '44 in white.

Abner did the maths.

The Heinrich Himmler of this world...

...was just a boy of fourteen years.

The conundrum, it was one that stabbed right at the heart of his own hypocrisy.

The train shuddered to a stop at Landshut Railway Station, its steam whistle piercing the morning air. Without a home address, Abner and David departed south for the centre of town. They would start with what little they had – Heinrich's school, Landshut Grammar Academy, which was also his father's place of work. Joseph Gebhard Himmler was the reason the family was in town; he was the newly appointed deputy principal.

Abner looked up into the sun. It was almost noon. They had roughly four hours before school ended for the day.

Skipping the playground, Heinrich Himmler looked lost in an imaginary world, one born of his only-child design. His head, light like a balloon, trailed his body as he grasped for, but missed, the leaves that swirled about him. Singing to himself, his satchel banged at his waist, pushing his hips along the playground with each jump.

Pop... from the bag a ball worked itself free.

Distracted in an instant, the boy's eyes lit up. Hunched over, like he was catching a chicken, it took more than a few fumbling seconds for him to corner the bouncing thing.

Under the shade of an elm David shuffled on the spot as he watched Heinrich flitter his way back to his father's office.

A surge of nervous energy numbed his fingers.

He is waiting for his father, perfect.

Against the brick, the boy began to play handball with no one but himself. The schoolyard around him was deserted, all students and teachers having already left for the day. Playing at the crest of a rise, behind him a bed of gravel led down to the northern shore of the Isar River.

David moved to the bank; there was a bench there that faced the water.

Twice, within a matter of minutes, he watched Heinrich swat wildly and miss wide. Each time his ball ran along at speed down into the long grass at the extremity of the schoolyard. As Heinrich trundled down to the perimeter, blissfully unaware how pathetic his hand-eye coordination was, David prepared himself. A third miss was inevitable... it would be his chance.

This plan, it would be an exemplification of the flexibility Abner championed.

Why follow the pair home? They could be done before tea.

Abner would of course scold his weapon choice. He always recommended a more impersonal approach, but no, he would stick to his guns, figuratively at least.

Another miss!

The ball came rocketing his way, gaining speed on the decline.

Steadying his smile, he pushed up from the bench.

"Ist das deins?" – "Is this yours?" David held out the yellow ball as Heinrich slid on his heels down the hill.

"Ja…" The boy approached slowly. He snuck a glance back up the hill, the office but a small square at its peak.

David kept his hand outstretched, enticing the boy forward. His German was basic at best, so he nodded with his head a silent 'come and get it'.

The tension between the pair – that of a stranger exaggerating his innocence – was fairy tale-esque in its malevolence. David could feel it, he let the moment linger, leaving Heinrich no choice but to approach.

"Danke." The boy's steps were short, his own hand extended in a reach.

"Ja." David smiled.

Heinrich stopped short. "Du kannst werfen."

"Ja." David tilted his grin, not registering the words.

Heinrich looked puzzled as he moved to within a metre.

David looked up from their meeting hands, his eyes narrowed.

One more step…

…Then he purposely fumbled the ball into the gap between their fingers.

"Ooh." Heinrich moved on rubberised reflex. Slowly, clumsily, he lunged forward, closing the gap further.

And that was when David pounced. Using his already outstretched hand he snatched Heinrich by the collar. The boy's eyes flashed wide like dinner plates, but before he could react David swung his other hand around – the one that had been behind his tailcoat.

Quick as a flash, David stabbed upward, driving his six-inch blade deep into Heinrich's sternum. The blow, severe enough to lift the boy, shifted his weight onto the handle of the knife.

Their faces were inches apart. David was carrying him now.

Heinrich was gasping short sharp breaths, his face a picture of incomprehensible shock. David could read his confusion up close like the pages of a book.

A thrill electrified his spine. Ever so slightly he leant forward and sniffed the boy's face. The smell of sweat, pubescent sweat, not yet acidic, was on him.

With Heinrich's legs dangling a foot from the ground David carried the boy back to the bench and placed him down in a seated position. His head slumped forward, bending his neck at a forty-five.

One blow was enough, David had known that instantly, but he was conscious he was being watched... and graded. He withdrew his knife, in doing so releasing a flood of Heinrich's blood into the curve of the wooden seat. To finish, he calmly, almost gently, re-inserted the knife between the third and fourth rib on Heinrich left side. The boy went into cardiac arrest instantly as the tip of the blade touched his heart.

David straightened and peered up towards the school, every cell in his body pulsing. The yard was empty still.

Perfect timing.

With no sense of hurry he produced a silk handkerchief and cleaned his hands. He looked down, pondering the body of the boy below him. *This test was not random, nor was it paid for. For some reason boy, you had this coming.*

This boy was an Abner prophecy, somehow significant. Abner had kept the facts to a minimum as a way of testing his moral condition.

He needn't have.

For cause, for prophecy, for money or for nothing, the thrill of it was enough.

David could feel something inside him shifting. The rhetoric of his youth, an ever-present oppressor to date, was dissolving. Right now, looking down at the crimson puddle flowing from boy, he felt something, something different, and it felt good.

Abner watched from well down the riverbank. He was acting as spotter and assessor in one. With the summer sun beating down on his back he still could not warm the chill that had settled at the base of his spine. The irony of the killer, the justification and victim was not lost on him. What he had just witnessed was a clinical display, devoid of all emotion... and it unsettled him.

Princip, the Black Hand and the city of Sarajevo, God help them... they had no idea what was coming.

Chapter 12

Location: .... 48.1351 N, 11.5820 E
Present day name: .... Perlacher Forest, Munich, Germany
IDTF Classification: . Tear Four
Date: .... June 25th 1914

Roy heaved his guts up. He was on all fours, his body in sensory overload. He hadn't moved yet from the spot where he'd landed, about three metres from the Tear opening. The inertia of Spike's push had carried through the Tear and sent him crashing forward into a densely packed forest. He was lucky he hadn't knocked himself out on any number of branches.

"Woooo!" Spike screamed. "What a fucking rush!" He was bouncing around like a bull rider who'd just completed his full eight seconds.

Roy let out another pitiful dry-retch.

"Wow, Royston, you all right?" Spike came over with a hand over his mouth, trying to hide a smile.

"Yep... I just need a second" With his cheeks bloated, it was all he could muster.

How wrong he'd been. It seemed stupid now, but the trip through the Tear was not what he had envisaged. Expecting a multicoloured wormhole, the like of which he had been promised by so many sci-fi movies, or possibly a light-speed rollercoaster past billions of stars, hell, he would have been happy with a trip through Wonka's magic tunnel. Instead he got blinding white light, blackness, a sucker punch in the guts, and the feeling of braking suddenly with no seatbelt on. The entire experience had lasted less than a second.

The lack of the spectacular had made emergence all the more jarring. With no lead-time to prepare, his mind had bent hard on the other side. One second he was in one place, the next in another.

Roy looked down into the mess that was today's lunch. He threw up a hand. "Maybe..." *Maybe Spike was fine because his underdeveloped mind did not even register the change. Yep... uh... no...* unfortunately the moment for defence passed when he heaved again.

Shielding his eyes, Roy rose to his feet. As he did a new world came into focus. Unlike at the time of his departure – three minutes ago – Perlacher Forest now actually resembled a forest. Rising all around him, like Indonesian scaffolding, spindly pines alternated with silvered birch, black, white and black again. Ground level visibility was surprisingly good; the trees were all old enough to have dropped most of their lower branches. Over ankle high brush Roy's view stretched on and on, his focus only fading at the edge of visibility into a whitewash of mist.

"Anytime you're ready, Professor." A voice, Clarke's, came from behind him.

Roy spun around to see the rest of his team watching him with varying levels of intrigue. Clarke, Spike, Panatoli and Heathcote were waiting together, along with another man. He was dressed differently to the rest of them; instead of Army fatigues or a safari suit, he had on a brown suit and flat cap – the soft round type with a small peak in the front.

"This way about fifty metres…" said the new man in the tweed, his American accent thick with a Latino flavour, "…there is a clearing up ahead."

Roy picked up his backpack and gave an apologetic wave. He tacked himself onto the end of the group as they set off in single file.

"You feeling all right back there, darling?" Loretta whispered over her shoulder. She was one step ahead of Roy in the line.

"Yeah, thanks." His pride hurt more than his stomach now. "You feel anything?"

"No." She tapped her curves. "I wish, but you don't get these by having a soft stomach."

"Right, did I miss anything?"

"What, while you were down there looking for that thing you dropped?" Loretta laughed. "…Poverino. Don't worry you weren't the only one, I am pretty sure I saw Heathcote almost faint while he thought nobody was watching." She rocked her head as she walked, the motion transferring down though her curves. "Um… what did you miss? Not too much. The guy up there in the suit is from Alpha Team. His name is Roman. He's taking us to the main camp. He said they have already done some reconnaissance and have a pretty good idea of where we are."

"'Where' or 'when'? The difference is pretty important."

"Oh sorry, yeah, *when*. That is going to take some getting used to."

"Really!" His voice pitched up an octave. "So…"

Loretta was smiling to herself – that should have been a sign. She continued walking, her steps purposely lackadaisical. "Apparently, we are prehistoric, there may or may not have been a mention of dinosaurs."

"What! Really?" Roy stopped in his tracks.

Loretta turned to face him, her eyes rolling. "No, you idiot."

Bravo Team entered the clearing on the tail of Roman. The grassed meadow was round, like a crop circle and had a line of tents strafing its circumference. One side was hidden in the crescent shadow of the low afternoon sun.

Dead centre of the scout-like set-up was a welcome party waiting patiently to greet them.

"Wow," Roy breathed. Alpha Team looked like a bill-poster for *The Untouchables*. Four dapper men in sharp suits stood in what seemed strategic stages of recline.

"Welcome." An African-American man in the middle strode forward to greet them, his voice a deep baritone.

He was shorter than Roy, but looked as thick as a post. He had a gruff draw to his battle hardened face. A steely pair of black eyes pinched tight above a salt and pepper beard that rose high on his cheeks and looked ocean washed, like a crab boat captain's. It contrasted with the skin of his bald head, which glistened and was razor blade smooth.

The man extended a hand to Clarke. "Major... I see you have brought some new friends." He was looking over her shoulder at Roy and the rest of Bravo who had stopped just short of entering the campsite.

"I'm afraid we were forced into a roster change, Captain. There was an incident in Israel after you left."

"I see," the man said. "I guess we should start then with some introductions." He moved to greet the rest of team, while Clarke hovered behind with the watchful eye of a mother. "Welcome everyone. My name is Captain Kordell Mason, but you can call me Mason. I am in charge of all tactical operations relating to these Tears, and since this whole side of the Tear is considered a tactical operation, that simply means I am in charge over here." Mason strode before the line-up of Bravo, like an officer on inspection duty. As he moved from shadow to sun Roy could better appreciate his outfit.

Wow, when the hell are we? He looked as dapper as a 120-kilo keg of muscle could. Like a 1900s gangster cum modern day barista, he had on green and red suspenders, high-waisted brown suit pants and a wide brown tie.

Mason was still talking. "Using your knowledge, it is my responsibility to track down and neutralise the anomaly of this world. Your previous team proved themselves quite useful in that endeavour, but that fact means little now. I will be looking for you to step up to the plate and fill the void." He spoke with a cold efficiency and seemed completely unperturbed that the previous team might be dead.

It was not comforting.

Bravo Team stood in a moment of silence not sure who should go first. Finally Roy stepped forward. "It's a pleasure to be here sir, Jacob Roy, professor of history at Oxford University."

"You're my new Ashbury?"

"Ah... I believe so."

Loretta was next in line. "Loretta Panatoli, professor of linguistics at the University of Florence."

Heathcote puffed his chest. "I am Doctor Brian Heathcote, leading particle physicist in my field. I am here to oversee all Tear related operations."

"Leading doctor...really?" Mason looked on curiously, "I'm guessing maths is not a strength of yours?"

Heathcote couldn't compute the second choice conundrum of his claim so Mason spelled it out.

"The leading particle physicist in your field doctor, was part of the previous team."

Heathcote stiffened. "Actually..."

But his retort was cut short.

"Right, well I guess that leaves me." Spike had his thumbs in his belt. "Sergeant Stanley Doran's mi name, but you can call me Spike. Served with the Major in Afghanistan, back when she was a Captain. I got a late call up once things went south in Jew-town."

Roy noticed that one of the soldiers behind Mason prickled. *Spike...*

"Hmm..." Mason fanned his fingers through his beard. He turned to the men standing behind him. Roman, Bravo's initial chaperone, had joined the rest of his crew. "...This here, is the rest of Alpha. We have Beckett and Roman, Roman is who you met earlier, they are my fellow Army Rangers." Roman was Hispanic and Beckett a thick-necked Caucasian. "Next is Simeon, he's our representative from Israel." A serious-looking man raised his hand. He had wide-set eyes, a sharp nose and black goatee. He was the one who didn't seem to appreciate Spike's Jewish comments. "And lastly there is Gerhard, he is German Special Forces..." Gerhard was blonde with a severely pot-marked face. "...He along with yourself, Ms Panatoli, make up our German speaking experts."

With the introductions concluded, Mason turned back to Bravo's opposing line. "Now, ladies and gentlemen, the information you are all probably dying to hear..." A whiter than white smile split his lips, "...The current date, give or take a few days, is June 25th 1914."

———

Roy's mouth hung agape... again.

He felt a weight press upon his shoulders. *This is right in my wheelhouse. 1914... that means... WWI!*

"How certain are you that we are pre-war?" Clarke's question broke him from his stupor.

"Hundred percent." Mason answered. "We have used the last two days for excursions into the surrounding land-scape. Contact was made with a farmer about three miles from here and a date ascertained. Yesterday, Gerhard and I conducted an expedition up into Munich for confirmation." Mason picked up a canvas satchel he had at his feet and handed it to Roy. "Professor, in here is a collection of everything we could find and gather without raising suspicion. There are newspapers, flyers, catalogues and even a couple of borrowed books from the Munich municipal offices. I'll need you to look through them and see if anything stands out."

"Oof. OK." The pouch dragged Roy's arm down in a way it hadn't for Mason. He draped it over one shoulder.

"Right..." Mason continued, "...now that everyone is here we need to get to work on locating the anomaly. Roman, Simeon, I need you two unpacking the supplies that Bravo have brought through. I need a balloon up asap. Gerhard, get yourself acquainted with Panatoli and bring her up to speed on your conversations yesterday. Beckett, take Heathcote back over to the Tear site and help him with whatever instruments he needs. Get to know each other; from now on you both are officially Base Control. Spike, I need you to set up Bravo lodgings for tonight. Then you can liaise with Roman, he'll find you something to do. Roy, like I said, I need you on those papers; Professor Panatoli will help you with the translation as soon as she is ready." His orders flowed thick and fast, all Roy could do was nod. Finally Mason turned to Clarke. "Clarke, you, me, main tent."

There was the briefest pause before the camp scattered into motion.

Chapter 13

"Yo Hillbilly, quit wandering and get over here."

Spike snapped from his daze. He spun around with a 'who me?' expression slapped on his mug, pointing to his own chest.

"No, the other fucking Hillbilly. Get your ass over here." The soldier named Roman was staring at him. He clapped his hands. "C'mon."

Spike dropped his head and jogged over.

"It's Doran right?" Roman asked when he arrived.

"Yeah."

"Hmm." Roman inspected him through one squinting eye. "Give me a hand, grab this case, haul it over to that other clearing."

After the campsite scattering Spike had had lodgings for the night set up in no time, for some reason though he had delayed in seeking out Roman. As he and Roman each carried a case toward the clearing, Roman stopped him mid-stride.

"Stanley Doran, right?" He spoke with a laid-back, slightly menacing Latino accent. Spike didn't want to say 'gang-banger' because he'd never met one, but he couldn't help but think of that scene in *Training Day*, when those 'guys' have Ethan Hawke in the bath.

"Yeah, I said so already."

"*The*... Sergeant Stanley Doran?" Roman was squinting again, regarding him from the side. "...The one from 'Rockslide Push', Korengal Valley 2015?"

"Yeah..." Spike shifted on the spot. The mere mention of the mission turned his stomach. *Rockslide, how did Roman know about Rockslide?* It was supposed to be classified.

"Motherfucker..." Roman reached out a hand, a single gold-toothed grin forming on his face "...I thought it was you."

"OK..." Spike took the man's hand.

Roman kicked his head back. "I was part of the sweep team that came in to clean up after that mess. We got to have one hell of a hunt because of you. Rockslide Retribution, that's what we named it. Insane how the Army let us off the chain."

Spike did his best to ignore the bog of anxiety he could feel rising, locking his ankles knees and thighs. Rockslide, it was something he never spoke about.

"Yeah, I heard you guys really took it to them." He forced a smile. He had heard rumours that the Army had brought in the elite of the elite. He had thought it was Delta, but Roman didn't look Delta.

Roman gave him a jab on the shoulder. "We could never get close though to the numbers you put up that night."

"Yeah, it was a hell of a night." Spike had danced this jig before, with the doctors back in London. He had become adept at suppressing that night; it was funny how Afghanistan bestowed that ability on all of its visitors.

"You come up all right after?" Roman seemed relaxed now, his shoulders had dropped.

"Yeah, I was hit twice, but nowhere important."

"That's right. I remember hearing you were in London, pretty banged up. So you're some type of hero now? How many medals you get for it?"

"Just one, a Distinguished Service Cross. But they classified it. Can't even show nobody. Hasn't got me laid once." This same part of the play always lightened the mood; it was his 'get out of jail'.

"No justice, eh?" Roman shook his shaved head. "Makes sense then, about you and the Major. That why she called you up for this?"

"Suppose, she'd never say but."

"Well, either way it's good to have you, you're already more competent than Bravo's last rent-a-guards."

"Rent-a-guards...? Thanks."

"Anytime Hillbilly."

"So..." Spike clapped his hands. "You really going to call me Hillbilly?"

"Sure as shit I am." Roman's squint was back. "You may be a hero, but don't forget you're our P.O.S hero now."

"Right." Spike smiled. *P.O.S – piece of shit*. He could live with that.

The pair arrived at the clearing to find Simeon waiting for them. As Roman knelt down over a pelican case slightly larger than a businessman's – unclipping the sturdy latches – he looked up at Spike. "You ever set up a high altitude HFECS balloon before?"

"I never even heard of one. Should I have?"

"No, and don't worry, neither had we. HFECS, it stands for 'High Frequency Communication and Surveillance' balloon. DARPA dug them out of storage for us. You'll see it's 60s tech, but RND made some modifications on the fly. The additional 'E' stands for a simple electromagnetic radar they bolted on the side." Roman removed a super-reflective silver package that was folded tightly down to the size of a pillow. "This baby right here is our eyes and ears. It allows us to talk to each other team-to-team, and back here to base without the need for satellites."

"Nice." Spike's eyes shimmered with a slight glaze.

"After all the science shit Zhu did inside the first Tear he came up with the idea of strapping this electromagnetic receiver on the side for the second." Roman pulled a tissue box-sized contraption out from the bottom of the case. "It's our main tool to get a lead on the anomaly."

"Or to see if there even is one." Simeon chimed in half-heartedly. He had been standing behind them, watching in silence up until then.

"Exactly..." Roman continued. "In Simeon's Tear, we didn't get no 'ping'. So we knew whoever travelled was already dead. The balloon sends out some kind of electromagnetic wave, and waits for a discrepancy in the reply. It works exactly like the 'ping' of standard radar. We then get fed with a heading and approximate distance."

"So I'm right in saying these anomalies are giving off a unique signature?" Spike was catching on.

"Yeah, Dr Zhu discovered it. They are apparently measurable when compared to every other Ectype around them."

"How?"

"How? How the fuck should I know? Do I look like I have a fucking PhD? If you want the physics you can ask ol' fat ass back at camp."

Spike smiled; it seemed Heathcote already had another admirer.

"I can live without them."

"OK then, heads-up. Even though this seems like a magic balloon, don't think that once we launch it our job is done. It is still very much a work in progress. DARPA have had fuck all time to perfect Zhu's idea, so it has some serious technical restrictions."

"Like?"

"Like first, it's common for comms to drop out. Depending on the atmosphere and angle of our short wave radio signals, they can have trouble cutting through clouds to reach the repeater. Second, and most importantly, it has massive limitations when it comes to the accuracy of the radar."

"The tolerance?"

"It depends on the proximity. The receiver can only give us results as one of a bunch of predetermined possibilities, 0, 1, 5, 10, 20, 50, 100, 250, 500 and so on, then it gives a percentage tolerance to help fill in the gaps. If positioned directly overhead we can have an accuracy of less than twenty metres, but the further away the balloon is from the anomaly the greater the discrepancy. At ten kilometres it might be one or two K either way, so ten to twenty percent. At a hundred it is roughly thirty each way, thirty percent. Get to a thousand and it blows out to five hundred either way, so it's pretty much useless."

"Right, so the closer the better."

"Yeah. The balloon was used successfully in Tear Two to narrow down our search area in Manhattan, but because our Tear Three guy was a no-show, this will only be the second time we can test it and hope to get a 'ping'."

"Can we launch more than one to triangulate a location?" Spike held up the case he was carrying.

"Nice, exactly. You're getting this now, Hillbilly. We will be throwing them up one after another to pinpoint a location. This one will get launched here. Then, depending on how far away this fucker is, we can travel closer and launch another. We have six in total and can always request more be sent through."

"OK. OK," Spike nodded. "I think I get it."

Roman continued. "The balloons are powered by solar cells and batteries that are good for about ten 'pings'. They have a basic flight system that allows them to anchor above the launch site, but being balloons they are at the mercy of bad weather. The longest we have had a balloon last is three days before it blew off course and became useless." Roman was rummaging around in the bottom of the case. "Here, familiarise yourself with this." He passed Spike a device that looked like a beeper, answering the question before Spike could ask. "Yep, that's a beeper. Young buck like you, you probably never fucking seen one, hey?"

It was true.

"We have gone all kinds of old school without the use of satellites. That thing will display a direction, a distance and a tolerance. You can keep that one, we're all supposed to have one."

"Thanks." Spike turned the piece of prehistoric tech over in his hands. It was black, about the size of a cigarette case.

Roman had removed all the components from the case and was starting to assemble the balloon. "Make sure you pay attention now because there is every chance you will have to launch one of these when we split."

Kneeling down, the two quickly fell into an efficient step.

"Socket."

"Here."

"Screwdriver.

"Here."

"Flathead, Hillbilly."

"Here."

Roman stopped short of tightening the last screw. "This is going to be a steep learn for you Hillbilly, but you'll be right. Just remember you ain't got to wander around camp like a lost puppy when Clarke ain't around. You got picked for a reason. A good reason."

"Thanks..." Spike paused, not sure how far he should push, "... Sanchez."

Roman cocked an eyebrow. "Fuck d'you just call me?"

In the main logistics tent Mason and Clarke were standing over a spread of laminated maps. With Mason's palm planted firmly over lower Bavaria, neither had eyes for the table.

"Tell me what happened in Israel."

They were only a metre apart.

Clarke's back was arched, her hips pushed forward. She reached up, and released her hair. "Israel can wait."

Dragging her hips along the table edge she moved in to within an inch of his face and stopped. Her breath escaped from barely parted lips. "Miss me?"

"Lane. Stop." She was so close only his eyes could move across her face.

"What... It's been two centuries."

"We can't."

She smiled, a controlling, knowing, smile. "Fine..." But did not move, not even a muscle.

The pause between them, it ached.

Mason couldn't bear it any longer. Sweeping the table clear, he grabbed her around the waist and pulled her close.

Chapter 14

Location: .... 31.0461° N, 34.8516° E
Present day name: .... Jerusalem, Israel
IDTF Classification: . Ridge / Tear Three
Date: .... April 15th 2017 / December 0032AD

The soldier strode with purpose through the outer tent. Computers – more suited to a laboratory than excavation – ran the length of the room, wall-to-wall. The absence of any disturbed soil did not surprise him in the slightest.

This was no archaeological dig.

His palms were slick. The cool breeze of his perimeter post had abandoned him long ago. His psyche teetered on the edge of reason, on the precipice of delirium. Between beats of his heart his periphery throbbed. Lost to a tunnel of black, his vision collapsed in from both sides.

What is this place?

But he knew the answer to his own question.

This place is a monstrosity, an unfathomable blasphemy, an act of heresy... This place, it cannot be allowed.

He clenched his fists, his adrenaline surging.

I was... right. The Americans... this is their doing.

His country seemed content to sit idly by while their American puppet masters had their way with the world. But this, now, was not just about influencing the future for further self-gain. This was not about oil, arms or world policing... this was an attempt to rewrite the past. This was a threat to religion. All religion. It was a passive attack that would affect the faith of billions and drive the wedge even deeper.

He was wracked with thought.

How could man be so audacious as to tamper with God's plan?

How could America dare to create a fake messiah?

Just as he was a soldier of Israel, the man also considered himself a soldier of God... *Then may God forgive me for what must be done.*

Through a vale of strips the soldier cut.

The second tent was clearly in shutdown mode, all of its inhabitants far too busy to pay him much notice. There were maybe eight in total, fewer than he expected. It seemed as if the primary American team had already left.

Perfect.

He knew that the second, Bravo, was mostly made up of the legitimate scholars.

Two men in lab coats rushed past him. He felt their excitement, their enthusiasm.

Right, he will be here.

Pausing in the middle of the tent, the soldier looked to the ceiling. Reciting a prayer, he unslung his rifle, and started firing.

Professor Susan Ashbury sat in a sealed quarantine pod. She was in the middle of her second debrief session when she heard what sounded like gunshots. She pushed upright, momentarily dumbfounded. From the corner of the room she stared out through the glass, over the makeshift command centre. Focusing her attention on the hanging opaque partitions between the second, outer laboratory, and her third, Tear Tent, she felt her body tighten.

The flaps hung deathly still.

Silence now.

Ashbury waited, for something, anything. It was like hearing the screech of tyres and no crash.

Across the table her subject seemed puzzled. The sounds for him were just another foreign sensory experience heaped on top of an already surreal world. The man sitting in front of her was extraordinary, sure to go down as the most significant 'discovery' in the history of the world. Discovery, it was a loose term. As yet they had not worked out how best to explain where he had come from. The truth, about where he had been stolen from, was certainly not an option. He was an unexpected bonus from the mission. A spontaneous decision by Mason, he was unique to Tear Three. The thought of bringing someone back had not even been entertained during the first two.

She was snapped from the thought by the sound of more gunfire. She turned to her subject. "Did you hear..." but stopped herself. He was staring at her, reading her fear.

The tent flaps parted. She held her breath.

An Israeli soldier sliced through, rifle first.

Thank God... The phrase held new meaning now.

Up on her feet she hammered on the inner glass of the quarantine pod. The soldier was about forty metres away, separated from her self-contained box by an expanse of desks and equipment.

Ashbury banged on the glass again. "Hey! Over here!"

A wave of relief flooded through her as she watched the soldier's ears prick.

"In here."

As the soldier turned, slowly, almost curiously, she caught his face for the first time. Her own dropped. *No...* A chill crept over her shoulders, and spilled down her back. *...This can't happen.*

The solider had blood smeared across his neck and chin. His face, flat and pale, lacked all emotion. Locked in an absent stare, the solider tilted his head... raised his rifle... and fired straight at her.

Thud! Thud! Thud!

The sound was somehow muted. Glass splintered in front of Ashbury's face, but did not shatter. She stumbled backward and half fell, half dived to the ground. Snapped from her trance she looked up. The bullets were dead on, tightly grouped... she would surely have been hit if not for the bulletproof glass.

Panic gripped her. She turned to her patient, he was still sitting in his chair at the debrief table, a blank look plastered on his face.

"Get down! Now!"

The words were foreign to him, but the tone was not. He dived below the table as another volley of bullets thudded into glass.

Ashbury raced over on hands and knees and grabbed her subject by the arm. They would be sitting ducks if the soldier reached the pod before she could lock it down.

"Stay here! Do not move!" She yelled above the dull hammer of more bullets. She pointed to the ground. "You got it? Stay!"

Crawling for the door, she flinched down as each new bullet pounded outside. Underneath the keypad she reached up and punched in the four-digit PIN, 25-12.

The sliding glass door hissed, then cracked an inch. *C'mon c'mon c'mon.* Head, neck, shoulders, she pushed through then... into a whole new world.

Almost instantly, bullets exploded around her. The world was so much louder now, deafening gunshots echoed like cracks of thunder. Ashbury cowered down as tight as she could. With her hands over her ears she glanced up at the external keypad, she had to get to it before the solider rounded the corner and had a clear line of sight.

She pushed herself halfway up, leaning her back against the wall. Reaching the rest of the way, her hand quivered above the keypad. Finding the large red 'lock' button she smashed her hand down.

The debrief door hissed shut.

Ashbury slid back down. Without the PIN code the debrief pod was inoperable, her subject was now safely locked in the cell. Conversely, though, she was now locked out and completely exposed.

A new barrage of bullets caused her to cry out, shaking the wall – one, two, three, four, five. There was silence next as the firing ceased abruptly.

Ashbury snuck a glance around the corner of the pod. The soldier had made his way halfway across the room. He was now about twenty metres away, attempting to reload. The space between them was filled with three long rows of end-to-end desks – in an old-school NASA-type arrangement – facing the non-existent Tear.

Shit. It was as good a time as any. It was time to move or die.

Taking her chance, Ashbury dived forward – toward to the soldier! – and slid to a halt up against the front of the first row of desks.

The soldier, having seen just a blur, now focused his attention on the three rows of benches in front of him. Eyes cold, his face in a trance, he resumed his blind firing.

Closer to her hunter now, Ashbury was thrust into an all-new world of pain. On her forearms, she had no option but to push ahead, her right shoulder tight on the final row of desks. To her left was a void that housed the Tear ramp and podium.

Debris from surrounding tabletops was thrown into the air like confetti as the bullets clanged off the metallic workbenches.

Ashbury kept crawling, pushing her side against the desks for cover.

She looked up.

Noooooo.

She had only another two desks before she would run out of cover.

With the solider still three rows towards the room's entrance, he, she and then the Tear ramp were all now directly in line with each other.

He stopped firing.

Ashbury froze. Scared to even breathe, she heard something worse than gunfire. It was the sound of boots jumping on and over the first separating row of desks... The soldier was making his way toward her!

Her mind scrambled. She was out of options. He would be on her in seconds...

...But then something truly spectacular happened.

Ashbury had her back against the desk, her arms around her knees. She was facing out, staring directly at the ramp, so she caught it all. It started with a crack louder than any gunshot, and was followed by a blinding incandescent burst, as if a massive, room-sized light bulb had blown.

It was the Tear... it was opening!

Ashbury had forgotten all about Major Clarke and Dr Zhu! They had been left behind with a Detachment-Array to facilitate the break.

Her face lit up, she allowed herself some hope. *They were coming back through?*

Hang on... Her face contorted back to despair. *...There was no way they could be prepared for this!*

Variables raced through Ashbury's mind. She heard the soldier leap down and up again, into the second row.

"To hell with this." Damned if she was going to wait to be killed. Pushing off her behind she shot up like a sprinter off the blocks... and then took off running for the Tear.

The soldier was just metres from the final row of desks, *and the bitch beyond them*, when the Tear opened. His whole body seized and he rocked like a statue back into the desk he had just scaled. In his arms his rifle sagged. His eyelids fluttered, as if trying to wake themselves from a dream. *So this was what all the secrecy was about.*

Transfixed on the golden rip, it took him more than a moment to realise his quarry was making a break for escape.

The woman sprinted for the Tear.

The soldier reacted late.

She was almost completely up the ramp by the time he could raise his rifle again, take aim and fire.

Ashbury dared to dream. She was less than a metre from the Tear when the first bullet zinged past her. Her legs pumped hard. Behind her a volley of automatic fire cracked. Only inches away, her face pushed into an invisible layer of warmth.

Her world flooded gold.

Ashbury disappeared into the Tear the exact moment before a bullet was due to smack straight into her back... She had made it. She was through.

Major Clarke watched the identical Tear-opening light-show, except in her case she was sitting cross-legged on the most powerful weapon known to man... in the middle of the Judaean desert.

"Finally."

She and Dr Zhu had been waiting patiently for the last thirteen hours for the Tear to reopen. Zhu had not been ready to affect the break the last time it was, so all unnecessary crew had been sent through ahead. An hour later then, with the Detachment-Array set, all that had been left for them to do was bake.

The Tear had been open only seconds before Clarke sensed something was wrong. Sitting almost directly in front of the opening, she felt something zing past her, just inches from her head.

She flinched. "What the...?"

Another high-pitched whir whistled by, so close she felt the air break in front of her nose. She could have sworn they were bullets, only she'd heard no gunfire.

Clarke had no time to compute, because in the next instant Professor Susan Ashbury burst through the Tear in a shower of blood.

A volley of automatic fire had been milliseconds from hitting Ashbury as she disappeared into the Tear. Now, following her through, the bullets burst through both the Tear and her chest in perfect synchrony as she appeared on the other side.

Ashbury's face was a picture of horror. Thrown forward, arms splayed, her knees gave out. She landed face down and slid a full two metres on the grated gangplank before coming to a halt at the ramp's halfway mark.

Clarke sprang into action. Vaulting off the metre-high Array with a feline grace, she yelled as she sprinted, gun in hand, up to the mouth of the Tear. "Zhu! Get the de-fib!" He had dived behind another crate to her right, his face plastered with abject terror.

She ran slightly to the side as bullets continued to split the air around her. Her mind was racing, but instantly on point. *Was this an attack on the other side? By how many? Whoever it was they were sure as shit trigger-happy.*

The smart move she knew was to prop and defend this side of the Tear, but who knew how long it would remain open? She could not afford to wait for another cycle if she let this one shut.

She knelt down on the edge of the gold, the atmosphere around her literally vibrating. *Ah fuck it.* Defence had never been her strong suit anyway.

She reached for her belt and produced two stun grenades. Pulling the pins on both, she released only one spring-loaded handle. Waiting... "One, two, three..." she reared back and threw the first grenade through. She followed it immediately with the second, this time without waiting for a delay. "...Four, five... wait for it."

On the other side of the Tear the soldier was still firing. After watching the bitch vanish right before his eyes, his utter disbelief had quickly given way to rage. His finger, white with pressure, had not relinquished the trigger. Whichever hell she was in, he would send another thirty bullets through for company.

It was at the end of his second clip, with his muzzle glowing red, that two objects came flying through the gold. The first spun end over end in an arc right at him. He locked on the object, but the blur of rotation made it difficult to focus. Time slowed, frame-by-frame, as his eyes peeled. A band of green on black, a body of perforated holes...

He recognised the grenade a second too late.

A blinding, million-candela explosion rocked the room. Ear-bursting with its ferocity, it made his jaw lock open, and for an instant the oxygen was sucked from his lungs.

The soldier stumbled backward and fell onto his arse. His view was blocked now by a row of desks in front. He could only listen as the second grenade landed on the metallic desktop, skidded across its top, and fell down at his feet. His eyes went wide, the worst possible thing they could do...

Clarke had no way to listen for the explosions. Next to the Tear, with her back up against an imaginary wall, she had to time her breach perfectly. The second stun grenade should be going off... "Now!"

She rolled sideways, gun up at the ready.

From windswept desert, she emerged into a cold, crisp, fluorescent silence. Scanning the room down the sights of her M4 Carbine, she felt the hairs on her arm prickle.

Smoke puffed in a plume from behind a desk two rows ahead.

Suddenly there was movement from the cloud.

A pistol emerged.

Clarke dived instinctively for the ground and pressed herself down as it started firing blindly. Bullets raced overhead through the space she had just been occupying.

Flat on the ramp she was completely exposed, there was no cover for miles. Her only saving grace seemed to be that the shooter was firing blindly and burning through rounds. Counting them out, she pressed her face down and covered her head with one hand.

But hang on...? No bullets were making contact around her. All were sailing high into the Tear above her. ...*Does he not know?*

Taking her chance, she unclenched, steadied herself, and pushed her cheek up against the stock of her rifle. *One look was all I needed.*

Three two one, click click click... the clip ran dry, but still whoever was on the other side of the desk kept smashing his finger down.

For seconds nothing happened.

Ears burned in search of anything.

A crop of hair dared to rise over the lip of the desk...

BAM!

Clarke fired.

She carved a canoe into a forehead sending brain matter and pink mist fizzing into the air. She heard a slump, and then nothing.

Long after the shot she lay still, intently focused down the sight of her rifle until finally she let out a calming breath. *One look is all I need.*

Turning finally to her right Clarke surveyed the tent in its entirety. "What the fuck happened here?"

Her gaze was drawn to the splintered debrief pod. A set of terrified eyes, peeking over the lip of a table, met her own. "Where is your..." she started, but stopped. "...Fuck! Ashbury!"

Launching off her stomach, Clarke spun on her heels... and sprinted back 2000 years.

Chapter 15

Location: .... 51.5074° N, 0.1278° W
Present day name: .... London, England
IDTF Classification: . Ridge
Time: .... April 15th 2017

Galvin at Windows. The Hilton on Park Lane. Top floor. Fuck-knows how many Michelin stars, but enough.

Luckily the 360-degree views of London were amazing, because the company wasn't much for conversation.

The woman sitting across from Magnus Thorn sat in silence, deep in concentration. She obviously couldn't do two things at once. Picking at her lobster tail with a sterling fork, her birdlike mouth was mincing what tiny bits of white flesh she was able to extract.

Torrid small-talk aside, the woman was immaculate. Tall, even for a sub-Saharan, she was slender, with velvet brown skin that glistened brighter than the Scandinavian variety he usually coveted. "I don't want anymore." She pushed her plate away like a child. She had given up on the tail, not even attempting the claws.

"That is fine." He liked them thin anyway.

The table, the best one in the restaurant, was his, all year round. He had a rolling reservation for whenever he felt inclined. He'd paid more for lunches he hadn't had at this restaurant than whatever she could order today.

The woman dabbed the side of her mouth with a napkin. "So Lucius..." It was an alias he used – from the Latin word for 'light' – he thought it fitting. "...You haven't explained exactly what you do?"

"OK..." His women usually started with *'How and why did you find me?'* But this one was cutting right to the part she felt most pertinent, *'How much money you got?'* "...I'm in waste management." His *Sopranos* moment always brought him a smile.

"I've never met a garbage man like you before..." She smacked her lips together on a silken napkin. They obviously didn't get HBO in Nigeria. "...I'm not sure I believe you."

He threw a hand across his heart. "You don't believe me? That hurts."

Did it? Not really. Thorn had worked hard this last quarter-century. Under his umbrella were all manner of legitimate, borderline and illegitimate operations. Damned if he could remember, but there probably was a waste one in there somewhere. "I'm just simple a man, one who, for the most part, likes to sit back and watch things happen as they should."

"For the most part?"

"Well, looking forward, there are always a few things worth changing."

"Hmmm, whatever." She wasn't buying his theatre, but her attempted nonchalance wasn't fooling him either.

From their darkened sockets his icy white-blue eyes evaluated her, all of her.

"Did you think this was just a casting couch meeting?"

She squirmed slightly at his directness. "Isn't that usually how these things go?"

He felt a bristle down his spine; oh how the conversation had livened. "And if you're right? I'm old enough to be your father. Does that bother you?"

She eyed him pensively, her light green contacts participating in the decision-making process, tipping the scales. "No..." She dragged a solitary finger across her red smacked lower lip. "...That would be fine."

That's right, it'd be fine.

As imposing as ever, Thorn had lost not an inch in his sixty-five years on Earth. His muscles, more taut than swollen now, were thinner sure, but harder. He looked like a bear fresh from hibernation, dangerous just the same. Dressed in a Desmond Merrion pinstripe, his silvery mane was cut just above the collar. It matched perfectly the laser sharp moustache sitting over his curled lip.

Finally, the woman broke from their stare and looked around the restaurant. "It must be a pretty large waste kingdom you run?"

"Well, there is a lot of waste out there. Think about it, can you remember who cleaned up the shit in the tip where you used to forage? It was probably one of my companies."

Her head snapped around, eyes narrow, burning. "Excuse me?"

"What? You didn't think anybody knew? Honey, that kind of stain is impossible to fully wash off. You can flip the cushion and drape it in as much fur as you like, but it will always be there."

"A... I..." she was at a loss, "...how dare you?" She threw down her napkin and pushed her chair back. "Give me one reason why I shouldn't walk out of here right now?"

Challenge accepted. "Because, all this cock teasing aside, you're here for something, same as me... Change."

Her eyes pierced the metre or so she had physically withdrawn from the table. "You have something wrong with you..." She almost spat the words. "...You know that."

Funny, it wasn't his first accusation. What had his last conquest called him? A bipolar-bear? Well, he had torn her apart like a bear, so it was kind of fitting.

"Diagnosed bipolar? No," he said matter of factly. "'Diagnosed arsehole... well maybe, so I'm sorry, that was rude."

She cried a laugh, a solitary exasperated laugh. It was not at him, but at herself, at her predicament. He could almost see the pit of internal confliction pulling at her stomach. It was making her sick. He didn't mind.

"Lucius, this is about the strangest thing I have ever done in my life, and you are about the strangest man I have ever met in my life."

Of course... If only you knew.

"You know I wasn't always like this." His face softened.

"No?" Hers did too.

"No."

"Well... then... let me ask you a question."

He watched as she consciously decided to change tack. Committing to her craft, she pulled her chair back to the table, cocked her head and rested her elbows on the edge. Pushing them together her small breasts rose up from her little black dress. Goosebumps rippled over mounds that held firm.

"You do this often, don't you? Fly women from all around the world for your amusement." A shoulder strap of her dress slipped, but she stopped short of putting it back.

"Yes." There was no point in lying; they had turned a corner together.

"Well..."

Bing! Interrupting her, Thorn's phone chimed from inside a pocket close to his chest. *Damn it, just as things were getting interesting.*

He held up a finger. "Hang on to that thought."

With his date looking less than impressed, he reached inside his jacket, pushed aside another device in there, and groped for his mobile.

Placing it to his ear he gave a wink before answering. "Hello..."

Thorn's cockiness faded quickly though as he listened.

"You're downstairs... now? I thought we said three o'clock?"

His gaze was now fixed on a spot on the table.

"What do you mean emergency? You're a physicist?"

"Germany...? Today...?"

"All right wait there. I'll be down in a second."

Without so much as looking at little Miss Naija, Thorn pushed back his chair and bolted upright. Clicking his fingers, he pointed to his own shoulders. A second later a waiter arrived with his overcoat.

"What are you doing?" The woman managed through a dumbstruck face.

"I have to go, something has come up."

"Seriously!? You're joking. I've been on a plane for the last nine hours and you're leaving?"

Thorn regarded her. It was a shame. Even enraged she looked good. "Stay if you like... leave if you don't."

And with that he was gone.

Downstairs, Thorn pushed through the front entrance before the doorman could see him coming. "Mr Thorn I... I'm sorry... your car, it is still being brought up."

"I'm walking."

He skipped down the front steps at pace, buttoning his coat as he went. At the bottom a black cab was idling.

Leaning on the half-opened back door Tabatha was waiting for him. "I've got five minutes," she said.

"What have you done to your hair? Is that pink?"

"Really..." Her disgust was pure teenage "...that's your hello?" She turned and stuck her head in the cab. "We're leaving."

"Tabatha... stop."

"You forget Magnus, you're not my father."

"Please, this is silly. Just step out of the cab, I'll have a driver come and get you."

"I can't, there's a plane waiting for me."

"You said that already, but I'm still not following. Germany...? Why are you going to Germany?"

"For work."

"Our work?"

"My work."

"In Germany?"

"Yes Magnus. You know I can't talk about it, so don't even."

"You can't talk about it!? I'm paying for your research, surely that..."

"Gives you no rights whatsoever to push the boundaries with my nine-to-five. We agreed on that when you found me at Cambridge."

She had him there. He regarded her. She was strong and smart, his protégé, that's what he loved about her.

"If I won't at least get our weekly consult... then an idea of when you'll be back would be fair."

"Magnus..."

"What...? Not as your father, just as a concerned investor."

Her face softened as she filled then emptied her lungs. "I've been called into the field. There's been a discovery. Someone may have beaten us to the punch."

What...? The shock on his face betrayed him.

"Magnus..."

But suddenly her voice was miles away... *The only person who could have beaten her to the punch was... standing right in front of her.*

"Magnus... your face...?" She cocked her head, tipping her Perspex glasses to one side. "You already know, don't you?"

"What...? No..." It was the truth; he had no idea what she was talking about. What she was saying, it was not possible, not for years, seven to be exact. "It's Zhu, isn't it? Is the little old Chinaman dragging you about?"

Her eyes narrowed. "Is that what this is about?"

"No..."

"It is, isn't it? These meetings, they're a way for you to keep track."

"Tee..."

"You don't need me, you and I both know that. So what else could it be?"

How wrong she was. He thought about the device in his pocket, the one where his mobile phone should have been...

...The one that now, may or may not have been vibrating!

Stopping, or more so freezing in mid-motion, Thorn's face dropped again, lower than before, if that was even possible with the all Botox he was rocking.

So caught up in the exchange he had not quite noticed it at first. On the outside of his overcoat he slapped at his chest. As he did the device in his pocket vibrated again.

He looked down... but if his phone was in his hand... then...

All confidence evaporated from within him. *No, not again? Surely not?* He jammed his hand half in, half out of his pocket, his face trying to contain his surprise.

"What?"

"Nothing."

Fuck. It couldn't be.

Thorn had a hand in his jacket; twisting his fingers he grasped at the other device. Half extracting it, he stole a glance. About the size of an old analogue Nokia, the letters 'TSL' were emblazed on the device's shiny stainless steel side. *T... S... L... If only she knew.*

"What's that?"

No... not yet. It could ruin everything!

"Nothing."

Nothing. This couldn't have been further from the truth. He had carried the TSL around diligently for a quarter-century without so much as a peep, and now three signals within six months!

The device's thin blue screen was illuminated... *Fuck!* It was no mistake.

Tabatha was watching him still, waiting to see where his bizarre display would lead.

"I've got to go..." She fell into the cab and pulled the door shut. Through the open window she regarded him one last time.

"What is it you want Magnus...? What is it the great Magnus the knowledgeable wants? Do you ever stop to think about that simple question?"

His eyes were lost in hers. *YOU!* His mind would have screamed had it not been elsewhere, crashing in a crescendo of realisation.

"Tee..."

She shook her head and stared at him, her eyes past sadness, verging instead on pity. "You really have no idea, do you?" She turned to the driver. "I'm ready. Let's go."

As the cab pulled away, Thorn's grip on the moment faded with it. Lunch, Tabatha, the TSL, like waves they were smashing him one after another before he could rise again for breath.

"Who was that?"

Standing with her arms crossed, his Nigerian princess was standing behind him at the Hilton's entrance.

He turned to her... she was everything he needed in that moment, a reminder of who he was... he was Magnus fucking Thorn... A man who could fuck the world, without the world having any idea who was fucking it... or her.

"Shut up and get in my car."

He needed to work up a sweat to really get his brain working... because if what his last five minutes had told him was true, then literally, for the third time in six months... his world had just collapsed.

Chapter 16

Roy wiped a forearm across his brow. The late evening air was like soup. All he was doing now was shuffling clamminess from one spot to another. The humidity though was not the sole reason for his perspiration. It was make or break time. He was no longer just a passenger on this mission... he needed to prove his worth.

After the Alpha/Bravo schoolyard line-up, Roy had taken his newly acquired reading material – Mason's notes – along with his backpack, over to a secluded corner of the camp. He had found what looked to be the communal mess area. A simple unwalled camouflage marquee housed a table and fold-out chairs. Freeze-dried food scraps and playing cards littered both.

He swept his hand across the table clearing everything into a bin. "I call Gin."

In a couple of hours at most Mason would want to see some kind of progress, *shit*. The pressure, Roy could feel it forming a pit right about his sternum. Judging by the sizeable paper stack in front of him, he had at least half a day's reading to get through, not including the time it would take Loretta to translate.

Remember the glass is half full. His brother's voice sprang to mind.

Yeah?

Yeah, it's just that it's half full of piss.

Right.

Right, and we pay eight quid for a taste o' that Foster's piss, so lap it up.

It was a joke they often shared. How his brother could be so positive after his last two years was something that amazed Roy. How he hadn't learnt yet, that drinking Foster's wasn't patriotic, was another. There was some truth to his mantra though; *the challenge would serve as motivation...* Maybe if he said it enough times, he might start believing it.

Roy splayed the stack of papers out in front of him. He was after an overview, so he could make a priority pile for Loretta to start on. Although he couldn't make sense of all the German titles, he was immediately struck by the thoroughness of Mason and Gerhard's collection. A wave of optimism swept over him. Aside from the obvious newspapers and political flyers, he was in possession of a pretty important collection of records.

'Munich and surrounding provinces Mortality Records 1850 – present.'

'Munich and surrounding provinces Birth Records 1850 – present.'

'High income tax returns 1910, 1911, 1912, 1913.'

'Current Local and Federal Government Cabinet positions.'

'The Dual Alliance 1879, Germany – Austria-Hungary.'

'The Triple Alliance 1881, Germany – Austria-Hungary – Italy.'

'Crime statistics 1850 – 1900 and 1990 – present.'

How did they get half of these? Roy pulled a chair and shuffled it close. Mason's comment of 'borrowing' from the municipal office took on a new meaning now... *they had raided the city archives!*

The German documents would have to wait until Loretta arrived to help translate. In the meantime Roy figured it would be best to start with a list of any and all significant events he was aware of.

Ten years was probably suitable.

Support had given him some handy tools. He rummaged through his backpack and produced an iPad and fold-out solar charger. The iPad was loaded with a Library of Congress-level (160 million-plus pages) encyclopaedia of world history. The technology was a godsend, because while he could recite 95 percent of any necessary facts, he wasn't *Rain Man.* He could use it to nail down the exact times of events, or find the name of some butler's mother's brother to the archduke of wherever-land.

Roy set about brainstorming significant events. His hope was to cross check them against information in Mason's documentation, to confirm whether or not they had actually happened inside this Fourth Tear. 'Significant' was an ambiguous classification that bothered him, the decision of how detailed to make his list was vexing, especially while all knowledge of the traveller remained hidden. Motive, race, gender and age were just some of the many factors that could influence what a certain individual considered personally significant. One man's hierarchy of importance was never going to be the same as the next.

Roy decided to break his significant event list into four categories: **Deaths** (more specifically assassinations), **Inventions, Revolutions** and **Miscellaneous**.

The elephant in the room, WWI, he would tackle separately; it deserved the most thorough examination. The Great War hung over the start of the century, and in turn his mind, like a black cloud. If they were asking him, he could not imagine a scenario in this Tear that somehow did not involve it.

Roy dabbed the end of his pen on his tongue. Before he started, he wrote down something that had been on the tip of his mind ever since Mason had divulged the arrival date. It was one name, and one date.

Archduke Franz Ferdinand, 28th June 1914.

He tapped the pen over and over on the date... "I'll come back to you."

Deaths and Assassinations:

1900 – Umberto I, King of Italy.

1901 – Queen Victoria, United Kingdom (Natural Death).

1903 – Aleksander Obrenovic, King of Serbia.

1905 – Theodoros Deligiannis, Prime Minister of Greece.

1908 – Carlos I and Luiz Filipe, King and Crown Prince of Portugal.

1910 – King Edward, United Kingdom (Natural Death).

1911 – Pyotr Stolypin, Prime Minister of Russia.

1912 – Jose Canalejas, Prime Minister of Spain.

1913 – Mahmud Pasha, Grand Visor of the Ottoman Empire.

Roy screwed up his face, *that's a few*. His pen tapped away. It was strenuous, but through six degrees of separation he could, in theory, link all in some way or another to Germany. Still, it didn't feel right, the connection, he was sure, would be more obvious. "No," he called it. There was no way keeping any of these people alive was worth travelling back in time for.

Inventions:

1901 – Marconi and the first transatlantic wireless signal.

1903 – The Wright brothers' first flight.

1904 – Radar.

1905 – Plastic, and Einstein proposes Theory of Relativity.

1908 – The Model T Ford, Detroit.

1913 – Assembly line production, stainless steel, and ecstasy.

Some interesting possibilities. Maybe the traveller has stolen the recipe for ecstasy, and just wants everyone to have a good time? OK, he was being ridiculous.

He noted that the control of radio, flight and especially plastic could be financially lucrative, and he made a mental note to try and check up on the whereabouts of Einstein. Albert was to become a significant player in the future atomic arms race.

Revolutions:

1900 – Boxer Rebellion in China.

1905 – Bloody Sunday, and the Russian revolution.

1905 – Norway breaks away from Sweden.

1907 – Romanian peasants revolt.

1908 – The Young Turk revolution.

1910 – Portuguese revolution.

1911 – Chinese revolution overthrowing the Qing dynasty.

Roy immediately drew a line through all except the Russian and the Young Turks of the Ottoman Empire. But even then, *why travel inside Germany if your intentions were to disrupt an event half a continent away?*

Anything else he could think of: Miscellaneous.

1903 – Bolshevik party founded in Russia, and women of the suffragist movement found the WSPU in the United Kingdom.

1904 – The Panama Canal breaks ground.

1900 and 1907 – The Hague conferences establish 'The Ten Rules of War'.

1911 – The Mona Lisa is stolen.

1912 – The Titanic sinks.

Again, nothing really concerning Germany. Roy smiled; the *Mona Lisa* theft was kind of cool though. Vincenzo Peruggia, dressed like a tradesman, simply walked out of the Louvre with it under his arm. *Had a pair of nuts on him like wrecking balls.*

So far Roy had three pages of scribble, and nothing he was confident enough to proclaim an option should Mason walk in. It felt good though to get everything down on paper. By eliminating smaller options it reassured him that his, and probably the whole team's assumptions, were on point. *The time was 1914... this Tear was about war.*

He allowed himself an assumption. *Someone has come here to affect the outcome of the one or both of the world wars. The question was though: Does someone want to prevent them? Change their outcome? Or profit off them?*

This world was currently in the imminent shadow of WWI. It was the obvious next avenue of investigation. Again Roy would break it down into four groups. This time they would be: **People, Conflict, Treaties** and... Roy looked to his circled scribble... **Franz Ferdinand**... the most famous shot in history.

People: Are they still alive, and in position?

Kaiser Wilhelm II – Emperor of Germany.

Alfred Von Schlieffen – Deviser of the Schlieffen Plan to win WWI.

Helmuth Von Moltke – German Army Commander who failed the Schlieffen Plan.

Paul Von Hindenburg and *Erich Ludendorff* – German Generals.

Franz Joseph – Emperor of Austria-Hungary.

Georges Clemenceau – Prime Minister of France.

David Lloyd George – Prime Minister of United Kingdom.

Winston Churchill – Influential British politician.

Woodrow Wilson – President of the United States.

Nicholas II – The last Tsar of Russia.

Vladimir Lenin – Bolshevik revolutionist.

Killing any one of these men could have a drastic impact on the outcome of the war. Without some, WWI may even have been avoidable.

They were all names Mason needed to be aware of. Roy paused on his list. Somehow it did not feel complete. If he kept himself strictly to WWI then, yes, it made perfect sense, but this was no university paper. He was not here to stick to rules; he was here to find results.

He scribbled down one more name. Even if he would not come to power for another twenty years his name may as well be included... It was Adolf Hitler.

Conflicts that preceded WWI

1900/14 – German alienation of the United Kingdom via its naval expansion.

1904 – Russo-Japanese war.

1908 – Austria annexes Bosnia.

1912 – First Balkan War.

1913 – Second Balkan War.

Could one man influence any of these conflicts?

It was the million-dollar question: could one man influence 'any' conflict? Roy was sceptical. Either way it didn't matter, geography was again an issue.

Why travel inside Germany if you are intent on affecting a conflict half a continent away?

Treaties

1839 – The treaty of London – The United Kingdom and Belgium.

1879 – The Dual Alliance – Germany and Austria-Hungary.

1881 – The Triple Alliance – Germany, Austria-Hungary and Italy.

1890 – The lapse of the Reinsurance Alliance – Germany and Russia.

1892 – Franco-Russian Military Convention Alliance – France and Russia.

1904 – Entente Cordiale – The United Kingdom and France.

1907 – Anglo-Russian Entente – The United Kingdom, France and Russia.

If any one of these treaties failed to eventuate, then the alliances of WWI could look very different right now. He remembered that some of the books Mason had obtained related to treaties, he made a note to start Loretta on them.

Next on Roy's hit list was one event that he knew with certainty hadn't happened yet in this new world. It was without doubt one of the most important events in recent human history, and arguably the most famous precursor to any war ever fought. Universally know as 'the shot that started the WWI'... it was the assassination of Archduke Franz Ferdinand... and it was due to happen in three days.

At the end of its tether, Roy's pen lid flung off to the side. Had he been drumming that hard? His mind seized the opportunity to take a break; it had been begging for an opening to procrastinate. He leant back on his chair and stretched his arms high, a difficult manoeuvre, considering how far he had sunk into the soft camp chair. Endless possibilities swooped his brain, like bats in cave, each one demanding attention, pulling him in different directions through time.

The next assassination would be no different. No matter how full he imagined the glass of optimism to be, trying to predict the broad and far reaching implications of any deviation to Franz Ferdinand's assassination would be like trying to count the ripples created by an anvil landing in a pond – if that anvil were dropped from an aeroplane.

How do I even start? It was a semester-worthy topic.

"You look like you need this more than I do," said a voice from behind.

Roy turned to see Loretta. A true sight for sore eyes, she was carrying two mugs of steaming coffee.

"My God, you read my mind." Roy reached with two hands for the boiling ceramic.

"How is your study going?" she asked.

"Ummm…" He rocked his head side-to-side, letting his black locks fall.

"That bad?"

"No, not really. It's just there's a lot going on around this time, there are so many important people and events happening, I'm terrified I will miss one."

"Well, all you can do is your best…" her touch was soft on his shoulder, "…start at the top and work your way down."

"That would be smart, but I have no idea where, when or what the top is. It differs depending on motive. Call me crazy, but I thought I should start at the bottom and cross off events and people I don't think are viable."

Loretta placed her mug down and began to roll up her sleeves. "What can I do?" Her auburn hair was tied up; she looked more ready for work in a legal practice than in a camping tent.

"Thanks for the offer. If you can confirm a few things for me, like the titles of these books, that would be a good start." Roy pointed to Mason's collection. "Am I right in thinking this one is a deaths record for the province?"

"It sure is. Do you need me to look someone up?"

"No, but thank you. The deaths are just a list of names, I can probably tackle them. I was hoping to use your expertise on some of these others." Roy picked up the one he thought pertained to treaties. "It will be dry, but I need to know if this book relates to the Germany, Austria-Hungary and Italy Alliance, and if it is still in effect."

"Sure thing." She blew the dust off the cover of the leather behemoth. Before she opened it though, her eyes scanned the pile on the table and fell on a tabloid. "Although how about I first catch up on some latest early-century gossip while I have my coffee?" Loretta picked up the daily Munich newspaper. "I can work out if there is any scandal afoot. You never know, some Duke might be sleeping around and affecting the course of history."

Roy let out a laugh. "Sure thing. Although I think it will be more shocking to find a Duke who is *not* sleeping around."

"Ooh... ah..." next to him, over the lip of her coffee, Loretta was taking the mickey out of the *Munich Weekly*. Roy was happy to have another person around; his task had seemed lighter the moment she had walked into the tent. Coffee in one hand, he balanced the mortality records on a knee. It was a brick of a thing, with over fifty years of names listed. He would start by scanning it for all the names he had listed above in his WWI register. Franz Ferdinand, it seemed, would have to wait a little longer.

It was an arduous task, scanning page after page of elegantly handwritten calligraphy.

Wilhelm, Moltke, Schlieffen, Ludendorff...Hitler. No, next page.

Wilhelm, Moltke, Schlieffen, Ludendorff...Hitler. No, next page.

Working his way from 1850 until the very end of the 1880s, he was not only looking for the exact individual, but any direct relative, like a father or grandfather.

On the seventy-third page, as his eyes were on autopilot, he had to do a double-take. There were two entries. Both were dated the 20th April 1889. *Jesus... he stuck gold.*

A Hitler – 51 years – Braunau Am Inn – Murdered.

K Hitler – 28 years – Braunau Am Inn – Murdered.

Roy flipped the page back and forth, first in amazement he had found something, then quickly for another reason.

Was that it? Just the two? Why was there no mention of anyone else?

"There should be another, where is the child? Is he dead also?" Roy said to himself out aloud. His thoughts were spilling out his mouth uncontrollably. He was so consumed with the book he had forgotten he wasn't alone.

Loretta looked up from her paper. "You're not talking about the Himmler child are you? Poor thing, what a tragedy."

Roy's ears pricked. He turned to her, his head in slow motion. "What did you say?"

"The Himmler murder. It was all over this newspaper. Such a despicable thing, to take the life of a child. No wonder the massive press." Her concern – maybe rightly so – seemed only for the child's life.

Roy had different ideas. His mind started to spin. "Murdered here..." His words fell out slowly, "...in Munich?"

"No, in Landshut."

"Loretta, how old was he?"

"Fourteen. Roy... Why are you giving me that look?"

"Loretta, this is very important, where is that story? I need all the details."

"Here." She passed Roy the paper, but of course he couldn't read it, so she recited the facts as she remembered. "His name was Heinrich Himmler, fourteen years old. Poor thing was stabbed to death in a completely random attack. Happened at his school, in a town called Landshut, about an hour from here. There is a massive manhunt going on."

Roy sprang to his feet, his hands scrambling across the table.

"What are you doing?" Loretta popped back.

"C'mon, we need to find Clarke and Mason." He scooped up the death register, the newspaper and also the criminal records journal for cross-reference.

"What? I don't under..." But before Loretta could finish he was off and running.

Roy had been hard at work for nearly two hours and, like the sun over the pines of Perlacher Forest, his mind had almost set. But how quickly that had changed. He was full of energy now, giddy with excitement. For all his brainstorming, analysing and assumptions about WWI, he had found two clues in the space of seconds that pertained to WWII...

How amazing it was... he had proven his worth.

Chapter 17

Location: .... 48.1351 N, 11.5820 E
Present day name: .... Perlacher Forest, Munich, Germany
IDTF Classification: . Tear Four
Date: .... June 25th 1914

Roy hammered on the main operations tent. Its plastic door flapped backward in waves, out of sync with his blows.

"Mason, Mason!"

"What?" Mason grumbled without opening.

Roy burst through. "MasonI'vefounditwe'vefounditHitlertheparentsdeadin1889Himmlertookilled..." He began to turn blue. "Huuuuuuuuuuuuuh." He loaded up a breath.

Mason raised a big bear paw, cutting him off. "Layman's terms Professor. Slowly. What have you found?"

"Sorry..." Roy's chest was heaving. "...We've found three murders, murders that should not have happened... big murders!"

"All right, hold it right there." Mason cast a sideways glance at Clarke.

She gave him a nod.

"Professor, I want you to compose a presentation. Clarke and I are going to gather everyone." He looked at his watch. "Roman and Simeon should have had a 'ping' by now. Their report and your new developments are something we all need to hear."

Roy and Loretta stood at the front of class. With hands behind backs, they shuffled from one foot to another like schoolkids waiting for their shot at 'show and tell'. They had the eyes of the entire IDTF team upon them.

Roy, trying to slip back into his Oxford lecturer persona, clapped his hands together more like a late-night TV host. "Good evening ladies and gentlemen. Thank you for coming out tonight." It was fitting; the sun had indeed set. The camp was now lit by 12-volt LEDs. "Now, I want you all to imagine the best way to prevent sixty million deaths..." His effort to get everyone thinking brought him nothing but silence, long silence. "OK... anyone? Any ideas?" He surveyed the tent to see only blank faces. A few in the back were already on the cusp of sleep. He looked to Loretta for help. Maybe this wasn't the right crowd to be trying this on?

"I got ten bucks says Hitler's dead." Spike yelled out, breaking the silence.

And like that, the room erupted.

It caught Roy completely off guard. His comatose group had transformed suddenly into an unruly mob. They were yelling and pointing at each other, completely oblivious to his presence. He felt like Michelle Pfeiffer in *Dangerous Minds. Was somebody throwing paper across the back?*

He could only make out pieces of the group argument. It somehow revolved around betting. Everyone it seemed was in on it.

"Fuck off, Hillbilly, I had dibs on Hitler." Roy heard a shout from Roman.

"Eat shit Hernandez, I said it here first." Apparently Spike was calling Roman 'Hernandez' now.

"This is bullshit, since when was the bet back on?" came from Beckett's vicinity.

The bickering affirmed Roy's suspicion on his crowd demographic. He would have to cut to the chase, if he could ever get a word in again.

Mason cut in with his booming voice. "All right, all right, children, let's settle this down. I'm happy you're all getting along, but Roy has a presentation to finish..." The crowd simmered down to a murmur. "...And just to clarify, you can all go to hell, I'm not paying out on Big Adolf, we all agreed no betting this time round."

Roy resumed the floor. "Thank you. I appreciate everyone's..." *What was the right word?* "...Enthusiasm." *Yeah.* "Although, I would have taken that bet if I were you, Captain. You'll see why soon." He turned back to the group. "Please allow me to get to the point. Thanks to the efforts of Mason and Gerhard procuring municipal archives, we were able to find some inconsistencies unique to this world. By inconsistencies I mean murders. Murders that had not happened in our world and could not have happened here without manipulation by a third party." Roy looked down his nose at the group, over his non-existent glasses. The time for levity was over. "Using this particular book," he held up the mortality records, "and cross-referencing it with this one," he continued, lifting the crime registry, "we were able to ascertain that one A Hitler and one K Hitler were murdered on, or possibly slightly before, April 20th 1889, in Braunau Am Inn. It's a town on the German-Austrian border."

Roy had used his preparation time to study the crime registry; he was looking for a matching entry to confirm the Hitler family deaths. Fortunately, as well as confirmation, the registry had provided some basic information on the murders. It listed both causes of death as 'revolver wound'. Klara's entry also had the additional note of 'fall from height'.

Most notable though, was the information that was not listed in her entry. Absent was any and all mention of 'with child'. Roy had seen that exact phase used throughout the book so he knew it was a possible listing.

Why did hers not have it? Had the birth already occurred?

What of baby Adolf then? Why was there no third death listing?

Roy's audience could now be heard murmuring about the A in A Hitler. He pressed on with his presentation; it was time for another surprise. "Contrary to most of your assumptions, the A Hitler referenced here belongs to one Alois Hitler, not Adolf. Alois was Adolf's father. The K accompanying it stands for Klara, Adolf's mother."

Spike interrupted again. "Same difference, it still counts just the same. Someone has obviously gone after the parents to prevent him from being born at all. It's a murder, without a murder... potential murder... but still with a murder... two of them." Spike was lost in his own theory. A few others were scratching their heads, not sure what to make of his murder logic puzzle. Spike counted his fingers and nodded to himself. "Yeah, I'm right, aren't I?"

"Yes Spike, it's true that by killing a person's parents you can wipe them from history without having to kill them directly." Roy confirmed. "But the kicker here, is that Adolf Hitler's actual birth date is April 20th 1889. His parents were murdered on the day of his birth. This raises some startling questions for us, like: had Klara already given birth? If so, then why is there no death notice for baby Adolf? And why, if you wanted to nullify Adolf, would you bother to wait until the birthdate to kill the parents?" Roy let the questions sink in. "Surely it would be an unnecessary hassle, that is of course unless you wanted the baby to be born..." Roy had questions for days, but finished with that last troubling suggestion.

Clarke decided to join in the conversation. She was at the back of the class leaning, with arms crossed, against a tent strut. "So, even though his parents are not, are you saying that right now Adolf Hitler could still be very much alive?"

She had hit the nail on the head.

"Maybe someone took the baby to dispose of the body elsewhere?" Spike offered.

"Possibly." Roy couldn't say either way. "I think there's every chance he could be dead, but without records to prove it, we have to assume he could still be alive."

Clarke had another, more pressing, question. "OK then, whose side is this traveller on?"

Her point was valid, but so were a million more. There were an infinite number of questions to ask; Roy could see that everyone in the room had their own. Unfortunately for them all, he did not have the answers. No one did, except the anomaly.

Roy did, however, have one theory. "Hopefully the circumstances surrounding this next murder tip the scales of the anomaly toward 'good'." He was aware of the oxymoron: a 'good' murderer. "Heinrich Himmler, Adolf Hitler's most senior deputy, second-in-charge of the Nazi party, and the chief coordinator of the Holocaust... was killed three days ago in Landshut, about seventy kilometres from here... He was only fourteen years old."

The death of a child got everyone's attention, regardless of the man he was going to grow into.

"The credit for this find belongs to Professor Panatoli; she was the one who discovered the news article pertaining to Himmler..." Panatoli blushed at his selflessness. "...His death can be counted as the third murder that was not supposed to happen in this world. It could be an unintended butterfly effect of another of the traveller's actions, but I highly doubt it, the killer it seems has an agenda."

Clarke was quick. "By my calculation that is twenty-five years between events Professor?"

Spike was running through his fingers again. "Why the big break?"

Both interruptions caused the floodgates to finally burst.

"Did he commit other murders in that twenty-five-year span?" Simeon shouted.

"Could he be waiting to kill people before significant events take place?" Beckett got in also.

"Does that mean World War II is not going to happen?" Gerhard's was probably the most pertinent.

Everyone was shooting questions at Roy. It was catharsis, catharsis through inquiry.

Finally, Mason intervened. "Enough with the questions! This is nothing new to us people." He looked around shaking his head. "We need to focus on what we know, not what we don't. Professor Roy and Professor Panatoli have given us two solid leads to start with, which is one more than we could have hoped for." He turned to Roy and Panatoli, half suggesting, half pointing to two empty seats. "Thank you both, if you have nothing left to add?"

"Of course." Roy nodded. "I haven't quite finished, but everything I have so far is listed in here." He handed Mason his work, then took a seat alongside Panatoli.

"All right, Alpha, Bravo, this is a start that gives us some much needed direction. As you all may be aware, the potential list of rich travellers suggested by Support is non-existent. There is no need to check up on anyone to see if they are leading different lives, because not a single one of them was alive in 1889." Mason turned to Heathcote. "1889 to 1914, that reminds me. Heathcote, if we now have to assume the Tear has been opening and closing for twenty-five years, why is it only getting volatile now?"

Heathcote went wide-eyed. "Ah... I... Umm."

Loretta gave Roy a nudge. "Like an arsehole who brings a meal to a cinema... he's looked disinterested the whole presentation."

Mason spoke over Heathcote's stuttering. "Get that information back through the Tear to Dr Zhu ASAP, we need everyone working on answers. Now..." He turned to Roman. "You, Mexicano, get your arse up here. What does our search engine have to say?"

Roman pushed off his knees, a barely audible "Puta" escaping from under his breath. As the engineering specialist on this mission, it was his responsibility to report on the HFESC balloon and any 'pings' it may have received. He took the cigarette he had been rolling and placed it behind his ear before shuffling forward in his own time.

Roman's look was not exactly GI Joe inspiring. With eyes that feigned laziness, a buttoned collar, dead-straight hairline and wispy moustache, all that was needed was a white singlet and teardrop tattoo to really scare the shit out of Middle America.

Little did Roy know, but Roman couldn't have been further away from the gang-banger that many pegged him – by looks alone – as being. From South Central Los Angeles, finishing school with honours had been easier for him than surviving outside the school gates. Few had questioned his reading habits though, after he beat a rival half to death with nothing but a copy of Sun Tzu's *The Art of War* – know thyself, know thy enemy and know how effective a fifty-page book rolled into a knuckle brace can be.

"All right." Roman smoothed his hand over his scalp and grabbed the back of his neck. "How many people I killed and I get nervous doing this shit."

"Anytime Pedro." Spike prompted, his smile wide.

Roman snapped up. "Very funny, Yokel."

Roy coughed out a laugh. For some reason a bit of casual racism seemed acceptable on this mission.

Spike and Roman continued to give each other grief.

"Redneck."

"Mexi-can't talk?"

They had obviously become fast friends.

"Huh hmm." Mason's cough interjected.

Spike zipped it as Roman resumed his fidgeting. "All right, let's just fucking get it over with." He looked sideways at the crowd. "Someone's here... We put the balloon up an hour ago and we got a 'ping'. Results came back at 100 clicks. Eastward bearing. Tolerance of thirty percent. That surprised me and Simeon. Considering Munich is five-K north of here, we were expecting to find him there."

Roman spoke in fragmented sentences, but Roy didn't care about that, he was more concerned with what a 'ping' was. It sounded bloody important and this was the first he'd heard of it. He looked around expecting to see some other confused faces, but everyone seemed on top of it... *Fuck.* This mission and the whole experience was flying by at breakneck speed; there was so much he felt in the dark on.

Roman continued. "We checked it again. Same result. Makes sense now that I've heard about this Landshut business. It is one of the towns in our search parameter. We had already started working the seventy to one-thirty tolerance. I have made a list of potential towns to the east of here that this guy could be hiding in." Roman handed Mason a folded sheet of paper.

"Thank you Roman..." There was a pause in the room. "...You done?"

"Yeah."

Mason opened Roman's note and scanned the page. There were seven towns on the list that fell in the approximate range. Next to each was listed the distance and direction from Munich.

– Landshut (73km) and Dingolfing (104km) were slightly north-east.

– Burghausen (111km) and Braunau Am Inn (124km) were directly east.

– Rosenheim (67km) and Bad Reichenhall (131km) were more south-east on the way to Salzburg (140km).

"OK everyone, that's enough for now," said Mason.

The group stood as one, and made its way to the flapping exit door. A quiet rumble bubbled away as each member voiced one concern or another.

"You can stay." Mason's voice cut through the noise.

Roy was trying to hide in the crowd, but he knew. "Me?"

Mason didn't say; he didn't have too, so Roy let the crowd dissolve around him. Clarke had remained at the rear; apparently she didn't need an invitation.

"This is going to be a wild goose chase," she said, once the room had cleared.

Mason ignored her pessimism. "Professor, where was your investigation heading next?"

"Well..." Roy's sweats were back. "...I was going to focus on the assassination of Archduke Franz Ferdinand, it's supposed to occur in three days' time."

"This guy seems more intent on dealing out death rather than preventing it," Mason countered.

"Yes, I agree, but knowing who he has targeted so far, it might be possible that this traveller has a somewhat noble agenda. If he does, then there is no bigger event in European, or possibly world, history that screams for intervention by an idealistic saviour. There would be no need for further influence on WWII if you could just prevent it altogether. And there is no better way to do that than to prevent WWI in the first place."

Mason ran his fingers through his beard, fanning it outward. "You think preventing both wars is possible by saving just one man?"

"I believe so."

Clarke spoke from behind. "What are you using for evidence, your opinion?" She forced Roy to turn back and forth as if he were the subject of a parental inquisition.

"Isn't my opinion exactly why I was brought along on this mission?"

Mason was next. "Where does it take place, this assassination?"

"Sarajevo. It's in modern day Bosnia-Herzegovina, although right now, in 1914, it has been annexed by Austria, much to the displeasure of the Serbs."

Mason opened Roy's notes. "I see here you have prepared a list of significant individuals important to WWI. Wilhelm, Schlieffen, Ludendorff and the rest." Mason was reading the list of Germans only. "Considering what we know about Hitler and Himmler, I want you to prepare a similar list in relation to WWII this time. Focus only on those vital to the Axis powers. This guy could be working his way through the Nazi party."

"And... Ferdinand?" Roy tried.

"Leave him with me."

Roy waited for more, but nothing came. "Of course." He would do as instructed, but he was getting frustrated that the assassination was not getting the time it deserved.

"Thank you, Professor..." Mason interrupted his thoughts.

Roy took the hint and made his way to the exit. He had a lot of work to do; there would be little sleep for him tonight.

"What do you think?" Clarke moved to the front now that she and Mason were alone.

"He's good."

"Surprisingly good." Clarke pursed her lips. "Serendipitous really, especially considering he wasn't chosen for his historical pedigree."

Mason shook his head. "So we lose Ashbury, and you replace her with someone we've had under surveillance for weeks? That was risky, very risky."

"Surveillance is a strong word, it was just a wiretap. We were right though, our man tried hard to contact Roy earlier this week. He has been calling everyone close to him, it is definitely a goodbye tour."

"Does Roy have any idea?" Mason asked.

"No."

"Will he help us once he does?"

"If this guy somehow travels underneath our noses, Roy is our contingency. He will be able to lead us straight to him."

"And if he doesn't?" Mason pressed.

"Have we not learned that professors are replaceable? If Roy is of no use to us, I have no problem obtaining 'clearance' to find another." Clarke paced the room, her boredom obvious.

"Hmm. And what about your boy?"

Clarke spun. "My boy? Who, Spike? He's not my boy."

Mason studied her defensiveness. "That's not what I heard."

"Don't be a dick."

"What of the rumours? About the drinking?"

"Bullshit." She spat. "Blown up to keep him in London while the whole thing blew over." She looked at him and frowned. "I expected better from you. You know what happened over there. I think he sure as hell earned the right to spend his time however he saw fit. If he were knee deep in pussy you would all be slapping him on the back. Instead he cracks one night at the bottom of a bottle and he has to come back to a battalion shrink."

"You can't piss away PTSD, Lane."

"It's not that."

"You sure? You sound a little sentimental."

"Fuck you..."

"Watch your tone Major." Mason's glare lingered. Rank, it was a constant issue between them.

Clarke didn't back down. "He's part of my team, not yours, so enough with the inquisition."

Thinking it best to leave it Mason looked down at the notes in front of him, the beginnings of a plan formulating in his mind. "OK, I see two obvious destinations. Both with confirmed third-party interference. We will need to check both Landshut and Braunau."

"You're not thinking of splitting up are you?"

Mason flipped between laminated maps. "The way I see it I will take Alpha..."

"I said, we are not possibly splitting up?"

"Enough Major!" Mason's snap had more weight than a slap to the face, but Clarke's glare met his head on. Rank, age, experience and sexual tension, their struggle could simmer only so long.

"We have nine hours until dawn..." Mason's jaw clenched. "Prepare your team for an excursion to Braunau."

Clarke's eyes burned, but she bit her tongue. She turned for the exit.

"Lane..." Mason called after her, "remember that on this side of the Tear, whatever this is..." he pointed at the gap between them, "...does not change anything."

She threw up a stern salute. "Yes... Captain."

Chapter 18

Location: .... 51.5074° N, 0.1278° W
Present day name: .... London, England
IDTF Classification: . Ridge
Time: .... April 19th 2017

Magnus Thorn had never actually stopped on Westminster Bridge, not for anything longer than a cursory glance through a heavily tinted Maybach window.

"Hmmm." It was indeed a fantastic spot to take in some of London's more iconic sites. Little wonder tourists swarmed the sidewalk around him like ants.

To the north, the Thames snaked its way past Queen's Walk and the massive London Eye. Victoria Embankment was on his left, its tree-lined boulevard in full bloom, while behind, to the south, was the quintessential London postcard, the Palace of Westminster and Elizabeth, aka 'Big Ben', Tower.

Thorn squinted through the extra-long lens of a digital SLR; the glare of an overcast sky bounced from both above and off the murky river below. The camera was a prop, but he clicked away anyway, trying to blend in with every other loser doing the same.

He flicked the floppy collar of his grey sweater. *Fucking London, it's supposed to be spring.*

To go with his mothballed tracksuit and camping-style wide-brim, he had on glasses that he did not require, contact lenses, a wig, prosthetic nose and crooked teeth dentures. Today, he wanted to look every one of his sixty-five years.

Shooting absently, this way and that, he could feel a familiar thrill boiling inside of him. It had begun in his toes, rising slowly, warming him against the stiff London breeze. *It was almost time to send another back...*

Ever since Abner, the fateful soldier, there had been only three others. But today, today was the day... In the middle of London proper he was finally ending his self-imposed abstinence. He was doing so in response to the arrival of two convenient and correlating needs.

One, he needed his soon-to-be-friend's hacking skills. And two, this man... well, he needed his son back.

Thorn dialled the number of the burner he had memorised.

A woman answered. "Lucius?"

He ignored her greeting. "Approaching you, the lost-looking man about forty metres to your right, in the blue suit." He was talking to an actress whom he had hired anonymously. The pair spoke via concealed Bluetooth ear buds, with her being under strict instruction to simply repeat what he said, word for word. She was to meet his traveller on a bench at the entrance to the London Eye Ferris wheel. Thorn had an uninterrupted view of it from his vantage spot on the bridge.

Thorn adjusted himself against the stone balustrade, pointed his camera and zoomed in slightly. "Don't waste your time, the real rainbows aren't seen from up there."

"Waste a' time that wheel, the real rainbows ain't seen from up dere." The girl's recital was close enough, her Scouse accent though an assault on the ears.

Thorn watched as Eden almost walked straight past the woman. "Huh... excuse me?" The code phase – coming from a twenty-something bohemian looking female with dreadlocks and a Sea-Shepherd t-shirt – surprising him.

"Seriously but, iss a shit view. You'll get a much bet'a one from the bridge over dere." Thorn was being cheeky, alluding to his real location. He was also enjoying himself, turning up the accent, trying to imitate how a young girl might talk these days.

Eden's overwhelmed eyes looked down on the girl.

"Quit staring at my tits would ya?" *Yep, this was fun.*

Eden stiffened, his eyes darting everywhere now, except at the girl.

"Ah jus' fuckin' with ya, let's get serious now."

"Who are you?" Eden finally found his voice.

"Someone wit' more to lose than you. Separations only temp'ry, a caution 'til we get to know each other. So, first things first. Canyoudoit? The program, s'it possible... yet?"

"It's already done."

"Done? Already?"

Thorn watched as Eden shuffled. "But... but, I'm not handing anything over until I get some answers."

"Course, course, I'm not an unreasonable man... or woman. Fire away."

"It's a ground breaking idea, with complicated code, like nothing I have ever heard of, let alone seen before..."

"That's not a question, I t'ought you had questions."

Eden grabbed his elbow, unsure of himself. He spoke hesitantly. "It's code from a future you have visited, isn't it?"

Thorn was impressed; the man at least deserved some credit for the idea. "Future travel ain't possible, I explained that already."

"OK, but surely someone that has invented travel between universes…" Eden took the USB drive out of his pocket, shaking it to emphasise his point. "…could write this code?"

"Who says I invented it? I just realised a potential. Been a long time since I sat down in front of a truly capable computer, I've lost the touch I used to have."

There was a pause between all three of them, as Eden seemed to contemplate the corner he was painting himself into. He was looking the actress deep into her lazy eyes.

"What guarantees do I have?"

Thorn smiled. *What guarantees do you have…? What choice do you have?* "Absolutely none."

"And when I arrive at my time…?"

"…The world, my friend, will be your oyster."

Thorn's actress was really working herself into the role. Nuts out, like a back-alley tomcat, she was leaning back, her arms splayed wide. With her mouth open, working overdrive on a piece of gum, she was occupying Eden completely, making it easy for Thorn to assess him via his lens.

Poor bastard. Eden for his part looked very much the semi-professional junkie, sweating, shaking, trying to score on his lunch break.

"I'm sensing some apprehension." Thorn prompted him back to the moment.

Eden was really working over his elbow. "What if I fail?"

"From what you told me, you'll be either dead, or on the run." It was blunt, but true, Thorn was sugar-coating nothing. "But how about this? If you fail, seek me out in the new world." Thorn tapped his forehead. "Two years, you say? Think I'm in Grenada around then. Explain everything. My technology will be available. I can send you back to try again." Thorn surprised himself with this one. *Don't go getting soft old man.*

Thorn took the opportunity to scan his surroundings. It was time he pretended to take some photos of other things. If anyone had been watching he would have been focused on the one area for far too long.

He was still listening though. "So…" It was crunch time now.

"OK, let's do it. Here…" Eden moved to give the actress the USB.

"Wow, wow, wow! Don't go giving it to this random bitch. I don't ever plan on seeing her in person." The actress seemed uncomfortable cursing herself in third person. "Keep that to yourself. Give it to me when we meet."

"When will that be?"

"Two days. Use it to say your goodbyes if you haven't already. I'll contact you with an exact time and location…" Thorn squinted one eye and clicked a close-up of Big Ben. "I hope you know you're getting this a hell of a lot cheaper that any of your counterparts."

Eden bit back now, finally. "Not really. What you can do with this code is limitless. I'm glad I won't be around to see you unleash it."

Thorn took some shots of an approaching black cab. He was slowly working his way back around to the goodbye proceedings. "I guess then, that's why this marriage works so well…"

"Fine, so, are we done?" Eden had found some confidence.

"Anxious to leave are you?" Thorn smiled. "Why the hurry?" It was time for some fun.

"Fancy taking me home?" The actress recited Thorn's words without really registering them. "You can have me if you want, consider it a departure present." She blushed now.

"Ahhh..."

Thorn felt a rush. This was not part of the deal, but hey, he liked this Eden guy. "Rainbow..." He whispered the codeword, he didn't want his girl repeating this part. "Love, you had better not repeat this, but I'll triple your rate if he says yes. Actually, don't even wait for an answer, simply take his hand and show him a real good time."

Thorn was just about to complete a 360-degree rotation back to the pair when he noticed something odd out of the corner of his lens. That something was someone, sitting about twenty metres away near the entrance to the aquarium, a man of Indian appearance... he was staring at Eden!

"What. The. Fuck." Thorn mouthed.

The Indian started speaking into his newspaper.

"Shit!" Thorn shouted. "Quick, give him your earpiece!"

"Quick, give him your earpiece?" His actress recited awkwardly.

"No, you stupid bitch! I'm serious! Give Eden the fucking earpiece now! And stay exactly where the fuck you are!"

"What? What about my..." She dropped the act, and turned in her seat.

"NOW!"

People next to him on the bridge turned to look at him as the actress handed Eden the earpiece.

"What's your game, motherfucker?!" Thorn barked.

"What? What do you mean?" Eden mumbled.

"The Indian man behind you reading the paper! Don't turn around! Is he yours?"

"No, definitely not! I... I... don't know what you're talking about."

Both men were working themselves into a state.

"Did you notice anyone following you today?" Thorn was firing off questions, trying to formulate a strategy at the same time. "Have you noticed anything different at all since you got in contact with me?"

"No, and no." Through the zoom Thorn could see Eden was sweating.

"Fuck. All right, say goodbye to Courtney as if nothing is wrong, turn and walk south down the Queen's Walk toward Westminster Bridge." Thorn did the maths. "You are going to walk straight past the fucking guy. Keep your eyes down. Let's see if he gets up after you."

Thorn zoomed out to capture the entire walk. *How could they know about this meeting? Were they onto him, or Eden? Could he be compromised?*

Just as he had suspected, as Eden passed, the Indian man rose from his seat and set off after him down Queen's Walk. He was doing a shit job of talking into his collar as he floated thirty paces back.

All right... It was a spanner, but one he could deal with.

Once both men turned onto Westminster Bridge, Thorn made his move.

"Finish crossing the bridge. Stay on the north side of the road. Walk past Parliament on your left. Take the first set of stairs on your right down into Westminster Station." Thorn was walking as he spoke, his words cutting in and out on his breath.

"Where are you sending me?"

"I just fucking told you! Westminster Station."

"But..." Eden's voice cracked. "But I need to get home?"

"Home?" Thorn scoffed. "Get a fucking grip you pussy, you are never heading home in this world again." The bipolar bear was stirring. "Take the stairs. Down in the concourse, immediately to your left, you will see a disabled toilet. Enter it and leave the door unlocked."

There was silence over his earpiece.

"Did you fucking hear me?"

"Yeah."

"Yeah, you got it?" Thorn pumped.

"Yeah, I got it." Eden was clearly struggling. "Disabled on the left."

MI6 agent Danish Parrera skipped the steps, two-at-a-time, down into Westminster Station. Under the chunky concrete roof of the main concourse he surveyed the throng of post-work commuters.

He'd been trailing Eden for over a week now – oddly, only breaking for the short 'family trip' out to Oxford as a US Army chaperone. He knew the guy well enough now to be confident the meeting beneath the Eye was no regular catch-up. The way the pair were getting on, it was obvious the dreadlocked girl was a plant.

Watching Eden cut his way through the station crowd, he was hoping, actually, he was almost certain, he was now on the way to meet the voice on the other end of his earpiece.

A businessman yapping away into a Bluetooth earpiece pushed past him, blocking his line of sight. He wasn't the first, so Parrera was ready. The station was home to three tube lines, the Circle, District and Jubilee. It would have been the perfect place to lose a tail... *if he hadn't seen his man stopping for a piss.*

Parrera looked down at his watch; it had been over five minutes since his man had entered the single disabled toilet. Something was wrong, he could feel it.

"Is there a second exit? Has he given me the slip?" He was questioning out loud as much for himself as for those on the other end of his radio.

"Fuck... Something is wrong."

He made the call, directing his voice this time straight into his collar. "I'm going in.

"Hold... we are... our way." His back-up came through in a broken crackle, the signal struggling to penetrate the heavy concrete interference. "We... stuck... crossing Westminster Bridge... I repeat... hold..."

Parrera ignored the directive. His eyes were fixed on the toilet door, his blinkers on. Slowly he navigated the crowd, inching toward the door.

Was the lock showing unoccupied?

The crowd sliced across his vision.

Shit. It was unlocked.

He reached the door. Knocking softly, he called out. "Is anyone in there?"

No response.

Placing his weight on the handle, Parrera leant forward.

The door cracked an inch.

Suddenly he felt a shove from behind. The wind was taken out of him. A sting stabbed his back... and then he saw blackness.

Thorn was hiding in plain sight on the other side of the concourse, waiting patiently for the Indian to make the first move. He could see the man was anxious, consumed entirely by the blue toilet door. *Oh the wait for back-up...* it always seemed an eternity in the heat of the moment.

On cue almost, curiosity got the better of the Indian.

Wait... wait... now! Thorn pushed off from his newspaper stand, timing his run. At the point of some imaginary triangle he was breathing down the Indian's neck just as he cracked the toilet door. In one fluid motion

Thorn blasted him in the back with a 10,000-volt taser, caught the weight of his suddenly limp body, and used his shoulder to roll through the already half-open door.

It was a beautiful manoeuvre.

Eden nearly hit the roof. Pressed hard against the grime-covered wall he scooched left, like a jailhouse escapee, as two men crashed through the door and fell at his feet.

One looked dead, the other, about a hundred years old.

"Quick, grab his legs." The older one looked up from his knees completely disregarding his state of shock. Eden recognised the voice, but the old wrinkled face delivering the orders did not match.

"Lucius...?"

"The legs, Eden! Quick!"

With no idea why, Eden did as he was told. He leant down and grabbed hold of the limp man's shoes like he was collecting spilt potatoes. Dropping a heel, the man groaned. *Shit...* he was not actually dead, just unconscious.

Moving away from the door, the old man reached out and properly locked them in.

Stepping backward, Eden looked down at his hands. Suddenly foreign, dirty, criminal, he didn't recognise them. *What the hell am I doing?*

The old man was jumping from side-to-side over the body, rummaging through the unconscious Indian's pockets.

"Fuck, nothing. No ID, no wallet, no phone."

"Fuck? What the fuck..." Eden had no idea what that even meant or why it was relevant.

The old man was into the Indian's jacket now. "No identification means MI6, and MI6 means back-up."

"And... just who the hell are you?" Eden managed to spit out.

The old man seemed confused, then laughed, all annoyance and aggression dropping from his face.

"How rude of me, I forgot all about this." He reached up and lifted his hat, the brown tufts of his wig lifted as one, to reveal a layer of silver underneath. The old man stuck out his hand. "Eden Roy, Magnus Thorn. I'll be your chauffer my friend... to another world."

Chapter 19

Location: .... 48.1351° N, 11.5820° E
Present day name: .... München Hauptbahnhof,
.... Munich, Germany
IDTF Classification: . Tear Four
Date: .... June 26th 1914

The entrance to München Hauptbahnhof was bursting with people. They flowed out in waves, in sync with precision, minute-by-minute, locomotive arrivals. In a city of just over half a million, it was incredible to think that this 19th century building accommodated twenty thousand travellers every day.

Roy stood in the centre of the Bahnhofplatz like a child on excursion. A wave of surreal feeling pushed him back and forth, toes to heels, as he absorbed his absurd new surrounds.

The forecourt, like Munich itself, was in the midst of a prosperous transition. The benefits of the second Industrial Revolution could be seen everywhere. Horse-drawn carts still lingered, but they looked tired clopping past the shiny new automobiles that lined the streets around the station. A newly installed electric tram dinged from somewhere behind Roy, its installation a benefit of the citywide electricity rollout. A *tramcar ride*. He rued the missed opportunity. At dawn he and his team had instead walked the five-kilometre journey north from Perlacher Forest.

Roy leaned forward and peered down the line of his now four-member team – Bravo had been cut by one when Heathcote had stayed behind with Beckett. All were staring up at the station, mouths slightly agape.

"Du siehst gut aus." Loretta spoke in German as she caught Roy's eye.

"Huh? What does that mean?" His reply was a whisper. They had been instructed that English was to be kept to a minimum where possible.

"Just commenting on your outfit." Loretta gave him a wink. "Good choice."

The team had been up most of last night. An inordinate amount of that time had been wasted on choosing outfits. While the importance of fitting in to early century Germany could not be understated, the process had wound up more than a little out of hand.

To his horror, Roy had been called upon to sit in on the change room and give his 'historical recommendations' – a ridiculous task only exacerbated by the presence of Loretta. Her choices had left him a stuttering mess.

"What?" She had said... jiggling. *"No good?"*

"Um, I think the tavern wench look may have gone out a couple of centuries ago, but if anyone could pull it off..."

Fuck. It was real palm on forehead stuff from him. She though had been too busy laughing to take any offence.

Where Loretta had made light of the dress-ups, it had been a far frostier story with Clarke. She fussed over her new wardrobe with both more care, and uncertainty, than Roy pegged her for having. Where Loretta had said *"What?"* with a smile, Clarke's rendition had a side of "... *the fuck you looking at?"* attached.

After what felt like an eternity trying to balance style, warmth and, most importantly, tactical practicality, it was eventually decided that both women would wear a female suit-type equivalent to the men. Short jackets were accompanied by pants – shockingly – that were puffy at the waist but tight at the bottom. Loretta's suit was predominantly crimson, Clarke's blue with pinstripes. Both toned down the butch with a small flowered fascinator upon their heads.

In an outfit befitting his name, Roy picked for himself a stone-coloured, crosschecked, three-piece. Beneath his buttoned vest, a white, linen, collarless shirt had a small dark pearl button at the neck, where a traditional tie would sit. He finished with a gold pocket watch and pair of shiny black leather boots.

During the change room session it was decided by Clarke – for the sake of travelling ease in the still misogynistic era – that the four would be separated into two pairs. The two women would travel under the guise of wives to the academic pair of Roy and Spike. Vienna was the supposed destination, a lecture on history their intended purpose.

Loretta nudged Roy, returning him to the moment. "Uh, thanks, I suppose."

"Hmm, I concur," Spike was pretending he knew German... and English. "We look like fucking ancient James Bonds."

"Jay Gatsbys?" Roy offered. "It's going to be written soon, in eleven years, I think."

"Never heard of him."

"What was it DiCaprio said in the movie?" Loretta said. "You can't repeat the past?"

Roy tried on his best debonair, "Why of course you can..." But he sounded more Connery than anything else.

"Here comes our man." Clarke cut through their quoting session, gesturing toward the station entrance.

Gerhard was walking toward them.

Clarke stepped forward to meet him halfway. The two exchanged a quick word before Gerhard passed over some papers.

Returning to the line-up Clarke handed each of them a ticket. "Alpha are boarding their train now. Ours doesn't leave for another forty minutes." She paused at Spike and Loretta. "Let's split up and try and blend in. Roy and I will meet you both at platform four in twenty minutes."

Spike and Loretta moved off, arm in arm, leaving Roy alone with Clarke.

"That was some good work last night…" Clarke started. "But I think this Braunau avenue of yours will be a big waste of our time." She was not so good at compliments.

Roy took a breath. He looked longingly into the crowd, already envious of Spike and Loretta. "I just presented the facts."

"This lead is twenty-five years old, the trail will be stale." Clarke kept at it.

"But…" Roy stopped. He didn't want to argue.

"If it were up to me, we would all be heading to Landshut…" She was talking to herself now as much as him. "He has to be there. We could cover much more ground together, and end this thing quickly."

Why she was airing, Roy didn't know. What he did know was that Alpha Team would be travelling to Landshut — the recent murder of Heinrich Himmler there took precedence for the main tactical team. And Bravo would travel to Braunau to investigate the Hitler murders. Mason was hedging his bets with the split. Both cities fell inside of the 'ping' parameters so, however unlikely, Braunau was still a possibility. Both teams were to travel by train with orders to launch a balloon in their respective towns – the results to be correlated through Heathcote back in Munich.

Roy stared forward, trying not to acknowledge the silence that had fallen upon them.

"What do you think?" She sought validation.

God... "Umm, I think Landshut and Braunau are both small scale towns. I can't imagine our anomaly has settled in either for the last twenty-five years. They were destinations of purpose for him. I think if he didn't immediately leave Landshut after the murder, we will find this guy on the move very shortly."

Silence fell again. *Wrong answer.* Together they stood still, each leaning on their respective luggage. Devoid of interaction or even fake affection, they were nailing the married couple look.

After another five minutes Clarke broke the deadlock. "Let's move."

Roy and Clarke traversed the crowded platform four. Waiting on their right, a potbelly-black locomotive headed a row of ornate green carriages. Through an obstacle course of loose baggage, ticket inspectors and lost-looking children, they could see Loretta and Spike waiting.

A piercing whistle split the steam soaked air.

"Historical tour 101," Spike said, much too loudly as he waved for their attention. He had a cheesy grin and swept his arm low. "First stop, the birthplace of the devil."

"Spike, you idiot, quit the English." Clarke moved past him and grabbed for a polished silver handrail. "Let's move."

As the two soldiers led the way up into the train neither noticed that Loretta was holding back. Scanning the platform from side to side, she was wringing a rolled up newspaper with both hands. Just as Roy was about to ascend she grabbed his arm and thrust the newspaper at him. "Did you know about this?"

Roy took the paper, but kept his eyes on hers. Now that he was close he could see she was fighting back the urge to cry.

"Well?" she pressed.

Studying the front page, he couldn't make out much of the headline except for a bold number '5'. Underneath was a picture of what looked a town hall.

Loretta read his mind and translated for him. "It says 'Five Dead in Archive Slaying'... Did you know that's how they got you your books?"

Roy was speechless, the shock on his face obvious enough to her. "I... I..."

"OK, I'll take that as a no?"

"Yes, I mean no, of course not."

She softened. "I'm sorry I had to ask."

"That's OK."

The silence between them spoke volumes.

"...Mason and Gerhard?" His was a rhetorical question.

"Has to be." Loretta answered anyway.

"Jesus... Surely not?" His denial was half-hearted because he had known the truth instantly.

Loretta dropped her finger on the front page, crinkling it in his hands. "They were five innocent civilians."

Roy was again lost for words. Murdered civilians were horrible any way and every way, obviously, but the accumulative consequences of death inside this Tear were a whole new factor he couldn't compute. They were immeasurable.

The enormity of the potential losses was making his head hurt. "It's not just five people, it's five potential future generations... If this is true..."

"Roy...." From Loretta's right eye her first tear fell.

"Yeah..."

She looked nervous to say, "I thought we were the good guys?"

"Me too. I mean. We are. But somehow I don't think it's that simple anymore."

"What do we do?"

She was staring at him, expectantly. Roy's mind was racing, but he didn't want to let it show. He was aware of the role she wanted him to play. Her eyes screamed for reassurance. She needed him to be strong, and she needed him to lead... but he was just... well... he didn't know what he was... but whatever it was, it wasn't enough.

He took a deep breath to calm himself. "OK, does Spike know?"

"No, he saw the paper, but couldn't read it."

"OK, keep it that way for now."

"OK."

"OK." The word bounced between them.

He reached out for her shoulder.

She leant ever so slightly into it.

"...OK."

As far as Roy was concerned right now, in terms of trust, the Bravo foursome had just splintered into a twosome. He wanted to believe he could trust Spike, but the odds that he was innocently unaware were not good. "Quick, we had better hurry before someone comes looking for us. We can talk more on the train."

"Should we...?" Loretta looked down the now empty platform. "This could be our last chance to get back to the Tear."

It was a warranted question.

Roy summoned all the courage he could. "Zhu and Richards will hear about this, I promise. But remember, without our help, there may not be a Zhu, Richards or world at all to go back too." He loathed to guilt Loretta into it, but he needed her just as much as she needed him. He craned low, looking deep into her eyes. "I give you my word I won't let anything bad happen to you."

He just prayed he could keep that promise.

"Yo Royston, you better not be hitting on my wife?" A voice came from above them.

Roy would have hit the roof if there had been one. It was Spike; he had obviously come to check why they were taking so long.

Fluttering her eyelids, Loretta snapped seamlessly into her role. "Oh, how I have missed you 'mein schatz', my sweetheart. I just finished a cigarette, but thank you for saving me from this scoundrel."

God, she was good.

"Baby this is 1914, not 2017, and we are flying first class, everyone is smoking up in here."

The two were hamming up their marital improv. Roy remained silent; he was busy viewing Spike under the light of new information. He watched as first the luggage and then Loretta boarded. *Did he know? Surely not? You're in denial... of course he knows.*

The locomotive steam whistle blasted twice to signify the train's imminent departure. Roy surveyed the platform one last time, his heart heavy.

What have I got myself into?

Chapter 20

Location: ....48.5442° N, 12.1469° E
Present day name: ....Landshut, Germany
IDTF Classification: .Tear Four
Date: ....June 26th 1914

Abner's wicker chair creaked as he tilted his head back and let the sunshine bake his face. Seated outside of a patisserie facing Landshut Railway Station, it felt great to be out in the open again.

"Another coffee?" David's empty espresso cup clattered on its saucer.

With eyes closed, Abner spoke softly. "No..." It had been three days, but still he was weary. "Our train leaves soon enough."

The fervour prompted by a child's murder had swept through the town as expected. Police presence on the streets had intensified tenfold, and townsfolk were on high alert. Landshut, however large, still had a small town feel. It was the kind of place where two foreign heads could easily come under suspicion, regardless of guilt or innocence.

"Look at these people, David... Really look at them."

From the café frontage, the pair had an unobstructed view of the square. Observing the trajectory of social change was still a marvel for Abner. The gift of knowing where it was all headed highlighted the nuances of the time. A man whopping his son openly in the square drew not a single glance. A couple doing everything in their power to resist the pleasures of touch; he wanted to scream at them to kiss. A group of four men leaving the rail station... well... they had a peculiar look to them. It was nothing overly obvious, but it was something.

David noticed them too, except he was more blunt with his summation. "Abner, look at that negro..." He straightened up in his chair. "How on Earth could he have paid for that suit? Look at him Abner, fancy negro, leading that pack of men like that."

"Watch your tongue." Racism, Abner would have none of it.

Though he couldn't properly appreciate it, David did have a point. It was not the invalidity of the black man's attire, but instead the strangeness of his apparent entourage.

Abner narrowed his gaze as the men fanned into a 'V'. The group, it looked just as diverse as its apparent head honcho. One Latino, one poster-boy Arian and one maybe slightly Middle Eastern trailed their leader, a leader who, if he was being specific, was probably African-American.

As the group approached, crossing the square, Abner traced each individually over the lip of his cup. It was indeed an odd ensemble, by any standards, not just 1914 small town Germany. Closer now, the looks of the American, Mexican and German were obvious, but Abner could see that the last man he first thought to be Arab, was instead almost certainly Jewish. He had a specific look that Abner had not seen in twenty-five years, but one he knew well from numerous visits. If they had been in '92 he'd have called it easily, but here in '14 it was more diffi-cult... because the country in question did not exist yet.

The last man is Israeli.

The more he watched, the more the group intrigued him. There was minimal interaction between the men; each seemed to know his role, and as such moved with purpose. What was clear was that they were no tourists; not one had ventured so much as a glance at the iconic Landshut clock tower shadowing the square.

Could it be...? His imagination was escaping him.

No... He was certain that what it was hinting at was not possible. *Remember the terms of travel, old man; this is your universe, your universe alone.*

Yet his eyes could not lie.

It was the little things that only someone like him could pick up on – the way the German carried his pack, the way the Israeli was scanning anyone who ventured too close, the way the American stopped on a dime, spun and delivered what seemed to be orders with a curt efficiency...

The group... it was military... proper military.

Lacking the pomp and ceremony that the 1900s demanded, the team resembled rather a cold, calculated, late-century strike team... like one he himself had been a part of in a previous life.

Abner looked to David; his boy had dropped the jokes and was evaluating the group for himself. "See boy. Those who are quick to talk learn nothing. Let's go."

As the pair rose, David collected their bags. "And what of them?"

"There are others who can do our bidding." Abner turned back for the café. "Wait here."

Inside he made a beeline for the elderly woman behind the counter. "Hallo..."

"Fertig?" – 'Finished?' the woman was wiping her hands on her apron.

"Ja."

"Netter Kaffee?" – 'Nice coffee?'

"Na sicher." – 'Of course.' His smile was exaggerated. "Köstlich." – 'Delicious'.

"Danke."

"Interessante landschaft auch." – 'Interesting scenery too."

The woman's eyebrows lifted. "Wirklich, wie?" – 'Really, how so?'

"Gut..." – 'Well...' Abner offered her a shake of his head as he guided her gaze out into the square. "Ich möchte keine probleme verursachen. Aber diese männer sprechen Englisch." – 'I don't wish to cause trouble, but those men out there are speaking English...'

"Ohh."

...Her intake of breath, it was all he needed.

Three minutes later, Abner was back outside. David greeted him with a knowing nod.

Abner answered the unspoken. "A small town seed of suspicion can grow wonderful things."

David's smirk formed independently of all other facial muscles, such a rare occurrence it was. "Throwing a town full of cats among four unknowing pigeons. Impressive."

With that the two of them proceeded to the station in silence. The sky above had darkened now, just like their mood. As Abner entered the railway station he paused for one final glimpse back. The men, they lingered still.

"Abner."

"Yes."

"What is it?"

"Nothing, boy."

But that was a lie. The sense of foreboding that tugged at him, it was an assurance, as good as any, that he would see these men again.

⁂

Mason was short and sharp. Every second they wasted was another step the anomaly could be making away from Landshut.

"Roman, Simeon, onto that balloon, I need a 'ping' ASAP. Gerhard, the school, you and I will start there and then move onto the parents' address. It's going to be radio silence until the balloon is up. If anything goes wrong, we rendezvous back here at the station at 2200. Let's sync now."

Each man reached for his respective pocket.

"I'm still not used to wearing one of these, Boss." Roman flipped open his ornate gold watch. "Fucking forget to keep it wound."

"Well, unless you're a bitch, wristwatches weren't worn by men for another couple of decades." Mason didn't have the time for him, literally.

As the foursome synchronised their watches, none of them noticed the beady set of eyes studying them from the patisserie window. It was a weird thing for four grown men to do in the middle of the street, the kind of thing that could easily draw the ire of an elderly townswoman on high alert...

Unfortunately for Alpha, they had local eyes on them now.

Chapter 21

Location: .... 48.2557° N, 13.0443° E
Present day name: .... Braunau am Inn, Austria
IDTF Classification: . Tear Four
Date: .... June 26th 1914

Salzburger Vorstadt 15. The birthplace of Adolf Hitler. Roy's heart was thumping out of his chest. This house had always been on his bucket list. It was one he thought he might forever miss out on after the Austrian Government released plans in 2016 to push for its demolition. Never in his wildest dreams did he imagine he would get to view it with the authenticity of a 1900s setting, without a single tourist out the front on the end of a selfie-stick.

Roy threw up a hand to shield his eyes. Through a squint he took in the patched and faded façade of the sandy-coloured three-storey building. Something struck him. It was after midday, mid-June, yet the second storey windows were all completely closed, possibly it seemed even boarded shut.

"He was born on the second floor, that was the Hitler's rented residence. They shared this building with two other families." Roy had played tour guide since they had arrived.

"Looks like someone has shut up shop." Clarke had also noticed the windows.

Roy couldn't understand why. "I am certain the Hitlers rented, so there is no reason for it to still be empty. The building was owned by a family called Biegel; I always remembered them because of how it sounded a bit like bagel."

Clarke turned to Loretta. "Enquiring about lodging on the second floor could be a legitimate avenue. Do you think you can manage?"

Loretta nodded. "Kein problem." Her German was on point, accent and all.

Clarke turned then to Roy and Spike. "Otherwise what other options do we have, historical or tactical?"

"That big wooden door on the left..." Roy answered. "It leads to an internal staircase from where you can access the individual apartments. Or, we can follow the laneway on the right. There will be access from the rear." He was fast approaching the limits of his memory; he had after all only read about the place in other people's books.

Spike shrugged. "Back sounds good enough for a breach."

"OK, let's make a decision before we start to draw attention," said Clarke.

"Right," Roy agreed. "This house is not yet a historical landmark. Aside from some murders a quarter of a century ago, there is no reason for us to be staring."

"Hallo..." Loretta spoke into a wall of timber. Pressing the side of her face close, she listened for a reply.

Nothing.

She reached tentatively for the dinner plate-sized door knocker. A brass-moulded lion's head held a heavy ring between its snarling jaws.

Clarke gave her a thumbs-up.

"Hallo jemand da?" Loretta said again, between booms this time.

"Hello... BOOM... is anybody there? BOOM." Roy understood that much.

"Ja!" Finally a voice – short on breath, and patience – came from the other side.

Loretta pushed back expectantly, but still the door remained closed. Without really thinking, she knocked again. "Ich möchte ein zimmer mieten."

"Scheiße halt!"

"Entschuldigung bin ich richtig fragen."

Roy had extinguished his limited German, he and the rest of the team were now in the dark on what was being said.

There was silence now on the other side. Loretta tried some more, "Ist dein zweiter stock vorhanden." But still the door remained closed. Turning to the group, she threw up her hands. "What do I do?"

Where Loretta was whispering, Clarke was pushing, full noise. "What did you say?"

"I said we would like to rent a room. I asked if the second floor was available?"

"Tell them we have gold."

"Really?" Loretta screwed her face up. "Gold? What we are pirates?"

"Go on." Clarke shooed her back to the door.

Loretta waved a hand across her throat. "No, maybe we should..."

"Just do it."

Before the two could mime argue any further though, the latch of the heavy wooden door clattered.

All four shot to attention.

The door creaked in just enough to reveal a pair of squished eyes set close on a puffy face. Below the cautious expression – underneath a bloodstained apron – a hard looking chest and belly filled the slim gap.

"Ja?"

The man's look warmed slightly when he met Loretta's smiling face. "Hallo."

"Hallo...?"

The two broke into a rapid fire conversation in German. From just his tone, Roy could see the man was not accustomed to renting out rooms, but as the conversation continued Roy could sense a shift. He watched as Loretta went to work on the jittery man. To start, the flirting seemed innocent enough, but it soon became obvious she was playing a role. A smile here, a flick of the hair there, Loretta had switched on her sex appeal and was ratcheting the dial to eleven.

Roy's eyelids fluttered, disbelieving what he was seeing. He was clued in to the game yet, still, Loretta's laugh was like a magnet, drawing him in. He turned to Spike who was watching also. "Is she...?"

"Yep..." Spike puffed his chest with pride. "That's my wife."

It was amazing. The woman had a gift.

Roy had another, equally scary thought. *Hang on, has she done this to me?*

"Dein name?" Loretta's sudden use of broken English brought all on the outs back into the conversation.

"Deryk Biegel." The man waved his hand in an arc to accentuate the obvious. "This. Father building... Now mine."

Deryk swung the door open another foot so he could regard the rest of the team, and more specifically Clarke, directly. "You pay gold... ja?"

"Yes." Clarke had none of Loretta's charm.

"The word for gold is the same in English and in German," Loretta clarified, reading all their minds. "I think Deryk was listening a little harder than we figured."

Roy watched as Deryk nodded. His attention was bouncing between Loretta and Clarke, a discord playing out between his brain and his dick, between greed and lust.

"English?" Clarke had all the patience of a border guard immigration officer.

"Ja ein bisschen." Deryk replied – obviously only a little.

"Room. Rent. Gold. Yes. No?"

"How... long?"

"One night."

"Lass mich das gold sehen." Deryk again reverted to German. The broken multi-language conversation was confusing the hell out of Roy.

Loretta translated for them. "He wants to see the gold."

Clarke reached for her belt and produced a nugget. The size of half a fingernail, it was far too excessive for one night's accommodation, but she couldn't exactly ask for change. Deryk's eyes widened at the sight of the nugget. Impulse seized him and he grabbed for it greedily. Clarke instinctively pulled away, swatting his hand like she was smacking a child's.

"Ah ah."

A reflex of revulsion more than caution, the affect of the slap was instantaneous. Offended all the same, if not more, Deryk recoiled. As he cast a red face Loretta's way, his shame quickly turned to anger. "Fine. You. No stay."

Loretta tried to smooth things over. "Please Deryk, eine nacht?"

But Deryk glared with an evil eye straight through her to Clarke. "Zwei. Zwei stücke gold."

Roy didn't need a translation; he knew what 'zwei' meant. Clarke it seemed did also.

"Two! You want two?"

"Zwei, zwei."

"No fucking way! I'm not getting barrelled by some sack of sweat, it's one or nothing."

"Fine." Deryk smiled. "Fuck. You. And fuck... off." His broken English insult would have been funny had it not been so serious.

And that was when things escalated.

Deryk, fat with a smug smile, turned away from the door and made to slam it shut. Just as he did though, Clarke rammed her boot forward, sliding her toe at speed into its bottom.

The heavy door crunched her boot, but she held firm.

Deryk snapped around, his face a deeper shade of red.

Clarke met his face with a smile; it was Loretta though who spoke for her. "Entschuldigung, wir kommen rein" ... *Sorry Deryk, we are coming inside.*

Deryk's pupils dilated at the sight of the two women, suddenly emboldened. A realisation washed over him, the time for jokes was very much over. His sympathetic nervous system made its calculations. Flight or fight, the choice was made...

And then he ran.

Spike sprang into action, as if he had been awaiting this exact eventuality. "Yee-haw!" He pushed past Loretta, and dived sideways through the slit in the door.

Clarke hesitated for only a second. Turning to Roy, she yelled, "Cut him off at the back," before she too then shouldered her way inside.

Roy looked around dumbfounded. *Who, me?* He turned to Loretta for reassurance, "Did she say...?"

"The back? Yeah."

...Shit.

Inside, Deryk's residence was a labyrinth of junk-laden corridors. Boxes, machine parts and books were stacked to at least head height, allowing only a slender line through the already narrow ground floor.

Spike broke into the entrance to find himself at an immediate disadvantage. Somehow, within the few seconds Deryk had on him, the big guy had managed to escape around multiple quick corners. It was an unbelievable feat for someone his size.

Spike heard something crash, a tower of junk collapsing in the next room. It was all he had to go on. Using his hands like paddles he forced himself forward as if he were striding through waist high water.

Behind him he heard Clarke crash into the house. "Fuck, what the fuck is this!"

"Clarke!" He laid his boot into a stack of sodden cardboard boxes. "This way."

Up ahead, keys jingled on an iron ring. Spike bolted the last few metres for an opening to his left. Family photos, black and white images of a young family of three whizzed past on his periphery. He rounded a timber doorframe – into what seemed to be the kitchen – just in time to see Deryk glance back from outside. The kitchen was less cluttered; a whole leg of beef sat half carved on the bench, dripping blood onto the floor. Spike was in free air now, five metres only from where the man had disappeared into the light of the outside. He broke for the exit, "I gotcha now fat boy."

Traversing the building façade, Roy dragged a hand along the sandstone as he half ran, half skipped ahead. As he reached the building's edge he took a left-hander around the alleyway entrance. The surface was jarringly uneven, irregular shaped bluestones jutted haphazardly from the floor.

The efficiency of the lane's water run-off was the least of Roy's concern though, because, as he squinted into the shadow, he was met with a most dreaded sight: Deryk, the rolling meatball of a man, was bounding straight toward him.

Twenty metres away, Deryk was already at pace and seemed to be gathering momentum with each elephant step. Roy gulped hard as Deryk waved a hand feverishly, willing him to get out of his way.

"Mo...ve!" Came a breathless yell.

Over Deryk's shoulder, Roy saw the smaller figure of Spike round the alleyway. The pair locked eyes, and Roy's, wide with apprehension, could read in Spike's plainly, *'Stop him!'*

"Nnnnnnnnonononono. Stopstopstop."

There was no way around it. A collision was inevitable. Every bone in Roy's body tensed. His mind screamed as his feet planted themselves, in defiance of all logic. *What are you doing!?*

Was it heroism? He doubted it. Paralysing fear? Most probably.

Either way, it was too late...

Deryk cannoned in Roy, shoulder down, front-row-rugby-style.

The force of the impact had Roy's feet off the ground. He flew backward a full metre. As Deryk rolled on – his legs chugging like a Mack truck over roadkill – Roy landed hard. His breath evacuated his lungs at vacuum pace. The shock of the sudden lack of oxygen quite possibly the only thing keeping him conscious.

He had failed miserably.

Yet, as his head bounced once, then twice, on the blue-stones, instinct kicked in. Roy threw a hand up and around anything he could. He found purchase, a solid, meaty, tree-trunk ankle. He yanked on it with all his might, just in time, before it stomped him flat.

"That was some thing you did back there, taking him down like that." Spike handed Roy a moist towel. It was the closest thing they had to ice. "Cap'n courageous, if you ask me."

Roy put the towel to his forehead. "It was nothing. I fell, he tripped."

"Sure. Whatever you say." Spike pulled over a rickety wicker chair. The mesh of the seat was long gone. Next to Roy he straddled it backward. "You play DT in high school or something?"

"DT?"

"Yeah DT, defensive tackle."

Roy let out a laugh that split his side. "Oh, God that hurts... Spike I'm Australian?"

"So... You ain't got no football?"

Another chuckle, this time holding his ribs. "Stop making me laugh... Yeah we got football, but you got to see it, it's different."

"Different as in...?"

"As in no pads."

"Nice... That how you get such a hard head."

Australian Rules, or any other type, Roy didn't play. His sports as a kid were the kinds that tended to have 'clubs' instead of 'teams'.

"No, contact wasn't really my thing in school." He thought of his boxing with John back home. "But, hey, this'll be my second black eye this week, so maybe I'm getting somewhere."

"You think you'll be staring down killers next?" Clarke was leaning against the door, entirely unimpressed. Neither Roy nor Spike had seen her appear.

"That wasn't really my point."

"Sure."

Waiting in what appeared to be the dining room of the Hitler's old residence, it was only Roy who realised the trio were milling in the possible location of Adolf's birth, and death. Almost entirely empty, the room was slick with a blanket of dust and, from the ceiling, spores hung like miniature stalactites turning from a creamy white to furry orange.

Roy heard a laugh, and then playful gasp, coming from the kitchen. It told him Loretta was still OK.

After the calamity in the alley, Spike had pounced on Deryk's back like he was on *COPS*, and subdued him with a rear naked chokehold. Together they had carried Deryk upstairs and tied him to one of the only bits of sturdy furniture left on the second floor, a cast iron stove in the kitchen. While Clarke and Spike had discussed what to do with him, Loretta had pounced on the chance to try a civil approach first.

"Fuck..." Clarke looked at her watch, a G-Shock she was not supposed to be wearing "...What is she doing?"

Roy shrugged, his brain felt like mush, he was happy enough to rest.

Clarke though was getting antsy "Fuck it, let's fan out. Fat chance of it, but start looking for clues. Blood stains, photographs, whatever."

Roy leant his head back. *Fuck me... really?*

He followed Clarke from the dining to children's room. She was sweeping for clues while he wandered, half asleep, pretending to do the same. They had been looking for not more than five minutes when Spike called from another room. "Ah... boss, I think I have something."

"Where are you?" Clarke called back.

"Here."

She rolled her eyes. "Here where idiot?"

They found him in the front, in a stale, timber-wrapped room – one with a dust-free square against the wall: a clue the room was once a bedroom.

"Shoot me down if I'm wrong, but I'm pretty sure this is a bullet hole." Spike was standing by a window he had pried open. "Needed some light. Then I seen this." He pointed to a splintered hole in the architrave a little lower than eye-level.

Roy looked past his arm to see the window revealed a view of the street below. Looking down, something about Klara's death twigged in his memory.

"What'd you reckon?"

Clarke moved closer and squinted into the hole. "Let's dig it out."

Spike jimmied the architrave. The bullet had passed clean through it. He was just about to dig into the render of the wall when the group heard the kitchen door creak open.

Silence.

"Huh hem." Loretta coughed from somewhere down the hall.

No one moved.

"Um. Hello?"

Roy, Spike and Clarke looked at each other, waiting. Clarke breathed through her nose. "This had better be good."

Filing back into the lounge, they found Loretta waiting for them.

Only when she was certain she had their attention, did she proceed, strangely, to take a bow. "Men are... fucking pathetic." She laughed as she rose. "No offence boys."

Roy's nod was the universal sign for 'meh'

"It really is like stealing candy from a baby. Another half hour and he would have given *me* some gold." She was clearly enjoying herself.

"Professor," Clarke spoke through clenched teeth, "if you want to go back in, feel free. Otherwise, spill your shit and spill it quick, I have bigger things…"

"Ah… I'm not sure anything can be more important than what I have just heard." Loretta corrected her with a solitary finger.

"OK, I'll bite." Roy too was conscious of the need to speed things up, he had an idea bubbling away inside. "The bow? Please elaborate."

"Well, I have just had quite an 'interesting' chat with our new landlord." Loretta settled against a wall because there was nowhere to sit. "His initial anger was an obvious roadblock, but thankfully he's a nervous one, our Deryk. Unable to help himself, he was soon asking all types of questions about where we are from, why we are here and, of course, why we had him hogtied to a stove. I persisted with the Americans lecturing in Vienna story, but as you can imagine he wasn't really buying it… so…" She brought two fingers up to her lips and puffed slowly, sensually, on an imaginary cigarette "…I reintroduced him to Lorrrr-retta…" Her Rs rolled vivaciously. "She always gets me out of trouble."

"Oh, you're breaking my heart." Spike dropped a hand across his chest.

"Hang on mein schatz, you will be happy I did. Together we started down the life story road." She looked at Roy. "You said the Biegels rented this place to the Hitlers. Well, Deryk is a Biegel. 'Who knows?' I thought. If Deryk had lived here his entire life maybe he remembered something about the murders?" A grin was forming on her lips that she couldn't contain.

"And?" Clarke was interested now.

"Let's just say we don't have to worry about your nuggets of gold anymore, because I've just mined some of my very own."

"Professor... enough."

"Well, where do I start? How about..." Pausing to build tension she splayed her hand wide and counted down her fingers. "Uno, he HAS lived here his entire life. Due, he DID know the Hitlers. Tre, he WAS here that night twenty-five years ago. Quattro, there WAS a birth. Cinque, he knows ALL about the murders, including who died and how they were killed. And sei..." She needed another hand. "...If we can believe him, he supposedly even confronted the killer."

You could have heard a pin drop in the room.

"Fuck, honey you are some piece of work." Spike exhaled.

"He confirmed the birth?" Roy asked equal parts shocked and impressed.

"Si, even remembers the little one's name. One, A... dolf... Hitler."

Clarke was shaking her head. "I don't believe it. Are you telling me, first stop, first local, twenty minutes in, and you have gotten us an anomaly description?" It was as close as she could get to a compliment.

"All without a pressured interrogation." Spike was extra impressed he wouldn't be needed.

"Well, I wouldn't claim all the secrets." Loretta smiled cheekily. "Just, you know, middle aged, short brown curly hair, brown eyes and a deep scar across the chin." She was purposely casual. "But hey, you guys said you found something better...?"

Chapter 22

Location: .... 48.5442° N, 12.1469° E
Present day name: .... Landshut, Germany
IDTF Classification: . Tear Four
Date: .... June 26th 1914

"...M as... up... ow!" Mason's earpiece crackled to life. He could just make out the sound of Roman's voice.

Fantastic. He turned from the kitchen sink to Gerhard. "Roman and Simeon have launched the second balloon; any minute now we should have clear coms."

"Perfect timing." The German had heard the broken transmission also. He sat with his chair pushed back on two legs, feet up on a table.

"Right then. Let's wrap this up." But before Mason could move, his earpiece fizzled again, this time with static.

Be patient, Roman.

White noise cut in and out. Mason had little choice but to listen.

The next sound to cut through though pricked his ears. Similarly broken, it was a rustle, like nylon on nylon. Someone was moving quickly, brushing past or through an obstruction. *Goddammit Roman, hang on, the balloon is still not at altitude.*

A voice then made him stop what he was doing. "Komm... aus... dein... obenen... händen."

The back of his neck bristled. *Was that German!?*

"O... uck... Simeo... you... left." His earpiece stuttered. It was Roman again, yelling.

A loud static CRACK split his eardrum. "Argh fuck! What the fuck?"

Even through the interference it was clearly a gunshot.

Mason's ears burned, searching the silence.

"Fuc...Mason...you...ther...?" Roman's voice broke through again. It was getting clearer with each transmission, but it wasn't happening fast enough. The balloon was still too low.

"Roman! Come in, Roman!" Mason spoke into his concealed throat mic, his voice clipped with urgency.

"...Affir...tive.. Mason... we... re under atta..."

CRACK CRACK CRACK!' Three quick gunshots echoed through the interference.

"Fuck! Roman, report!"

Silence.

"ROMAN?"

More silence.

Mason didn't need to be told, something was clearly wrong.

"Roman, sit tight. We are on our way."

Mason peered up from the floor, and the splodge of blood on it he'd found himself staring into. He took a deep breath and refocused on his immediate surroundings. He had to deal with his own problems before he could start on Roman's.

Before him, sat a sick, sorry and broken Joseph Gebhard Himmler. Joseph was the father of Heinrich, the murdered boy of Landshut. As if the death of a child wasn't torturous enough, the man's current predicament was affirmation he had seen better days.

Joseph sat naked, tied by hand and foot to a chair in his own kitchen. His face was a bloodied mess, smashed to pieces in a quick fire interrogation. Next to him lay the unconscious, possibly dead – no one was keeping track – body of his wife, Anna Maria.

"Joseph, I wish I could thank you, but I'm afraid you have been disappointingly unhelpful."

Joseph stared at Mason through the one half functioning eye he had left. Far too concussed to offer much – anger, sorrow and confusion had passed him long ago – now he just sat like a vegetable.

Mason knelt down, eye-to-one-good-eye with his captive. He spoke as if to a child. "We have to leave now. But remember what I told you, he was going to grow into a cunt anyway." He rose and moved back to the sink. Facing out over a row of indoor herbs he studied the yard outside. The faucet squealed as he washed the blood from his hands. From one knuckle a small piece of tooth clattered down onto the metal before disappearing down the drain. The absurd act had a patience about it. He closed his eyes, feeling the cold water rush between his fingers. "Gerhard... wash the house."

Gerhard still had not moved from his seat at the table, he was eyeballing the side of the Himmler man's head, studying him like someone would a job well done. Joseph had no left hand side vision, so he never saw Gerhard raise his silenced pistol. "Sünden des sohnes." The German spoke calmly in his native tongue, before he fired a shot into Joseph's brain.

Mason did not even flinch. He wiped his hands on a tea towel, and neatly folded it back over the oven handle. "We dealing out one-liners now?

"Sins of the son," Gerhard clarified. "I thought it was fitting."

Mason nodded to the wife on the floor. "Make it quick."

Gerhard was up now. He gave Anna Maria a nudge with his boot. She stirred groggily. Gerhard looked up – surprised and a little fearful – he hadn't expected movement. "She is alive."

"And?"

"And, well…" He paused. "A woman is still a woman, Ectype or not."

Rational or not, Gerhard apparently had some sort of misguided line.

Mason watched the German's body tense in anticipation of his own reply. But he didn't bother with a retort. He just drew his pistol and ruthlessly fired a shot into the back of Anna's slowly lifting head. The force of the point blank bullet hammered her forehead down onto the kitchen floor, it bounced three times as her body went limp.

"Remember, the original Anna has lived her life. These things, they are just duplicates to be deleted, like copies on a computer." Mason picked up a candle from the table and handed it to Gerhard. "Now… the rest of the house." His meaning was plain. "Make it quick too, something tells me we are not done yet with death here in Landshut."

Roman and Simeon were pinned down. Their refuge, the last house of an abruptly dead-ended street, was a two-storey bluestone. Still warm, the cottage had been strategically abandoned by its owners within seconds of them barging in. Minutes later, they'd been surrounded… and that was when the all-out assault had begun.

They lay crouched besides opposing windows, Roman at the front, facing the street, Simeon at the rear, covering the yard they had just crossed. They kept in each other's line of sight through the kitchen doorway.

"Ey, this is embarrassing!" Roman flinched down as a bullet punctured the glass next to him. "Pinned down by a fucking musket brigade."

"I'm pretty sure I saw someone with a pitchfork out there." Simeon was laughing, but it was not at all impossible he hadn't. "Next to that guy handing out the torches like candyfloss."

It was night outside. Shadows of red licked in through the windows, and danced across the walls inside.

"Nothing like a lynching to really rally a town," Roman yelled loudly, as the onslaught of bullets ceased temporarily. "Mason's gonna have our nuts for this."

"I can't understand it, how the fuck did they find us?"

Thirty minutes earlier

"We ready?" Roman lifted his empty HFECS case up onto a rusted out 44-gallon drum.

"Good to go." Simeon was kneeling next to the assembled balloon.

"All right." Roman had out the final checklist. "GPS anchor established?"

"Check."

"Elevation parameters set?

"Check."

"Solar coils primed?"

"Check."

"Commencing launch. In... three... two... one."

The heating coils glowed to life.

Leaving Landshut Station, it had taken Roman only one pass around town to identify a suitable launch site. A scrapyard to the north of the station would suffice. Being a Sunday, the junk filled wasteland was conveniently unattended.

The sun had almost set on them now. All around, the rust-riddled ruins baked in the last few seconds of sun before succumbing to the slow moving shadow. Like a rising tide the yard was turning from orange to red to black.

The launch demanded dusk at least, the last thing Roman needed was a bunch of locals screaming 'alien'. When unpacked and assembled the balloon concertinaed out from its tight folds into a surprisingly large ten-foot sack. Its foil skin was super lightweight and incredibly thin. In the breeze it rolled more than flapped, like liquid silver.

"Releasing anchor in... three... two... one..." Simeon's hands sprang open as he released his grip on the balloon's rigid, circular mouth.

Floating before them for a second, its heating coils glowed red in their fight against gravity, tipping the scales ever so precariously toward ascension.

"C'mon." Roman resisted the urge to reach out.

With each centimetre of altitude the balloon's rise began to gather speed.

"Fucking A." He clapped. "Give it ten minutes and we should have coms, another ten after that and we can ping this prick."

"You still got eyes on?"

"Yeah, a bit to the left, you got it?"

"Yeah."

Together with Simeon, Roman still had his neck craned skyward when he heard what sounded like footsteps in the mud...

A cough and then voice pulled his gaze back to Earth. "Wer bist du?"

Roman did a double take, but recognised the uniforms immediately.

...Oh fuck.

Two men, each with thick blue jackets on, were staring at them curiously. Both looked far too regal for scrapyard employees. On their heads, stiff, cake-tin-style hats were the type with a small peak in the front. From tasselled shoulders, two rows of gold buttons led down to a hip holstered revolver on each. One, assumedly the sergeant, also had an ornate sword swinging from his belt.

"Was machen sie?" said the sergeant.

"Fuck." Roman let slip.

"Was machen sie!"

Roman and Simeon had no idea what the officers were saying. They looked to each other like children caught with the cookie jar.

"Was machen sie!" The sergeant repeated again, a third time now.

An awkward silence ensued as all four men stood frozen in position.

"Was machen sie!"

"Yeah, we fucking heard you the first time." Roman bit back.

The Germans seemed to be thrown by the English, and the level of tension between the group – already unnaturally high – ramped skyward. Roman could see the junior's hand shaking, while the sergeant shuffled his stance, bracing himself for something.

What the hell is going on... this is not a standard police stop.

"Wow wow wow. The last thing Roman wanted was bloodshed. He raised his palms slowly, conscious not to flinch "Sorry. We are lost." He pointed between himself and Simeon. "American. We don't speak German."

The junior officer looked past him to the array of equipment spread on the ground behind them. He pointed. "Was ist das alles?"

That one was obvious. "Hey, that's not ours, that was here when we got here."

His lie got him nothing in the way of acknowledgement, or disarmament. Instead the officers turned to each other and began whispering as they pointed from the equipment back to the front gate.

"They can't understand us. What do we do?" Simeon muttered under his breath.

"If they reach, we put them down." Roman's smile was clenched. "Make it non-lethal if possible."

"Fuck, my gun is on the crate behind me."

Simeon and Roman's three-piece suits did not allow for hip holsters. Instead both had been issued the shoulder variety to wear beneath their jackets. Unfortunately for Simeon he had shrugged off both jacket and holster during the balloon assembly.

"Work something out. If they move, you take the left, I'll take the Zorro on the right." Roman said.

"Fuck, we're fucked."

"Hör auf zu redden!" The sergeant – taking umbrage with their conversation – screamed at them. Like the sky above, the situation darkened suddenly. Both officers started yelling animatedly at Roman and Simeon. "Auf den boden runter! Auf den boden runter! Auf den boden runter!"

"Calm the fuck down! We don't understand you!" Roman kept his eyes glued on the sergeant. He could see a bead of sweat escape the man's cap. "Get ready..." he spoke out of the side of his mouth "...Zorro is getting itchy fingers."

"Fuck. Fucking idiots." Simeon was totally exposed.

Shaking, sweating, choking, it was instead the junior officer who flinched first. As his little finger felt for the metal of his weapon, Roman could see it on his face, he couldn't help himself.

"Don't you do it..."

But it was too late. As the junior officer jerked at his weapon, the sergeant followed suit a split-second later.

The standoff broke into a blur of movement. From three separate firearms – all at various stages of draw – three shots rang out. Milliseconds apart, they echoed through the scrapyard, like from a within a metal cave.

One bullet hit the ground, one sailed wide right... and one hit flesh.

Both police officers dropped.

The sergeant was dead instantly. Roman's bullet had entered his left eye-socket and blown out the back of his skull.

The junior officer's collapse was slower. He coiled over with a loud "hoof" as the air evacuated his lungs. Slowly, bent at the waist, he fell from his knees to the floor.

Roman turned to Simeon; he was kneeling in an extended lunge, the pose of a man who had just thrown something... something very hard.

"You all right?"

Rising, Simeon patted down his chest. "Yeah. Fucker must have missed by inches. I felt it pass me wide." He gestured then to Zorro's missing eyeball. "Nice shot."

"Stupid motherfuckers... I didn't want to do that."

Simeon was smiling.

"What's so funny?"

"Well, did we just have our first Mexican standoff? I was just thinking your mama would be proud."

Roman was crossing the patch of no man's land. "Who says this is my first."

The junior officer had now curled into a ball on his side. Clutching his stomach he was writhing in pain. Roman observed the man's predicament; he had the handle of Simeon's knife protruding from his abdomen.

"Impressive."

Roman nudged the officer with his foot. The man shimmied up in the dirt, like a wounded animal. His hands were slick with blood. As he tried to crawl, one clutched at the knife while the other fumbled at his waist. Reaching for his utility belt he extracted something.

"You cheeky fucker." Roman caught on a second too late, it was not gauze as he had assumed, but instead a standard issue officer's whistle.

"Shit…" It was all he could manage before the officer blew with all the breath he had left.

At the front of the yard the gate burst open. At least ten officers streamed in, all with their weapons drawn.

"Simeon! We got move!" Roman spun on his heels.

Simeon didn't need to be told. At the sound of the whistle he had snatched up two separate shoulder holsters and was now loosing off shots blindly as he ran.

The pair abandoned their remaining equipment and sprinted for the rear of the yard. Roman had barely a second to glance skyward before the first shot whizzed past his head. The balloon was but a glint in among the stars, high enough to be safe.

Abutting rough parkland, the rear of the scrapyard was a wall of green. Crashing into the thick brush, Roman was plunged into a world of darkness.

Spurned on by yelling, Roman ran. Branches whipped at his face and logs smashed at his shins. Navigation, it was impossible. With his eyes closed he let his body take over. Chugging his legs, his hands led him forward.

Suddenly, breaking into open air, he skidded to the edge of an embankment and looked down into a small creek. Moonlight glistened white off the water. Another step and he would have tumbled straight over the ledge.

On the other side of the creek a field led to what seemed to be a rundown residential block. Roman could see the faint flicker of candles in only a few windows.

Options, A B C raced through his brain, the creek, the field, the street…?

Bark exploded off a tree next to him jolting him back to his ledge. Cries of murder intensified behind him. The German police regiment following them had obviously found the bodies of their fallen comrades.

Roman jumped and slid feet first down the slope. Splashing into the creek, his boots filled to his ankles.

Simeon splashed down next to him, panting. "Where are we going?"

At the bottom of the embankment now, the pair was out of danger, temporarily. Shots still continued to burst through though, showering them with branches.

"That house up ahead…" Roman pointed. "We need to make a run for it. You got smoke?"

"Yeah." Simeon reached for his second shoulder holster; hanging from it were four small grenades. He grabbed one shaped like a soft drink can; it was green with a yellow band around its middle. He pulled the pin and launched it into the open field between them and the house… Then they ran.

Present

"Oh fuck! Simeon on your left!"

The top of a head appeared through the kitchen window just above where Simeon was crouching. With the hat, a revolver rose over the sill.

BAM! Roman fired. The man fell backwards. Alive or dead, Roman was not sure.

"Fuck, Mason are you there?" He tried into his mic.

"Ro... c... in... man," came a stunted reply.

"Simeon, the coms are almost up," yelled Roman, ducking down as a chorus of bullets ricocheted off the stone around him.

He got no reply other than footsteps. Simeon was on the move.

"Affirmative Mason. We are under attack!" Roman spoke down into his mic again. CRACK CRACK CRACK. He leant sideways and fired three warning shots through the front window.

Their advanced weaponry was the only thing keeping them alive. Roman heard Simeon now above him, on the second floor. Firing two shots over the back, towards the scrapyard approach, he was picking off any officers stupid enough to leave the cover of the creek. Roman snuck a glance at the streetscape. Reinforcements had arrived from town. Under the light of burning torches they were busy fashioning a barricade from an overturned horse-cart.

Both sides settled in... it seemed a siege had begun.

"How have you not realised we don't speak fucking German?" Roman yelled into the air, a thick vein bulging from his tattooed neck.

A monotonous echo trumpeted from a megaphone outside. "Kapituliere dich! Du bist umgeben! Kapituliere dich! Du bist umgeben!"

"Where the hell is Mason?" Roman cursed. Radio coms had been operational for the last hour, but Roman had heard nothing. He flicked open his pocket watch. The time was 2205. He yelled up to Simeon above. "Looks like we have missed our train... Simeon?"

"I think we have bigger problems..." Was all he heard from upstairs before the sound of breaking glass interrupted Simeon, and the 'VROOSH' of flame-catching accelerant engulfed the house.

Roman felt heat scorch the side of his face. Flames licked the stone façade and reached with fingers of red into his broken window. There was another crash as more Molotov cocktails – they wouldn't have that name until 1939 – smashed into the ground floor.

"They are going to burn us out." Simeon began shooting again; Roman did too, trying to hit what flaming wicks were visible in the dark before they were thrown.

As if on cue Roman's earpiece crackled to life. "You guys need a hand?" It was Mason.

"Fucking hell boss! You been waiting out there for things to really go ass up?"

"Quit your whining. We've been securing transport."

"What's the plan? Because we have about three minutes before we're barbecued." The smell of petrol was burning his nose.

Finally a cocktail hit its mark, this time landing through a window. A crackling came from a bedroom as smoke started to fan across the roof and up the stairwell.

Mason's voice cut through again. "Gerhard has worked his way down into the crowd. He is going to pop smoke at your door. I am on the road to the north and will light up the street. Give it exactly nineteen seconds from my first shot, and then make a run for me. I am in one of only two cars up here."

"Roger."

Short and sharp. There was no need for questions.

If the ethical actions of the Alpha were not already in question, then what happened next would have sent shivers through the United Nations War Court.

Gerhard, who was standing in among a crowd of gawking townsfolk, initiated proceedings. Dispatching his smoke grenade with all of the precision of a soccer hooligan he popped the canister perfectly at the base of the front door.

With a 'POP HISSSSSSSS' grey smoke was jettisoned low across the sidewalk. Expanding quickly it dirtied the flames – from orange to crimson – that had taken hold on the doors and windows of the façade.

Gerhard rolled quickly into a nearby laneway. The surrounding crowd had not more than a second to question his behaviour, before the booming thunder – and 900 metres per second force – of Mason's M4A1 Carbine descended upon them.

"Copies anyway..." Mason repeated a mantra to himself as he stared down the barrel.

Thirty rounds... four seconds... one spent magazine. Coupling this with three-second rapid reloads, he was able to drop three magazines with a second still to spare.

The suddenness of the barrage was as disastrous as it was shocking. Anyone who didn't dive for the ground was dispatched there moments later, full of lead. Bullets hammered through the crowd, into the side of the make-shift wooden barricade the police were using to orchestrate their siege. Essentially flanked, the police were carved from their soft underside by a weapon that no one in 1914 could imagine, let alone comprehend.

Timber shattered, glass shattered, stone shattered, bodies shattered. One and the same all manner of debris was spewed into the air.

Once the firing had ceased it was a full two minutes before anyone dared to raise their heads, the location of the suspects the furthest possible thing from their minds.

A De Dietrich-1905 sat idling right where Mason had said it would be. Roman was the last of the four to arrive. Vaulting into the back, he lowered himself into an elevated rear bench seat that was already chock-full of luggage.

He surveyed the scene over the waist-high windowless car body. The orange hue of the now raging house fire illuminated a deathly still streetscape. The ground, covered with blood, glowed unnaturally bright, rain-soaked without rain. In the reflection of the flames, the crimson lake revealed only death in its inverse image of the world.

"God help us," Roman whispered under his breath.

"Hey." Mason threw something in his lap before slamming on the accelerator. "Tell me this is not for real."

Roman fumbled on account of the sluggish take-off. He looked down to find Mason's balloon beeper. He had not even realised that, in the confusion of the scrapyard, he had completely abandoned his own. He flipped it around in his hands.

'500. E. 50%'

Roman stared at the overly simple one-line screen. "Five hundred kilometres east?"

"You can read."

"Yeah, but..." He wanted to share Mason's doubt, but he couldn't. He knew the readout was not wrong, it had no reason to be wrong, he'd watched the balloon sail to safety himself.

Mason read his silence and took it for confirmation. "When will we get another 'ping'?"

Roman was still not properly computing, his mind unable to comprehend what had just happened.

"Hey! I said..."

"Within the hour."

There was silence in the car, the anxiety of the beeper a convenient cover for it.

Had they really just done that? Roman looked around the cabin as wind buffeted them all. Was it only he thinking it? *Had they really just murdered all those civilians?*

"Roman! Switch on." Mason downshifted around a corner. "I need you to get this information to Bravo. They are our most mobile option now. We are useless until we can find another rail station. Get onto Heathcote as well; we need to get a message to Zhu... This fucker is on the run."

Chapter 23

Location: .... 48.1351 N, 11.5820 E
Present day name: .... Perlacher Forest, Munich, Germany
IDTF Classification: . Ridge
Date: .... April 20th 2017

Dr Ronald Zhu sat inside his makeshift Tear Four office, hunched over his makeshift laboratory table. A lamp burned close over his shoulder. His tortoiseshell glasses were perched precariously at the end of his nose. Squinting through them, trying in vein to increase their magnification, a trickle of sweat dropped and ran down one lens.

His breath was measured as his scalpel descended.

No one could be allowed to know what he was doing. It was a lie that could bring down an entire career... the ultimate conundrum, for an impossible task.

But he would have the last laugh he knew... because nowhere in the rules did it say he couldn't delaminate his Rubik's cube.

The phone on Zhu's desk erupted. Rocking side to side with an analogue wail the thing moved a full inch.

"Ah dammit!" He seethed, clutching his finger.

Dropping the cube he sucked on the razor thin cut. A laugh escaped him. How stupid would he sound explaining this to Medical?

He snapped up the receiver, his smile wide. "Hello... Ya... Huh...? What!"

His jovial tone evaporated almost instantly. "Well, lock down the building! You must do it now!" It was as forceful a command as he could muster. "Is the lead holding? ... OK, I'll be there right away."

———

Zhu shouldered through the quarantine doors, his feet shuffling in Adidas slides. The Support room was abuzz with more activity than ever before. A clamorous clattering of fingers bashed away at keyboards, phones wailed incessantly and technicians scurried from desk to desk with papers held high.

His entrance, however, was important enough to halt everyone and everything in their tracks. A hush fell across the room as all eyes looked to him.

"When exactly did it open?" He asked the closest man in a lab coat.

"Exactly..." the balding man turned to his screen, "... seven minutes, forty-three, forty-four, forty-five seconds ago."

"The readout?"

Before the man could answer, Zhu's second-in-command skidded to a stop at the desk. Her name was Tabatha Stan-Lakely, or Tee for short. With clear Perspex-framed glasses, she had a bright pink streak through her hair that stood out against the peroxided rest. "Sir, we assumed it was just another standard opening, we didn't want to bother you. But then... the reception team sir... they got..." She put a hand over her mouth and sucked in a sob.

"Another blackout?"

"Worse this time."

She was young his Tee, and struggling. A gifted Cambridge grad – smarter even than he, Zhu was sure – she was a spritely girl of the crusader ilk, like most gen Zs nowadays. "They're in a bad way sir..." her eyes were watering, "...they're still in there."

Zhu pulled a scrunched handkerchief from his pocket and blew his nose. "You said radiation on the phone?" he reminded her.

Tee straightened up, pulling both her lab coat down and herself together. "Sir, it was just like usual. The Tear was preceded by the same audible cues. There were no warning signs..."

"The signs have been coming for weeks now Tee, just subtly enough to keep us off guard. The visual distortions we had just two days ago, that was our warning... my warning."

"Doctor..."

"Go on Tee, please."

"The audio cues were indistinguishable, same as always. But, upon appearance, the visual apparition was immediately disturbing. Where the gold should have been, we had nothing but blackness."

Zhu looked to his right, through the glass observation window. The pane was dark; the entire room behind it was dark, so dark it was actually just a solid black mass, blacker than any black he had seen before. *Impossible...* Even without lights in the Tear Tent, in theory light should have been spilling in from his observation room and then bouncing back, but it wasn't.

Tee read his thoughts. "The lights inside blew out almost instantly. I know how this might sound, but to me it looked like an explosion of... darkness." She hesitated as she too looked to the observation window. "It was the antithesis of an explosion. The Tear seemed to spew out a vacuum that consumed, absorbed or drained, I don't know what to call it... all the life out of the room."

"Where are the readouts?" Zhu asked for a second time.

Tee passed him some paperwork. He thumbed through it as she gave a summary. "That immense radiation spike is the Tear opening..." he was looking at the abnormal graph on page two. The actual peak was not visible, the parameters were so far off. "It peaked..." she didn't want to say it, "... at 16,775 rems."

"Good God." Zhu pushed his glasses. "I've never seen a figure that high."

"It dropped almost instantly back down to three rems milliseconds later, but it's now slowly on the rise again. It's currently at seven rems."

"So basically you are saying a neutron bomb's worth of radiation detonated in that room, dissipated immediately, and is now charging back up again?" Zhu's question was rhetorical.

Tee didn't have the answers. No one did yet, that was his job. She just stared at him with watery eyes. "You need to see this." She turned a monitor around. The screen was a blue, orange and indigo coloured display of the Tear Tent. "It's our live infrared feed."

Zhu felt a stab in his gut. On the screen, spaced randomly in a sea of blue, were four human-shaped orangey-red blobs. All were keeled over. All were not moving.

Tee read off her tablet. "The US military Nuclear Weapons Archive assumes that anything in the vicinity of 8000 rems – Roentgen equivalent man – will permanently incapacitate a solider. The radiation causes a metabolic disruption that interferes with the central nervous system. Those men in there became instantly disorientated and fell into comas mere seconds after the exposure."

"Are they dead?" Zhu already knew the answer.

"No, not yet. But they will be. Their bodies are cooking themselves from the inside out." She wiped at a tear before it could fall.

Zhu pulled the nearest seat, alternating his view between the screen and the window. It did not seem real; what the pixelated truth exposed of the horror behind the black. He collected his thoughts while Tee waited patiently for orders. A plan was formulating in his mind.

"The radiation doesn't explain the absence of escapable light; we need to assume those two anomalies are mutually exclusive. The infrared visibility is our first clue and should be our starting point. IR wavelengths are longer than those of visible light. Get a team working on the maximum wavelength size that the Tear is absorbing. It might shed light, pardon the pun, on what type of energy the Tear has moved onto absorbing."

Tee nodded and made to leave. Zhu called to her. "Tee..." she turned slowly, her eyes red. "Why have we still not retrieved the reception team from the room? Was the scrub team not standing by?"

"Coronel Richards has quarantined the room." Her voice was now just a whisper. "No one goes in or out except on his orders. He's in the debrief room if you want to see him, but be careful, he's on a warpath." Clutching her iPad to her chest, she scurried off.

Zhu turned back to the blackness. He didn't need science to explain the intricacies of what he knew, the deep-seated feeling in his gut told him all he needed.

The Tear is collapsing. And soon enough, Munich, Europe, our world, the solar system... he had no idea where it would stop *...was going to collapse with it.*

Zhu was dancing his pigeon claws over his computer, punching in equations when Colonel Richards stormed into the Support Tent.

"Where is Zhu?" Richard's voice boomed through the laboratory. He was a man of few words, so the entire room stiffened when he spoke. Most in there had never heard his voice until now.

"Yes, yes, I'm here." Zhu strained his head up over the partition of his desk.

Richards strode over to his workstation, an entourage of two immaculately dressed soldiers flanking him on either side. One had a briefcase handcuffed to his wrist.

"It is good to see you're awake doctor." Richards didn't allow Zhu a response. "I need a situation report. The President has got an itchy finger and is dying to try a nuke on one of these things. Give me a reason to convince him otherwise."

"OK, well let me assure you that as of right now that room is rather safe. Extremely dark, but rather safe."

"And fifteen minutes ago?"

"Well... not so much. But, by learning our lesson from the design of the Israel tent and isolating the Tear to its own room, we pretty much saved all our lives. It seems the seven inches of lead plating we installed as a precaution was not overkill."

Richard's silence prompted Zhu to continue. "Colonel, I can't assume to speak for your, and certainly not the President's, plans, but I do know one thing – our number one priority right now should be getting word to Mason and Clarke. The only way we can shut this Tear down is from their side. That bomb your boy has strapped to his wrist is absolutely pointless on this side. Flexing your muscles here won't do a single thing but make a giant hole."

The solider with the case glared at his 'boy' reference.

Richards stroked his moustache. "The President's scientific advisers seem to think otherwise."

"And you're going to take the word of some men half a world away? Sir, Alpha, Bravo, they need to know about this. To put it plainly, the only hope we have, is that they hurry the hell up and find that anomaly."

Richards eyed Zhu. Zhu could see his mind ticking, its tell was the artery bulging just behind his ear. He obviously had instructions he was – right in this moment – choosing to either follow or disobey. Finally he spoke. "You have seventy-two hours doctor, three days, that's all. Then pointless or not, we're nuking this thing."

Zhu gulped. *I hope the universe even has seventy-two hours.*

Chapter 24

Location: ....48.1351 N, 11.5820 E
Present day name: ....Perlacher Forest, Munich, Germany
IDTF Classification: .Tear Four
Date: ....June 26th/27th 1914

Heathcote's arse was perched on the side of a crate, half on half off. Sweat patches soaked both his underarms and the back of his shirt where his ponytail rested. He had paper in one hand, and a pen in the other. A lid between his lips muffled everything he said. "Huh. Uh huh. Yep."

Mason's dictation was coming in thick and fast. In nearly complete darkness Heathcote's writing screwed sideways across the page. The only source of illumination he had was a soft golden glow coming from over his shoulder. "What...? Hang on, say that again... Heading east, south-east, got it."

Heathcote and Beckett were currently in the depths of the forest, back at the site of the Tear. When Heathcote's base camp sensors had activated twenty minutes ago the pair had begrudgingly rolled from their tents, into the night.

Apart from the voice barking through their earpieces, the scene surrounding them was completely... ordinary. The Tear opening had been as uneventful as they imagined, like any other they had witnessed before... that was until Mason had burst through the radio.

Finally Heathcote's earpiece fell silent. His ear was burning. He looked across to Beckett, who was standing immobilised, like a dimly lit street sign. "You heard all that?"

"Yeah." Beckett had all the charisma of the proverbial saturated cleaning implement.

"It seems your janitor-boy Roman has dug his team a pretty deep hole." Heathcote's crate had substituted for a high horse. "I hope Mason comes up with a better plan than what he just spewed; it pains me to think the fate of our universe now rests in the hands of Kangaroo-Roy and Loretta-Loren, or whatever their names are."

Beckett stifled a yawn. It was only in the heat of battle that his synapses truly fired. "Masonknowswhathesdoing." He pointed to the Tear. "Howlongwegot? Time to get a message through and get them balloons in return?"

Heathcote turned to study the Tear, his eyes glowing like a conquistador with gold-lust. "I fail to see why not, it looks completely normal to me. We should have maybe another forty minutes."

"OKletsdoit." Beckett hocked up a ball of spit from somewhere down in his guts.

Both of them were drawn to the glow, across a soft carpet of leaves, like moths to a flame. The Tear gave off an iridescent shimmer, sporadic ripples coursing down its length from top to bottom.

"Fetch me a...?" Heathcote was about to order Beckett to get him a communication capsule, when the Tear pulsed, heavier than usual, pulled in like an inverse bubble... and shot something out of its middle.

"Nooo..." Heathcote's face contorted and his hands rose in an instinctive effort to defend himself. He tried to duck, but his size did not allow for reflexes; all he could mange was a cowering flinch.

An object sailed threw the air toward him, spinning end on end... before it bounced innocuously off the fat of his stomach.

He let out a shrill scream and dropped as if shot.

"Hmph." Beckett's grunt was somewhere between surprise and laughter. A smile spread across his lips as he bent down next to Heathcote and picked up the offending object. It was a communication capsule – Dr Zhu had beaten them to the punch, literally. He unscrewed the cap of the cylindrical steel capsule as Heathcote watched on.

"Excuse me, what do you think you are doing? That will be for me."

Beckett regarded Heathcote and proceeded anyway. He pulled out a thick wad of A4 paper, and began to flick through the sheets.

"You think you're going to be able to understand those calculations?" Heathcote snapped from the ground, as he rolled over, trying to rise.

Beckett reached the final page and paused. On it, scribbled in red marker were four large sentences...

'Hurry up!'

'The Tear is collapsing.'

'You have seventy-two hours.'

'Nuke is now in play.'

Beckett flipped the page around. "I think this one is self-explanatory... dickhead."

Chapter 25

Location: ....48.2557° N, 13.0443° E
Present day name: ....Braunau am Inn, Austria
IDTF Classification: .Tear Four
Date: ....June 27th 1914

"Hey..."

Roy felt a kick against his cot. His eyes cracked open. Rubbing them free, the shadowy figure of Clarke materialised over him. Her face, backlit by a kitchen candle, was darker and more serious than usual. She watched him for an awkwardly long second before turning back into the light of the kitchen.

"Get up."

"Huh... Wha... is everything OK?" Roy pushed his body up with his elbows. Across from him, Loretta was fast asleep in her bed. Next to her, Spike's was empty.

As Roy shuffled slowly into the kitchen his hands alternated between covering a yawn and adjusting his suit-pant braces.

"Royston, you look like shit buddy," Spike greeted him.

"Thanks, what time is it?

"One am local."

Spike and Clarke were sitting at the small wooden dining table. Spread out between them was a map of Europe. Resting dead centre on it was a balloon beeper. To one side Roy could see his 'significant events' report was sitting on top of a stack of other books.

"Is something wrong?"

Clarke took charge. "Sit." Underneath the table she kicked out the chair opposite her. "We've had word from both Mason and Heathcote. Neither's news was good. Alpha have been compromised in Landshut. About the same time, Heathcote received a message from Dr Zhu."

Roy took a seat. "Is everyone...?"

"Alive?" She finished for him. "For now, yes. More to the point, before they got themselves into a world of shit, Roman's balloon was able to correlate a reading that Spike's received while you were asleep. The anomaly, he's on the move."

Roy looked down at the upside-down map. Vienna was circled in red.

Clarke confirmed his suspicion. "Judging by a '250, E, 40%' ping we received, and cross-referencing it with the '500, E, 50%' that Alpha did, we think he has moved to Vienna..." She paused. Roy sensed something in her tone, possibly doubt. Across the small table he was close enough to see wrinkles on her face he had never noticed before. "Mason wants us in Vienna."

"If it's decided, why then, can I ask, have you woken me?"

Clarke surveyed him. "Professor, we received word from Heathcote that we have roughly seventy-two hours before the Tear either collapses or the idiots back home try to blow it to hell."

"What...?" Roy leant back in his chair. "Since when... I thought we had more time... and what do you mean, 'blow it to hell'? How can that even be an option while we are still in here?"

Clarke gave his shock little credence. "I am sick of chasing tail on these missions. We need to get on the front foot and set a trap for this bastard." She swivelled the map around so now it was facing Roy. "Professor, I believe you may have been right in your summation," but her tone negated all praise. "The anomaly, he's heading south, to Sarajevo."

As much as Roy wanted too, he was smart enough not to say 'I told you so'.

Clarke reached to her left and opened a book titled *Bradshaw's Continental Railway Guide*. Roy knew it well, *is that a first edition? God, how much did that cost?* With the book in one hand she drew a line on the map from Vienna to Budapest to Belgrade; it was then only a short dotted stretch to Sarajevo.

"Professor, we are going follow Mason's orders and travel to Vienna. But once there we are going to intercept the famous Orient Express Railway and use it to travel south."

"And Mason?" It was the elephant of insubordination in the room.

"We don't have time for whatever the fuck Mason thinks." Clarke snapped. "Three days Roy. We have three days to get from one side of Europe to the other and back again, while finding an anomaly in between."

Roy held up his hands. "OK, I was just saying."

"Now, by my calculation, using the overnight express from Belgrade, we can be in Sarajevo by nine am tomorrow, the 28th."

Roy gulped. "Sarajevo on the 28th? Do you know what day that is, what happens that morning? It doesn't allow us very much time."

"It actually allows us no time, for error or fucking around, that is why I woke you. We need to act fast. You have to use this morning to prepare everything you can on the assassination of Franz Ferdinand..."

"Royston" Spike re-entered the kitchen. His hushed tone was appropriate for the hour at hand, but still strange coming from him. "How y'all doing?"

Roy had been working now for nearly two hours. It was that time of night where it could be either very late, or very early, he didn't know how he preferred it. "All right I suppose, I could murder a coffee though."

"Ain't got nothing for you there, sorry." Spike pulled a chair to sit backward. "But I got something else you might be interested in."

"You're not here for...?" Roy shook his head. Fatigue had dulled his mind.

"Intelligence?"

"Yeah."

"Fuck no, you can save that shit for Clarke. Just tell me who I gotta shoot and I shoot. The why of it all?" Spike shrugged. "Is a 'meh' for me." He reached down to the front of his pants. Fumbling around, wrist deep, he pulled out his hand, and placed a small object on the table with a metallic clunk. "So this... is for you."

It was a handgun.

"Spike..." Roy straightened.

But Spike spoke for him. "It's a Luger-P8. Absolute classic." He pushed it toward Roy. "I think you should have it Royston. You know, just in case."

Roy eyed the weapon the way Australians usually did – like it could go off any second. He had never been this close to a gun before. "Take it." Spike pushed it forward.

Slowly, not wanting to offend, Roy let his academic fascination get the better of him. He picked up the pistol and felt its weight in his hand. A surreal power cursed through his palm.

He didn't have to be a history professor to know what type of pistol it was; the esteem this model commanded was legendary. The Luger was a pistol that was soon to become infamous as one of the most coveted Axis wartime collectables. A trophy to be looted, even hunted for, from WWII Nazi officers.

Roy was mesmerised. He caught himself staring, lost in the pistol's allure. Placing it back on the table he pushed it to Spike. "I don't need a gun, do I?"

"Well, no. No one ever needs a gun... until they need one."

"I... I wouldn't know what to do with it."

"Oh hell Royston, shootin's the easy part. The hardest part will be keeping it from the Major, she will lose her lid if she done knew I gave it to ya."

"Where did you even get it?" Roy only realised now he should ask.

"It was Deryk's. He told me I could have it."

Somehow Roy doubted this. "Shit Spike, still, I just... I just don't know." He looked for another excuse, any excuse. "Don't you want to keep it? These pistols, you know they are worth a lot of money back home."

"Pffft. Don't worry, I got one already, granddaddy brought one back from Normandy. Tracked a Kraut three days just to get it."

"Oh..." Roy was running out of ideas. "What's going to happen to him?"

"Who, my granddaddy?"

"No Spike, Deryk."

"Oh, nothing. I got alls we're gonna get out of him. We'll cut him loose come morning. He's jaded, but he knows he's lucky, so I don't think we'll have a problem."

"Are we going to compensate him?" It was stupid, but it was a thought that had been playing on Roy's mind.

Spike shrugged, it seemed his default response. "If it will make you feel better, I can talk to Clarke about some gold." He pushed back from the table and rose to his feet. "It's kinda pointless though, considering..."

There it was again, another vague reference to a mission parameter well over Roy's head. "What... why?"

Spike spoke casually on his way out as though he was in the loop. "He'd have to spend it quick, don't know what the going rate for gold would be in black-hole-land..." His voice trailed away as he left the room.

Roy looked down. "Hey..." The Luger was still resting on the table. "Hey Spike, you left..."

But Spike was gone.

Roy sighed. "Shit." He looked around the room, somewhat ashamed, before he dragged it off the table.

Chapter 26

Location: .... The Orient Express
Present day name: .... Somewhere in transit between Austria and Serbia
IDTF Classification: . Tear Four
Date: .... June 27th 1914

The *Orient Express is an intriguing beast, as opulent as it is mysterious. Beginning in 1883 as a means of travel between Paris and Constantinople, the journey via rail has developed itself as much a reputation as the final destination. Traversing some of the more curious states of our time, through Romania, Bulgaria, and Hungary, travellers can bear witness now to places that previously one could only view down the extended arm of eastern secrecy.*

Roy closed Bradshaw's Railway Guide and rubbed his eyes. Seated against a window, he stared out as the train took a long sweeping right-hand turn.

With just a small crane of his neck he could see the entire the starboard side. Ahead, white over black, the locomotive chugged through a column of steam carrying it down its length. With the steam dissipating at around the restaurant carriage – the third after first-class – two lions were visible stamped within a gilded circle of vine.

Gold against the royal blue wagon, it was the logo of 'Compagnie Internationale des Wagons-Lits' – the owner of the Orient brand.

Snaking his eyes further forward, past the locomotive, he saw where a crystal river – the path of which they were tracing – wound lazily through boulders the size of cars. Across its bank, stretching up at a forty-five, a forest of tiered pines ascended into cloud.

As Roy's forehead fell softly against the glass, his breath fogged the window. With a sigh he wiped at the film. It was enough to draw his gaze back to the cabin.

He was the only one awake.

On one of two opposing bench seats, the seat opposite him was empty. Its vacancy struck him again, as it had all journey. There was something about it, something that tugged at him inside. Not just physically empty, the seat 'felt' empty, almost permanently so. *Was it the seat, or the pit inside of him, yearning?*

Like a long paused video, his mind ghosted an image across from him, one burned forever into his retinas. His wife, Georgina, he could almost see her now sitting, gazing out of the window, her eyes full of wonder. They had taken a train across Europe, the first summer after he had decided to stay in London. West-to-east, countless months, no jobs, no money, no worries. Bouncing from castle-to-castle, church-to-church, beach-to-beach... life had never been sweeter.

Roy's focus sharpened as his world softened. His wife's blonde hair, like silk, pushed back behind her pixie ears, fell to just past her shoulders. With ear buds in her ears she had a hand on her chin, pushing her gaze skyward. The joy in her face was effortless, it was what he loved about her, it was impossible to resist, such vibrancy.

He couldn't help but smile.

She looked at him as he stared at her, she caught him often, *what?*

He opened his mouth to speak, but stopped, lucidly aware that the very act would shatter him back to reality.

What you listening too?

A love song playlist.

Chingy, One Call Away?

Her smile turned to a pout and she popped her tongue. Her freckles scrunched up her nose as she pulled a face.

Boney M, Sunny, actually.

What about Meet Her at the Loveparade?

She rolled her eyes, *You're such a loser.*

Guilty as charged he thought, in that moment he had been the happiest loser alive.

A piercing screech of steel on steel jolted Roy from his daydream. Georgina's image disappeared instantly, replaced again by an empty seat.

Pitched high, the chalkboard-splice, he knew, was a byproduct of the train's frustratingly slow speed. Fifty-five kilometres per hour... their pace, or lack of, was making him nervous. His team needed every minute they could manage. The timing of events to come could not have allowed for any less leeway. It would have been laughable really, if it wasn't such a horrendously heavy burden. *All of a sudden the Tear is collapsing... just as we are thrust out on our own... on a collision course with history.*

Roy looked down into his lap, at his notes. Close enough to done, it was about time he briefed... "Clar...." His voice was hoarse, he had been silent for so long. He cleared his throat. "Huh-hum... Clarke."

Clarke opened her eyes. Loretta did too.

Clarke looked around the cabin, her priorities immediately mission conscious.

"Where is Spike?"

"Ah, he needed some air," Roy lied. Spike had asked him to cover for him for ten-minutes... an-hour-and-a-half ago. *"Got to sample myself some 20th century lager in the restaurant cart."*

"He will be back any second, he told me to get started without him." Another lie.

Roy shuffled his notes, contemplating where to start. He was sure whichever way he chose would be either too little or too much for Clarke.

Short and sweet, save yourself.

"Archduke Franz Ferdinand, heir apparent to the Austro-Hungarian throne, was born on December 18th 1863, and died June 28th 1914. Which is..." Roy tilted his head, it felt weird to say, "...tomorrow."

He pulled a photo from his notes and placed it on the table so the others could see. Looking up at them was a square-headed, bruising sort of a man. While a pompous military uniform and thick overhanging moustache suited noble preconceptions, the man behind them could have easily been a local blacksmith. His thick chest and neck held up a stiff jaw and full cheeks.

"While there have been many influential assassinations throughout history – Julius Caesar, Alexander II of Russia, Abraham Lincoln, and Mahatma Gandhi are but a few – Franz Ferdinand's though, stands above them all in significance. Not merely an important assassination, his death can legitimately stand as one of the most important events period, in all of human history. A match to a powder keg-mix of obstinate leadership, intricate alliances and extreme nationalism, his murder would be the catalyst for approximately eighteen million deaths in WWI, and arguably sixty million more in WWII."

This was all high school stuff, so he was skimming.

"Only a nephew to the Emperor Franz Joseph, Ferdinand was never slated for greatness. His position on the ladder of ascension would change dramatically though during adolescence, with three important family deaths. The first – a cousin, when Ferdinand was just a boy of eleven – would bequeath him an enormous fortune and estate, making him overnight one of the richest men in Austria. The second, in 1889 – the suicide of only child Crown Prince Rudolph – bumped the tracks of ascension to his lineage. And then the third – his father Karl Ludwig in 1896 – suddenly had him assuming the title of Presumptive Heir to the Empire."

"Dio…" Loretta breathed "…like that John Goodman movie, King Ralph. Where the whole royal family dies?" It was weird what movies she had seen, but Roy couldn't throw stones, he'd seen it also.

"Right. Now by all accounts Franz was kind of…" he looked for an appropriately PC title, "…dim. Often ridiculed, rarely respected, and flat out disliked by the Emperor, the extent of his disparagement was so extreme it was even decreed that none of his children could ever assume the throne. Super harsh stuff…"

Clarke cut in. "Right, Professor we get it. We know who he was… or is, a dumbass royal who lucked onto a throne."

Yep, it was only a matter of time.

She wasn't finished though. "Let's speed things up, why was he so important? Bare facts only."

"OK. Um… it was in two respects…" Roy balanced his palms like scales, "…life and death. First, in life, it was well know that Ferdinand was a staunch conservative with deeply anti-war views. There is a very real possibility that the tension of the time, between just about everyone, could have been managed had he lived and ascended the throne. Most historians believe the question – of whether the assassins inadvertently harmed their nationalist ideals instead of fostering them – is a legitimate one."

He pulled a map of Europe from his notes.

"Now to really understand the importance of Ferdinand's death, it is important first to acknowledge just how large the Austro-Hungarian Empire is." He pointed to most of Eastern Europe. "Aside from Austria and Hungary it currently encompasses modern day Slovakia, Croatia, the Czech Republic, Bosnia/Herzegovina, half of Poland, Ukraine, Romania and, most importantly for our mission..." His finger fell down on the paper, "...a section of Serbia. It is an enormous empire and, like all overgrown empires, it has some serious problems controlling its territories. Serbia especially, was, or is, a thorn in the great Austro-Hungarian side. It is full of pan-Slavic nationalists who yearn for greater autonomy and the formation of independent Balkan states. Most importantly though for the annals of history, Serbia is also aligned with Austria-Hungary's greatest rival... Russia."

Roy looked at Loretta, she was listening intently. Clarke was more difficult to read. *I'm losing her.*

"Bear with me a second, because even though I am going back, this is extremely important. After Austria-Hungary annexed – a fancy word for 'stole' – Bosnia and Herzegovina in 1908, the fragile balance of power in the Balkans was disrupted. Correctly sensing the growing animosity of Serbia, Austrian Army Chief Franz Conrad von Hötzendorf asked his German ally Helmuth von Moltke where they would stand should Austria-Hungary decide to make a *pre-emptive* strike and invade Serbia."

Loretta cut in. "This 'von Moltke', he was in your notes of significant people, yes?"

"Correct," Roy replied. "That is because Moltke replied... that not only would German be happy to deviate from its current alliance terms of defensive assistance only, but should Russia choose to defend Serbia, it would help by declaring war on both Russia, and its ally in the west also... France."

"The war was just an obligation of honoured treaties?" Loretta summarised both his speech and thirty years of history with one succinct sentence.

"Correct. The guns of war had been loaded. Austria-Hungary and Germany stood on one side, Serbia, Russia and France – unbeknown to them – stood on the other. All that was needed was a reason to pull the trigger... and along would come Archduke Franz Ferdinand... to walk right between the crosshairs."

"What a cluster-fuck," Clarke said; at least she was awake.

"Tomorrow morning, despite numerous warnings of an assassination plot, the Archduke still continued..." Roy scratched his head "...or will still continue with his visit." He moved to check his beloved Seiko Tuna. Seeing his wrist was empty, he remembered and reached for his pocket and the pocket watch inside. "Funnily enough Ferdinand is actually set to arrive in Sarajevo any minute now. That shows just how behind we are." He replaced his watch in his inner jacket pocket. "Anyway, after his imminent death tomorrow, the government of Austria-Hungary will determine, rightly or wrongly, that the assassin – a pan-Slavic nationalist named Gavrilo Princip – was acting in conjunction with the Serbian military. Effectively, in their eyes, making the killing an act of war..."

"Starting... World... War... One," Loretta finished for him.

"Right." Roy took a big breath. "And so it goes, that in just one month from today, on the 28th of July, Austria-Hungary will invade Serbia. Russia will declare war on Austro-Hungary. Germany will declare war on Russia. Germany will pre-emptively attack France through Belgium. The United Kingdom will declare war on Germany. The colonies of France and England will be drawn to Europe. Japan will sense an opening in the Pacific and declare war on Germany. And, eventually, the United States will join the war in defence of the Allies. The juggernaut of World War One will have begun... with an enduring legacy, that it all happened, because of one man."

Chapter 27

Location: .... The Orient Express Restaurant Car
Present day name: .... Somewhere in transit from Austria to Serbia
IDTF Classification: . Tear Four
Date: .... June 27th 1914

The Orient swayed gently as Roy wandered through the hall of the third passenger car. He reached out to steady himself, but thought better of smudging the star speckled window to his left. Not wanting to accidently knock, he pressed a palm on a cabin door to his right, planted himself, and rocked awkwardly with the train. It looked ridiculous, like he was surfing.

He was on his way to the restaurant car. It had taken every bit of bullshit he had in him to persuade Clarke to let him go. Under the impression Spike had been missing only fifteen minutes, he didn't want to think what would have happened had she known it was verging on nearly two hours.

From behind the cabin door an elderly looking man poked his head.

"Hello." Roy threw up a shy wave that almost tipped him over.

The man mumbled something in German that didn't require translation. Raising a hand of his own, he 'shoo'ed Roy away from the door, actually 'shoo'ed him. *Really, I'm the asshole? Bloody Spike!*

Stepping into the restaurant car was like stepping into the ballroom of a live-action Cluedo board. An aroma of spicy tobacco was sharp on the nose, it seemed to permeate from a full wrap of Persian carpet wall and ceiling coverings. A large mahogany bar dominated the interior of the cabin. Polished to a mirror finish, it ran down the right-hand side for more than half the carriage length. Behind it, a Monopoly-man looking bartender was polishing a bottle of top shelf gin with a cloth.

A procession of three interconnected chandeliers served to draw Roy's eyes down to the seated section of the restaurant. It was there that he found Spike.

With his head swaying over a glass of beer he seemed too preoccupied to have noticed much of anything, so Roy took a minute to watch. Sitting at a small two-seater bar table, he turned to the person next to him and started talking, his hands flailing animatedly as he did.

Cheeky bugger. Roy smiled. Spike was a little drunk... and he wasn't alone.

"I tell ya, it'll change the darn world." A slur was there, but only if you knew him. "E for Electricity, M for Mass and C... C is for Calculus. Then you done times the whole lot by two... it'll gives you E=MC2... Trust me darling, it is going to change the way you think of the universe... and planets... and shit."

Eavesdropping from behind, Roy let out a small chuckle. Spike was talking to a lady. She was young and pretty, in a classically Middle Eastern way. Her eyes, large yet thin, sat naturally shadowed under a pair of sculpted eyebrows.

Spike placed a hand on the back of her chair. "Now darling, you got to keep this next part super secret." He pulled out his HFECS beeper. "But I'm working on a device I'ma call the Sp'I'ke phone, kinda like this 'ere beeper thing, except way cooler. 'Magine talking with your friends back in Paris while you're 'ome in Istanbul. I can show it to you maybe, maybe in your cabin…"

Roy ears pricked. *OK Casanova, Istanbul is not even Istanbul yet, and there is no way I am losing you again.* He moved in between the pair. "Professor Stanley Doran, why here you are, I've been looking for you all over." Roy's eyes flashed wide, trying not so subtly to cut through Spike's booze haze.

Spike looked over his shoulder, completely oblivious. "Royston!" he cried with surprise. "Welcome to the party! Lem'me introduce you to Helena, she a friend of mine."

Roy turned and bowed his head. Helena nodded receptively. "It is a pleasure to meet you, Helena. My name is Professor Jacob…"

"She's a student in Paris…" Spike interjected innocently before Roy could finish, his excitement abounding. "Guess what she is studying, Roy? Come on, guess."

Roy shook his head. "I have no…"

Spike threw his hands in the air. "She's gonna be a scientist! Jus' like us! I jus' finished telling her about them lectures we gave in Vienna."

Oh God.

At least he was sober enough to remember the team's cover story, but Roy could not even imagine what other liberties Spike may have taken with scientific history. He turned to Helena. "Helena, I am so sorry to be rude, but could I please have a word alone with my esteemed colleague?"

"Wow wow wow, Royston what are you doing?" Spike eyes turned sad, like a puppy. "No. Helena darling, don't go."

She rose slowly. "Of course, it was a pleasure to meet you both. Thank you for the drink and conversation Professor Doran, and..." she looked at Roy, a hint of intrigue behind her cinnamon coloured eyes. "Professor Jacob... Royston." Before Roy could correct her, she softly placed a small kiss on both their cheeks. "Should either of you like another drink, I am in the first-class carriage, the 'neon' room."

Both men watched, hypnotised by hips, as she then sauntered out of the restaurant without once looking back.

Spike broke the air with a whistle. "Neon room, eh... the party room? Hang on...?" He twigged. "What did she mean by 'either of you'?"

"Huh?" Roy played dumb. "I'm not sure."

Spike was too in love to care. He motioned after her. "Should we go?"

"Don't even think about it!"

"Oh Royston, don't do me like that. Did you hear what she said? She called me... 'Professor'." Spike was bouncing in his seat. He drew out "Professsssssor" one more time to himself.

Roy rolled his eyes. "Next time Professsssssor you might want to try doing Einstein some justice. E is for energy, M is for mass, and C is the speed of light."

"C is speed?" Spike whistled. "Really? You sure?"

"Yeah Spike."

"Hmmm, who'da thought?" Spike turned to Roy straight on and placed a hand on his shoulder. "I like you, Royston." He nodded repeatedly as if convincing himself. "Sit, sit. Let's finish these drinks."

Roy looked around. It was late, the bar was clearly shutting down, but they weren't the last in there. Reluctantly he said, "Two minutes..."

Leaning in close, Roy didn't know why he was whispering, but he was. "Do you realise you have been gone for two hours? There's no way I would have been able to cover for you if Clarke hadn't been asleep for most of it."

Spike nodded some more. "Like I said, I like you bud. Y'all don't have to worry about Clarke, she's all bark that one. Don't get me wrong I love 'er like a brother, but fuck she's all yap yap yap sometimes."

Spike had a sloppy little chuckle to himself. Roy snapped side to side. It was irrational, but he was terrified Clarke was somewhere listening.

Spike's eyes were a little red. One drooped lower than the other. The thought occurred to Roy that he now had two clear options in front of him, *cabin time or question time?* He was aware which was the responsible option, but something inside glued him to his seat.

"Spike. How do you and Clarke know each other?"

Spike did not seem surprised at all by the change of topic, the circumspect part of his brain clearly not firing. "We was in Afghanistan."

"Whereabouts exactly?" Roy tried to keep himself casual.

"We was posted in the Korengal..." The question seemed to send Spike into thought. He stared blankly into his glass. "...Fucking shithole."

Roy was conscious to tread lightly "Can I ask how it came to pass that you can avoid her 'bark' so easily?"

Spike's eyes opened a little. It took him some time to answer. When he did it was immediately obvious his mood had darkened. "There was ten men in my squad. Clarke was our CO." He spoke in short sentences, as if narrating a replay in his mind. "Our job was to set up a forward operating base about a click from the main base Dallas. The mission was codenamed Rockslide Push..." He paused. Lost in his beer, he had yet to blink. "We was attacked nearly every hour as we dug ourselves into that Godforsaken ridge. Fuck. We thought we were on top of it. But the second night, before we could resupply, about fifty of the fuckers came for us..."

Roy wanted to tell Spike to stop.

"...Eight men died that night... Clarke and I were the only ones to survive. We fought six hours in the dark, until she was knocked flat by an RPG. Unconscious was the only way she was ever going to allow a retreat. I carried her the whole way back to Dallas. We was getting shot at the entire time."

Roy felt terrible, what had he done? He had never seen Spike this despondent.

Spike wasn't finished though. "The rules of war went out the window that night Royston... I done things I needed to do, and things that Clarke ordered me to do, both were just as bad as each other. Them decisions haunt me most nights. But it's them decisions that mean Clarke don't need to question my loyalty, or ability, ever again." The sombre topic seemed to sober Spike up. He looked up from his beer glass to Roy's apologetic face.

"Spike... I'm... so..."

Spike saved Roy the embarrassment. "...It's all good Royston. Shit happens, especially in Afghanistan. Let's just hope it comes easier for us tomorrow."

After what seemed an eternity of silence Roy finally found his voice. "So second string professor to second string soldier, why didn't Clarke choose you as the first choice for this mission?"

Spike looked down at himself. "Ain't it obvious. Look at this fucking mess." He chuckled. "After Rockslide I got stuck bouncing between German hospitals and leave allocations I chose to take in London. I was right to go for the first Tear, but I had to dance the quack dance for nearly three months before they let me strap the boots back on."

Spike made to rise. Roy reached out with a hand. "Spike if I can, one last thing? Before, in Afghanistan, you just mentioned rules of war going out of the window... What exactly are the rules of engagement for us inside these Tears?"

Spike studied Roy. The segue was seamless, but both men knew the question was way too loaded to be spontaneous. Spike shrugged. "There are none, Royston. Ectypes aren't covered under no Geneva. I don't like it, but Clarke and Mason have made it pretty clear we're here to save our own skin, all else comes in second to that..." With that he stood and made for the exit, all of a sudden a picture of responsibility. "Let's go bud, we got a big day tomorrow."

It took everything Roy had to not skol the two glasses left in front of him. "Hang on..." he looked up, "...wait for me."

"Goes without saying that we'll be keeping this to ourselves?" Spike was walking in front of Roy as they traversed the second-last sleeping cart.

"Of course." Silhouettes whipped past the window to Roy's right, a full moon hung above. "However comfortable you are, I'm not really keen on Clarke's bark."

Spike was running his hand up and down the glass leaving a set of smudged tracks. "You know, two more minutes and I was outa there. Reckon I could chalk Helena up there as a win, even without the... you know... win." The old Spike was slowly making his return. "Think they got a name for it?"

"Huh? A name for what?" Roy was focused on using his sleeve to wipe Spike's tracks as he was leaving them.

"Inter-d'I'mensional relations?" the 'I' in his d'I'mensional twanged with southern pride.

Roy laughed. "I'm not sure, you could have been the first."

"Hmm..." Spike bounced along, the spring back in his step.

"Not to bring you down at all Casanova, but you did have an unfair advantage, dazzling her with that beeper of yours."

Spike stopped dead, halted by a thought. He proceeded to slap at his pants and jacket. "Fuck. My beeper, think I musta left it at the bar." He repeated his dance again checking every pocket a second time. "Yep, I reckon I did."

As he made to turn, Roy stopped him. "Hang on, I'll go. You need to get back to our room, Clarke will lose it if I return without you, tell her I stopped to use the bathroom."

"Shit. All right. You're probably right." He gave Roy a soft jab. "Don't go snaking me though you sly dog, Helena is mine."

Roy held up his left hand, showing his wedding band. "Seriously?"

"OK, OK, OK. Just be quick then."

Roy yanked sideways on the restaurant handle. The door had a glass inlay with a yellow 'dining' leadlight woven through the middle. It slid on heavy iron tracks into a cavity. To his surprise Roy entered to find that the cart was not completely empty, he had been sure as he left it was well past closing.

"Le barre se ferme." – "The bar is closed." – The bartender, jacket off, looked now like a snotty poker dealer.

"Huh? Oh OK, I'm aware, I just left..." Roy's words fell away when he saw a man... not the bartender, but another, standing by the table where he and Spike had been sitting. He had something in his hand that he was turning it over, up and down, side to side.

Oh God... It was the beeper.

Roy had stopped only a few paces in. He was staring with all the subtlety of a child.

"…Le barre se ferme."

The bartender's words were miles away. Staring as he was, Roy was willing the examination to be just a passing, drunken, curiosity.

Please… just put it down.

As he watched though, something about the man caught his eye. Other than the intent with which he was studying the beeper, there was something about his appearance, about his face.

Why do you look familiar?

His mind, working with a lag, couldn't quite place it. The man was young. His face, white and cold like porcelain, had thin lips, a downturned mouth and eyelids that seemed to blend into his cheeks and brow, causing his blue eyes to bulge from his head. The most striking feature of all, and the one that had initially drawn his attention, was the man's hair. It was jet black and slicked to the side.

Roy's mind spun. It was an iconic look.

…Add a thick block moustache… No… surely not?

He subconsciously took a step towards the man. He had no idea why, but his legs were not his own. "Adolf?" He whispered, a question to himself.

No, it can't be. A doppelganger, maybe?

How old would the original be in this world, twenty-five?

Wrestling, conflicted, he was all the while shuffling forward like a zombie toward the table.

…It is possible.

"Adolf?" He heard himself again say out loud. Was he really calling to the young man? Acting on mesmerised autopilot, he was halfway down the bar. Somehow the young man had still not noticed him.

"Adolf?" Again, louder this time. His own voice sounded foreign to him.

What are you doing? Shut up!

Two more steps. "Adolf?"

That was when a voice came from his periphery... "It's David."

A man rose slowly from behind Roy. Sitting under the dark green shadow of a wall-mounted lamp, he had been shaded from view as Roy entered.

Roy snapped from his trance. Spinning around, he watched as the man extended to full height, inhaled sharply through his nose, and let out let out a long slow breath. "The boy's name... It's David... like the star."

The new man positioned himself in front of the dining room door, effectively sealing off Roy's path of retreat. He stepped forward, his chest expanding as he did, until both stood face-to-face.

The distance between them was awkwardly inadequate. Roy could feel the man's breath competing with his own. Helpless to resist, he could do nothing but stare back.

There was a chilling pause. The bartender and man with the beeper both stopped what they were doing, as if the silence was a cracking gunshot. They watched intently as Roy and the man evaluated each other from a distance of mere inches. There was a palpable tension between them, so much more than necessary for such an innocuous event.

Why is he being so aggressive... so protective?

After what felt like an eternity, Roy spoke. "I... my... apologies, I must be thinking of someone else..." The man's face remained impassive. *What the hell is going on here?* "...He looks..." Roy grasped for another excuse. He dared to sneak a peek back at the 'boy' at the bar "... like a friend of mine."

Finally the man in front of him moved. He craned his head to catch Roy's as it returned to the front. Continuing his roll he tipped his neck back and forth again twice over. Roy heard multiple cracks as he did. He measured his words and spoke purposely, slowly. "The way your friend was talking before, it looks like you both may be imagining things."

What!? Roy's mind exploded. He tried not to let his shock translate to his face. *Had this guy been listening to Spike the whole night? Eavesdropping?*

The man's face was cold, only the slightest curl of a lip accompanied his shot across the bow. Behind the eight ball, Roy somehow found his feet. "The true sign of intelligence is not knowledge, but imagination." It was a quote from...

"...Einstein." The man acknowledged.

What the... Who is this guy? Fear now took a stranglehold over what little courage Roy thought he had found. He longed for a second to compute. He tried to look around at the room, but the man was so close he was occupying his entire view.

The head in front of him was plain enough. It had brown hair, brown eyes and the beginnings of brown stubble. Roy's eyes lowered to his chin... there was a deep ugly scar that ran vertically down its length.

Oh shit!

"I best be leaving." Roy fumbled backward a step... the wrong way! Away from his exit, away from Bravo's cabin!

The man's cold eyes did not budge. "Before you do... Jacob. Could you please oblige me with the time."

What? He knows my name? Shit, shit, shit. Stay calm, stay calm, stay calm."

"Of course." Roy gulped. He cocked back the sleeve of his jacket...

No.... Fuck.... The pocket watch!

But his realisation was a second too late.

Before he could correct himself and reach for his jacket the man cut him off. "You don't belong here Professor. But something tells me you know that already."

The cabin shook as it constricted in on Roy, he felt its blood-red walls press upon his peripheries, pressurising the room, suffocating him. Roy took three steps backward, the man's eyes boring into him, pushing him backward with a physical force.

"Who are you?" He spoke with a sociopathic lack of emotion.

"I... I... don't know what you're talking about?" Roy dragged his heels.

The man matched him, slow step for slow step. "I think you do, Jacob." His 'Jacob' sliced through Roy like a knife. "I can tell you're the smarter of your little pair."

"You're... wrong," was all Roy could manage, his voice breaking with a pathetic desperation.

The man could sense it, smell it on him. "Why are you here, Jacob?"

"I just came back for my..."

"What?" The man smiled, wanting to him to say it. "Your pager?"

"No..." but Roy's mere acknowledgment of the word was damning.

"Jacob. I will ask this only once..." Something slid from the man's shirtsleeve. Roy caught a glint of polished steel "...Where, are, you, from?"

Fuck. Say somewhere, anywhere... "No... where."

Roy had backed up now past both David and the bartender, almost all the way to the opposing cabin entrance now. His retreat had put maybe five paces between him and the man. He was perspiring madly, his shirt collar, and the pearl at its centre, were slicing into his throat. His mind raced. *Could he turn and run?* No, the door was shut behind him; he would never make it through the bottleneck in time. Even if he could, what was there at the front of the train? His team was all in the rear.

That was when he heard the familiar clatter of iron wheels sliding across metal, and a spring-loaded groan of tension... The door behind him, it was opening.

"Was ist hier los?" A voice came from behind him. The bartender was the only one who understood exactly, but the inference was clear, *'what is going on here?'*

A regal looking man in an Orient Express Officer's uniform almost bowled into Roy's back, he took a swift step around him on his course for the bar, clearly annoyed it was still open. The officer was now in between Roy and his aggressor. He looked down and noticed just as Roy had, the knife in the man's hand. "Was ist hier los?" The anger in his accusation had turned now to concern.

It was as good an opportunity as Roy would ever have. He summoned all his courage, dropped the hammer... and ran.

Slicing sideways through the guillotining restaurant door with millimetres to spare his body braced for pain, for the plunge of a knife somewhere in his back or a hand pulling him at the least.

...But neither came.

As the door crunched closed Roy could hear the muted sounds of a struggle behind him, a cough of surprise, a blood-soaked gargle, and the slumping of weight on the floor. His breath caught in his throat. *This couldn't be real, this couldn't be happening; you were supposed to wake up before you died in a dream, right?*

He raced down the thin carriage corridor like his life depended on it, cabin doors whisking past on him on the right. Reaching the next sliding door at full speed, he used his momentum to yank the door open in one continuous motion. As he turned to slam the door behind him, a chilling sight turned his blood cold. At the other end of the carriage, through the restaurant's stained glass window he saw two figures, his aggressor and the Hitler/David boy, they were stepping over something, or someone, moving his way.

Roy slammed the second airlock door shut, his menacing view replaced by the floating letters of the 'First Class' leadlight. *First Class!*

He had an idea. He raced down the aisle, paying attention now to the cabin doors. "Hydrogen, Helium, Lithium, Beryllium…" He was talking to himself as he ran. "Boron, Carbon, Nitrogen, Oxygen… Shit!" His mind went blank.

This is eighth grade science, c'mon! He had made his way to room nine. He searched his brain for an answer. *What's next?*

"Fluorine, Neon, Sodium!" *That's it.*

Roy wrapped his knuckles on door number ten.

"Helena!" He tried to sound as calm as possible, but there was no time. He looked right, down the long corridor to the door at its end, his view was obscured.

"Helena! Quick!" They would be on him any second.

He heard a latch on the other side of the cabin, and felt the door start to slide. A face appeared through a gap too thin for recognition. He had no time for permission, he could explain later, he hoped. He barged shoulder first through the gap, and fell into a heap on the other side.

"Professor Jacob?" The view of Helena in a floor-length nightgown greeted him from the floor, her Middle Eastern features glistened in the silvery vale of the moonlit cabin. "…I assumed you would be the one to remember your periodic table."

Roy was panting, he waved his hand across the door. "Please, just lock the door."

With a face of mild confusion she turned and obliged. No sooner than she had, Roy heard footsteps in the corridor, two pairs. Still on his back his eyes searched the slit of light at the bottom of the door. Like a crummy horror film he waited, expecting a shadow to step across and interrupt the beam at any moment.

Helena watched him in silence, then knelt down next to him, breaking his trance. "Professor, breathe." He hadn't even realised he was holding his breath. She placed one hand on his cheek, literally pulling his gaze away from the door. "What's wrong? You look like you have just seen a ghost."

If only she knew how right she was.

Chapter 28

Colours bled on the back of Roy's eyelids as if he were watching them across a wet roadway. Slowly the neon shapes sharpened down the lens of his mind. The red of a Burger King entrance, the blue of a TDK sign, and the yellow of a globe encircled Les Mis billboard drifted free of the Pollocky mess. Floating forward and to adjacent corners of his view, the lights structured Roy's world. He was both aware, and not, of his surrounds. The smell of sewer steam, the crispness of winter against his cheeks, the cobble beneath his soles, an acappella rendition of 'Silent Night', his senses shot from input to input without focusing on any detail specifically. He was conscious of the absurdity, but completely comfortable... he had been here before.

"Roy, what time you got?"

"Boh?" He looked up and over Georgina's head at Eden his brother. "Don't stress mate, we got time." Roy had his hands wrapped around his wife, her face was buried into his chest. He rubbed her arms as she looked up at him with her freckles.

"You're really still going?"

"Babe, the midnight screening…" he smiled a cheeky smile. "It's tradition."

She didn't argue. The whole thing had been her idea, a way for him to bond with his brother. She had had no idea their collective nerd forces were strong enough already.

"When are they ever going to show a movie I want to see?"

"It's Christmas Eve, *Love Actually* is on repeat on nearly every channel tonight, you don't need a cinema for it."

"You!" She gave him a squeeze. "So what are you seeing then, something highbrow that you can lord over us pop culture consumers?"

"Highbrow?" He feigned offence, "It's the Prince Charles babe. That's not the spirit." But oh it was, it was exactly the point of the independent Leicester Square institution. "It's *The Warriors*, a proper classic."

"Pffft…" Her smile was wide "…you're both losers."

"C'mon you two lovebirds." A soft voice from behind interrupted them. "H is almost out." It was Florence, Eden's wife. She was holding her son Henry, just as Roy was holding Georgina, although at eight and swaying on tired legs, he was buried more so into her waist. The five of them had been out for Christmas Eve dinner. Thai, Florence's way of feeling closer to home come Christmas, and then a movie for the boys, that was their tradition. It was as close as their tiny, multinational, five-member family got to turkey and stocking fillers.

Georgina studied her barely lucid nephew and cocked an eyebrow her sister-in-law's way, "Vino?"

"Absolutely. Let these idiots brave the cold, H will be down in no time, we can get the fire going at mine."

"Settled then." Georgina turned back to Roy. "I'll grab a lift with Flo, pick me up on your way home?"

"Sure," smiled Roy. "Don't get too..." but he stopped, winked and slipped his hands a little higher, "...actually, maybe."

Georgina let out a cry. "Ah ah ahh, dreaming mister." She slapped his chest. "But, if you are not too late I might have a surprise for you, something I was going to save until tomorrow."

"An early Christmas present?"

"Only if you're home early."

"You're both making me sick." Eden rolled his eyes. "Even more than usual. What are we, fifteen again?"

"Ah excuse me, fifteen?" Georgina threw a hand across her heart. "Speak for yourself and your delinquency, I was a lady, and a lady waits until marriage."

"Pffft." It was Roy's turn to laugh.

"All right, all right." Georgina smiled. "You can both piss off now." She reached up onto her toes, planted a kiss on him and whispered in his ear. "I'm serious though mister, best surprise you will ever get. Don't be late."

"Got it." He kissed her once more and held the embrace for an extended second, soaking in her warmth. Jokes aside, of which there was always a few, it was during simple moments like these that he felt the full weight of how much he loved her. Locked with his lips on hers, his world had a habit of compressing down to a two-foot radius. It was like there was a *Truman Show*-style spotlight constantly on reserve, waiting just for them to block out all the noise.

"Remember..." He looked deep into her eyes, "...*Love Actually*, BBC Two."

"Dick."

With one last playful slap across the chest the couples split like a school dance, the boys crossing Leicester Square, while the girls and Henry made for the pedestrian lights of Charing Cross Road.

Time, the most pivotal few seconds anyway, they always had a habit of skipping.

Four tyres screeched, an engine screamed on redline, a kerb smashed by torn suspension... it was a symphony of catastrophic imminence. The Square, awash with more people than Roy had realised, froze in unison. The carol bells ceased to swing. All eyes darted as one to the street. Like a hidden wave the speeding BMW blurred between the gaps of the parked cars.

Roy didn't need to see this, not again.

"Jacob..." Roy felt a hand pulling him from nowhere. He blinked, half in, half out, of consciousness. Was he asleep? Suddenly he was transported to the very lights his wife had been waiting at. Only the traffic pole was no longer upright. His head snapped from side to side down the cobbles, digesting the carnage. The view punched the air from his lungs. He tried to move but his feet were clamped to the pavement, bogged in an invisible sea of quicksand. An ear-splitting silence spilled from his mouth. A tear, cocked at the ready, knowing events before he could, spilled down his cheek.

He. Had. To. Move... If only... This time could be different.

But this was how it always was, his nightmare, this was how it finished, with him locked in the torturous prison of his mind's creation.

"Jacob..." Again, the voice. But he was alone at the lights. Eden had disappeared.

"Hey, wake up, we are here." An invisible hand shook him, rocking him on his frozen heels.

"Hey." The voice, it reverberated around the entire Square like a voice from God.

"What? Huh?" Roy's eyes snapped open. His face was licked with sweat. He looked up into a face, just inches from his own, but saw nothing but a blur. Not yet out of the wake, his eyes were grasping frantically at the dissipating fog that was him, saving his wife... This time he could do, he had to do it.

"Hey..." the face above him was blurry. It was Helena's, but not. It was Georgina's, but not. It was the doctor at St Thomas, Dr Chapman's, but not. Dr Chapman, she had looked younger than Roy thought possible, there was no way a kid could be sure about these things, right? *Check again, you have to!* Roy's mind screamed. But she didn't have to.

Dr Chapman, she was how Roy had come to learn the surprise his wife had in store for him. It was a discovery left only for an emergency room doctor to make.

His Georgina, before she had left him... she was pregnant.

Chapter 29

Location: .... 43.8563° N, 18.4131° E
Present day name: .... Sarajevo, Bosnia and Herzegovina
IDTF Classification: . Tear Four
Date: .... June 28th 1914, 0935 hrs

Abner stepped down from the train onto the open air asphalt platform. Ahead of him a jet of steam shot out from beneath the locomotive with little regard for disembarking passengers. The rapidly expanding mist glistened in the early morning sunshine, refracting laser thin rainbows as it swelled. Within seconds the platform and all on it were shrouded in an impenetrable cloud of white.

With David in tow, Abner cut through the haze. They were on a strict time-frame; they could not afford a confrontation.

Across the street now, he watched a specific group of passengers linger long after the train's departure. The trio included the drunken blonde 'professor' from the restaurant, as well as two new individuals. The new additions surprised him somewhat, both being women. One of them, the one with jet-black hair, was pacing up and down the platform. She was irate. She had clearly lost something... or someone.

He couldn't help a smile.

The latest in a series of disturbing coincidences, the events of last night were unfortunate to say the least. What had started with the group of men in Landshut, and continued with the drunken faux lecturer, had culminated in the appearance of 'Mr Jacob Royston'. He was the third strike, the affirmation of all of Abner's suspicions.

How did he escape?

Standing in the hall of first class, David's desires had been clear, he had pressed for a resolution. *But eight, nine, ten or eleven...?* They had had no idea which cabin Jacob had entered. With two bodies – the bartender and his boss – still to haul overboard, Abner did not need the attention.

It was the conservative choice, the right choice. Yet he could not help but feel it was a decision that would come back to haunt him. All night, round and round his mind swirled, all passages of thought leading him back to one fact.

He was no longer the only traveller in this universe...
Someone is here...
But are they here for me, the boy or the history of this world?

"Who are they, Abner? Austrian spies? Serbian anarchists?" David was studying the group with contempt.

Abner felt for the deep indentation in his chin. "Neither," he said. "But remember these faces David, their destiny is now intertwined with our own."

"Should we... before they get in our way." The boy's bloodlust was blinding him.

"No. Now is not the time. We have bigger fish to... save. Remember, we must be diligent to not affect the coming events in any way. It is the reason we have left our arrival until now. The slightest deviation or the most innocuous event could potentially derail our goal. A shootout now, here, would surely draw the ire of all those involved today, rendering our plan useless."

David contemplated the response. Abner looked to him as he did. It was obvious the boy had a million questions. Abner could acknowledge that now, emboldened by the events in Landshut, it was only a matter of time before he chose to challenge his 'prophecies'.

"David..." *After today you will never have a need to question again, because after today the world will be changed, and even I will not know what is in store for it beyond.* But he said nothing of the sort. Instead he picked up his long rectangular case, it was an irregular shape for luggage, but it perfectly housed his Barrett M90 sniper rifle. "Let's go, we have just over an hour until 10:45. You need to get in position and I need to find the palace."

"Goddammit." Clarke was pacing back and forth.

The platform she was standing on was now empty, save for a single lonely figure walking towards her.

Roy had held off disembarking until the final possible second. He walked slowly, his soft arms hanging from stooped shoulders. His bloodshot eyes sat atop black bags and stared blankly at his feet.

Clarke cast a deliberate stare at Spike. She didn't say anything, but she didn't have to. *You are fucking lucky, Lieutenant.*

Spike looked sheepish but fine, only the affliction of regret, not alcohol, weighed upon him.

Roy rejoined his team. His eyes, flat, looked almost two-dimensional.

"Where the fuck have you been?" Clarke's scowl hid an air of relief.

He opened his mouth to speak, but couldn't. The where, the how, he did not know how to begin. Before he could find the words, Loretta stepped forward and placed her arms around his chest. "Roy, we thought…"

He placed one hand on her back, the other rested limp by his side. "It's OK, I'm all right." Whether it was true or not, didn't matter.

"What happened?" Her head was on his shoulder.

"Well…" He pulled back "…I think I just met our anomaly."

Chapter 30

Location: .... 43.8563° N, 18.4131° E
Present day name: .... Sarajevo, Bosnia and Herzegovina
IDTF Classification: . Tear Four
Date: .... June 28th 1914, 0939 hrs

Roy stood in front of his team. "So as you can imagine, it was a little weird this morning..." A ring of stunned faces watched him intently, waiting for more. "The whole experience was painfully reminiscent of my high school years, utterly perplexing for the females involved."

The remainder of his night had been no less awkward than his entrance into Helena's room. His embarrassing recoil from her touch had led to a rather muddled conversation explaining that he, with all respect possible, had no intention of a midnight rendezvous. *No, I'm sorry, but I can't, that's not to say I wouldn't, because I would, but, it's just... I...*

"Roy, who gives a fuck about Helena..." Clarke snapped. "All the shit before, you're sure of it?"

"Right, sorry..." Lying supine, staring the whole night at the roof of Helena's cabin, he had replayed the events a thousand times over, so much so, it seemed now that they had happened to someone else. "...Yeah, I'm sure."

"You did all's you could Royston, I shoulda never have left you." Spike extended a hand. "I'm sorry."

Roy took it gladly. "It's not your fault." Yes, or no, it didn't matter.

Spike placed his free hand on top of the lingering shake, locking it down deeper than any apology could. "I mean it, never again."

"Thanks Spike."

Resetting himself, Roy took his hand back, pushed his hair behind his ears, and ran both hands down his cheeks. "All right..." He retrieved his watch from his jacket pocket. The significance of the act struck him – he would never mistake its location again. The intricate details of the thing popped now from his palm, the engraved silver cover, the sepia stained dial. "It's 9:40... We are running out of time, and history. We only have half an hour until the *first* attempt on Ferdinand's life."

"Right." Clarke snapped a look around. "Everyone in." The group huddled in like she was quarterback. "It looks like we are back to chasing tail. But I can assure you this fucker has fucked us for the last time. Right here..." She turned to Roy, tapping his skull, "...we have all the facts we need to turn the tables. So tell us professor, what's next? Where will your new friends be heading?"

Roy was ready for her figurative bus. The presentation he had prepared last night before leaving to find Spike was waiting to go. He just couldn't believe he only was getting to it now, here, in the early morning sunshine, on a train platform in the middle of Sarajevo.

"OK, in half an hour, at 10:10 local time, Franz Ferdinand and his four-car motorcade will drive along the Apple Quay. It is a road that runs along the Miljacka River about a kilometre south from here. Seven assassins will be stationed along the route. They are members of a group calling themselves the 'Young Bosnians'. They are just a bunch of kids, eighteen- to nineteen-year-olds – only one, the organiser Danilo Ilić, is older than 20. That being said, they cannot be underestimated. The group have been financed and weaponised by the notorious terrorist group the 'Black Hand'."

"Black Hand…?" Spike had taken a knee. "They Muslim?"

"No, The Black Hand are a secret military society formed by officers of the Serbian Army. They were, or are, led by captain Dragutin Dimitrijević, so you can expect these schoolboy assassins to be significantly armed." Roy looked about the group, seven assassins onto four, make that two soldiers… their odds were not great. "The assassins will be positioned on the three bridges that cross over the Miljacka River – the Cumurja, Latin, and Kaiser. At 10:10 an assassin named Nedeljko Čabrinović will make the first attempt on Ferdinand's life, but it will be unsuccessful. The successful attempt will come thirty-five minutes later at 10:45, outside of Moritz Schiller's delicatessen, right next to Latin Bridge. The fateful shots will be fired by an assassin named Gavrilo Princip."

Like a television chef, Roy pulled his iPad from his backpack and loaded a map of the area.

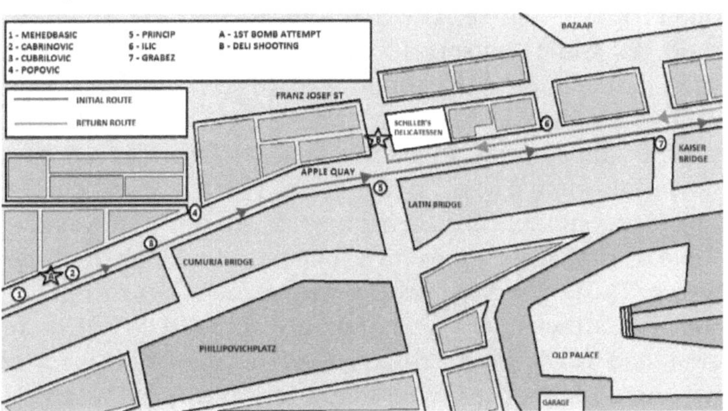

"This is something I prepared earlier. Right here at 10:10..." Roy pointed to the 'A' next to Cumurja Bridge."...Nedeljko Čabrinović throws a bomb that bounces off the hood of Ferdinand's car. The surprise attack causes Ferdinand and his entourage to speed east – along the blue line – to the Town Hall, thus giving the remaining assassins no time to act. At 10:45 after concluding formalities at the hall, Ferdinand, stupidly or gallantly, whichever way you look at it, decides that before leaving town he wants to visit those injured by the bomb. He retraces his route west down the Apple Quay to do so. Observe the red line."

"He retraces the same route?" Clarke shook her head.

"Correct, but wait there's more ineptitude to come from his attaché. When at the Latin Bridge, the driver of Ferdinand's vehicle mistakenly turns off into a small side street. Upon being ordered to reverse and continue down the quay he promptly stalls the car outside of Moritz Schiller's shop..." Roy pointed to the 'B' on the map. "Fortuitously for the Young Bosnians, Gavrilo Princip – assassin number five – is inside the deli commiserating the busted mission with a meal. Seizing his opportunity, he exits just as the car stalls and fires two shots at point blank range into the open topped vehicle. The first shot will hit Ferdinand in the neck while the second will hit Ferdinand's pregnant wife Sophia once in the abdomen." Roy paused. He looked around his huddle. He didn't want to say he was finished, but he kind of was. "I cannot believe I condensed that down into such a basic explanation. There is so much..."

Clarke cut him off. "Yeah, yeah, we get it Roy. Save the extra facts for the return journey." She looked at her watch. "We only have twenty-five minutes now to get to that first attack. Here is what we are going to do..." Clarke snatched Roy's iPad. "Spike, your number one priority will be to get another balloon up. Do you think you can get one up in time?"

"Ah…" Spike's fingers flipped in front of his face as he counted. "Will be touch and go. If not for the first attack, definitely for the proper one. It's just that…"

Clarke cut him off. "No excuses, I just need it fucking up, we will be running blind and deaf without it." She studied the map. "Find a rooftop of the south side of the river, just near this Phillip thing." She pointed at the parkland named Philopovicplatz. "It should give you a bird's-eye view over the deli. Loretta, you will go with Spike and wait for him in the park, I need you out of harm's way to look after the luggage."

"OK, I can do that." Loretta nodded.

Clarke turned to Roy. "Roy, you and I will hustle to the site of the first attack. If your friends are game enough to show their faces, I will need your eyes to point out the anomaly or this Hitler baby."

"Right." Roy gulped.

"The way I see it, the only way the anomaly can guarantee Ferdinand's life is by taking out the final shooter…" She looked expectantly at him, the rhetorical question clearly not."

"I agree…" Roy coughed. "Acting prematurely could risk creating alternative unprecedented versions of events. The earlier the anomaly acts, the more variables he introduces to the situation. A different assassin could assume Princip's role, or the final shooting could happen elsewhere."

Clarke was pleased enough. "OK, assuming as much, we will make for the delicatessen after the bombing. Let it be known that our priority here is the anomaly, and the anomaly only. The Hitler boy, the assassins, Ferdinand, I don't give a fuck whether they live or die. Saving Europe is none of our concern, saving our own world is." She checked her watch one last time. "The next train back to

Munich rolls through here at 1500 hours; that gives us five-and-a-half-hours to get this job done and then get back here for the long ride home."

Roy looked around the huddle. It was a short cycle through the three other faces. Each one conveyed his or her emotions differently. Clarke's was focused, Spike's was keen, Loretta's was courageous... he just wished he could share their optimism.

Chapter 31

Location: .... 43.8563° N, 18.4131° E
Present day name: .... Sarajevo, Bosnia and Herzegovina
IDTF Classification: . Tear Four
Date: .... June 28th 1914, 1005 hrs

Roy and Clarke shouldered their way through the throng of onlookers. A bank of loyal monarchists lined the footpath that ran between the Apple Quay roadway and the Miljacka River. All were waiting patiently for a glimpse of the heir to the throne, none even remotely aware of the terrorists within their midst.

Clarke came to a halt twenty metres short of Cumurja Bridge, the first of the three bridges. Roy almost ran into her back. "You might want to keep moving." He whispered.

She didn't have enough space to really turn, so she tilted her head back to lend him an ear. "No good?"

"Not if you intend on keeping all of your limbs. Čabrinović's bomb will detonate just over there." Roy pointed to the road a few metres away.

"Is he here now, can you see him?" Clarke asked.

"Who Čabrinović, or the anomaly?"

"Either, either? Is there anyone here you fucking recognise?"

Shaking his head, Roy turned to survey the crowd. A densely packed sea of bodies jostled before him, making it impossible to get a lock on individual faces. Even if he could, he had no idea what Čabrinović, or for that matter, five of the six other Young Bosnian assassins even looked like. Gavrilo Princip was the only one he could envisage. As the man who had fired the fateful shots, his mugshot was infamous in the annals of history.

"No one is here that I can see."

There was a clatter of applause from down the street. "I think the motorcade is arriving, quick another few metres, move up onto the bridge." Roy ushered Clarke from behind.

As she moved, she talked into her collar. "Spike? Spike are you there?" Roy could hear no reply in his earpiece as he watched her. "Spike? Is that fucking balloon up yet?"

Nothing.

Clarke led the way, pushing toward the bluestone bridge. The footpath they were on rose like a ramp as it turned to meet the slightly higher overpass. People had crowded onto the elevated section, using it to try and get a better view. Clarke charged straight into their midst. Blatantly she shoved one man straight in the back to create room for herself and Roy. Like falling dominoes, her push rippled forward. As each row tipped, heads snapped back, looking for the source. The closest man, a lumberjack looking thing, spun with rage in his eyes. Clarke met his glare with ice of her own. Tracing her body down, the man's bushy frown quivered ever so slightly as his gaze fell upon her open jacket. She had her Ka-Bar knife unsheathed inside. The ominous jet-black blade did all the talking. In his eyes, it was obvious the Ferdinand-juice was not worth the crazy-bitch-squeeze.

"Here he comes." Roy broke Clarke from her hackled stance.

The four-car imperial motorcade was a hundred metres away, travelling slowly, at a purposeful 'let me wave to my subjects' pace. Roy could make out Ferdinand now; he was in the second vehicle – a brand new Gräf & Stift Double Phaeton open-topped touring car. His extravagant top hat set him apart, the peacock feathers extending from it reaching a full foot into the air.

Sixty metres now.

Roy had to consciously peel his eyes from the motorcade to scan the crowd. He and Clarke were the only ones looking the wrong way, not clapping.

Thirty metres.

The passage of time slowed Roy's mind, as if he were in a dream... *this, was, history!* He looked to Ferdinand, every fibre of his being wanted to scream, like the organiser of some demented surprise party.

Twenty metres.

His body tensed.

And then it happened... Just like history said it would.

Nedjelko Čabrinović stepped forward from the crowd, a visible trail of smoke fizzling from the stick of dynamite he clutched in his right hand. Roy and Clarke spotted him simultaneously, along with most of the crowd.

A collective gasp emanated from the sidewalk.

Without fanfare, or so much as a call to God, Čabrinović tossed his bomb, straight-arm, in an arc at the moving second vehicle. To the horror of all watching – and those in the royal motorcar – the bomb found its mark, and landed square on the bonnet.

Clarke snapped to Roy.

"Watch..." He had time to reassure her, because just as he predicted, and just as history dictated... the bomb failed to detonate.

Čabrinović had mistimed the fuse. Completely bewildered, he stood alone, three paces into the cordoned off street. He, Clarke, Roy and the entire crowd, watched in suspense as the bomb, its wick still sizzling, slid down the length of Ferdinand's bonnet, bounced against the frameless windscreen, and fell off the side of the car onto the roadway below.

Sensing the danger, Ferdinand's driver – Roy knew his name to be Leopold Lojka – slammed on the accelerator. The Archduke – oblivious thus far – was thrown backward in a huff as his car launched clear of the bomb.

The third car of the motorcade, trailing directly behind Ferdinand's, reacted similarly, unfortunately though it was not as lucky. Just as its front wheels passed over the dynamite stick, the burning fuse disappeared into its nitroglycerine end with a penultimate puff. There was a momentary pause, just enough for the faintest of hopes to surface.

Roy winced, first, early, because only he knew... and a second later, the dynamite detonated.

The explosion launched the head of the car at least a metre off the ground. Exposed in the open cabin, the two front-seat passengers were jettisoned backward, blood spraying up onto their faces from below. A concussive shockwave punched through Roy's chest. His retinas flashed white. Like flash photography of old, the short and sharp burst, burning hot, was followed then by a seemingly excessive discharge of white smoke. The blanketing cloud did an ample job of stirring the crowd into a panic. Roy and Clarke were the only two that had not dived for the ground or scattered. They stood absurdly still, surveying the chaos.

From behind, the rest of the motorcade roared past the incapacitated vehicle, leaving it and its passengers to bleed out. While both soldiers would sustain major injuries, screaming as they were, Roy knew they would at least live.

Through the panicked crowd Čabrinović was frozen stiff on the road, his eyes slowly alternating between his open palm and the damaged car. He mouthed something to himself. A prayer of forgiveness or failure, it was all the same.

Clarke made to move towards him. "Wait." Roy placed an arm across her chest. "He is no threat... just watch."

Čabrinović pulled something from his pocket, it was too small to see, but Roy didn't need to, he already knew. Čabrinović placed the capsule in his mouth and bit down hard. Leaving nothing to chance, and with a sense of theatre not yet realised, he turned then, screamed and ran straight back into the horrified crowd. With his arms outstretched he reached the river unaccosted and hurled himself over the balustrade, down into the murky water below.

"Fuck me." Clarke breathed.

Roy let the absurdity of the moment hang in the air. "Wait, it gets worse."

Unbeknown to Čabrinović, the waters of the Miljacka River were at their lowest point in nearly a decade. Rather than plunging into the murky waters to die a cyanide-induced death, he instead landed face first in a three-inch shallow pool. Stranded and badly injured, he lay spreadeagled in the mud with no other option but to wait for the poison to take effect.

"Jesus. What a way to go." Clarke was leaning over the bridge staring at his half submerged body.

Roy watched knowingly. "I wish I could say it was over." He felt like some sort of macabre Nostradamus commentating Cabrinovic's demise... Because at that moment, down on the riverbed, just as he knew he would, Cabrinovic started to stir.

"The cyanide pills that all the assassins have been given are out of date." Roy said. "The crowd are soon going to realise he is alive. They will drag him out and beat him half to death before the police can arrive..." The whole thing was a historical curiosity he had smiled at in the past – or future. Now, being there he felt nothing but sadness. "...I couldn't make this stuff up if I tried."

Clarke watched as the crowd started to gather up against the balustrade of the Quay and point down. "Serves him right..." she spat. "...Failed with the bomb, failed, with the pill, and failed with the jump. Fucking idiot." She pushed off. "Let's move. I need you scanning the crowd. Otherwise..." she looked to her watch, "...we have thirty minutes to get to that deli."

***

Spike pushed back from the rooftop ledge. "God dang sorry son of a bitch."

He was four storeys up, overlooking the Apple Quay, and had just witnessed the first attempt on Ferdinand's life. *So Royston was right.* He reached sideways and snapped shut the stabilising legs of his sniper rifle. Not that he didn't trust the professor, but he had set it up on the parapet just in case.

He turned around to the mess of components spread out on the tarred rooftop. He had only been halfway through the launch of the HFECS balloon when he had first heard the crowd start to applaud. *I told her I wouldn't get it up in time. Fucking impossible with one person.* Now that all the excitement was over it was time to get back to his task. *Twenty more minutes and it should be done, another ten after that to get to altitude.* He looked at his pocket watch. It read 10:15. *Half-hour till go time... It will be close.*

Chapter 32

Roy stared in wonder at the scene that surrounded him...

On his left, two children kicked a can between them. Almost running into a woman carrying a leg of paper-wrapped meat, they dodged her cursing and skipped past two elderly men who were setting up fishing rods – the two obviously knew something about the shallow river that Roy didn't.

While the day-to-day lives of these turn of the century Serbians was fascinating, sure, Roy was marvelling more at what he couldn't see, rather than what he could. He could see no heavy police presence or criminal investigators. There were no street closures, photojournalists, news reporters or gawking civilians either. To his amazement, the scene was completely ordinary... The heir to the throne of the kingdom had just survived an assassination attempt not more than twenty minutes ago, and it seemed as life was back to usual!

Keep calm and carry on Sarajevo?

On Clarke's heels, Roy had migrated up the Apple Quay some three hundred metres. He was now standing on the corner of it and the Latin Bridge, across the roadway from arguably the most photographed delicatessen in history. Schiller's Deli was a three-storey sandstone building on the corner. Its green door, recessed up the laneway, sat past two adjacent full-length corner windows.

Clarke cracked her knuckles, breaking the silence between them. "How long?" She had a way of talking without looking at him that made him feel expendable.

"Ten minutes." Butterflies stabbed at Roy's gut. *Ten minutes!*

"I need you inside the café."

The blood drained from his face. "Me? What, on my own?"

"You are the only one who knows who we are looking for."

"But..."

"It's not a request, Roy. Get on your fucking bike and move. We don't have time for you to pussyfoot."

Her comment stung, and not just for the obvious reasons. In the last three days he had felt something within himself shift, something he couldn't put his finger on. It was a feeling of something... anything... that was a whole lot better than the nothing he was accustomed to.

Without another word he lifted his chin, straightened the pearl on his half-collar, and marched across the road to the café entrance.

The bell above Schiller's entrance chimed as Roy pushed through. Dialled to eleven, the 'ding' may as well have shaken the ground beneath him. With his pupils wide he looked up at the bell and then out to crowd.

No one inside the deli, not even the clerk, bothered to look up.

You're fine, you're fine, you're fine. He let out a pent-up breath and wiped at a bead of sweat on his sideburn.

Inside, Schiller's was a comfortably sized delicatessen. Around the L-shaped frontage ten or so tables – each with red and white checked tablecloths – faced out to the Quay and laneway. Towards the rear, a glass counter – holding a huge metal cash register – had salamis hanging above. Behind it, a wood-fired stove was filling the room with an aroma of freshly baked bread.

Roy glued his eyes to the floor as he passed through the row of tables. It was not until his knees hit the counter that he dared look up.

From the rear of the deli he scanned side-to-side, studying what little he could of the backs of heads and sides of faces he could see. It took only a moment for him to find one he recognised. Sitting on his own, on a table by the laneway window – blissfully unaware of anything except the half-eaten sandwich before him – was the small, dirty-looking-pixie-head of Gavrilo Princip... the fifth Young Bosnian assassin.

Jesus Christ, HE'S here!

Roy swung his gaze left then – toward the Quay and the river-facing window – looking for either train passenger. Table by table he moved until... he found a pair of black eyes staring directly back at him.

Oh God...

Hitler, or David – Roy wasn't sure what to call him – was sitting bolt upright in his chair burning a hole of hate straight through him. His eyes screamed murder, and his teeth reared in a growl. He didn't, but he may as well have dragged a finger across his throat.

Jesus Christ, THEY'RE BOTH here!

Each man had a table against adjacent sections of the L-shaped frontage; Roy was at the counter. Together they all formed a triangle in the deli, with Princip now closest to the exit.

David snapped his head to Princip. Roy did the same. Princip was toying with a meal, wistfully gazing out the side window, completely oblivious to the stares burning him from both angles. Roy felt David's glare snap back onto him, and then back again. He could see the confliction burning through his fists that were clenched on the table. Princip shuffled in his seat, forcing David's glare to linger.

Roy didn't know what to do. He was faced with the absurd scenario of watching a man, watching a man... eat a sandwich... while both had murder on their mind. His body bristled with electricity; a layer just above his skin prickled his body like a cheap suit. He could hear his own heart pounding. He could feel his pulse throbbing behind his ears. *I am standing inside a powder keg! And either of these two could strike a match any second!*

Roy remembered Clarke's instructions and whispered into his throat mic. "Clarke."

Nothing.

"Clarke." It was futile; the balloon was not up yet.

Running the maths, Roy's eyes darted to the exit and back to David. He would have to run straight through his line of sight to make it to the door. His feet shuffled. *Bowl over whatever you have to, just do it, run!* But as he took his first step, he heard something that made his heart sink. It was the rattle of clapping, and the rumble of engines. The choice was no longer his to make... Franz Ferdinand's motorcade was returning.

David's ear pricked, but no one else in the deli moved. Roy watched in disbelief as a black car appeared outside of the river-facing window. *This couldn't be happening. Not yet!*

The car slowed before turning into the adjacent laneway to the deli. Roy's eyes moved from one window to another like pages of a book.

No...

It was through the second, in the middle of Franz Joseph Laneway, and in full view of Gavrilo Princip... that the car promptly stopped... just where history said it would.

Roy didn't need to hear through the window to know what was being said; it was obvious confusion was reigning. A man in the front stood up in his seat and began yelling, from the back another pointed forward while the first pointed back. The driver, Lojka, was frantically crunching the gear lever, sweat already leaking from his brow.

The car lurched backward a couple of feet trying to turn. It hopped once, then twice, before the engine coughed out a plume of soot and stalled again. It was now precariously placed with its nose toward an opposing shopfront, and its rear toward the deli.

Back inside, Princip was staring through the glass like a child at the zoo. His sandwich fell from his hand to his plate, and was met there a moment later by a dollop of incredulous drool. Roy could almost see the synapses firing in his brain as he realised the fortuitous opportunity in front of him.

He started to rise from his chair.

Roy snapped to David. *Are you seeing this?*

But David was seated still. His eyes darted from Princip to the window, to the door, and back again, but still he remained seated.

Why are you not moving?

Princip pushed back from his table on wobbly legs, knocking over his chair. He stumbled toward the door, pinballing from one table to another.

Roy's fists clenched, he wanted to scream. *Why is nobody moving!?*

That was when David sprung to life. Like a leopard he was up and slicing through the maze of tables with silky grace. Swiftly he gained on his fumbling prey...

But Roy could see it was not going to be enough.

Princip was at the door now.

David was still six paces behind.

He can't possibly intercept.

Princip pushed through, out into sunshine.

David caught the door before it could close.

Hang on... Roy stiffened. He kicked off the counter and sprinted after them. *...I'm not getting left behind.*

Chapter 33

Location: .... 43.8563° N, 18.4131° E

Present day name: .... Sarajevo, Bosnia and Herzegovina

IDTF Classification: . Tear Four

Date: .... June 28th 1914, 1045 hrs

With a double-handed shove Roy burst from the deli into sunshine. Ahead, he caught both Princip and David, one fumbling, the other stalking. It was a bizarre procession he was joining. David was only a second behind the Young Bosnian, while he himself was only a further few back again.

Thankfully or not – Roy didn't know – he could now make out the barrel of a concealed handgun jutting from the end of David's sleeve.

Out on the street chaos was slowly erupting. Gawking locals, having parked their bemusement, were crowding the vehicle, hands extended like zombies, trying to get a touch on the royals. Up in their seats, Ferdinand's soldiers were literally using their feet to kick them away.

Roy watched helplessly as Princip strode with purpose, oblivious to his entourage. He thrust a hand into his jacket pocket and pulled free a fist full of metal. With each step he turned, more and more side on, until Roy could see the sun glistening off his extended pistol.

Consumed by the masses, Ferdinand and the occupants of his vehicle were completely unawares.

Princip was less than five metres away.

Fuck, it's going to happen. What is David doing? He still had his pistol up his sleeve.

Words caught in Roy's throat, he was unarmed, what he was even doing out there was beyond him.

Two metres.

Four feet! History says he fires from four feet! Roy's mind screamed for David to intervene.

Princip stopped at four feet. Steadied... And then all at once his body exploded.

Roy was floored by the blast. Falling like an ice-skater onto his arse, his legs swept from under him as his upper half flailed.

But the blast, as shocking as it was, was no explosion. It had instead come courtesy of a bullet... a supersonic bullet.

As the shot blew Princip's body clean in half, the accompanying pressure wave of the cannon sent his upper section cartwheeling into the air for blood to spray out in a 360-degree rotation. Time slowed for Roy as he watched with absurdity his first dead body – or half-a-body – arc through time and space, and crash down metres from its complement. He turned back to the set of crumpled legs... only to see David standing next to them, completely still, as calm as you like.

People flashed into motion as Roy sat glued on his backside, the flurry of mayhem accelerating his world back up to speed like an analogue VHS. A high-pitched scream emanated from the royal car. It was Sophia, her face was covered in speckled blood and she was losing her mind. Roy could now see why... because David had raised his pistol and was pointing it straight at her.

Pushing himself onto his elbows Roy craned his neck around the scattering crowd. He was looking for... Clarke! He found her, pushing her way through from the across the street. "Clarke!" His voice was hoarse.

She couldn't hear him over the pandemonium.

"Clarke..."

But it was too late, because just as she saw him, CRACK! A shot hammered like thunder over the crowd... David, he had pulled the trigger.

No! Roy snapped around with dread in his heart, to see that David had fired... over Sophia's shoulder... into the head of someone behind her! Another Young Bosnian assassin!

The man – or more so boy – dropped like a stone.

Shit... Roy had completely forgotten. *Mehmedbašić, Čubrilovicć, Popović, Ilicć, and Grabež... There were still five, or now four more in the crowd.*

BOOM! Another sonic wave cracked like thunder from above. A man to Roy's left was thrown sideways as if hit by a truck. Another assassin! A gun that he had just drawn was thrown into the air.

Roy did the obvious maths. *There is a sniper somewhere! And possibly three assassins left!* It was all he had time to compute before the first shots cracked around him. A bullet smashed at the roadway next to his hand, rocks ricocheted into his face, *fuck fuck fuck*, his mind screamed, he was on his arse and completely exposed. *Get moving!*

Still facing forward, he scrambled backward like a crab. "Clarke..." He yelled as he did. She was closer now, just on the other side of the motorcade, maybe fifteen paces away. "David..." He pointed as he crawled, "...is Adolf!"

With two hands on his pistol, David was sweeping the crowd. His ears pricked at the sound of his own name. To Roy's horror he spun on his heels to the source. David's eyes met his own in a flash of red.

Oh shit! Bad idea, bad idea!

David raised his pistol and pointed it right at the middle of Roy's forehead. Roy's eyes locked onto the end of barrel. He saw nothing but the black hole... and then a blur of motion in his periphery.

BANG!

He felt the air break next to his head... then nothing.

David's bullet missed by millimetres, because at the very last moment... he was tackled side-on by Clarke.

If it were even possible, that was when all hell broke even looser.

With Clarke and David crashing to the floor, a soldier in the front seat of Ferdinand's car sensed the break in danger. He rose, drew his pistol – with far too much pomp and ceremony – and trained his sights on the wrestling pair of David and Clarke in front of him. As he did, two others from the surrounding motorcade joined him.

Roy watched helplessly. *They are going to shoot the wrong people!*

But just as the soldiers were about to fire, shots instead echoed out from the within the crowd...

It was the remaining three Bosnians! They were using the panic as cover and camouflage to fire from across the Quay!

With Franz Ferdinand still their obvious priority, the Bosnians blanketed the royal car in bullets. Their first volley of shots hit two of the royal soldiers in the back, dropping them in unison like synchronised divers. Flanked and sandwiched, the third soldier flung himself forward, out of the vehicle. Falling on the same side of the car as the wrestling pair of Clarke and David, he was now under the same cover as his initial targets!

BOOM! Another sniper round fired. Civilian, soldier or assassin, a scream was cut in half.

With the crowd thinner now, Roy caught sight of three men standing at the mouth of the Latin Bridge. With a simultaneous puff, another volley of shots spewed forth from their line.

The royal car took the brunt of the damage. In the backseat Ferdinand dived over his wife Sophia in an attempt to cover her. Frantically screaming at his driver to find a gear, his cheeks glowed beetroot red. As more shots emanated from the bridge it was third time unlucky for Lojka the driver. Hit in the chest, he rag-dolled in his seat before a gurgle of blood popped from the corner of his mouth.

At the same time as those in the royal motorcar were shielding themselves from the Bosnians on bridge, on the opposite side of the immobilised lump – on the floor in front of the deli – David and Clarke were engaged in a fierce hand-to-hand battle. Clarke had sprung to her feet first and was raining down punches as David scrambled backward. The surprise of her tackle had evened the gender gap in their comparable sizes, but David was doing an ample enough job of defending himself from below. He found purchase off the pavement, rolled backward and launched to his feet in one fluid movement.

The scales of the fight tipped now that David was up. Though roughly the same height, he had at least twenty pounds on Clarke. His face contorted – the shock at having a woman tackle him replaced by rage – as he threw a series of rash haymakers her way. Clarke parried the first and second, but could only catch the weight of the third with her forearm. Even under a block the blow staggered her. Sensing her weakness, David wound up and rained down another combination of heavy blows. Clarke caught them all, but as their accumulative force hammered her down to one knee, a fist broke through and connected with her temple.

Stars speckled across her vision as she reached to steady herself.

David, now with a second worth of space, looked around for the pistol that had been thrown from his grip. It was only a few metres away, but he withheld a dive toward it. Instead he smiled, wound up for a knockout blow, and launched at Clarke with all his might.

Fat with arrogance, his finishing blow was sledge-hammer heavy, but markedly slow. Clarke saw it like a watermelon. She slid right, pushed off the ground, and delivered with precision, not power, two short sharp jabs of her own.

David's nose cracked in a fountain of blood. His eyes lit up, slick with tears, and he let out a rage filled scream. Her own head thumping, Clarke was desperate to level the odds once more. Rolling the dice, she spear-tackled David, shoulder into abdomen, and launched both of them back to the pavement. Manoeuvring sideways like a crab, she slid to his back, wrapped one arm around his neck and squeezed with all she had left.

Roy had pushed back far enough now to find himself at the entrance to the deli, in the stone nook housing the entrance.

The scene in front of him was one of utter chaos. Microcosms of battle raged across the street. The few panicked royal soldiers still alive fired indiscriminately on the crowd as the Young Bosnians danced among them. From the cover and confusion of the civilians the assassins quickly wrested the upper hand, pushing those not already wounded into a coward's retreat. Meanwhile, Clarke and David were sprawled on the floor; there was a sniper somewhere picking people off, and Spike... well Spike... *Shit, where is Spike?*

Roy tried his throat mic. "Spike! Spike where are you?"

Static. Nothing but static.

Hang on. Static. His face lit up. *There was static! The balloon must be up!*

He heard a reply through his earpiece. "...ing...oon."

Shit, it's still not high enough.

"Spike, we need your help!" Roy screamed anyway.

His earpiece crackled again. "...I'm goin... or... sniper."

Roy looked up from the random section of shirt collar he was talking into. The area on the other side of the royal vehicle was now almost entirely empty. With all remaining civilians having run for cover, the only three figures remaining were those of the Bosnians.

The blood drained from his face... they were beginning to make their way across the street!

Only one soldier of Ferdinand's guard remained. He was the man pinned down on Clarke and David's side of the car. With gallantry that could only be described as blindly idealistic he stood fully upright and returned fire over the vehicle. Bullets pinged all around him as he got off one, then two shots – but it was no use, the weight of return fire was too great. The soldier was hit seconds later. Pockets of blood puffed through the back of his jacket and he fell to the floor wheezing.

BOOM!

As if on cue the sniper returned to play. With devastating force the centre member of the advancing Bosnian line was catapulted forward as a bullet like a sledgehammer smashed into his back.

Hope... it reared its head, but Roy's delight was short-lived. The remaining two assassins continued their march forward, almost robotically stepping their way over their comrade's dead body. Well aware he couldn't be sure whose side he was on, Roy waited expectantly for another sniper round...

The assassins were twenty metres from the car.

Why is he not shooting the other ones?
Fifteen metres.
C'mon...
Ten.
Whatever the reason, Roy realised... the sniper won't stop them, can't stop them.

A wave spilled over him as he looked at the royal car. *Ferdinand is a sitting duck.* From head to toe, his body felt electrified. Unaccustomed to the sensation, he didn't give himself time to question the absurdity of the decision before him. He just made his choice... and sprinted for the car.

"...ike!"

Spike was bounding up a flight of stairs when his earpiece crackled. Taking the steps two at a time, his legs pumped hard, pushing him towards the topmost doorway. Looking across from his original balloon launching position, he couldn't be one hundred percent certain where the sniper's shots were coming from, but the rooftop of the 'old palace' was his best guess.

"Royston! Tell Clarke I'm going for the sniper."

Spike reached the top landing. Without even catching a breath he planted his massive boot dead centre of the door... and charged through gun up at the ready.

Chapter 34

Location: . . . . 43.8563° N, 18.4131° E
Present day name: . . . . Sarajevo, Bosnia and Herzegovina
IDTF Classification: . Tear Four
Date: . . . . June 28th 1914, 1051 hrs

Roy sprinted out into the open... The hell he was thinking, he had no idea, he just ran.

Crossing no man's land, he raced right past the tangle that was Clarke and David. Locked together in a mad scramble of limbs, they were rolling in a cloud of kicked up dust. Moving too quickly to focus on who exactly was on top, Roy had no time to stop and help.

...Clarke, she would have to handle herself.

Clarke had an arm around David's throat. Her eyes diverted to Roy for a split second as he skirted by. Impossibly quick, it was an opening still, an opening David had been waiting for. Shifting his weight he elbowed her backwards, hard into the abdomen. Clarke gasped as one of her ribs cracked.

She felt her grip slip.

David was ready. With one move he transitioned from defence to attack, twisting his body to face her. From his top position he locked his hands around her throat. He dropped his face to within inches of hers, his mouth seething with hatred.

Clarke gasped for air, and tried to pry open his vice-like grip.

But it was no use; he was too strong.

Her peripheries compressed; spots, black like ink, dotted her vision.

She had to do something. She tried to bring her ankle up as high as she could... If she could just reach it...

Crouching low as he ran, Roy was less than a metre away from the royal automobile when another volley of shots cracked from the quay. Diving the remainder of the way, his back smashed with a thud up against the driver's side door.

One, two, three, deep breath, deep breath...

Dragging his gaze away from the dead eyes of the last royal soldier, Roy took a second to peek over the convertible body at the approaching assassins. They were so close now he could make out their faces! *Shit shit shit.*

Without even thinking, he reached above his head and yanked on the driver's side handle. Lojka, his chest full of lead, was slumped over in his seat. He slid out on his own when Roy opened the door. As Roy clambered up into the vehicle he met the terrified eyes of Ferdinand in the back seat. There was no time for introductions.

CRACK CRACK CRACK!

Roy ducked down under the steering wheel, just as a trio of bullets ripped open the seatback right where his head had been. Under the dash he found what he was looking for. *Tell me the engine has cleared!*

He cranked the ignition... *C'mon!* ...And the car roared to life.

To their horror, the Bosnians – realising what the bizarre man behind the wheel was trying to do – broke into a sprint.

With his head still down Roy grasped for the stick shift. It was only up or down. With no idea which way was drive he slammed the lever down and floored the accelerator... only for the car to launch backward in reverse!

Fuuuuuck! It was too late to change.

Crouched low in the seat Roy kept his foot glued to the floor. Driving completely blind, he heard bullets smash through the already broken windscreen above him.

Roy felt the bump of the kerb.

Oh shit...

He braced for what he knew would be next...

Because a second later... the car smashed backward through the window of Schiller's delicatessen!

Aside from the obvious destruction a motor vehicle can cause to a building, the movement of the royal vehicle from streetscape to shopfront had another, more unintended consequence. The cover it was providing the wrestling pair of Clarke and David from the advancing Bosnian assassins had now completely disappeared.

There was a strange pause in proceedings as both pairs, first, watched in disbelief as the car launched into the shopfront and, then second, took a moment to realise they now faced a completely new threat.

David was still straddling Clarke, his hands around her throat. He looked to the Bosnians with the surprise of a backstage crew with the curtain lifted.

The Bosnians, for their part, didn't know what to make of them. The sight of two supposed civilians wrestling seemed completely unrelated to their royal plot.

Their momentary indecisiveness was all the prompting David needed; he sprung from atop Clarke like a cat and dived for something to his right... it was the pistol he had neglected to pick up previously. In one fluid motion he collected the weapon, somersaulted forward, and came up firing. With David now off her, Clarke too reached for a weapon. She pulled at the hem of her pants to reveal a small Beretta concealable-handgun attached to her ankle. Still on her back she drew and also fired on the dumb-struck assassins.

The odd pair teamed together perfectly. David's bullet hit the closer of the two while Clarke aimed hers at the furthest. Both men dropped dead before either could realise what was happening.

Clarke had no time to relax though. She swung her pistol around to where David had rolled, only to see that he was up and already on the move, making a break for the smashed-in delicatessen entrance. She tensed, her finger depressed ever so slightly, but she didn't pull the trigger.

"Fuck!" She yelled into the air... she needed this guy alive.

Watching helplessly as David disappeared into the deli, Clarke was left on her own, on her back, in the middle of the now strangely deserted street. The silence though was short lived, because as she dragged herself to her feet, she heard the distinct wail of antiquated sirens in the distance. If things hadn't gone to enough shit already... the local police were on their way.

Inside the royal motorcar Roy stirred at the sound of the approaching sirens. Slouched in the driver's seat he reached groggily for his forehead. Working his hand around he felt a gouge just above his hairline. Probing the mush, he winced as a line of blood dripped down his face.

Wiping at the warmth with his shirtsleeve, he smudged blood across one eye, painting his vision an eerie shade of red.

Red-filtered or not, inside the delicatessen destruction reigned. Flying in reverse, the car had impacted with such force that it was now completely inside the building. In front, through the smashed shop window, rays of sunlight caught on the cloud of dust lingering in the air. Below, bricks lay strewn all around and underneath the vehicle. At the rear, having snowploughed a stack of wooden tables with its boot, the vehicle had almost reached the sales counter.

A yell from behind dissected Roy's fog of concussion. His senses, still adjusting, took a second to compute the cry of a female voice.

"Shut up bitch!"

Another, or maybe the same voice again. "You. Get up. Move!"

Roy spun to see... David!

He was barking at Ferdinand, dragging the sluggish royal backward by his collar over the boot of the car as he did. "If it wasn't for me, you would be dead already. Get moving!"

Ferdinand was clearly feeling his own effects of the crash. His face was covered in a layer of white dust. It puffed from his moustache as he landed awkwardly behind the vehicle. David propped him with a shoulder until he found his feet. Roy caught himself staring, he knew it didn't matter in 'his' world, but still, he was relieved to see Ferdinand alive in this one.

"David..." he croaked. "Let him go."

Again, he had no idea what the hell he was doing, but he was about to find out how right he was about the anomalies' noble intentions.

David looked across. And without hesitation, from a distance of only three metres... lifted his pistol and fired directly at Roy!

Roy dived down across the passenger bench seat.

But he was too slow...

He felt something sear his upper arm. Hot like a blow-torch, it was numbness more than pain, but he cried out just the same. *Dumb idea! Bloody dumb idea!*

Off balance, under Ferdinand's load, and with the rear of the vehicle jutting up on an angle, David's bullet had sailed wide, just. It passed through Roy's seat back, grazing him, before smashing into the dash.

Roy tensed for another shot, one that would finish him, but in that instant he heard a familiar voice. It was one that he normally tried to avoid, but right now it was sweeter than a symphony to his ears...

"FREEZE MOTHERFUCKER!"

...It was Clarke.

She stood in the unhinged delicatessen doorway, her pistol gripped tight between both hands. She had her sights peeled down the barrel at David, who was holding Ferdinand in front of him now, around the neck.

As Clarke inched her way forward, Roy watched David adjust himself until only a slither of one eye was visible. The two, their faces, they could not have looked any different. Clarke's glare was burning with such ferocity through Ferdinand it was like he wasn't even there. David's in return, was a dispassionate veneer, his cold and black eyes had yet to blink. Anxiety, uncertainty or stupidity, it was impossible to read which way he was leaning.

"Don't even fucking think about it." Clarke was talking just to have something to say, but the comment may as well have been in another language how little David responded, a shuffle slightly to the right was the only clue he had even heard her. With each step she took he countered with a manoeuvre further behind Ferdinand. Ferdinand for his part was coming to his senses, slowly at first, and then quite quickly, he transitioned from groggy, to wide-eyed, to terrified as he focused on Clarke's gun pointing through him.

Roy watched on with bated breath the slow hushed dance. The silence inside the deli was deafening. Outside though, the incessant wail of the police sirens was growing louder. *They are going to be here any second.*

David broke the icy impasse. "I know who you are..." He said to Clarke as she slid another foot forward like a chess piece. "You don't belong here."

"Neither do you," she countered. "From what I heard, you should be in Vienna around now, sucking dick like some art school faggot."

Did David know what she meant? Yes, or no, he hid any confusion completely. He tilted his head, looking at her with condescending sympathy. "Your insults mean nothing, because you clearly know nothing. I see it is indeed only Abner who has the gift of foresight."

"Is that what you call him...?" Clarke cut in, police sirens echoing. "Abner?"

David's smug look evaporated with his slip. If it was even possible, his eyes narrowed further. Clarke motioned with her pistol at Ferdinand. "Has this Abner been whispering fairy tales like this in your ear while he has been taking you from behind for twenty-five years. Your boyfriend sounds like a hell of a guy, I'd really like to meet him... How about you tell me where you're supposed to rendezvous."

David flashed in anger. He couldn't help himself. "Vile whore!" he spat. "How can you deny Abner's prophecy after what you witnessed today? He has proven that this man must live. He must live for the safety of our world."

"Not my world…" Clarke almost smiled before… CRACK! She fired a shot right into Ferdinand's chest.

"Noooo!" Roy ripped at the backrest he didn't realise his fingers were digging into.

The bullet slammed into Ferdinand's chest… and passed straight through into David. Both men fell backward together against the deli counter, coming apart only as they slouched to the floor.

Roy bolted to his feet in the driver's seat. "What did you do?"

But Clarke was already moving to the bodies. "Saved your fucking life that's what I did." She wasn't even looking at him. "Shut up and come help me."

Roy was numb, too stunned to move. It was only when he heard a whimpering from below did his trance break. His view was drawn down to the back seat he was now standing over. Down in the rear foot well, a muffled cry was emanating from Sophia Ferdinand. She was curled in a ball, one hand over her face, the other clutching her pregnant belly.

Shit! Roy had forgotten all about her. The two locked eyes before he placed a finger over his mouth in the universal sign for 'sssshhhh'. Tearing off his jacket, he threw it over her – it was all he could think to do – before he clambered quickly out of the vehicle.

At the counter, Clarke had stepped straight over Ferdinand and was kneeling next to David. She put two fingers on his neck. "He is still alive. We need to get him out of here."

"Huh?" Roy only had eyes for the Archduke. Doctor or not, it was immediately obvious the royal was dead. The gaping hole in his own chest didn't need a PhD to diagnose. The wound, just above the heart, was oozing a slick of blood as black as night.

"Roy!" Clarke was struggling to roll David's dead weight.

"Yeah." But his voice just a distracted whisper.

"Switch on."

"How could you...?" Moving to David now, Roy could see that both Ferdinand's and the boy's bullet wounds did not exactly line up. Because of their differing heights and angles David's was higher and more to the left, through the shoulder.

Roy had a sickening thought... *She had shot strategically THROUGH Ferdinand!*

He turned to Clarke who was busy plugging David's wound with gauze. "You did this on purpose didn't you? You just condemned this world to war so you could keep David alive?"

Clarke heaved David's unconscious body back up to a seated position. "Fucking hell Roy, his name is Hitler, and he is the only lead we have to find the anomaly. Fuck Ferdinand, and fuck this world, because if we don't get out of here this second, it is going to be us that are fucked next."

Clarke and Roy broke through into the rear laneway of Schiller's delicatessen. Between them they half carried, half dragged David's limp body over the cobblestones. Out front, the wail of oncoming sirens was soon accompanied by the sound of screeching tyres... the police, they had finally arrived on scene.

"Fuck." Clarke shrugged herself free of David.

Roy almost collapsed under the added weight. He was exhausted, mentally and physically. He threw out a hand for a metal trash can to prop himself up. As he did, the sight of his silvery reflection triggered something in his memory.

"Clarke, the balloon..." He wheezed through deep breaths. "I think the balloon is up."

Clarke keyed her mic. "Spike! Are you there?"

Nothing.

"Spike...we are in the rear laneway."

Roy looked up at the line of blue sky between the tall alleyway walls. That was when he heard the rumble of an engine.

His microphone crackled. "BEEP BEEP!" The sound of a horn echoed from both the alley and his earpiece. "Behind you!" A female voice did the same.

Clarke and Roy swung around. A car was almost on them. It bobbled over the uneven cobblestones and lurched to halt just short of their toes.

Loretta rose from the driver's seat... "Well, don't just stand there, get in!"

Roy could have kissed her there and then he was so happy. Cracking the back door he toppled onto and over David as he heaved his limp body up onto the bench.

Clarke vaulted herself into the front passenger side. Without even a thank-you she was straight onto her mic. "Spike! Where are you?"

Nothing again.

She turned to Loretta with more aggression than was necessary. "Where is..."

But she was cut off by an unfamiliar voice that crackled to life in all of their ears. "Spike... Was that his name?"

Roy's blood ran cold. He recognised the voice immediately, but he was the only one in the car who did...

...That was because it belonged to Abner.

Chapter 35

Location: .... 51.4613° N, 0.1156° W
Present day name: .... Brixton, London, England
IDTF Classification: . Ridge
Time: .... April 22nd 2017

The analogue clock centre-dash ticked over to three... am. Sitting in the driver's seat of the onyx-coloured Bentley, Magnus Thorn was reclined far beyond the driving position, staring out into a starless sky. Between his teeth he tugged on a cigar. Like a flare, a glow washed the cream leather interior red. Thorn was savouring a moment, while he had one, because the melodramatic crescendo playing out in his head was about to reach an intriguing climax.

In the dead of the night Thorn's Bentley was near on invisible. Parked at the outer edge of the supermarket car park, it belonged to the darkness like a cat did the shadows. At the opposite end of the lot, a soft red and blue glow emanated from a Tesco sign that hung above two battered looking glass doors. As enticing as the neon was, it was nothing but a lure, a human-sized insect zapper.

Not your average vehicular stable, this particular car park was a fitting example of the 'finest' the lovely suburb of Brixton had to offer. Trolleys littered the lot, broken bottles splashed on asphalt like blood on tile, tossed down into the arena from a six-foot concrete ring. Two overhead lights, still intact, failed dismally to provide haven, casting instead a line of shadow more menacing than the darkness itself.

Thorn, reclined as he was, was comfortable with the setting. He had chosen this place himself, for the exact reason. He needed the lot to be empty both now, and... in 2014. That was because finally, after more than forty-eight hours of God-forsaken-fucking-around, it was almost time... His fifth traveller was ready to go.

For Eden Roy the danger outside the Bentley had nothing on the climate inside. Seated in the passenger seat, suffocating, his eyes were burning from the haze of cigar smoke. Unable to hold himself any longer he stifled a sneeze, spluttered, and began to cough uncontrollably.

"Eden, Eden, Eden... Relax. Here take a breath." Thorn lowered the passenger window. "Try and keep it down, I don't want to have to scrub you from this universe and the next." Thorn butted his cigar against the steering wheel, singeing a circle on the immaculate leather. "Better?" He lowered his own window and flicked the stump out.

Eden collected himself, but refused to look at Thorn. Instead he stared into the night. "Can we just get to the point? What are we even doing here?"

"Oh Eden." Thorn pushed out his bottom lip. "I know the store is closed, but I'm sure we can get you a chocolate milk somewhere else."

"Really... seriously?" Eden turned in his seat. "You're going to joke about this, now?" He was trying to sound annoyed, but in truth he was more defeated than anything. For the last thirty-six hours he had felt more captive than equal in this extraordinary 'business' transaction.

"There is no need to be a dick, Eden. You know what they say about making sure you leave the ones you love on good terms." Thorn softened. "I would hate for our last words to be nasty."

Eden slumped back. "You said there would be a pod."

"There is. It's over there."

Eden followed Thorn's finger into the darkness. Up until now he had thought the car park completely deserted, but now he saw it, a large silhouette, barely visible in an adjacent corner. Whatever it was, it looked to be idling, a steady puff of fumes from its tailpipe the only give away of its existence. He squinted. It was no 'pod'... it was a van.

"There is a black minivan parked in the corner. You see it?"

"Yeah." But Eden was confused.

"Well, I present to you, your chariot... Here" Thorn reached into his jacket pocket and threw Eden a set of car keys. "Now I know its no DeLorean, but don't worry, what it lacks in speed, it makes up for in style. There'll be no need for eighty-eight miles per hour with her."

Eden frowned. "I don't get it?"

"What? The eighty-eight miles...?" Thorn looked surprised "C'mon..."

"Yeah, I fucking get that." Eden snapped. "I don't get the van, where is the pod? Is this some type of rip-off?"

Thorn's face hardened, as quick as a bear trap he swung the back of his hand up into Eden's face. His boxing glove-sized mitt connected sweetly with cheek. "Don't go falling apart on me Mr Roy... I don't appreciate being sworn at, and I certainly didn't like being called a cheat."

Eden's eyes were wide. Not hurt, just stunned, it was the kind of slap that hit nerve more than flesh. He looked down at his lap like a battered wife.

Thorn's face softened into a merry smile. "My apologies... you know I wasn't always like this." He nudged Eden with the same mitt. "Anyway, the van? It is the reason why I haven't sent anyone back in a while. I needed to develop a more discreet way to transport a giant fucking time travel capsule around the globe. My solution: why not make the pod and the mode of transport one and the same?"

Eden turned the key over in his hand. "If the engine is already running, then what is...?"

"The key is for the rear double-doors. All you have to do is get in the back and hit the green push button. Its impossible to miss, it's the only button in there. Everything else is already set."

Eden didn't know what to say. He was struggling with the thought of saying 'goodbye' or 'thank you' to the man he considered a maniac seated next to him. But being the last conversation he would ever have in this universe, the decent human inside him needed to end things courteously. "Thanks I suppose..."

Thorn smiled, his backhander instantly forgotten. "You're very welcome."

Eden made to reach for the door, but Thorn stopped him. "Hang on a second." He reached into the backseat. "I feel a little guilty about Westminster. I know the whole 'Tasering a government official' really ruined your departure plans, so I got you a little something to make up for it." He pulled from the backseat a single strapped leather bag. "It's a little 2014 Christmas present, a starter kit."

Eden opened the satchel and immediately stiffened. Thorn kept talking as if his were a completely natural gift. "Two hundred thousand pounds in cash, a 9mm Glock, an old iPhone 5, and a passport with a new name. Consider it an insurance policy should you choose to abandon your endeavour and abscond to Majorca. Or... if this is after all one big scam and you don't travel anywhere, feel free to come back outside and use the gun to shoot me. I'll be waiting here just in case."

Eden studied the money and the weapon; he had never seen a gun or so much cash in one place before. "And if I don't... abandon?"

"Then check the internal zipper."

Eden pulled a manila folder from it. Attached to the folder was a BMW car key. Thorn answered Eden's question before he could ask. "It is every single life detail about one Lamar Tobin... his family, his address, his work, and all of his movements in the week leading up to the crash. It's everything you should need to find him."

"And the key?"

"Think about it... There are a million ways to skin a cat, Eden. I'm just providing you with some tools. It's up to you to decide what you're really seeking, a simple prevention, or the retribution you deserve?"

Eden ran his hand down the tinted rear Mercedes van window, until it came to a rest on the door handle. His heart was heavy, not with a fear of where he was headed – as he had suspected it would – but rather of what he was leaving behind. Knowing even that he was headed to an exact copy of this world, he suddenly felt a strange attachment to the one that he had called home for so long.

He scanned the car park, never before had an asphalt wasteland looked so good. Heavy with nostalgia he pulled out his 2017 mobile phone, he had one last call to make before it became useless, one for closure.

The phone rang and rang before the voicemail finally clicked in. *"Hi you've reached Professor Jacob Roy, sorry I can't come to the phone right now..."*

Eden was almost relieved. He had no idea what he would have said had someone answered. The voicemail beeped. "Brother..." He paused. "I'll see you in another life, sooner than you think. I'll tell Georgina, Henry and Florence you say hello... I'm going to save them all, for you, for us."

Thorn snapped his Zippo between his thumb and index finger, simultaneously opening and striking a flame. He dragged down on a fresh cigar while he watched Eden disappear into the rear of the minivan.

"Any..."

"Second..."

"Now..."

The atmosphere immediately surrounding the van cracked to life... and that was when lightning struck, literally.

White-blue sparks split the air. Fingers of current shot out from within the van, passing through its black walls like paper. They began small, but expanded quickly, in all directions. The arcs multiplied, melding into one another until a blinding sphere illuminated all corners of the car park.

Suddenly, as violently as it had begun, the sphere contracted. The white light drew in on itself, through the van walls to a point somewhere within, compressing down to a point of magnified intensity. The windows of the vehicle glowed from within. With light came heat, bubbles welded themselves into the black paint as the van was assaulted from inside out.

"Three... two... one..." Thorn held two fingers up, like an orchestra conductor "...and..."

In a moment of unnatural silence, as if even sound waves were being consumed, the tight ball of light completed its cataclysmic display and collapsed in on itself perfectly.

"...Goodbye Mr Eden."

Opening the door to his Bentley Thorn fanned his arms out wide and proceeded to twirl on the spot. "And they all go wild." He granted his imaginary crowd a slow stage bow. "Thank you. Thank you. You're too kind."

Making for the van – he needed to check if it could run before calling his towing crew – Thorn was halfway across the tarmac when something happened, something that froze him in his tracks. Almost losing a loafer, he skidded to a stop on a pile of broken glass. His mouth fell agape, the cigar between his lips falling to the ground to tumble away in crash of ember.

A light. A sound. An event. An... He had no idea, and no words to explain it. It was simply... Gold.

It was something that he, the all-knowing Magnus Thorn, could never have possibly anticipated, because up until this very moment he had been oblivious to its even existence. It was a Tear... and it was opening.

A deafening crack preceded an explosion of light. Thorn waited for a flaming pressure wave to obliterate him, but instead an incandescent warmth washed over him, lifting him, taking his breath, his weight.

His van though was not so delicately handled. The Tear split the atmosphere at the exact point of the collapsed sphere, right in its centre. A red-hot ring of molten steel flared right around the vehicle, like a plasma cutter through a butter block.

With its walls, floor, roof and drivetrain sheared, the vehicle was no longer able to balance across axles. Collapsing in on itself, in an 'A', both halves slid in the inch or so that had been obliterated. But instead of coming to rest against each other as physics dictated they should, both halves continued somehow on a slide into nothing-ness...

What the hell? Thorn watched in amazement as the tail section of the van overbalanced and fell straight through the Tear, vanishing completely! The absent rear doors – off to fuck knows where – left him with a view of the Tear in its entirety. Like a golden eye, a jagged elongated oval starred at him.

"OK Sauron... I see you."

Panic, fear, Thorn felt neither. Strangely calm, as he watched shimmering ripples dance across the vertical pool, only answers flooded his brain.

He reached out a hand, closed his eyes and let one vision fill his mind.

Home.

Chapter 36

Clarke was pacing. With heavy feet she trampled a thin line back and forth through the ankle high grass. "Ten past?" She looked at Roy. "Are you sure he said ten past?" On the outskirts of town now, she had been simmering away just shy of a boil.

"He said ten minutes, which should make it about ten past eleven," Roy said.

Clarke checked her watch, killed some more grass, and checked her watch again.

"We will find him." Roy offered but immediately regretted the words. *I should have said Spike... we will find 'Spike'. But that was obvious, right, that he meant Spike?* Looking at Clarke, which one she wanted to find more, Spike or Abner, was impossible to read on her raven face.

A raven, it was stupid, but that was how he saw her now. Zoomorphism, he was pretty sure it was a thing, like a gruff bulldog of a man, or a weaselly car salesman, she too was similarly identifiable. The smartest of the flying variety, and possibly the craftiest of all animals, it would almost have been a compliment to be called a raven... *if they weren't such sinister cunts of things.*

Wow. OK. Where did that come from? Roy straightened against the post he was leaning on. He and Clarke stood, not looking at each other, as if she had read his thoughts. "I know Spike will be fine." Roy tried again, another futile statement, but still it felt good to reaffirm exactly where his loyalties lay.

"Oh you do, do you?"

"Yeah. I think I do."

"For the record Roy, after that bullshit in the deli, I don't really give a fuck what you think."

"Right..." It was as good a cue as any. Flicking open his pocket watch he saw they still had a couple of minutes so he pushed off the paddock fence. "I suppose I should check on Loretta."

Loretta was over by the gravel roadway, babysitting the 1908 Doriot-Flandrin she had earlier commandeered. Idling with the subtlety of a freightliner, it sat chugging up and down with a real mechanical vulnerability. With the rear door open, she was propped on the back seat, one foot kicking at the ground outside. She looked up as Roy approached, and smoothed down her jacket.

"We have a minute to ourselves?"

"Yeah, I suppose," Roy replied. "No word as yet."

"Darling, can you please let me have a look at your head and arm."

Roy felt for his forehead. The coagulating blood there had matted his hair and was in the process of crystalising. Twisting his arm, he spied next – through a tear in his shirt – the graze on his arm. Courtesy of the first bullet, specifically intended for him in his life, something about the wound thumped louder than his headache.

Three inches to the right, that was all it would have taken.

Transfixed on the burn, forgetting to blink, Roy's eyes both dried and watered. Awash with a pinkish watercolour his blurring vision dragged with it his focus into a haze. Like a pebble down through a murky pond, his thoughts sank past Abner, David, Germany, the Tear, his team and their mission, until they invariably settled as it always did, on Georgina. *Would she even recognise him now, after the things he'd done?*

"Hey..." Loretta finally prompted from the void.

Roy snapped too, blinking away a gritty reservoir pooling at each eye.

"I hope I'm not out of line..." She looked at him but stopped.

Roy met her eyes, they searched his own.

"But, do you want to tell me about her?"

Her hand was waiting, hovering above his arm. Somehow she had read his mind.

"I don't think I can, I'm sorry..."

Loretta's eyes did not judge; they looked too burdened by their own grief to call him out on his. A moment lingered between them as Roy stared into her welling eyes.

"But she would have liked you, you know. I see so much of her in you."

It was enough, enough to break the air that locked them. Loretta looked down, feigning a search for a bandage.

Roy found his voice again. "Are you OK?"

"Me? I'll be fine..." A sniffle told him otherwise. "I wish though I could say the same about..." her words fell away though before she could say who.

Roy reached out with his bad arm and gently, without actually touching her, lifted her chin. Supporting her eyes with his own he mustered all his will. "We will find him... I promise." It felt so good to not have to clarify whom he meant.

Loretta nodded and wiped away a tear. "I know."

"Now..." He seethed as his hand fell away. "Please tell me we brought some 21st century painkillers with us."

Her eyes brightened a touch. "Of course, military grade, no prescription required."

As silence fell over them, the banality of dressing Roy's wounds seemed to purge both of them. As Loretta wrapped his head delicately, the comfort of just having someone close soothed both Roy's body and mind. On his arm her linen gauze stood out as the cleanest part of his outfit. Jacket-less now and covered in soot, his vest and pants had moved from grey, well into the spectrum of black.

"Hey, can I ask you something else?" Loretta tied off the end of his bandage.

"Sure." Roy turned his wrist to twist his arm, impressed with her work.

"Considering what's happened, do you think there will some day be a history professor in this world, studying you and your involvement in this whole thing?"

The question was not what he was expecting. "Wow, OK, that is... interesting."

"I'm sorry. But, you know, it would almost be poetic."

Roy chuckled through his nose. "It's OK, it's just weird to think about... I suppose it all depends on Sophia Ferdinand. If anyone believes her that there were one British, one Australian and one American accents in the café, then it could make for some interesting historical analysis... or conspiracy theories."

Loretta nodded but left her response hanging, the question obviously a soft opener for something else on her mind.

"Why, what are you thinking?" Roy saved her the trouble.

"Nothing..." she began to pack her med-kit. "It's just that, after all you did... Ferdinand is still dead... And... Well, I guess I was wondering if any good can come of this, what we've done?"

"I don't know?" It was the honest truth. "It all depends on who gets the blame this time around. We left a lot of Serbian bodies behind. It would be easy to see the powers that be pinning it on them just the same. With so many sides in greater Europe, not just Germany and Austria, pushing for war, it could still be too convenient a theory to oppose."

"Do you think he ever even had a chance?"

"How do you mean?"

"Well my Nonna..." His look of confusion stopped her. "My grandmother... she used to say 'se deve accadere, allora accadrà' 'if it is meant to happen, then it will happen'. Is there is a chance something bigger than us dictated Ferdinand's death?"

"Clarke dictated he die." Roy's response came out shorter than he intended. He felt the burn of an anger he didn't know he was harbouring, then guilt. "I'm sorry."

"Don't be, I can't even imagine..."

"No." He stopped her. "You didn't deserve that."

The question of the universe's will still hung between them. "I guess I'm not sure." It was a useless answer certainly, but he suspected his opinion was not really the point. "Why?"

Her eyes fell on the rear of their car. "I was wondering what it could mean for 'him'?"

Roy joined her gaze. "David...?" Why he was so reluctant to use the boy's real name he didn't know. "You know I spent the better part of a year and nearly a million words arguing that without him peace was possible. It will almost be a shame to leave this world without ever finding out."

"It would also be a shame to be torn apart inside a black hole."

Roy turned to her. With a smile he feigned thought. "Hmmm... maybe."

"Hey, there's always next time." Loretta too allowed herself a thin grin.

"In another Tear?"

She shrugged. "You never know, who says this will be the last?"

"Right, this could be just the beginning of our adventure."

"To next time then." She raised an imaginary toast.

"Yeah, to next time."

It felt good to be once again on a familiar page, but the silence they shared was also telling.

"Actually..." Roy was the first. "...I'm not sure I could do this all again."

1132 hrs – twenty-two minutes overdue – was when Roy's earpiece crackled to life. The fuzz of an expectant transmission, that artificial sound of silence, it rolled in stereo from his left to right ear. He looked to Clarke back at the paddock fence. She had stopped her pacing.

Both of them could hear it... nothing, purposeful nothingness.

The static ached on, amplifying with each second. Roy's ears burned, searching for any sound while his eyes remained glued on Clarke.

She was barely breathing.

Finally, after what seemed minutes, she could help herself no longer. "You have been here a long time, I was expecting some bigger changes..."

There was the slightest crackle through the mic, the crackle of movement, a shuffle perhaps. They both heard it for what it was. A sinister smile split Clarke's lips. "What have you been doing for twenty-five years? Doesn't look like much. Oh I know, you wanted to be a daddy right? You know there are simpler ways to steal a child than travelling back a hundred years."

Roy flinched for an explosion through the mic, but Clarke kept at it. "So fiddling with the worst kids in history... was that your thing? Was that how you justified it? Did these kids have it coming?"

Another shuffle kept her rolling. "Are you trying to save your soul now with this whole Ferdinand jerk-off? Doing the future a favour like some lone ranger with a crazy side-kick..."

Finally, a breath exhaled slowly through the mic, cutting her one-way conversation. "Enough..."

Abner was surprisingly calm, emotionless. His measured words sliced through with an icy clarity as if the seas of static had been parted just for them. "I want to speak to Professor Jacob... and only to Professor Jacob."

"Um... I'm here." Roy started.

Clarke looked up from her notepad, her frown screamed 'stupid'. After three futile attempts to assert authority she had finally relented. She resumed her furiously scribbling before turning her pad like a television cue card. 'Good cop/bad cop.'

It was now Roy's turn to frown. What?

"Where is David?" Abner started, distracting Roy with his directness.

Roy glanced to the car, his eyes subconsciously darting to the boot. Clarke waved in his periphery like an air traffic controller. Slicing her hand across her throat in the 'kill it' motion she flipped a second cue card that read 'one for one' and mouthed the word 'Spike' with her lips.

"He's here." Roy did his best to reciprocate Abner's frosty tone, but it sounded only like he was lowering his voice.

"Alive?"

"Um…" Roy gulped. "I think it is only fair the questions flow one for one. We need to know what has happened to Spike. I can't give you anything more until…"

Over him, Abner slowed his words. "Is. He. Alive?"

Roy flashed back to the restaurant carriage of the Orient Express, the intensity of it. He stammered slightly and picked his shirt off his sweat soaked chest. He couldn't help himself. "Yes… He was hurt, but he is going to live."

Fuck.

He heard a huff from beside and could feel the burn of Clarke's glare. Through the microphone though he picked up the faintest, almost inaudible, exhalation. Something about the breath struck Roy. Held in a second too long, and let out a second too slow, it seemed… invested.

Roy prompted again, conscious to atone. "What about Spike?"

"Hmmm… Spike." Abner rolled the name over airwave. "…it's true, he doesn't look like a Stanley… Spike, he was gallant enough."

Clarke's jaw clenched. "You smug fuck! Where is he?"

Abner paid no heed to her re-entrance. His words, completely monotone, were for Roy only. "I watched what you did today, Jacob. Your trick with the car surprised me. After we met on the train, I did not peg you as the self-sacrificing type."

Was that a compliment? Roy couldn't help but feel he was being manipulated. "I guess I wasn't really thinking."

"Tell me, how did your heroics play out? Did he live, the heir?"

The question, the slight eagerness behind it, was an opening. Roy looked to Loretta, her eyes giving him all he needed. "Would it matter to you if he didn't? Would this trip back in time be wasted if he didn't?"

"Not necessarily."

"No?"

"I was sent for genocide, not war. Any extra, is purely for me and the boy."

I knew it! He is no anarchist. A conscious psychopath maybe, if such a thing were possible?

"...Sent?" Roy emphasised the distinction. "To stop a holocaust by stopping one man?"

"You disagree with the distinction?"

"No." *If only you knew.* Another thought struck Roy, a more administrative one. "So this moral agenda then, it is not your own? You are following orders?"

"I have been here for twenty-five years, Jacob, there are no such thing as orders anymore, just the inevitability of change."

"And what then would your employers say, if they knew who young David really was?" It was a leap, a risk.

There was a pause on the line. A nerve had been struck like a gong.

"You assume they don't." Abner's cover was almost seamlessly. Almost.

Roy felt a rush of trepidation. He was on the money, but had no idea what to do with it. Clarke motioned around him, holding and pointing to a hastily scribbled 'push'.

God, what was he doing? He had never been any good at poker. He looked at Loretta who was chewing her bottom lip; she gave a reassuring thumbs up.

Roy swallowed. "I know they don't."

"You do, do you?"

A cough. A lie. "A lot has changed since you left. If we have the ability to track you across time, did you not think we could track who sent you?" Roy hastened his next point before Abner could call him out. "You were sent to terminate the boy, weren't you?"

Abner seemed to contemplate the odds. His tone softened unexpectedly. "Do you have a family, Jacob?"

"No." Roy skirted the truth.

"There is something inside those that do..." his voice trailed away. "Every time I look at my son I am reminded of his potential, I must remember that he did six-million-times-over what I was too afraid to do once. That is my burden. That is my penance. That is the debt I owe."

Abner seemed to catch himself then. He paused, as if listening to his words again. As he did any softness in his tone evaporated. "What has happened has happened... What is done is done..." He was back in control. "Now all that remains is what lies ahead for both of us. So, I will ask you again like I asked on the train. Why are YOU here Jacob?"

Shit, Roy hadn't planned this far ahead. "Ah..." He tried to stall. "What if I said I'm just a lowly history professor, here for observation?" *Shit, who starts the truth with, 'what if I said'.*

"I'd say it's a long way to come for a field trip."

"Okay..." Roy was stumped, he'd exhausted his meagre tank of lies. Clarke was going to hate him for this, but the time for stroking each other was over. "I think you know it's for you, that we are here both for you, and because of you..." The truth – well half of it – was liberating "...we want to meet, maybe run a few tests."

Silence on the line.

"Tests?"

The smell of bullshit was thick; it reeked.

"Yes." Roy tried still. "Some simple tests."

"And if I decline?"

Fuck can I do this? "Well..." Roy felt himself blush, *can I really do this?* "We have David. I think... he would say that maybe you shouldn't."

A defiant laugh flashed over the line.

Oh God.

"David knew what we were here for. You 'think' he would say I shouldn't? Ask him yourself, I dare you." Abner laughed again. "Ask him what he would 'prefer' even, death or your extended company."

Fuck. Was Abner the one bluffing now? Roy couldn't tell, it sure as hell didn't sound like it. He had one card left to play though, running on instinct he thought on what he guessed was Abner's tell.

Roy stiffened; he needed every cell of confidence in his body for this to work. "I thought you might say that. But you see, his death was never an option, because we are not like you, we are not guns for hire." Both Clarke and Loretta were looking at him with quizzical concern; he was flying solo, off the range. "What WILL happen, should you refuse, is we will be forced to turn him over... to the Serbian authorities." Roy paused, on the other end the line crackled. "Your boy, the one you have groomed tirelessly to prevent from becoming the monster he could, will almost certainly – with the aid of Sophia's eyewitness accounts – now take over from Gavrilo Princip as the assassin of Ferdinand. He will become the face of WWI instead of WWII, and resume a legacy as potent as it is fitting, as one of the most culpable names in all of history."

Loretta bit down on the lip she was chewing and Clarke dropped her pen and paper. Roy could only hope Abner's was similarly poised. He himself was shaking, his body was calling him out on the absurdity of his performance.

A deafening silence ensued.

Finally, just when it seemed Abner was no longer with them, his voice seared. "The old palace, 1430 hours. The rooftop. Bring the boy. Call it a test, or call it what it is. Just know that I will not make the same mistake I did on the train, or when watching you through my sights. You have painted yourself red now, Jacob..." With that Roy heard the familiar click of a microphone disconnecting. Mesmerised by both the foreignness of his own words, and Abner's ominous threat, he was left staring ahead.

Clarke, having snapped from her stupor, trudged across his view. She banged on the car boot with a fist. "David, you still with us? Your deadbeat dad called, he says hello."

Roy felt a touch on his shoulder. It was Loretta, she had come up beside him. "Roy. That was... amazing. Where did that come from?"

He looked down at his hands as if they had just committed a crime. "I don't know."

She watched him, reading his thoughts. "We are still the good guys, Roy." It was her turn to repeat his earlier words.

He turned to her, present but not. "I don't think there are any good guys left."

Before Loretta could object, their conversation was interrupted by the click of another microphone coming to life. Roy braced for Abner to re-emerge from the silence, but instead a different, deeper voice boomed through. "Switch to your secondary channel Major." Another disconnecting click punctuated the transmission.

What the...? Roy fumbled with his radio trying desperately to remember the allocated back-up-channel, *nine, no, ten, no, eleven... there.*

He heard the voice. "...intercepted the entire conversation. Seems your bookworm has a spine after all. As for us, we will be coming hot. Current projections have us rendezvousing with you at approximately 1330 hrs. Balloon, recon, prelim. If you haven't already, get them done. I don't need to tell you that we need to flush this fucker out ASAP, then get home while we still have one."

Roy's head was spinning. With fear or joy, he didn't know? Was it possible to feel both? Hope, he allowed himself that much... Mason and Alpha Team were on their way.

Chapter 37

Location: ....43.8563° N, 18.4131° E
Present day name: ....The Old Palace of Sarajevo, Bosnia and Herzegovina
IDTF Classification: .Tear Four
Date: ....June 28th 1914, 1425 hrs

Mason advanced, back shoulder to the wall, down the expansive palace hall. From doorway to doorway he slid, strafing one foot over the other, in total silence. Floor-to-ceiling tapestries draped the expanse between each refuge. Brushing one he felt thickness push back against his leading arm. The old palace was littered with works, abandoned in the move. More hanging rug than master-piece Mason thought; Professor Roy had mentioned something of their significance, but that lesson had been pushed to the periphery of his mind.

His focus was on point, where it needed to be. Crouched forward, coiled like a spring, his vision was trained down the sights of his M4. The black assault rifle floated loosely in his grip. *Assault...* it could not have been a more fitting description of their current task, unless of course 'search and destroy' had suddenly become an honest Army idiom.

Why had Abner relented? For the sake of the boy? Who knew? Who cared? With enough balloons they would have found him eventually. He was just making life easier.

As Mason approached a T at the end of the hall, he looked to his adjacent wall. Clarke was there, mimicking his advance step for step. He held up a clenched fist and she stopped on a dime.

She was a good soldier Clarke, female or not, she was proficiency personified. She had handled herself with more poise than he could have hoped considering the shit-storm she was confronted with. He dropped to a knee at the edge of his wall, and covered her as she peered around hers. Respect, was that what he was feeling? Or was it pride? Lust maybe. A yearning... Love even?

She was considering his face now, momentarily lost in hers. "Pssst. What the fuck?" She waved a hand and indicated to his blind turn. "Let's move."

Mason nodded. She was right. It was nearly two thirty. They had to be back at the station before three. Her drive was warranted but, as always, her coldness a worry. He should have learned by now, that was their way about each other.

'0.20, E, 11%'

"Two hundred metres. Eastward heading. Twenty-metre variable..." Roman whispered. He did some mental arithmetic. *If Spike launched the balloon from the building below the park? And the park was a quarter-click across the street to the west, then...* "He has to be in the north-west corner, looking out over the river at the deli. It is probably where he set up his original sniper position."

"Copy," came a reply from Mason.

A minute later, another silent vibration. '0.20, E, 10%'

"Two hundred east from the balloon still. He is not moving. Keep your heading constant." Roman had one eye on his beeper; the other was peeled down the barrel of his Glock, focused on the head of his hostage at its end.

'0.22, NE, 10%'

"Two twenty now. He has potentially moved north, around the building edge. Adjust heading slightly to intercept." He was giving instructions to the advance team of Mason, Clarke and Gerhard on level three. He and Simeon had split once again and were on babysitting duties. They were holding David in what seemed an abandoned ballroom immediately to the left of main palace entrance.

Roman allowed himself a second, in between pings, to study his surrounds. In the middle of the room, directly above his head, a large peach-coloured void yearned for its long since pillaged chandelier. Below, the floors were slick with a visible layer of dust that seemed to float an inch or so off the parquetry. Ballroom or high school gymnasium? The room had a comparable feel.

David sat patched up and semi-conscious, tied to a chair at one of only two circular tables still standing. Coming to, at his white-sheeted table, the cheeky fucker even had the nerve to joke through bloodied teeth "I'm ready for my meal". His English accent was bizarre on the ears, it assailed at Roman's notion of history like little else had on the mission thus far.

"You know he can see the future." The boy tilted his head back and chuckled to the ceiling. "You have no chance!"

"Shut the fuck up!" Roman dropped the butt of his pistol on the boy's chin, clattering his teeth.

Vrrrrr Vrrrrr... '0.220, NE, 10%'

Roman snapped too. "Holding steady boss."

Using an Army issue iPad Roman had set the balloon to ping on overdrive, it would chew through the battery, but it meant he could get location results near on command. A sickening thought occurred to him. *'Location'*... there was something important he was missing about the distinction. *Location... fuck... not elevation... oh God, is he even on the roof?*

That was when Mason's voice crackled through his earpiece. "Approaching the rooftop service stairs now."

Mason, Clarke and Gerhard breached perfectly behind the force of Mason's boot. Rolling through the door on each other's tail they fanned out and had a 360-degree rotation cleared in seconds.

"Motherfucker..." Mason breathed.

"He's not here." Clarke finished for him

The group, back together, encircled an incidental air vent where Abner should have been. Mason spoke. "Roman, are you sure about your coordinates?"

"Hundred percent boss. It's still 0.20, NE, 10 percent." Came a reply through his mic.

Mason bent a knee and rested his weight upon it. He could have, should have, predicted as much. Their little jaunt through the palace had been too easy. With no guards, no roadblocks, it made sense now that they had been purposely funnelled to the roof. *So their rat was playing with his cats...* he smiled, ...*very well.* Deep down, a part of him would have been disappointed almost to find Abner had simply rolled over.

"OK..." The vent creaked beneath his foot. "This has just confirmed the calibre of man we're dealing with. There is only one explanation..."

"Yeah..." Roman's voice crackled through the mic again. "You're standing right on top of him."

Mason regarded his feet. "I suppose it's lucky then that there are three floors below us, and three of us here to search them." He scanned the cityscape around them. "Look around, locate yourselves. Use the buildings to make note of exactly where we are. This fucker is literally right below us. Clarke, you take the second floor. Gerhard, you take the first. Me, I'll take the ground." Clarke and Gerhard nodded without hesitation. "If it wasn't clear already, you both have operational freedom from here on. Don't take any chances. You cross paths with anyone breathing, put them down or pin them down." He checked his watch. "The clock is ticking, let's move."

"Commencing sweep of level two," Clarke logged.

Ten or so seconds of silence passed.

"Gerhard entering level one." The German spoke in a broken third person.

Another ten seconds.

"I'm in position on ground." Mason's husk was unmistakable.

The delay, Roman realised, was the time it took to descend a flight of the grand central staircase. Each member of the advance team was now alone on their respective palace floor.

Pacing the ballroom, Roman moved to a large arched window that faced the palace entrance. It didn't sit well with him, as it wouldn't with any soldier, that he was sitting underutilised while his team had been forced to split. He peeled a heavy plum-coloured drape and cast his gaze down the palace drive. The mile-long crushed-rock strip was dotted with weeds. At its extremity, just inside of the palace gates, he could see the figures of Roy and Panatoli sitting together in the front of one of their two vehicles.

"Roy, radio check."

"Ah, yep, umm, loud and clear," came a reply.

"Stay sharp, you heard the anomaly is not complying."

"Uh huh..." there was a pause on the line. "You know his name is Abner if that makes it easier."

"Right, it doesn't."

Roman let the drape fall. "Something doesn't feel right."

Simeon looked up. He was cleaning his pistol next to David. "No?"

"There's something about this building. This Abner asshole has effectively countered the balloon's advantage. What are the chances of that happening?"

"Coincidence, it happens, you know that."

"Is that what this is?" Roman was asking himself as much as Simeon.

"Of course. Why? What are you trying to say? That he knows about the balloons?" Simeon shook his head. "Impossible."

"Is it, really? Of all the possible sites in this city, right here, this palace, is where elevation has the greatest chance of fucking us. It's the tallest building for miles..."

Right then, from somewhere above, a concussive boom cut Roman's sentence. A rumble rolled like a choppy wave from one side of the palace to the other until it hit their ballroom. Plaster dust fell in white strings around them.

Roman eyed the ceiling. "Explosion?"

"We got him?" Simeon clapped his hands.

There was a pause as the two men waited for something more... anything more.

Watching, waiting, it was David though who vocalised the growing concern in the pit of Roman's stomach. "You realise that there is a three-in-four chance that that was one of your friends... getting got." He rocked back on his chair, a chilly smile across his lipless mouth.

Roman's earpiece erupted. "Advance team report! What was that?" It was Mason.

"This is Clarke. Sounded like a grenade. I'm on two, came from below me."

An aching silence ensued.

"Gerhard...?" Mason.

Nothing.

"Gerhard, report."

Nothing again.

"Roman, Roy..." Mason moved on, "...secondary team, report."

"This is Roman. Sounded like an explosion down here boss."

"This is Roy, I can see smoke coming from the first floor."

"Fuck." Mason was moving. "Roman. Get me another ping. There is every chance Gerhard has nailed the fucker and done himself or his radio in in the process."

"Roger boss, right away."

Roman ran from the window to David's table, to the other side, where his gear was stacked. Focused now, he could barely hear Mason and Clarke in his ear, planning to rendezvous on level one.

Simeon jumped out of the way as Roman scooped up a beeper and a small tablet. He jammed two cables from the tablet into the back of the beeper and both devices illuminated to life. Seconds later Roman had his thumb practically through the 'send' icon of the tablet – bashing it three times to be sure the screen distorted into a sea of purple.

"C'mon, c'mon." Roman stared at the tiny, rectangular beeper screen. "C'mon..."

The wait felt an eternity.

Finally, rhythmically, the black case vibrated in his hand. A hush fell over the three, even David, who had no idea what was going on, was sufficiently intrigued.

Roman slowly straightened. "Fuck me, he did it." He turned the screen to Simeon, the yellow backlight glowing in his palm.

'0 – 0 percent'

Simeon let out a breath as he clamped David's shoulder. "How about that you smug fuck? Your Nostradamus didn't see that coming, did he?"

David shrugged as much as his restraints would allow. He looked on defiantly, his eyes thin.

Roman bit his bottom lip and keyed his mic. "Roman to Mason."

"Send."

"The ping came back negative for any signature."

"Fan-fucking-tastic. We are closing in on the blast area now."

"Roger..."

Confirmation or not, Roman was unnaturally hesitant, the pit in his stomach had yet to close over.

Simeon read as much. "What's wrong?"

"Well... what if it is like I said? What if he knew about the balloon? What if he has found a way to manipulate it?"

"Impossible... Think about it logically, if you can't think of how he would, then what chance does he have?"

It was true. As rudimentary as the balloons were, there wasn't much that could go wrong with them. *Although...* A sickening thought struck Roman. *What if it's not the balloon he manipulates?*

He snatched for his mic. "Roy you there?"

"Ah, yeah," came a stunted reply

"History and shit, you know much about this building?"

"Some things..."

"OK. Tell me, did these palaces have there own armouries or blacksmithing areas?"

"Some did. This particular palace was built in the late 1400s by the first known Ottoman governor of Bosnia, Isa-Beg Ishaković, and expanded upon in the 1600s by Gazi Husrev-Beg..."

"Roy..." Roman cut him off. "Enough. Dumb it down. Yes or no?"

"Sorry... yes. In the basement."

"Did they work with much lead?"

"No, not really, too soft a material for weaponry."

"Shit." Roman deflated slightly, but his mind was still racing.

Roy's voice broke through again, "But Roman, I think I know what you're getting at. If you're after lead, then there's somewhere else you need to know about."

A sharp plastic stink cut the air. Hot biting fumes scraped the roof of Mason's mouth before burning his throat. The vein at his temple thumped, delivering his brain the first stages of an unmistakable nitroglycerine headache. The explosion... it was dynamite.

The room was a mess. Halved almost perfectly by darkness, smoke rolled along the ceiling like a thunderstorm, suffocating what few lights had not blown in the blast. From down on his knees, under the blanket of smoke, Mason could see a single shattered window was illuminating the lower half haze. Down a lane of destruction light shimmered from an overturned stainless trolley onto walls either side. The mix of off-white and pale-green tiles had on them already a slick coat of soot. *This floor looks more hospital than palace.*

Mason slid forward as if on skis, his rifle raised. Both he and Clarke had heard Roman's confirmation of the negative ping, but still they moved with caution, conscious of booby traps. *Fucking hundred-year-old dynamite, cough the wrong way on the shit and... well.*

Entering the blast zone, his suit-pant stretched tight around his thigh as his knee squished into a tacky puddle. Scanning side-to-side, it took a second for his pant to soak through, and another then for him to realise... *What the...*

Recoiling instinctively, his foot slipped, wiping a track through red. Falling backward onto his palms – as if playing Twister on one giant crimson pad – he only just kept his rump aloft.

Fucking hell. The pool was oozing from a torso half buried under a desk to his right... He was crouching in someone.

Mason whistled to Clarke.

Hustling over, she kicked the desk off the body. "Fuck. It's Gerhard."

Even in half, and smoking, it was obvious. The German's Aryan blue eyes stared lifelessly in different directions and no amount of burn could hide his pockmarked skin.

Clarke was kicking at the blast debris. "Looks like there are pieces everywhere. Too many for just one, could be multiple casualties."

Standing, Mason wiped his hands on his pants. "Bet you Abner's own booby trap backfired. Find me a definitive piece. I want confirmation of a second body." He turned his attention inward then, the demise of Gerhard barely registering. "Mason to Roman."

His earpiece crackled. "Yeah boss."

"Confirmation Gerhard is KIA. Stand by on the anomaly, awaiting a positive identification."

"Ah... Boss." Roman sounded less than relieved. "We could have a problem."

Mason slung his rifle over his shoulder. "What?"

"I got word from Roy. He has confirmed that this palace has a medical wing, apparently built after some rich fucker lost an heir mid-century."

"I'm aware." Mason cut him off. "I'm standing in the remnants of it as we speak."

"Shit."

"Roman, spit it, what's this about?"

"This will sound like a stretch... but I believe there's a way this Abner guy could have manipulated the result of the ping, especially the negative return."

"Roman, I am looking at pieces of the guy scattered around the room, and…" he looked at his watch, "we have less than an hour before the Orient fucking maroons us in this shithole."

"I understand sir, but please, if you are where you say you are, you at least need to hear this."

"Fine. Make it quick soldier."

"OK, according to the Professor, these palaces, especially the medical wings of them, often had a room dedicated to radium storage."

"Radium storage?" Mason couldn't hide his surprise.

"Yeah, radium. As in the radioactive shit found in uranium. Roy says it was discovered in the early 1900s and used for all types of stuff, cancer treatment, beauty, anything. He's got all the facts, but apparently there were even dedicated radium spas over Eastern Europe, it was a real aristocrat sort of thing."

"All right I get it…" Mason cut in. "There might be radium here somewhere. What's it got to do with us? How's he used it?"

"No, it's not the radium he could have used boss… It's the lead-lined room it's stored in…"

The smoke had almost completely cleared, but still the room was painted with what seemed a permanent shadow. Mason's eyes fell on a heavy looking metal door to his right. It had a circular glass porthole in its centre, solid rivets around its perimeter and a small illegible placard beneath.

He keyed his mic. "Found it."

"Psssst." He flagged Clarke and pointed to the room. She immediately raised her rifle to cover him as he moved forward.

Roman's voice played like narration as he slid his back along the wall adjacent the porthole. "The lead casing could be blocking, hiding or, however you want to say, fucking up the signal. He could still be in there."

The texture behind Mason changed as he transitioned onto the smooth lead sheeting. Next to his head he snuck a glance through the circular window.

Inside was a sea of crimson. He took a second, longer look, "There is a lot of blood in there…" - but his sentence fell away, "…oh fuck!" Abandoning all caution, he spun and yanked hard on the steel handle. Heaving the heavy door open as if it were hollow, he bolted in as Clarke yelled from across the room.

"What? What is it?"

Inside Mason skidded to a halt and dropped to his knees. "Hey, come on buddy, stay with me." He yelled over his shoulder at the entrance. "Don't come in here, Lane." Her first name, he never called her by her first name. "It's clear. Just don't come in here I said. That's an order…"

Clarke appeared at the doorway. There was no holding her back. "What…" A breath stuck in her throat as her words fell into nothingness.

On the floor up against the storage room back wall, seated in a pool of his own blood, was the body of Sergeant Spike Doran. Spike dragged his head up. His chest was pulsing, his mouth grasping for short sharp shallow breaths.

"Major…" His voice was a whisper "…I'm sorry." He hacked a splattering of blood from deep in his chest. His eyes pulsed wide with each cough. An unblinking tear fell from one into the speckling of red on his cheek. "I'm sorry. He knows."

Mason was using his bulky frame to block Clarke's view as much as possible, but her gaze inevitably found Spike's lower half. She covered her mouth, swallowing a sob. Both of Spike's legs were missing. Tourniqueted at the thighs by thick leather belts, the exposed flesh of his legs flapped over the broken white stumps of his dissected femurs. One of his sleeves was drawn up above the elbow, a harpoon-sized needle protruded from the soft underbelly of his arm. From the needle a teak stained hose led to an elevated jar that held a soapy concoction, it was a crude attempt at an IV drip.

The light behind Spike's vacant eyes was dimming. "Held out as long as I could." Still he tried a smile. "Fucker got me by the second leg."

"Spike." Clarke collapsed down next to him, pushing Mason aside. "Stop talking." She fumbled with her belt for a small water bottle. "Here, drink."

"Stop." Spike pushed her away by letting his head fall to the side. He closed his eyes and whispered again. "I'm sorry."

"Sorry for what Spike? What does he know?" Mason was standing now, over both of them, but even he had a hand to his face.

"Everything. He knows everything. Anomaly... Balloons... Where we..."

"The Tear?" Mason's hand drew into a fist. A tooth bit down on knuckle. "Does he know about the Tear?"

Spike seemed out now, his racing breath had slowed to a crawl.

"Spike!" Mason's voice boomed with double-edged concern. "Does he know about the Tear?"

"Mason!" Clarke snapped around. "What are you doing?"

"What? We need to know."

"Enough." She turned back to Spike and yanked out the rust covered needle. Looping his arm over her shoulder she tried to lift him. "C'mon, we are going to get you out of here."

"Major. Stop." Spike coughed. There was no fear in his voice, just resignation.

She glared at him from only inches away. "I'm not leaving."

"Stiff shit... because I ain't comin'." His head tilted back against the wall.

Clarke's eyes were heavy with a level of desperation Mason had seldom seen. "Damn you if you think I'm leaving you. You're not having that over me."

Mason could have sworn Spike smiled before he hacked again. His lungs took a second to re-engage, the gaps between breaths blowing out now beyond measure.

"Spike!"

"Lane." Mason's voice was soft, again her first name.

She snapped to him. "Don't you dare! We are taking him."

"Lane, it's too late, he's gone."

She turned back, in disbelief. Spike's eyes stared absently at the ceiling, his chest had stopped moving. Like his faltering body, the streak of a single tear had run dry before it could fall from his cheek. Clarke un-looped his arm and grabbed him by the collar, straightening his neck. "Spike! Wake up!"

Mason was suddenly beside her, his hand on her shoulder. "Lane, all we can do for him now... is find this bastard."

"Roman! It's a trap!" Mason was running through the medical wing screaming. "We found Spike, the second body was his! He's been tortured and used to cover for Abner." Mason was getting no reply, but he was on a roll, spitting out words as quickly as he could. "Assume he knows! Assume the anomaly knows everything! You were right, he was hiding in the room, the negative reply was false. Ping again! I repeat... ping again!"

Chapter 38

Roy shifted in the driver's seat. The burgundy leather of the Chesterfield bench seat burned his exposed forearms. He had removed his vest and rolled the sleeves of his shirt; still a pool of sweat was drenching his lower back. Air-conditioning, it would be another fifty years before Chrysler would be the first to offer it as an option. Roy squinted up into the sun like it was an overbearing parent. *Fair enough AC was a delusion, but hell was a roof shade too much to ask?*

The teams' parking effort didn't help Roy's burgeoning melanoma. They had their two vehicles, Alpha's stolen, and Loretta's commandeered, fanned across the palace drive, blocking the front palace gates.

Loretta, her upper half leaning over the seat back, was rummaging around in the rear as Roy sizzled. "There they are..." she turned back holding a straw boater for herself, and a felt bowler for him.

"Thanks." His looked like a prop from *The Avengers* – the British, not Marvel variety.

She pretended to flip down a non-present sun visor mirror and straighten her hair. "OK?"

"Of course." Amazingly, after all they had been through, she still looked immaculate.

They both stared ahead at the palace, an apprehensive silence falling again. While they were very much in the afternoon light, both were in the dark when it came to what was happening at the other end of the drive.

In the ballroom Roman could hear nothing but static. He scratched at the prickly regrowth spoiling his once straight forehead hairline. It had been nearly two minutes since Mason had entered the radium room, and still no word.

"Mason. Boss. You there?"

Nothing.

"Boss?"

The lead walls were almost certainly inhibiting Mason's signal. There was little to do other than wait.

Simeon wandered over, one eyebrow raised. "What's going on?"

Before Roman could offer an explanation, Mason's voice interjected mid-sentence. "...oman can you... hear me? I said... Ping again!" He sounded short of breath, his voice bouncing in step with his stride.

Roman didn't understand, but he didn't need to be told twice. He swept his hand across the table and snatched up his beeper and tablet as Mason relayed a broken set of instructions. "...Spike's body... tortured... he knows... hiding the whole..."

Roman fumbled with the tablet screen, the 'send' button glowed bright, lighting his face from below. But just as he brought his finger down...

"Huh-hem." A cough from his periphery stopped him dead in his tracks.

Roman leaned over the table; a paralysis of dread locked his finger as his head slowly turned to the entrance.

Abner stood between the ballroom double doors. He looked calm, grounded, as if he had been there for some time, waiting for someone to notice him. A pistol, balanced effortlessly between both hands, was pointed in their direction.

"You don't need that anymore." He gestured toward the tablet with a flick of his gunbarrel. "Here I am."

Roman was stuck, caught red-handed with his hand poised over the cookie jar. Simeon, next to him, was equally dumbfounded.

Roman let both the beeper and tablet drop to the table. Straightening slowly, he held his palms out. "Wow, wow, let's all slow down."

With a merciless disregard for theatre Abner moved his pistol the inch or so required to find Simeon's chest.

Roman read in the man's eyes...

He snapped left. "Simeon! No..."

Two cracks split the room, echoing through the expanse.

Simeon, the poor bastard, still trying to make sense of the situation, was catapulted backward in a spin. With his eyes still open, he fell face up next to David's chair.

David looked down at the body, up to his father, and back to the body. Tied still, he kicked at Simeon's shoulder with his heel. "How about that YOU smug fuck."

The satisfaction with which David echoed Simeon's earlier words chilled Roman's blood, he wasn't stupid, he knew he had seconds at most.

Up again now, David's eyes were full admiration. "You came..."

"You let them catch you." Abner spoke softly.

"They..." the boy tried.

"It doesn't matter."

Roman watched the reunion in disbelief. Taking his chance, but not wanting to make a sudden move, he slid his hand across his abs towards the pistol hanging from his underarm harness.

Without even a word Abner's gunbarrel stopped him, its black hollow-tip traced his movement.

Roman threw up his other hand. "Wow wow wait." For what he hoped, it didn't matter — it was the only thing he could sieve from the jumble that was his mind.

Shit... This was all happening too fast. Standing straight, gun hand on chest, there was no way he could possibly draw in time... but he had no choice. In Abner's face, in the nothingness behind it, he could read his fate clear as day.

Fuck you, you cold bastard. A look of defiance crossed his own. His brow furrowed. *I've taken better men.*

And so for the second time in 24 hours Roman reached, and again two cracks split the cavernous room. This time though, as the dust settled... Roman saw nothing but blackness.

A bevy of cracks popped almost as one from the palace.

Roy's ears pricked. "Was that...?"

Loretta's did too. "Gunshots, two of them?"

"I don't like this." Roy slid from the front seat; drawn to his feet he studied the stone building down the drive.

Clarke's voice cut in to his ear. "Roy?" Her tone was biting, more than usual.

"Yes, we're here."

"With Loretta?"

"She's here..."

"Have you heard from Roman?"

"Um... Yeah."

"We can't reach him. What were those shots?"

"Oh…" Roy caught on. "Um, no. I haven't spoken to him since…"

"Fucking hell Roy!" Her words spat like venom. "What can you see outside?"

"Um… Nothing." He was starting to sweat a non-heat related sweat.

"Nothing?"

"No, I mean yes. Nothing." The smoke from level one had cleared. The palace was looking as tranquil as it had when they arrived.

"Fuck! Roman! Where the you?" She was talking through Roy now, onto the open channel.

Mason's voice interjected. "Clarke… he's there."

"What's going on?" Roy wasn't following. "Who's there?"

Mason ignored the question. "Roy. Bring a car to the front entrance. Now."

Mason's inflection was clear enough. Roy wasn't going to ask again. "Right." He reached for the ignition crank. Loretta mimed him a thumbs-up and slid out toward the second vehicle. "Hang on." Roy stopped her. "Mason you said car, you mean cars, right?"

"Wrong…" Mason's breath was short, beneath it Roy could hear him shuffle, prop, and shuffle again. "…We only need one from now on."

Roy gulped. *Jesus, what was happening in there?*

Choke. Crank – clockwise quarter turn. Ignition. Timing stalk. Throttle stalk. Handbrake. Neutral. Crank – clockwise, a final half turn. Engine start… Nope.

"C'mon!" Roy banged at the wheel.

The process for starting the Dietrich couldn't have been any more complicated. With the tutorial he had been given long relegated, Roy was instead adopting another age-old tactic – the 'pull every lever you can see, curse and hope' manoeuvre.

"Here, give it to me." Loretta snatched the crankshaft from his hand and circled to the front of the radiator. "When I say go. Ignition, the lever on the left, and then give it some gas."

Roy just looked at her.

"Idiota. How do you think I stole that other car? My husband collected these pieces of shit." Loretta cranked a half turn. "OK now."

Miraculously the engine, in all its forty-eight-horse-power glory, roared to life.

Roy just looked at her in awe. "Should you...?" He pointed to the wheel.

"No." She jumped in the passenger seat. "Let's go."

No sooner had the Dietrich's wheels bitten into dirt, did Roy hear in the distance a sound that made his stomach lurch. It was a wail he was all too familiar with, a wail that only explosions and gunfire could bring... the wail of police sirens.

The palace drive was long and straight, maybe half-a-mile. On either side ten-foot hedges amplified a causeway feel. Like bulging dam walls they strained under the weight of overgrowth. Their peaks, leaning in for each other, were trying to complete an arc.

As heavy as she was, the Dietrich's acceleration was impressive. Foot punched to the floor, it took not even half the drive to hit top speed. As it did the engine transitioned from tractor chug to winding whirr.

"Mason, we're almost there." Roy spoke above the gale flowing over the windscreen-less bonnet.

On cue up ahead Roy watched the iron-studded palace door recede into the darkened entrance archway. Mason and Clarke leapt from the maw, both with rifles to their shoulders. Mason took a knee next to a corner of stone. As he swept his gun across the front garden Clarke skipped forward until she found cover behind a terracotta pot taller than she was.

As Roy skidded to a spongy stop beneath them, both hustled down the landings travertine stairs then dived into the Dietrich's rear bench seat. Mason had eyes only for Roy, while Clarke crouched low and backward, her brow and rifle the only things visible over the leather as she covered their six. Watching her so serious, Roy and Loretta instinctively slunk down in their seats.

"Take the service ring road." Mason pointed. There was no time for any 'hi, how are yous'. "We need to do a lap of the palace. Abner has David; they are making a run for it."

"What about the others?" Loretta cut in with a solid amount of nerve.

"There are no others," Mason spat from the side of his mouth. "Let's go!"

"What do you mean, no others?" Roy was struggling to compute the simple phrase. He made to rise, he suddenly wanted out of the driver's seat, but from behind Mason slapped a hand on his shoulder. "Roy, drive!"

Fuck. Roy reached for reverse, but before he could find the gear he stopped... because right then, in front of all of them, the most curious of sights skidded around the bend.

Chapter 39

"The shed..." Abner was short of breath, "...the shed is a storage garage." He was limping heavily, dragging an unresponsive leg behind him. "Arrgh." He seethed as his leg caught on a half-buried rock. A surge of pain shot up his left side.

The fucking Mexican had been quick, unbelievably quick. He had almost fully completed his draw. Milliseconds more and the bullet in his thigh could have done some more serious damage.

Abner was draped over David's one good shoulder providing directions. Locked together like a pair of corresponding crutches they supported each other across the palace rear yard.

"Left, towards the river. Follow the horses."

Through a smattering of trees a structure appeared. Annexed to the royal stables, the long-since neglected shed had imbedded weeds springing from the mortar of its bluestone walls, and holes through its slate roof.

Abner propped at the sliding barn door, balanced on his good leg, and used all his strength to haul the thing aside. Knowing what was waiting in storage for him on the other side, it was satisfying still to hear an intake of breath from David to his side.

Inside was overflow... from the royal garage.

Before them, taking pride of place among a bevy of future classics, sat two 1903 Spyker 60HPs. Original royal playthings, they were a his-and-hers set.

"I give you the world's first four-wheel drive racing car, six-cylinder, all wheel braking..."

Silvery-grey, the coffin-shaped racers looked as sleek as a turn of the century vehicle could. Large racing numbers on the flanks led to a sharp V-shaped bonnet. Off their front grilles sat two oversized golden lanterns. A signature of the Spyker brand, they looked more like copper diving helmets than headlights.

"Get in..." Abner pointed to the one with a black 5 in a white circle. He himself moved to the other, with a green 8 over yellow. "We're taking both." He spoke out ahead at the cars not noticing that David had remained at the door.

Abner popped the hood of 8 before turning to 5, and then back to the door.

"What are you waiting for? Let's go."

"Abner... who are they?" David's face was solemn. "I'm not going anywhere until I know."

He was serious, Abner could see that instantly. His silhouette, framed by the square of light behind him stood strong, with its shoulders back.

Abner knew, there was no point continuing the charade, not here, not now.

"They are from a different time, David. A future time."

The boy's face showed no emotion, no shock, no nothing.

"And. They are here to take me back…" Abner lowered the hood slowly "Because so am I." With a surprising turn of pace he slid back to David, and took him by both shoulders "But they underestimate us, boy. The gift of foresight has made them arrogant." He moved, still holding David, leading him to the cars as he talked, his voice tinged with a desperation that had not been present all mission. "Come, I have a plan, a plan that they will never see coming."

"Running? Is that your plan?"

"No David." Abner's eyes widened. "Munich is my plan… We are going to beat these bastards to their own portal, and shut down this world with them still in it."

From the bluestone cave a deafening twelve-cylinder duet fractured the air with symphony of backfire. The two cars shot out ahead of a cloud of dust like missiles from some great stone submarine.

For Abner it was like riding a bike. A smile split his lips. Straightening up, his thin Spyker tyres dug into the gravel and launched him forward with neck-wobbling torque. With speed the steering became loose and the car seemed to bunker down and tap into its rally-bred memory.

Out in the open David also found some sort of groove. With only one good arm to fight the lack of power steering he was finding it easier to turn with acceleration rather than the actual wheel. His Spyker looked to be on ice as it drifted from one overcorrection to another around the palace exterior.

"The gate David! Get to the front gate," Abner yelled over the roar of his sixty horses.

As the Spykers rounded the southern corner of the C-shaped palace, Abner had his eyes glued on the oasis that was the front drive. Enticing like a siren, the hedge-lined corridor consumed him completely. Drifting past the front entrance, almost sideways, he was blinded to the Dietrich sitting there and thus never saw its four occupants all watching him... their mouths agape.

CraCraCraCRACK. Automatic fire melded into one extended jackhammer. A line of bullets strafed the Spyker's side. Snapping his head to the bonnet, he saw bullets thudding down the length of his car quicker than he could follow, piercing the thin aluminium as if it were a bed sheet. From engine to cabin, it was the third and fourth rounds of the volley that found flesh, slamming into Abner's hip and abdomen.

"Argh!" He saw spots, fat black ones. It was his same wounded side. The nerve endings in it squeezed beyond their tether, logjamming his spine in their desperation to overcome him. As he fought to control the Spyker, he crunched down low, pinning his elbow between the car body and his own. Even with pressure on the wounds a pool of warmth soaked his seat.

Fishtailing like matching burnout lines, both Spykers entered the drive side-by-side. Only inches apart they accelerated away from the Dietrich. Abner looked across at David. His son's veneer of confidence had evaporated, the blackness behind his eyes was softer, the inky depth there now not so deep. The boy knew that inside Abner's cabin at least one bullet had found its mark.

"You OK?" Abner got in first.

"Are you?"

"Don't worry about me, just worry about getting to that train."

Abner looked back. The Dietrich, giving chase now, was just straightening onto the long drive behind them; they had a couple of seconds' lead at best. Inside the burgundy behemoth he could see four familiar faces.

Jacob...

Smashing his accelerator through the floor his fingers wrenched at the leather steering wheel. "Let's go!"

But just as his Spyker hit top speed, both in front and behind, a multitude of crises began all at once.

From behind, another volley of bullets ricocheted off the rear of his vehicle. Abner winced, before turning as much as his busted leg would allow to loose off some wild round-arm shots of his own. It was with his body facing backwards, his pistol poised over the rear, that he noticed the Spyker's totally exposed rear mounted fuel cylinder had been punctured. Dumping fuel by the gallon, petrol was jettisoning out in a perfectly cylindrical rod, just like the spout of a fountain.

Fuck...

He heard the sounds of horns.

Fuck...

Turning he could see that his predicament ahead was no better.

Blocking the gate some quarter-mile away – having skidded to a halt nose-to-tail – was a line of black police cars.

A procession of helmets scurried behind the line like they were running a trench. Popping over the bonnets one after another at least twenty officers trained their weapons down range.

Fuck... His path of escape had just become a bullet-ridden dead-end.

If that wasn't enough to crush a man's spirit, Abner's final labour would come in the form of a cough that spluttered from underneath his hood.

Black smoke spluttered from his engine as a second, third and fourth cough hacked their way free.

The Spyker began to lose momentum.

"Enough!" He cursed into the sky.

Speed, fuel, hope. All were draining into the gravel metre-by-metre.

Abner's chest expanded, his whole body swelling with a stubborn defiance.

Not while I'm still breathing...

He turned backward again to the Dietrich and loosed off the rest of his magazine, save for one round. Behind, the burgundy tractor braked and swerved, creating some much needed space.

Next he was up, scanning the side of David's Spyker; amazingly it was as yet untouched. Over the roar of the engines he yelled, "Keep it steady!"

Manoeuvring his car over, he closed the gap between them until the two cars were wheel to wheel. "I'm going to jam my accelerator!"

Abner searched his immediate surrounds. There was nothing. The cabin was not just bare, but stripped back for racing. He looked up, calculating the dwindling distance to the police roadblock. As he did, a new option, the only option, hit him.

A smile split his lips... *Let them burn.*

Sensing the occasion like a faithful steed, Abner's Spyker gave one last kick, pulling itself away from David's. Abner was two hundred metres from the line. Another five seconds was all he needed.

Four...

Leaning in, he caressed the wheel like a stallion's mane. "Get me there."

Three...

He was almost close enough.

Two....

He could see realisation dawn on the faces of the police line.

One...

There was no stopping him now.

Suddenly, as if on cue, the Spyker spluttered a final cough. As its engine stalled for good the cabin transformed instantaneously, as if the engines had just been cut on an aeroplane. With the thumping V6 absent, just a rhythmic hum of tyre remained. The mind-bending suddenness of the silence brought with it an unexpected clarity.

Abner looked back... to the one whom this was all for, David. Their eyes met for a moment. The boy, with uncertainty, fear and finally a deep knowing in his, was exactly that, his boy once again... and it was with that image in his mind... that Abner jumped.

Rocks, dust, blood, bone and Newton's second law in reverse, Abner tumbled across gravel for what felt longer than humanly possible. No longer able to differentiate between the broken or bullet ridden parts of his body he caught flashes of the world with each rotation, still shots of consequence slipped in among the chaos.

Up ahead, his Spyker – coasting on momentum like a train on rails – sailed dutifully forward. Next to him, David's own – its four-wheel braking system working hard – kicked up shrapnel as it skidded to a shuddering halt. Behind, the Dietrich also slammed on its brakes. The heavy crimson beast lurched forward, gouging a grove a full three inches into the drive.

Rolling still, Abner felt his immobile leg dredge a path through the gravel. Finding purchase on a rock like a ship's anchor, he was jolted to a sudden stop. With his lower half numb he came to a rest – his pistol in one hand, the other holding a clump of clawed dirt – in the middle of a bizarre three-step. The Dietrich was maybe a hundred metres back while the police line was another hundred ahead.

Pushing himself up onto his one good knee, Abner wheeled around in an arc towards his own, fast disappearing Spyker. On either side he saw police, with horror on their faces, dive for cover.

His world slowed as his focus narrowed.

The impact, it was like two mechanised rams butting heads. An ear-piercing clang was followed almost instantly, by an all-consuming, heavy metal on heavy metal baritone groan. Reverberating up the runway, it hummed through Abner like a speaker set to only to bass.

As the Spyker smashed deep into the police line its front found purchase. Digging down, the rear was vaulted skyward, its underside shooting up in an arc.

Pausing at its zenith, the car teetered on the precipice of destruction, undecided whether to tip back, or over. The petrol cylinder, exposed over the boot, twinkled with a glint of afternoon sun. Hanging in the air like a honey pot, still spouting its amber nectar, it was the exactly eventuality Abner had been waiting for.

He took a breath, aimed, and fired...

A sole-shaking explosion tore through the police line with such force it threw Abner back onto his behind. Three vehicles as well as the Spyker were instantly disintegrated. A rolling flame spread like a wave left and right, quickly enveloping those not directly impacted by the crash. Like a choreographed Las Vegas fountain, a chorus of ignition, then explosion, burst up from both sides.

Abner though was not watching the show. From his backside, he had already flopped to his left, spun 180 degrees in the dirt, and slammed a fresh magazine into his pistol. He glimpsed David, standing in his seat, staring over the bonnet of his Spyker in awe of the destruction.

"David!" Abner raised his pistol, and let rip with a volley of cover fire. "Go!"

Abner trained his attention on the Dietrich now; its four occupants had clambered up and out and were using the body of the vehicle for cover. He fired from his side, his world vertical. He just needed to give David some time, time to escape. If he could still ensure that, and then this would all be worth it...

But next to him a second rifle cracked to life.

What... no...

Turning his head he saw that David had rolled over the rear of his Spyker and was lying flat on its petrol tank facing backwards. He was firing with the dead Mexican's automatic.

"David...?"

But the boy ignored him.

Abner felt a stab of anguish. He knew what he was doing. "No!" he choked. "The train!"

Return fire cracked now from the Dietrich. Bullets pinged into the dirt around them, but Abner didn't flinch, he didn't care. Anger burned inside him hotter than the fire at his back. He screamed uncontrollably as he fired back.

"YOU...!" *You people, you've ruined everything.*

He was totally exposed in the middle of the drive, but knew he was safe, they wanted him alive. "You want me! Come and get me!" He screamed at the top of his lungs as he unloaded the remainder of his clip.

The firing from the Dietrich ceased. There was moment of silence. *Had he hit one?* He couldn't tell. He reached to reload, a final magazine. That was when he felt a set of hands from behind, yanking him underneath his arms.

Abner looked up, squinting into the sun. With his eyes awash, he felt, more than saw, his boy above him. No words were spoken... none were needed. Taking his weight both literally and figuratively, David dragged him up into his Spyker before he too clambered inside, and punched them the hell out of Dodge.

Chapter 40

Location: .... 43.8563° N, 18.4131° E
Present day name: .... Sarajevo, Bosnia and Herzegovina
IDTF Classification: . Tear Four
Date: .... June 28th 1914, 1455 hrs

After almost yanking the front door off its hinges, Mason spun the Dietrich around in a circle of dust. With the front-end spinning toward her, Clarke vaulted herself over the bonnet 80s style, and sprung into the front passenger seat. Not quite as game, Roy and Loretta fell into the back a few seconds later, completing what was effectively a reversal of their previous seating positions.

Roy was still arse-up as Mason gunned the Dietrich down the drive; the lurch sent his head and shoulders crumpling further into the footwell. All arms and legs, he righted himself just in time to see the rump of David's number five Spyker disappear through the line of destruction ahead.

Clarke propped her rifle on the dash and cracked off a burst of shots into the smoke. "Shit..." She racked back her sleeve, exposing her G-Shock. "The Orient leaves in five minutes!"

"The train?" Mason picked up her inference. "What makes you think...?"

"Think about it. If he knows what we think he knows, then he has to be heading for the station."

"Motherfucker..." Mason clicked. "He's going to try and shut us down."

"Wouldn't you?"

"Roy?" Mason boomed over his shoulder.

"Yeah."

"Which way?"

Luckily Roy had been listening, because he needed every possible second to get his bearings. He turned his face to the sun. It was commencing its lazy, late afternoon descent behind him. East, they were facing east.

"Um, north, we need to head north... which is..." he was whispering to himself, doing the N-E-S-W maths. "Left! Then we'll head straight, kind of... over the Kaiser Bridge. The station is on the other side of the bazaar."

Fortuitously – if one could call the death and destruction of innocent police fortuitous – Abner's plan to use his car as a rolling bomb had cleared the police roadblock. Flying headlong into the fire, the Dietrich bulldozed a pocket of clean air in front of it. Parting the smoke like the sea, flames pushed up and around the grille in opposing licks, creating a hole for the car to emerge unscathed and at full-speed.

Clarke shot up in her seat, scanning the road. "Left, there are tyre marks going left."

Roy watched Mason battle with the wheel, trying to manoeuvre the two-tonne beast left, even as a chorus of its own screeching rubber told him no. He was giving the Dietrich's accelerator no relief, and duly, its forty-five-horsepower motor was offering all it could.

"There!" Clarke raised her rifle as the Spyker came into view at the end of the street. "Quick, we're losing them."

It was true. Even as it was, obviously helmed by a novice, the Spyker was increasing the gap between them. Like a pinball the racer slung-shot from side-to-side across both lanes, only just missing oncoming traffic.

Traffic... that was one word for it.

A horse, clopping the bluestone, reared from its cart as the Spyker missed its head by inches. As it did, a bevy of barrels tipped from the flatbed it was pulling and spilled across the road.

Not even acknowledging the brake pedal, Mason dodged the barrels like he was racing slalom, left, right, left, right.

"Hold it steady, Goddammit." Clarke had her cheek pressed to her rifle. The Spyker was bobbing across all their views like a MiG dodging missile-lock.

Before she could get a bead on it, before any of them could get a bead on it, the Spyker veered wildly left around a bend.

Fishtailing out of control, the Spyker's arse bounced up onto the kerb with an axle-jarring jolt. Pedestrians dived for cover as it bunny-hopped sideways and into a collection of trashcans, launching one down the street like a spot-kick. While the screech of rubber heralded some warning, David's inexperience behind the wheel was impossible to factor. As the Spyker bounced off the kerb and found the road again Roy could only stare in wonder that no pedestrians had been hit... yet.

Right then left, the team gained ground with each corner the Spyker mishandled, but they could only watch on helplessly as on the straights the raw speed of the racer left them seemingly stuck on the spot.

On Roy's periphery shocked onlookers blurred into one continuous wall, their heads snapping back and forth in waves as first David and then they sped by. *A car chase, in 1914?* He could only imagine how unheard of this was.

From the brick enclaves of the downtown streets both vehicles burst onto the southern promenade of the Miljacka River. The low-slung sun assaulted Roy's eyes. Throwing a hand up, he caught the river whisking by somewhere below him on his right. As the Dietrich roared like a hungry lion chasing its far nimbler prey, Roy realised they were heading west now, towards Schiller's delicatessen again.

Ahead, the Spyker was the first to approach the Kaiser overpass. Veering in front of an oncoming truck, it launched skyward over the cobblestone bridge before bottoming out its suspension on the other side.

In its game of unexpected chicken, the truck was not so lucky, or so nimble. It swerved uncontrollably, up onto the footpath, before careering into a packed fruit stand. The truck crushed both the wooden cart, and the crowd around it. Bodies rolled like pins under the vehicle, painting the tyres red. Those not straight runover were tossed into the air and onto the road directly in front of the Dietrich.

"Oh dear God." Loretta covered her eyes.

Unflinchingly, with his eyes peeled, Mason kept his foot planted. Just as if they were barrels, he dodged one and then another pedestrian before – at the final possible moment – he braked hard and pulled right. With its tyres screeching the Dietrich missed a mangled local by only inches as it rounded onto Kaiser Bridge.

The Dietrich's wobbly suspension bobbed it like a ship over the bridge. Roy's view swung from sky to road to sky and back again. As he hit the arcing apex he couldn't help but look back at the destruction they were leaving in their wake, at how wrong he had been.

"Roy!" Mason's husk snapped him around. His question was obvious... the Spyker was nowhere to be seen.

Finding his own voice, Roy shot an arm between Mason and Clarke. "The station. It's on the other side of the bazaar. He probably took that laneway…" Roy pointed at an upcoming left. "If we do the same we can horseshoe around it."

"The other side of the bazaar?" Mason repeated.

"Yeah. If you go…" Roy tried again.

But Mason cut him off before he could finish. "There's no time."

"But the only other way is…" Roy's voice dropped away when he realised what Mason was saying. "We can't…"

But oh yes they could.

Mason punched the gas, launching the Dietrich past the final available laneway turn, and straight into the densely packed open-air market.

Built in 1462, Sarajevo's Bascarsija Bazaar was nestled in among a high-density pocket just north of the Miljacka River. Built, razed, condemned and saved thus far as history dictated it should, the maze-like avenue of inter-connected shops was about to have a new chapter of devastation inserted into its storied script.

The first merchant saw them coming. Positioned head-on in front of the entrance – as if his store was a ticket booth – he had full view of their approach. His eyes, dark with eyeshadow, pressed down with doubt before bursting wide with fear.

"Move!" Roy waved a hand from the back seat.

The man dived, not a second too early, before the Dietrich reduced his stand to splinters. Copper urns, glass statuettes, dyed linens and God-only-knows-what-else crashed off the Dietrich's hood as it ploughed through the tinderbox cart and into the slender, arched entrance behind.

Like a child staring out through a window and not fore-seeing a tunnel down the road, Roy's world immediately constricted. His mind struggled to process the instant change.

Stone streaked past, so close he could touch it. The roar of the engine – suddenly amplified within the seismic tunnel – assaulted his ears.

...We can't be doing this!

Down the alleyway, people, goods and animals spilled from each storefront over an endless blanket of overlapping rugs. Save for a thin line of exposed cobble down the middle, either side was stacked high with shit. Roy waited for the Dietrich to bog down, to snag or to be met head-on by something, but somehow it pushed on, its engine revving well past redline, if redline was even a thing in 1914. The sun's rays, obscured by low-hanging tarpaulins, split the path with sheets of brightness. Like guillotines of light they flashed from above as Roy passed under one, two, three, like a slow strobe. The deeper the car hurtled, the further Roy felt the market walls sandwich in. Screams echoed from everywhere. His senses overloaded. Mason's must have too, because just as they passed their next curtain of light... he hit his first pedestrian.

A local man, drawn to the commotion, stepped out from his shop. With a wicker broom in his hands, he was struck mid-stride by the front tyre of the Dietrich and launched back against his shop. Spinning like a top he bounced from the glass back again into the car, this time further down, along the side of Roy's running board. Rag-dolling a messy pirouette, front to back to front again, he hit every panel on his way down.

Roy could only watch as a blur passed him by, but to his horror, right before the man was set to fall off the end of the vehicle – into some kind of safety – his shirt snagged on the golden trim of the rear wheel arch.

Jolted against rubber, the smell of burning flesh assaulted Roy's nostrils. The man screamed as his skin seared. He tried to push himself away, but his arm caught in the Dietrich spokes, and snapped around violently, relieved of its connection to shoulder. As his one remaining arm flapped above – trying to find purchase on anything it could – Roy snapped into action. Leaning over the edge he reached for the man.

"Give me your hand!"

The man was manic, frothing at the mouth. His only hand left flailed madly.

Roy's fingers fluttered against a wrist, but found no purchase. He lunged further, tipping precariously... just as the Dietrich smashed through another storefront.

Debris rocked the car body, flashing past Roy's exposed head. The impact was too much, too much to correct. He began to overbalance, to tip.

Oh shit... he was going over.

But just as his feet lifted from within the car, he felt a hand on his back.

"Where are you going?" It was Loretta.

Hang on Loretta, that's it! With his torso now completely over the edge, Roy's eyes met the man's. His open palm came down just as he felt Loretta tugging him backward. His fingers clutched... at nothing but clean air.

"No!"

In the very instant he was yanked upward, Roy watched the man's shirt give way, and him drop beneath the wheel with a sickening pop.

Roy fell into the cabin and rolled backward into Loretta's lap. Her eyes fell onto him, a relieved smile on her lips. "Got you."

He was momentarily lost, his throat thick with words for a man history did not, and now would not, ever know. Before he could muster something, Clarke yelled into the air above her head. "Roy! Left or right?"

He propped up onto his elbows to see they had almost smashed completely through the bazaar; its end beckoned, growing like a light down a tunnel. Roy closed his eyes, envisaging the iPad map of Sarajevo. "Ahhh, right. Hard right."

"You sure?"

Finally he snapped. "Yes, I'm fucking sure!" He couldn't help himself, his anger finally bursting free of the dam that was his chest.

Clarke's head almost spun off her neck. She shot him a glare, but Roy faced it head-on, her bark the furthest possible thing from his mind. After seconds, seconds that they didn't have, and the jolt – and scream – of another human sized speed-hump, Clarke turned around. Roy turned too in his seat, to study their wake. *Goddamn*, it was unconscionable. Like a hot knife through butter they had cut an unmitigated swathe of destruction through the unsuspecting and totally unprepared marketplace. How many people were dead because of them he didn't want to imagine.

Like a *Dukes of Hazzard* set piece, the Dietrich burst from the bazaar's northernmost portal. Throwing off a blanket of dust, it launched over a set of three steps. Floating, its front wheels spun in slow motion as the engine revved the rear ones freely.

Like a bull rider relieved of gravity, Roy's limbs floated in front of his face. Time, it slowed somehow. Beyond his arms he watched Mason dance with the loose steering wheel. Separated from the asphalt, the man had been relieved of all control.

Roy's world crashed with the Dietrich. Dropped on its chassis, the two-tonne machine punched the roadway. Roy felt his coccyx hammer as the car's suspension snapped like a twig. Bouncing on a forty-five, the car suddenly found grip and slung right, sending him on a crunching slide into Loretta. Carried across the road by momentum, the Dietrich smashed against an adjacent row of shops. Roy threw himself over Loretta as the passenger side seared against brick. Sparks shot up, showering his back. Keeping his head down, he couldn't tell whether Mason was punching the brakes or if the car was bogging against the façade, but finally, somehow they ground to halt.

Inside the cabin only the sound of breathing remained.

As Roy slowly lifted himself off her, it was Loretta first who vocalised what they both were thinking.

"Fanculo." She whispered.

"That mean you're all right?"

"Not quite, but I am."

Any relief, though, was fleeting, because no sooner than Roy straightened did he hear a roar from behind.

In the front, he watched Clarke turn which way and that, searching for her rifle, but it was no use. On their inside, David's Spyker shot past, its silver body gleaming, rearing almost. Through the cloud of haze it burst, looking every bit a fifth chrome horseman... on a journey out of hell itself.

In the back of their wounded chariot a sense of familiarity returned to Roy. Between curiously onlooking locals, he noticed again the distinctive peeling of a passing green house door, and then a faded 'vacant' sign on a thread store shopfront.

"We're almost there!'

Mason spoke over his shoulder. "OK, there's every chance some sort of checkpoint will be set up looking for us. Get ready for anything."

Clarke cocked the bolt of her rifle; Loretta pulled a soft case full of ammunition across her chest. There was no reason to play coy now; they wouldn't be bluffing their way through anything now. Roy just sat, collecting his breath; he saw no point even in bothering to wipe the layer of dust that caked his face.

The station appeared at the end of the street.

"Fucking hell," Clark breathed.

The four hearts inside the Dietrich sunk as a one... because parked at the end of the platform... the Spyker sat idling away, completely empty.

Chapter 41

Location: ....43.8563° N, 18.4131° E
Present day name: .... Sarajevo, Bosnia and Herzegovina
IDTF Classification: . Tear Four
Date: ....June 28th 1914, 1503 hrs

A trail of blood like a line of red breadcrumbs trickled from Abner's leg. His suit pant was soaked through. Draped even as he was, once again, over David's shoulder, the pain in his side was blackout inducing.

It was after three – departure time. Save for the Orient, chugging on the spot a plume of smoke into the sky, the platform was empty.

"Izvinite, šta radite?" An Orient officer leaned from a door ahead before stepping down onto the carriage running board. The man had a clipboard in one hand and was waving them away from the train with the other.

"Odmaknite se od voza."

Abner didn't need a translation. He raised his free arm and fired a shot clean into the officer's forehead. With his eyes locked in shock, the man's legs crumpled beneath him before he fell sideways away from the train.

"They will want to take you back, take us both back," Abner coughed as he and David stepped as one over the body. "You, my boy, are more important than you can imagine... Whatever you do, you must keep pushing, onto Munich, into the unknown. You mustn't let them take you, under no circumstance."

"Stop..." David uncoupled their arms. He stepped up first into the doorway left open by the officer. "Where I go, you go..." But as he turned with an extended hand his words fell away.

Abner stood three steps back. Instead of on his boy, his eyes peeled down the length of the platform. "Remember David, how important you are."

"Abner. What are you doing?" David's voice pitched an octave.

"They're here..."

"And, so what?" David's hand was still outstretched. "We can head them off on board, from the back."

"No, we can't."

Abner was still not facing him, maybe purposely so.

"But..." David's retort caught in his throat,

Abner turned now to his boy, the corners of his eyes pressed tight.

"David. Go."

A piercing whistle shot from the locomotive. The whole train shuddered as its huge brake calipers released. Under the front engine, steel wheels spun on the spot before they found purchase and jolted the train forward.

"Abner...!"

But David was moving. Pushing back from the disappearing door he worked his way along the interior hallway, trying to keep himself in line. Through the glass neither man could hear each other, but from window-to-window Abner could read his boy's lips.

"Abner... don't do this." David's eyes were red with tears. Abner had never seen him cry before. *"Please, you can still..."*

But it was wishful thinking and both men knew it.

No, this would be where Abner's journey ended. With an otherworldly calm he spoke to himself as much as his boy. "If only the world could see you now... You have been all the son a father could hope for... and all the man this world needed you to be."

With one final longing stare he watched his son press a palm to the last window of his carriage. *"Dad..."*

Abner turned away from the train. As he jammed his last clip into his pistol he saw a black bob rise over the end of the platform ramp.

Right... the military bitch was first... *of course.*

Crouched low, she was running with both hands on a rifle to her side.

With the train accelerating slowly, still gathering momentum, she closed the gap quickly. Only metres from the rear carriage's aft most handrail, she was only a short sprint away from launching herself aboard.

Next to the body of the dead Orient officer, Abner dropped to one knee to aim. As he cracked off his first shot, though, his leg gave way beneath him. Catching himself with an outstretched hand, his shot ricocheted off metal.

The result was good enough. The woman flinched down, skidded to a stop and dived left. From the expanse of the platform she rolled like a cat down the metre or so drop onto the tracks.

With the chugging of its engine now one continuous rumble, the train continued to motor up to speed.

Another whistle pierced the sky.

Abner watched the final carriage pass him by. With his focus on the fast receding Orient crest emblazoned on the rear, he slumped down onto his buttocks and allowed himself a grimace-tinged smile.

He'd done it, David was safe.

Slower now than warranted, he drew himself back around, a sense of relief overriding the pain in his leg, hips and lower back.

Right where the woman had rolled, her head popped over the platform lip. With no train in sight for her now, he and the dead officer were the only things left on the platform.

Peering down the length of her rifle he watched her study him for the briefest second. She had him dead to rights if she wanted.

...But she couldn't, could she? No.

At the absurdity of the stalemate, Abner almost laughed. He raised his pistol into the air and fired lazily into the sky. "Try and drag me back alive, I dare you!"

The woman did not flinch an inch.

"What are you doing? I said..."

Those black eyes of hers, they burned with the intensity of a thousand suns, a hatred of incendiary proportions. It was while staring into them that the penny for Abner not only dropped, but shattered. It was in their hollows that he knew he was wrong.

Spike, he had withheld one last secret...

Her rifle cracked.

Resignation hit Abner harder than any bullet could. He felt a microsecond of hammering on his forehead... then nothing of his skull exploding.

Chapter 42

Location: .... 43.8563° N, 18.4131° E

Present day name: .... Sarajevo Train Station, Bosnia and Herzegovina

IDTF Classification: . Tear Four

Date: .... June 28th 1914, 1510 hrs

Clarke nudged the end of her barrel into Abner's chest, poking at him like child would a creature washed ashore. "You run into Spike motherfucker, you make sure you tell him who sent you down."

The Dietrich limped next to the platform, into the void of the departed steam train. Bobbling over the uneven rock it nudged right up to the lip.

Mason looked up the metre or so at her. "You done?"

Clarke abandoned her very loose vital signs survey. "Yeah." She leapt down from the platform landing with two feet onto the leather of the passenger seat.

In the back seat, Roy was now almost eye-to-eye with Abner's elevated corpse. Even to him it was obvious the formalities of an 'Anomaly Death Ping' were not necessary. A crater through the brain had a strange way of making that procedure irrelevant.

"Bastardo." Loretta, next to him, was burning her own hole through Abner's listless face. "He didn't deserve to sacrifice himself like that."

She was right. From afar, the romance of Abner's final sacrifice had been almost stirring. The significance of such an act, to have something like it locked away as your last conscious choice, that was a choice reserved for... *a hero*.

A familiar face imposed itself on Roy's consciousness, like a veil behind his eyes, obscuring what he was actually seeing... *a hero like Spike*.

Lost almost in Spike's bouncing smile, it took a second for Roy to realise there was in fact no lingering poetry on offer on the train platform. There was no cinematic bullet wound, final breath or slow closing eyes... just the stark reality of death. Punctured, broken and contorted, what remained of Abner was a sad, bullet-ridden mess, a mess that some poor bastard was soon to lump into a furnace and cook far beyond well.

Clarke nestled into her seat. "It's over."

"What about the boy?" Mason reminded her. "He's not just going to roll over."

"Well..." Clarke motioned to the tracks like someone who'd done her part. "You better get us back to Munich before him."

Mason wrapped his knuckles on the wheel. "We won't catch the train in this thing, she's on her last legs." He turned to the back seat "Roy!"

"Yeah?"

"We need another option."

Every damn time. "Excuse me...? Another option for what?"

"To get us home."

"Mason..." Clarke interrupted their exchange. She was whispering through the side of her mouth at his back.

"Not now Lane."

"Mason..." Her 'Mason', more forceful this time, was equal parts distracted. "Who cares where we're going... just... start... fucking... driving."

Both Mason and Roy turned to trace Clarke's gaze. Over the bonnet the magnitude of their predicament was as obvious as it was crushing. A veritable army, no, an actual army, was turning into the end of the street. One after another a line of flatbed troop carriers thundered down the main station road. Climbing down in waves from their back, at least fifty men swarmed into a pack. Like a throng of angry bees, they rolled as one, shoulder-to-shoulder in riot formation.

Clarke nudged him. "I said..."

Mason's eyes were darting from the tracks that disappeared right, to the road behind the procession of troopies that skewed left.

"They are not the local police..." Clarke was reading his mind. "There is no way we can shoot our way through that, don't even think about it."

A guttural grumble echoed from deep within Mason. Roy could see his mind ticking over. Retreat, it was obviously not an option he was accustomed to.

"Mason." Clarke grabbed him by the arm. "We need to move."

"Guys," Roy interjected. "This will sound crazy, but I don't think they are here for us. Whatever you do, do it slowly."

"What!?" Clarke snapped around.

"Look." He pointed. It was true not a single soldier had singled them out... yet. "I think they might be here to quell the coming riots."

Clarke spun back around in her seat. The soldiers were close now, so close they could all see the patches sown onto their black and red tunics – *SAJ Serbian Special Forces*. She turned back. "Riots?"

"Yeah, the anti-Serb riots." Roy nodded. "They kick off directly after Ferdinand's death. Two people are killed within hours – which has probably already happened – and a bunch of homes and businesses are set to be razed. It's going to last two full days, and descend basically into a spree of government sanctified ethnic hate crime."

Clarke snapped from Roy, to Mason, to the street and back to Mason.

Mason spoke for her. "We can't take that chance, Roy." His knuckles, taut with tension, were bulging white on the wheel. He floored the accelerator... only for the Dietrich to shoot backwards in reverse! As it did, he threw an arm backward over Clarke's headrest, locked his eyes on the road and shouted. "Everybody get down."

As expected, they didn't realise they were playing, the unsuspecting launch of the Dietrich was enough to draw the SAJ's ire. Whistles blew, shouting echoed... and then the front handful of soldiers raised their bolt-action rifles and fired.

Bullets cracked into the Dietrich's grille as it rocketed backward. Its hood ornament – a circle split by two arrows – disintegrated. Clarke returned fire as Mason swung the lumbering beast around 180 degrees. Righting the Dietrich back-to-front, or back-to-back, meant Roy and Loretta were now at the mercy of the onslaught. A bullet puffed through the leather backrest above Roy. Once again without even thinking he found himself over Loretta, shielding her with his body.

The lag between getting out of reverse and into drive felt like an eternity, but finally Mason crunched them into drive. He steered the Dietrich in a swerving retreat south from the station forecourt, just as a chorus of klaxons began sounding at their back.

"Clarke, time?"

She thrust her G-Shock forward. "1520… 28th of June 1914."

"Right." Mason was yelling over the lashing wind, doing the maths. "If Heathcote received Zhu's message around midnight on the 27th, then that means we have a little under thirty-three hours to make it back to the Tear before the deadline. It's thirty or so on the Orient, but the next train doesn't leave until 3pm tomorrow." He paused while he crunched in another gear. "What are our options? What other modes of transport are available?"

Oh God. Roy had an idea; he just couldn't bring himself to say it. Just the thought of it caused every fibre of his sole to quiver. His phobia, the emerging technology, 1900s statistics on its death rate, it was nuts to even think it.

"Roy? What is it?" Over him, firing shots backward, Clarke could see straight into his fear.

"Well, these soldiers, I'm pretty sure I know where they came from, and how they were able to gather at the station so quickly."

"Explain…" Mason looked into the space where a rear-view mirror should have been. "…Quickly."

"Well, the entire reason Ferdinand was here in Sarajevo was to observe a series of joint military exercises. They took place on the outskirts of town this morning. There was a host of radical new war mechanisms on display, automated rifles, long range cannons, razor wire and also… high altitude reconnaissance." He paused in the hope they were getting his 'drift'.

Clarke refused to spare him. "For fuck's sake Roy, spit it out."

"OK, by any chance has either of you had an experience with the Air Force? Because I think I know where I can find you something to fly."

Chapter 43

Location: ....43.8563° N, 18.4131° E
Present day name: ....Outskirts Sarajevo, Bosnia and Herzegovina
IDTF Classification: . Tear Four
Date: ....June 28th 1914, 1600 hrs

The Dietrich transitioned from dirt to grass and coasted to a stop. Roy's eyes jolted open, the way they always somehow did when it was his stop on the tube back home.

Fuck. How long had he been out?

He grabbed immediately for the base of skull. Sans a shot-out headrest, his neck, craned skyward all ride, had seized at ninety degrees.

He felt a hand on his knee.

"Feeling better?" Loretta was seated next to him in the backseat.

"Yeah, thanks."

"Sounds like you needed it."

He knew instantly what she meant. "Was I snoring?"

"Like a chainsaw. Lucky we haven't passed another soul for miles."

As Roy cracked his neck back into first position he could see they were off-road, well past civilisation. Having parked next to what looked like the edge of a pine forest,

Mason was wrestling with a thicket of blackberry, pulling it like a tangled sheet over the bonnet of the Dietrich. Clarke was behind him, her shoulder to a tree trunk, peering down the length of her rifle into the scrub.

"I'm guessing we're here?"

"Your aeroporto?" Loretta nodded. "Yeah, we're here?"

Neither of them laughed, that wasn't her point.

Thanks to his hair-brained suggestion, they finally had some semblance of a plan. Supposedly, a makeshift military camp – near on abandoned – was now only a short trek through the trees. As Roy hopped out of the Dietrich, he hoped for all of their sakes he was right... at least about the abandoned part.

"The Militärluftschiff II, M.II for short." Roy held out a reluctant hand. "I give you Austro-Hungary's finest, remaining, lighter than air flight-craft."

Crouched as they were, overlooking the football field-sized clearing, the Zeppelin below was impossible to miss. At well over fifty metres, it was tethered down, but floating still, about three metres above the ground. Crisply white, like fresh linen, it looked solid, yet exceedingly vulnerable. Its internal steel skeleton jutted from beneath its thin rubberised shell, like the emaciated ribcage of a rescue dog. In what seemed an afterthought, a tiny pilot's cabin and three large Maybach C-X engines were attached at even intervals down the floating underbelly.

"Weather permitting, those three engines, with two turboprops each, should be able to get us up to about 65 to 75 kilometres per hour."

"Hang on." Mason stopped him. "What did you mean, finest 'remaining' aircraft?"

"Well..." Roy didn't want to spoil their party. "...The Militärluftschiff III, this ship's successor, was destroyed about eight days ago, I think it was June 20th, in an accident over Fischamend. Some crazy pilot tried to loop it in a biplane. Instead he sliced the top, tore a hole and ignited the hydrogen that these things are filled with. The explosion killed nine people. The accident, if you can call it that, will, or possibly already has, led to the end of the Austro-Hungarian airship program."

"You're kidding." Mason shook his head.

"It's history." Roy offered. "Like I said with Čabrinovič on the bridge today... I couldn't make this stuff up if I tried."

"You said a plane was involved in the accident?" Mason's voice spiked with the originality of a new idea. "I can see one over there by the tree line." He was looking to the right of the Zeppelin, toward an assortment of temporary shelters. There, resting beneath a crosscheck of tarpaulins was the unmistakable winged shape of an aeroplane.

Roy had already anticipated the notion and was ready with his pin to pop his bubble. "Aeroplanes are not viable yet, not for what we need. That one is almost certainly an Albatros B.II or Aviatik B.I model. They were both short-range reconnaissance biplanes shared between Germany and Austria-Hungary. Unfortunately they can only carry two crew, and have a maximum flight time of a few hours at best."

"So, can it make it?" Clarke realigned the inquisition, her stare having never left the Zeppelin.

"I'm pretty sure, fully fuelled, it should be able to take us non-stop."

"Pretty sure? That's a big if."

"Well, soon these things will be crossing the Atlantic. That's a one-hundred-and-ten hour journey. Way I see it we should be right with thirty or so."

"It doesn't look like we have much choice in the matter." Mason had heard enough. "Major, you think you can work it out?"

"Of course."

Roy gulped. "So... you've never flown one?"

"No Roy," Clarke snapped. "It shouldn't come as a surprise that the military did not teach me to fly a fucking hot-air balloon."

"Technically, it's not a hot..." but Roy stopped himself, thinking better of the correction. Instead he turned to Mason for some help.

The man's face offered him little comfort. "No idea here. Clarke is our best bet. Was it choppers in Iraq or Afghanistan Major?"

"Apaches in Afghanistan."

A soft voice came from behind them, saving Roy some embarrassment.

"Where is everyone?" It was Loretta.

The question was a valid one. The makeshift base looked deserted, like everyone had up and left mid demonstration.

"We can only hope in Sarajevo, dealing with the riot." Mason brought his hand to his brow, furrowing his gaze. "Clarke, how many we got?"

"Four so far by the entrance. Allow maybe a handful more in that tent, could be a barracks. None so far at the bird."

"Right." Mason clapped his hands like a quarterback. "Roy, Panatoli, you two head straight for the M.II. Start untying the anchors. Clarke and I will sweep the camp and meet you there." He eyed both academics, regarding them a second longer. "I know I shouldn't be asking for more, but we're almost there I promise. One last push from you both and we're home."

Compliment, pep talk, thinly veiled orders, whatever it was, the acknowledgement for once was at least comforting.

"Questions?"

Roy and Loretta both shook their heads.

"Good, let's move."

Roy hauled himself over a wooden cattle fence. As far as he could see the Militärluftschiff was dormant, but still, as a force of some newly acquired habit, he hunched low as he ran, as if he were approaching a chopper instead of a blimp.

He and Loretta fanned out in a V, under the nose of the aircraft. With a clear line of sight down the belly, Roy could see that the aircraft was indeed unguarded, and that four ropes, two on either side, tethered it to the ground.

"We'll leave one tether in place until Mason and Clarke arrive." Roy moved to the port side.

"Right." Loretta took off towards the starboard.

Getting to work on his first set of knots, Roy realised how tired his body was, how much he was running on fumes. The rope was soaked through, as thick as his wrist, his forearms burned as he clawed at the clumped mess.

Absorbed in the knot, left over right, right over left, he was only halfway through when he heard what sounded like a thud in the mud behind him. The unmistakable squelch of footsteps on grass followed... and then a voice that made his blood freeze.

"Ko si ti?"

Fuck fuck fuck fuck fuck...

But cocking his head, Roy realised something was off. The voice, it wasn't directed his way, it had come from his right... from Loretta's side. He spun in horror to see a soldier standing over her, his back to Roy's side of the ship.

How could I have been so stupid? Next to the soldier hung a rope ladder, still flapping from use... The soldier had been in the pilot's cabin!

"Niko." Loretta lay her knot down slowly and rose to her feet. Her accent was flawlessly Serbian.

The soldier's shoulders relaxed somewhat at the sound of his native tongue. "Šta si radio tamo dole? Ne možeš biti ovde."

"Ah... Ja sam proveravala..." Loretta coughed. "Ah... ja." Her eyes darted over the soldier's shoulder at Roy.

Roy didn't need to be told see she was blanking. She had been caught red-handed with her hand in the honey pot, linguistic abilities or not, there were few lies capable of hiding the fact.

Roy watched the soldier shift, his stance open up, his hand slowly reach around his back, to a rifle hanging there. He realised he had to do something. He felt for the bulge at his own lower back. Like a heat pack, the piece of metal there had been burning a hole in his spine for the last two hours. It was the Luger that Spike had given him. Hidden in his satchel since Braunau, it was twice now he had been caught without it. First the Orient, and then in the deli, he had conceded at the palace that his stubbornness was not a good enough reason to flirt with the chance of a third.

Roy pulled the weapon. What he intended to do next, he had no idea. Something would come to him. Silently, he took three paces forward. It was wishful thinking, because nothing did.

"Hey...!"

The soldier spun in surprise.

Roy felt his tongue abandon him. 'Hey,' shit... that was all he had.

There was a silent impasse between the two. Roy was a kid, standing up to a bully for the first time, realising only as he did, the stupidity of the idea.

The soldier looked at him curiously, at the pistol shaking in his hand. "Spusti oružje." He spoke with a frightening calmness. He was young, maybe in his mid twenties, tall and built.

"Um..."

"Spusti svoje... You drop yours." It was Loretta who spoke for Roy, translating as she did. "Ili će on uskoro razneti svoje jebene mozgove... Or else he will blow your fucking brains out."

"Um, yeah..." Roy thrust his pistol forward. "...What she said."

The soldier seemed to calculate his options; his eyes darted from Roy to the rope ladder.

"Uradi to...! Do it!" Loretta commanded.

Finally, the soldier obeyed and let the sling of his rifle drop from his shoulder. He kept his eyes glued on Roy as Loretta continued to speak. "Položiti, ruke iza leđa... Lie down, hands behind your back." She leaned to the side of the soldier and looked at Roy with her mouth agape. "Where did you get that!"

"Spike gave it to me..." Roy looked at the weapon a little self-consciously. "It was Deryk's."

The soldier lowered himself to one knee as they spoke. Neither of them noticed him pause mid-descent.

"Well, thanks."

"You're welcome. I just hope this guy has no idea, that I have no idea how to use it... and that he can't speak English."

"You won't have to." Loretta scanned her surrounds. All three of them were in the aircraft's shadow. "What can we use to tie him up?"

Subconsciously, Roy followed Loretta's lead and subverted his gaze. With a complete lack of awareness he waved his pistol at the pile of supplies to his right. "What's that over...?"

And that was when the soldier struck. From Roy's periphery he launched off one knee, up underneath his pistol arm, and had the gap between them closed in an instant.

"Roy!" Loretta screamed.

But it was too late. The soldier cannoned into Roy's sternum and together as one they shot backward onto the paddock grass.

The Luger slipped from Roy's grip, falling beneath him somewhere during the crash.

Tumbling over, the men separated. Roy rolled over his back, splayed out and vaulted to his feet. The soldier wasted no time either. Pushing up from his belly, he had both fists cocked at the waist and his head tilted back. Like the fighting Irish, he assumed a classic early-century fighting stance.

Roy searched the ground for his pistol, spending time he did not have.

The soldier advanced, and lunged with a right.

The man swung like a freight train. Roy felt the air break in front of his nose. He flexed back, well after the fact. *Jesus*. Forgetting the gun, he slid backward and squared up. With hands on either side of his eyebrows, he peered with wide eyes through the small gap created. It was a technique that 'John the Swan' was halfway through beating into him back home, the 'if you're shit at boxing, at least be able to defend yourself' technique.

The soldier, emboldened by his near miss, reared back and threw for the stars. But Roy was on his game now; he stepped back – letting the punch sail by – before advancing in on its wake. With muscle memory taking over, WHACK, he delivered a jab straight into the soldier's nose. It was a flinch more than a punch, soft but quick, just hard enough to stun.

There was a pause between them as Roy let the soldier stumble back. He himself was almost as shocked; he had never hit anyone without gloves before. His middle finger swelled, but he felt no pain, his adrenaline was pumping hard.

The soldier's eyes watered. He let out a roar and charged, left, right, left, right, like a drunken bar fighter. The first pair Roy was able to step back on, but quickly the soldier was within his guard. Overwhelmed, Roy caught the third and fourth on his forearms just as they were about to smash into his ears.

Softened even beneath a block, Roy's brain rattled inside his skull. The soldier's explosion had brought him close, super close; Roy could smell his tobacco-stained breath. Full of confidence he grabbed Roy by the collar and reared his head back. He was going for a headbutt!

In that instant, like it had been sucked clean out of his ears, Roy's mind tagged out and his body took charge. Primed for a chance to fight on autopilot, on instinct, he felt his skin prickle and his fists surge with electricity.

The soldier's forehead bore down. The distance was perfect now... perfect for a short, compact uppercut!

Roy dropped his hips and pushed up with his legs. A shot cracked like gunpowder under the soldier's chin as his head jolted back like a whip. Roy used the space created to slam home another, and then another. As he did he heard the chatter of teeth on teeth, of enamel shattering enamel.

The soldier stumbled back, his legs wobbly, before he tripped and fell backward onto the grass. Standing over the man, Roy's body released him, letting his mind tap back in. Clarity returned, and that was when he saw it... the Luger... it was on the ground... right next to where the soldier had fallen!

Roy's heart sank. He knew instantly that this was it for him, the end of the line. There was no way he could beat the man to the weapon.

The soldier seemed to realise as much. Without a rush even, he reached for the pistol, smiling as he savoured the absurdity of chance over worth. He rubbed his battered chin with one hand while raising the Luger lazily with the other.

"Assass...in?" His attempt at English was impressive. "...Yes?"

Roy's shoulders dropped; he would have laughed if it wasn't so crushing. "If only you knew."

It was no use though, his words sailed well over the soldier's head. Roy didn't know what to do. He was completely helpless. He closed his eyes. If this was the end, then he didn't want to see it.

There was a creak of movement... Roy tensed, waiting for the pain.

Would there be pain?

THUD!

What...

Instead of a gunshot, a thick, sickeningly meaty thud burst forth, as if through a soup of flesh.

Roy's eyes fluttered open, his whole body was compressed down, frozen with anticipation.

Standing over the slumped form of the soldier was Loretta. She was holding the soldier's rifle by the barrel, baseball bat style. Her chest was heaving, her eyes were glued down... on a patch of red forming on the man's right temple.

The talons of tension released from Roy's chest, and it took a second for him to breathe. "Loretta..."

With his whole body tingling, Roy stepped over the man and into the line of her stare.

Her hands were shaking.

"Hey." With eyes only for her, as if she were his world, he gently released the weapon from her frozen hands and dropped it to the ground.

"I'm sorry." She mumbled, her voice soft. "I didn't mean too..."

"Hey, hey, it's OK." He grabbed her by the shoulders and turned her away. "You saved my life."

She seemed to come back to reality with his touch. "I'm sorry, I had to."

"I know."

"Is he going to be OK?"

"Of course," Roy lied.

"I didn't mean to... kill..."

"Hey, don't even say that..." Roy pulled her into a hug. With her head on his chest he looked over her shoulder. Whether she meant it or not, the soldier had yet to move.

"He was going to kill you." She was speaking to herself, justifying something she didn't need to.

"I know. Hey..." He pushed back, so they were face to face. "Thank you."

They were only centimetres apart. Her eyes had the beginnings of tears in them. Roy wiped at a blade of grass on her chin. "You are the only thing getting me through this."

The first tear fell down her cheek... and that was when she leant in and kissed him.

It was soft, so soft and only for a second. Roy let her lips take his. He was in shock, but not. For the second time in as many minutes he felt his brain tap out, and his body take over.

Pulling away, Loretta looked at him, really looked at him. No words were spoken, none were needed.

"We need to..." Finally she spoke softly, more to herself. "The ropes."

"Right..." Releasing her, Roy knelt down next to the soldier and collected the Luger. "Let's get you aboard; let me worry about getting these ropes untied."

"Are we right?" Mason's voice boomed from over by the barracks. He and Clarke were striding over. Clarke had a smattering of blood across her razor sharp cheek.

She pulled up at the feet of the crumpled soldier. "What the fuck is this?"

Roy was ready though. "He kind of sprung up on us."

"Really?" Clarke raised her eyebrows. "You did this?"

"It was a team effort."

She stepped straight on, patting him on the shoulder as she passed. "Nice work."

Roy felt a stab of guilt. The absurdity of being praised for bashing a man half to death, was it any worse than attempting to be modest about it?

"And Loretta?" Clarke reached for the rope ladder.

"She is on board already."

"Right..." she began to climb. "Let's get in the air."

Roy studied the grass directly below his feet one last time before he grasped the swinging ladder. "Right..."

Strangely, after everything, his fear of flying was the furthest thing from his mind.

Chapter 44

Location: .... 48.1351 N, 11.5820 E
Present day name: .... Perlacher Forrest, Munich, Germany
IDTF Classification: . Ridge
Date: .... April 22nd 2017

Dr Ronald Zhu pushed back his office chair and hoisted a red stamped 'confidential' folder high above his head. Next was his cement slab of a laptop, then a stack of oily pizza boxes. With his desk in a state, and his eyesight the way it was, the clean-and-jerk was necessary.

"Where the hell are you?"

In Zhu's defence, the mess was not entirely his own, because the desk was not entirely his own. Commandeered from some poor sap directly after the Tear Room meltdown, the 50s-style launch control behemoth had served as his workstation, sleep-station, and – ashamedly late last night, with a water bottle underneath – piss-station. *Had it been two days?* He reached up for his chin to what constituted his excuse for a beard. The facial hair to hair-from-mole ratio was tipping. *Where had the time gone?*

Zhu tossed aside the pizza boxes. They fell dangerously close to his yellow-filled Aqua-Pure bottle. "Where... are you?"

The source of his frustration – buzzing incessantly from some mystical chasm of secrecy his desk had no intention of revealing – was a certain instrument he had only just perfected. So new was the device – an additional irony – he had yet to even name the thing, and therefore could not properly curse it.

"FFFF..."

"Everything OK over there?" Tabatha Stan-Lakely popped her pink bob over the waist high partition.

Zhu looked up. "Tee. Sorry, excuse my..." The spark of an idea flickered his eyes from guilty to excited. "Hang on, perfect, can you come over here a second and help me? Bring that eagle eyed vision of yours."

Tee skipped around way too enthusiastically for the time of morning it was.

"What's up?"

"Listen..." He held up a finger. "Can you hear that?"

"The vibrating?" She let out a laugh. "You funny old thing, have you lost your phone?" Bending down on the side of the desk – turning her nose at, but not mentioning, his relief bottle – she rose with something. "What's this?"

The block in her hand looked nothing like a mobile phone. Rudimental in design, it was slightly bigger and visibly weighty in her palm. Looking like a bullion bar of stainless steel, a small blue pixelated screen on one side was the only indication it was anything other than a battering tool.

"Aha, Tee you truly are a lifesaver. That... is..." he paused, still unable to think of a name. "That... is... a little something I have been working on. Something that you of all people should recognise, considering..."

"Considering what..." Tee studied the brick in a new light now; something about its construction specifically looked familiar, like three days ago familiar, like Magnus Thorn kind of familiar.

"It's yours Tee. You were right."

Her mouth dropped. "No way?"

"Yes way.

"But my work... it was purely theoretical. How?"

"You're not giving yourself enough credit. The 'how' was the easy part, you had all the steps laid out like a set of subatomic IKEA instructions."

"But what about the Higgs boson particles? How did you...?"

"Got them no problem, as many as we need. It's amazing the lack of red tape one encounters when the world is about to end."

Tee looked between Zhu and the brick, she was cradling it now like a baby – her baby.

"I'm sorry I know it's a little larger than your design, but the rest should be pretty familiar. Just as you thought we could, we basically enhanced and miniaturised the principles of our HFESC balloons."

"Does it..." She looked scared to ask.

"Work? I think so. Just like you speculated, it detects disruptions to space-time on an interdimensional level. We should get an alert whenever either an anomaly or Tear has been terminated."

The vibration in her hand took on a whole new significance. "Hang on..."

Zhu smiled as the realisation dawned on her.

"Are you saying we are receiving this signal from a whole other dimension?"

"I am."

"And...?"

He gave her a shrug, his glasses sliding down as he did. "Maybe... It has never buzzed like this before outside of testing."

"Gosh, Dr Zhu." She held out the device, her face all smiles. "They've done it, they have found the anomaly!"

"Well, we'll need to get a message through to Dr Heathcote for confirmation, but yes it is quite possible." Pushing his glasses up his nose with one hand, Zhu made to take the device with the other. Before he could, Tee pulled the device back a touch.

"Hang on... if Richards knows the anomaly is dead won't he just order us to shut the Tear down straightaway?"

Zhu smiled at her perceptiveness – she was cluey, his protégé. He had realised it too, what Richards would say once he knew the anomaly was dead, what course of action he would order.

"It's possible. I was hoping I wouldn't have to tell him, that Mason and Clarke would be back by now. But now I don't think we have a choice. We are running out of time. If our world literally doesn't collapse in..." He looked up to the looming countdown clock at the head of the room. "Thirteen hours and seventeen minutes, the handicap of the President's useless nuclear blast will ensure it does not long after that."

"But Doctor..." Tee's face dropped, her enthusiasm giving way to an immediate desperation. "You have to wait, we have to give the tactical team more time. We can use this thing to somehow try and convince Richards and the President to hold off."

Zhu's face softened, he spoke softly. "Tee, we are scientists. It is our responsibility to analyse the facts, without emotion, and apply logic to this situation."

"But..." Her lip quivered. Somehow already she had a set of bags under her young eyes. "We have to try."

Bless her naïve heart he thought. The device was exactly that, them trying. He smiled a tender smile. "Of course my dear. I will try."

Tee, not wanting to concede, stiffened. A new vein of thought suddenly readable right across her face. "Doctor, we could delay them. Run interference?"

Zhu shook his head. "Tee, no."

But she kept spitballing. "We could get the word out to a select few. Ramirez, Mitchell, Petiffer, we should start with them, we can trust them. The Detachment-Array would be a good place to start. Maybe we can find a way to interlock it somehow…"

"Tee, please." Zhu tried to stop her.

"If Ramirez can manipulate the radiation readouts…"

"Tee!" Zhu was louder this time. "Please. You must stop. For your own safety."

"What…?" 'Safety', the word threw her. "Why?"

Zhu didn't need to say anymore, she knew. His familiar playfulness was gone. He reached out and softly took his device from her palm. He could see the cogs in her head aligning, the look of horror forming on her face.

"Doctor. What are you trying to say?"

"Tee, I'm sorry, but there are more lives at risk here than just the members of the tactical team, seven billion more to be exact."

"But Doctor…" Her voice was whisper quiet now.

"Tee, I'll delay as much as I can… but it's on them now to save themselves."

Richards was seated behind a boardroom table inside a room that served as both his office and the camp's crisis room. He had an array of LCD monitors behind him, and one brightly painted red telephone in front.

Zhu stood on the opposite side, tantalisingly close to the bat-phone. Standing even as he was, he was only just eye-to-eye with the seated General as he spoke.

"So Mason, he has done it again," Richards grumbled.

"Four times now."

"It's impressive... really."

"Agreed."

Extending his arm, Richards exposed a gold watch. Even on the last clasp, the thing was constricting his wrist. "Half a day to spare."

"Thirteen hours now." Zhu corrected. "According to the device sir, exact nullification was actually nineteen hours fifty-three minutes ago. We only received the signal once the device came online."

"Hmmm." Richards flipped Zhu's stainless brick in his palm. In his hands the device looked small. "I'm going to need a name for this thing. Give it some credibility when I tell the President."

"Of course." Zhu agreed; the thought had occurred to him. "Credit should go to its creator sir."

Stanlakely? Was it one word? No, Stan-Lakely, two words.

"Stan-Lakely...?" Richards repeated the name they had just finished discussing. "Really?"

"It is a scientific precedent."

Richards crossed his butcher's-block forearms. "Considering that she was willing to sabotage this entire operation, Doctor, I find your sentimentality a little hypo-critical."

"That may be true." Zhu took the jab. "But misguided or not, it is credit she undoubtedly deserves. I was thinking 'TSL-1' if I could be so bold as to make the suggestion?"

"Hmmm." Richards didn't seem convinced.

"She is an amazing physicist, by far the best we have. I have no doubt that it will be her soon standing where I am, as head of the operation. Hell, it's not beyond the realm of reason even, to suggest she will be at the cutting edge of Tear creation come another decade or two. This slip, I implore you, will be nothing but a blip on her record."

"Fine." Richard's whiskers blew. "But, I'll need to make an example. Correct her trajectory."

Zhu adjusted his glasses. "Umm... I'm not sure I follow."

"Don't play dumb, Doctor. I need another."

Zhu shuffled, "Um, might I suggest then, Ramirez, Mitchell or possibly Petiffer?"

Richards didn't even ask for an explanation, he just wrote the three names down. "Done."

Zhu let out a nervous chuckle. His claws picked at each other under stooped shoulders. "You'll pick one, right? Not all three?"

"I said I needed an example doctor, not a fucking Kumbaya. I'll pick as many as I fucking wish."

"Do I have your word at least that no harm will come to them?" Zhu was trying to extricate the knife he had inadvertently samurai-slashed through his team's back.

"What happens to them is none of your concern, Doctor."

"They are good scientist... good people."

Richards studied him. "Doctor, the fate of the world rarely falls to good people. You of all people should be aware that we can't achieve anything without a little sacrifice."

Zhu let out a defeated sigh. Touché.

How could he judge Richards when he himself was technically the greatest mass murderer to ever walk the Earth?

He couldn't, that's how.

Three Tears, twenty-odd billion people so far, with another five or so billion to come in this Tear Four. The numbers were incomprehensible, too large to even fathom, let alone solicit an emotional response.

The pair stood in silence. Zhu waiting for Richards to vocalise the course of action he knew was inevitable. Richards' cheeks bulged as his jaw clenched. Zhu could see the idea materialise in his mind. With so much death between them it was still amazing to see how quickly he could justify the problem of abandoning his own men to die.

"Doctor…"

"Yes."

"How long do you need?"

"Six hours on this side, maybe a few more on the other."

"OK." Richards was steely faced. "Don't delay for anyone. Shut it down."

She was somewhere under France, ninety-odd metres below the ground, or maybe it was Switzerland, she couldn't be quite sure. Having been in her golf cart-transport for a while now it was entirely possible she had skipped the border.

Her driver coasted to a stop, the battery-powered whirl of the electric motor cycling down.

"Thank you Private Grey." She tried her best to remember their names, even with the recent influx.

"My pleasure, Ma'am. Best of luck for this afternoon."

"I appreciate that. Will you be right to turn around? Hate for you to do a twenty-seven-kilometre loop just for me."

"That's all right Ma'am, there's a turning circle a little ways up."

Private Grey nodded and accelerated away in relative silence, leaving her alone in the concrete tunnel. Next to her the LHC vacuum tube stretched in both directions, disappearing at the extremity of her view as it rounded the gradual bend of its cross-country circumference. Looking like an aeroplane engine mid-service, the metre or so diameter pipe was covered in smaller hoses, electrical components and wiring. Nearly fifteen years old now, it was amazing the thing had only cost seven and a half billion Euros in 2010. It was a small price considering...

The soldier standing guard at her office door stood fast and shot up a salute.

"You don't have to do that, Barry." She placed a hand on his shoulder as she swiped herself in.

"Excuse me, Ma'am." Barry placed a hand across the door. "You have a visitor. Been waiting twenty minutes now. Had his own pass."

She looked from the handle to his arm.

Realising then he was blocking her path, Barry dropped his hand. "Sorry, Ma'am."

"Please Barry, don't even, thank you for the concern."

The wonders of a rank aligned world were something she would never get used to, that and being called 'Ma'am'. It had been three years now she had been a... *geez, she smiled, what was she again?* Her Department of Army, DA, rank was purely ceremonial, so irrelevant to her and her work she couldn't actually remember the correct title, *was it Major Major, Lance something?*

Barry wasn't done though; he leant in towards her, his voice softer than usual. "If I can be so bold, Ma'am, there's a bit of radio chatter, seems your visitor is required else-where... in pre-decon maybe?"

"Thank you, Barry." She smiled. "I'll make sure to tell him, but I can't imagine he'll care. The best of us he's supposed to be, but they obviously didn't factor tardiness into the selection criteria."

Barry nodded knowingly. "Deserves all the time he needs I reckon, what with what he put his hand up to do."

Her visitor was waiting where he always did, on the cot in the corner of her office, the one she spent more nights in than she did her proper bed.

The same line, always... she was waited for it as she walked in.

He pushed down on the mattress. "Tee, you know I'm going to miss these springs."

Yep, she rolled her eyes. "That's Professor Stan-Lakely to you."

"Right." He got up and took a bow. "How could I forget... the prodigious young professor sending me away?"

Tee scooped up an apple from the bowl next to the door and threw it at him. "I'm only two years younger than you."

"True, and you've been lead physicist here how long already...?"

"Three years, you know that."

"I rest my case." Her visitor took a crispy chunk, seething in an explosion of juice. "Has it really been that long since numbnuts kicked the bucket?"

"Please don't call him that."

"Sorry, Professor Numbnuts."

Tee rounded her desk, sat and swung her chair round to face him. "You know he taught me everything I know."

"Don't be modest, we'd still be chasing our tails if he was still around. The Gateway was your discovery, we all know it."

Tee searched her desk for the floating effigy of her and her mentor. She found it between her charging iPhone XX, and a very specific palm-sized stainless steel case with a blue screen. In the floating hologram, together with cheesy grins – her with her pink hair, and him with his tortoiseshell glasses – she and Dr Zhu could not have looked a stranger couple of scientists.

She sighed... Zhu had died before he could see their project come to fruition. Two years into her five-year journey a heart attack had taken him and, ready or not, the reins of the whole operation had been left to her.

Her visitor followed her gaze. "Am I going to get a memorial when I'm gone?"

Tee let out a laugh, heavy with realisation. "Not a moment sooner."

Off the cot the man bounced and scooped up her phone. "Right then." He placed the XX on its side, letting a latest feature of self-correcting-balance do its thing. Rolling to her chair he lifted her with one hand, spun her in a pirouette and dipped her just in time for the perfect shot.

From his arms, Tee looked up into his eyes, hers were suddenly watering. "What are you doing?" Her voice was a whisper.

The question was so much more than literal. His playfulness was a cover for something they were both refusing to acknowledge... and they both knew it.

"I... I don't know."

It was about the most honest thing she had ever heard him say, and it completely stumped her.

Instead of talking, together they looked to the phone once more. The camera, recognising their faces, snapped away and the holographic projector on her desk initialised automatically... A keeper it judged, worthy of light.

But as smart as their world had become, no advance in technology could gauge properly the sadness buried deep behind their eyes.

Tee looked to her desk for something – a stainless steel block – and then up into his eyes for what would be the final time.

"I've got something for you..."

"Hang on."

He leant in and kissed her.

"Magnus... They are waiting."

"Then let them wait..."

He was stalling, and she couldn't have been happier he was. Together in silence, their gaze fell upon the miniature version of themselves forming on her desk.

When finally the image had formed he spoke. "Tee, I'll be back, I promise."

The hologram, it was one that would remain in place for nearly thirty years, time-stamped and tagged. While its glow would fade in time, somehow the hope it brought her would burn brightly just the same.

Tabatha Stan-Lakely and Magnus Thorn – June 21st 2024.

Thirty years on... and still she would still be waiting for him to return.

Chapter 45

Location: ....48.1351 N, 11.5820 E
Present day name: ....Perlacher Forrest, Munich, Germany
IDTF Classification: .Tear Four
Date: ....June 29th 1914

David stood, like the trees around him, breathless. Concealed in plain sight, a slither of his body, like the crest of the moon, was awash, bathed in the reflection of the artificial campsite lights. Rain pattered the leaves above. Through the canopy it fell fat, matting his hair before washing away in rivulets the dried blood on his cheek. Peering from the blackness, his icy blues danced green. His focus, locked on the incandescent yellow of a specific, golden glow, was unwavering. His left eyelid quivered. *So this is how they arrived... and this is how they plan to leave.*

As if he were privy to a magician's secret, David watched wave after wave of man and machinery appear seemingly from nowhere. From the golden lake they marched – their faces as calm as the very surface from which they emerged – down the ramp, and straight into motion, as if enacting some prepared plan.

'Tear' was the name Spike had 'volunteered'. How apt it was. The golden pool looked to be doing exactly that, tearing a hole through the very fabric of the forest itself.

From the Tear one last pallet emerged. Different somehow, obviously precious, a tiny Asian man nursed it, patting it like it was alive, as it rolled to a stop at the base of the ramp. The Asian man fumbled with a whistle around his neck, his fingers, seized into a claw, struggled to find his lips.

Pausing as one, the camp froze at the sound of his three short sharp blasts. A collective breath was held as he approached a rectangle of black glass attached to one side.

With just a tap the glass illuminated white. Two days ago this seemingly otherworldly feat would have been amazing, too much for David to comprehend, but now he had eyes only for what the display flashed bright.

It was a set of numbers, counting down from sixty.

59:57

59:56

59:55

David watched still.

A countdown to Armageddon it was, but he was in no hurry, not yet.

He had an hour to wait, and wait he would... for the one who had started all this... The one they called Jacob.

They had been flying for nearly thirty-one hours, and still they were airborne. Unlike anything Roy had ever experienced, the Zeppelin seemed to hover on the spot, just below the clouds, as Eastern Europe flowed beneath them like a slow-moving treadmill.

Below the fog of his breath, expanding and contracting upon the louvre window, Roy traced a moonlit river. Thirty hours was an eternity to be left alone with one's thoughts. In the murkiness between wake and sleep faces flashed over the landscape below. He had seen so much death, a truly staggering amount, beyond the realm of comprehension.

Civilians, colleagues, friends, protectors... *good men*, he saw them all.

From one face to another, a constant question was woven like thread. It was a question that weighed upon him, one he could no longer contain. Roy tipped his forehead onto the glass, the small circle of condensation swelled as he exhaled.

Roman, Gerhard, Simeon and Spike, especially Spike, was that what they were... good men?

His head sank down the glass until his chin came to a rest upon his knuckles. A wave of emptiness swept over him.

Was that what any of them were...? Was that what he was?

He closed his eyes, but the darkness offered little respite. Somewhere, deep down a rabbit hole of realisation the answer beckoned. Like a trail of breadcrumbs the obvious enticed, until, before he knew it, he was descending uncontrollably into a mindful hell of his own design.

Right and just, was that what this cause was trying to be?

Then at what cost could their survival be justified?

Voices echoed in the dark. Zhu's, Spike's, Heathcote's and Clarke's, their previous comments flooded his mind. With clarity now they slotted together beside one another. *"Shut down..." "Detachment..." "It doesn't matter..." "They don't matter."*

The bottom of the rabbit hole, it came up at him at a thousand clicks.

To survive... That was their goal.

But to save their world... That was their mission

"Goddammit." Roy pushed his head up.
To suceed... at ANY cost.
He knew what that meant now.
To survive... they would need to exact the ULTIMATE cost.

Rain began to lash the Zeppelin as a grumble of thunder rolled like a bowling ball across the land. In the pre-dawn darkness it was difficult to see, but Roy could tell the weather was turning. The moon had disappeared behind the cloud, and a wind was now howling through the cabin.

Letting the darkness envelop him, Roy looked to Clarke and Mason over by the Zeppelin's steering controls; both were lost in the application of flight. Turning his attention to the cabin, he found Loretta in an adjacent corner. In what was not a large space, she had pushed herself as far to the side as possible and curled her legs up to her chest. Starring absently out of the window at the carpet of black below, she had hardly spoken since they had boarded.

"Hey," Roy whispered.

Loretta's head lolled to face him, streaks of mascara ran in lines down her face like a dried water-colour. Somehow still she looked beautiful, it was just in a different, vulnerable way.

"Did you get some sleep?" His voice was soft.

She offered a weak nod. "Did you? You look beat up."

He smiled. "After everything, it's strange, but I'll take beat up."

She let out a breath and smiled too. "Sorry..."

It was her first in nearly a day and a half and he was glad to see it. Stretching her shoulders back, as if shrugging off a cape of fragility, she spoke with a new energy. "Do you think it's true what they said, that David is really heading back to the Tear?"

Roy shot a glance at the occupied duo of Clarke and Mason. Facing forward, their figures were silhouetted by the incandescent glow of the control panel.

"I don't know. After all this, nothing would surprise me."

"Something's not right," she said, wiping at her cheeks, "I have a funny feeling about what's waiting for us down there."

"Well..." Roy nodded knowingly. "That's exactly what I wanted to talk to you about."

"Switch on, people." A voice from the panel interrupted them. Mason was looking back from the flight controls. "We're making our descent."

Rising from their seats, Roy took Loretta by the hand as they made their way to the front windscreen. He gave it a reassuring squeeze. "We're almost home."

Now at the control panel, it was obvious the weather was turning further. Driving 45-degree rain buffeted the Zeppelin and fell off the canopy like a continuous sheet around them.

"There it is." Mason pointed through the dark.

On the horizon Roy could just make out a soft dome-shaped glow. Like a sports field back home, it seemed to be emanating from a clearing in the forest.

Clarke looked at her watch. "Not bad..." it was a compliment for herself, "...still have time to spare."

As the Zeppelin floated closer, figures still too small to identify scurried about the camp. One in particular, smaller than the rest, caught Roy's attention. He had an unusual gate, more a hunched shuffle than walk.

"Is that...?"

"Fuck me." It was Clarke who was connecting the dots. She raised a hand to her head, shielding her eyes from the lights of the panel. "They're here already."

"What? Who?" Roy brought his hand up trying to do the same.

Clarke brought a fist down on the flight controls. She turned to Mason. "It's Dr Zhu and the Detachment crew."

With Mason silent, it was left to Roy to recoil. "Zhu? What's he doing here already?"

"Isn't it obvious?" Clarke was seething now. "...Motherfucker is here to shut us down."

Chapter 46

Location: ....48.1351 N, 11.5820 E
Present day name: ....Perlacher Forrest, Munich, Germany
IDTF Classification: .Tear Four
Date: ....June 29th 1914

Clarke swung from the extremity of the Zeppelin's rope ladder as it cut through the last of the low hanging cloud. Her body was taut, on an angle; her feet pushed almost horizontal as she looped only an elbow through one rung.

Below her Dr Zhu was waiting under the descending Goliath. In the canopy's rainless shadow, he was alone in a paddock of windswept grass.

Clarke jumped down the final two metres. "Are we interrupting?" Landing with a feline fluency, her shoulders slinked as she stalked towards him.

"Major Clarke, of course not." Zhu fumbled.

She pushed straight past him. "Jam it Zhu."

"What?" Zhu could only watch her back as she strode straight off. As he turned again, Mason was the next to descend. "Captain Mason..." Zhu tried to get his formal greeting back on track. "It of course fills me with joy to see that you both are alive and well."

"Really?" Mason was a little more diplomatic. "You going to tell me this is our welcome party?"

Zhu pushed his glasses up his nose. "Well, I am sure you can appreciate that there is..." he checked his watch, "...less than an hour until the nuclear deadline. It has been over forty-eight since your last contact..."

"Doctor," Mason interjected. "Even if I hadn't lost half of my team, and was willing to listen to your shit, it's a little hard to launch a fucking communications balloon while travelling in another fucking balloon."

"Of course." Zhu looked up at the enormous Zeppelin above. "I must say I am sufficiently impressed."

"Yeah, well you have Roy to thank for it."

"Ah, Professor Roy, fantastic."

Mason made to pass, but Zhu shuffled into his path, holding him up like a mouse might an elephant. "So there are others aboard?" He raised an expectant eyebrow. "By chance has another, maybe significant, local, happened to accompany you back? Another possible addition for the interdimensional case study."

"You mean for your collection?" Mason's nostrils flared. "Well, I was going to ask you the same thing, Doctor." He looked over Zhu's head, scanning the camp. "There's every chance the number one man on your shopping list... is here already."

Roy and Loretta had been reduced to passengers once more. In the main camp – situated within the larger clearing over which the Zeppelin was floating – soldiers hustled about, packing whatever had not been earmarked for 'strategic abandonment'.

Clarke was in the middle of the controlled chaos, barking orders. As people scurried past her, Roy could see that camp numbers had swelled once again to more than ten people. In addition to Clarke, Mason, Loretta and himself, there was Zhu, Jersey – Zhu's designated military escort – Beckett, Heathcote and three additional Detachment personnel. Thick-necked and stern-faced, the additional trio were the very definition of military grunts.

"Here, make yourself useful." Heathcote pushed a folded satellite into Roy's hands. "Take this to the Detachment-Array."

"Huh…" Roy hadn't even seen the man approach.

"I said the Detachment-Array…" Heathcote shook his head. His eyes were wide like 'come on'.

Roy took a second longer to regard the man. *Fucking Heathcote.* Unlike himself who looked like he'd been dragged behind a horse the last forty-eight hours, Heathcote looked much the same as the day they had arrived. He was still wearing the safari suit they had travelled in, and had only just the beginnings of a patchy stubble.

Heathcote, perplexed by Roy's inaction, looked to Loretta.

"What wrong with your boyfr…"

"Hey Heathcote…" Roy couldn't say what came over him, but as the words poured from him, he held the satellite away from his body… and straight dropped it.

Heathcote's head almost snapped off his shoulders he spun around so quickly. His mouth fell open at the sight of the crumpled instrument. Having a conniption of sorts, his words dribbled out. "I… Wha… Di…"

As the realisation of Roy's only possible reasoning occurred to the man, his rat face snivelled into a snarl.

"How dare you! I'm going straight to…"

But Roy could not have cared less where Heatcote was going. With a sense of urgency more than aggression, he snatched the man by the shirtfront before he could finish. "Shut up and tell me something Heathcote… What exactly does the Detachment-Array do?"

Heathcote's lips peeled back as he let out a conde-scending chuckle. "The name is obvious, isn't it? It detaches our two universes and severs the bond. Like pulling a leech."

As measured as he'd tried to be all mission, Roy felt the fingers of his free hand silently clench. "And that's it, we both live happily ever after?"

"Maybe, maybe not." Heathcote's turkey neck wobbled as he shook his head. "Why, what are you trying to insin-uate, Roy?"

Roy felt his fist rise behind his back. He'd had enough of the ambiguity.

Heathcote, Clarke, Zhu and even Spike, they had all alluded to the same notion of an impending cataclysm. In his heart he knew the truth, but still he needed it said... this world needed it said.

"I think you're full of shit, Heathcote." Roy yelled now "What happens to this world?"

Heathcote's eyes narrowed as he smiled. "Wouldn't you like to know?"

And that was enough for Roy to launch a strike.

Heathcote's eyes flashed wide as Roy fist came at him. The man floundered backward, fell to his arse and let out a shrill scream. "No don't!"

But Roy hadn't swung true, not the whole way anyway.

Standing over Heathcote, Roy didn't care enough to regard the man at his feet. Instead his eyes zeroed in on Dr Zhu. The Doctor was ahead, walking the path that led deeper in the forest, towards the Tear. He had Jersey Gianinni by his side, chaperoning him.

Roy spoke without looking down. "You're a piece of shit, Heathcote." He stepped over the man, his knee swinging close enough for Heathcote to flinch down further.

"Wait, where are you going?" Loretta called from behind.

Holding out his hand, Roy turned to her. "I need to speak to Zhu. You coming?"

"But... I... I don't understand?"

"There is something going on here, Loretta." Roy's eyes had softened again. "Something that no one wants us to know about. I've got questions, and I'm not going through another Tear until I get answers."

"Dr Zhu," Roy called out as he jogged. "Do you have a second?"

"Of course, Professor." Zhu nodded as he ducked beneath a branch. "If you can walk and talk."

Roy held the clump of tree to the side so he, and then Loretta, could fall into step behind Zhu. The old man was shuffling as fast as his frame would allow behind Jersey who was out front on point, leading the way. The route towards the Tear's smaller clearing was narrow, single-file mostly. A breadcrumb trail of green glow-sticks illuminated the way; like buoys in the ocean they bobbed at different heights across the undulating ground, casting a neon glow over the soft brush beneath their feet.

"Dr Zhu..." Drops of rain fell from leaf to leaf above, blinding Roy as they fell fat on his cheeks. "I need to ask about the Detachment-Array. Its purpose was something that was never communicated to Loretta or myself."

"The reason for that... is because it does not concern you." Zhu's tone was frustratingly chirpy, completely negating any rudeness on his behalf. "If everyone sticks to their respective field..."

"Then all we'll do is foster the ignorance pervading this mission..." Roy spoke over him, his voice more forceful than desperate. "We need to take our heads out of the sand, Doctor. Do you realise what is taking place on the tactical side of these missions? Do you realise what is happening out there?"

"Hmm, hmm." Zhu was agreeing, but with what part, Roy had no idea.

Before the Doctor could respond properly though, the foursome rounded a horseshoe in the track and broke into a clearing.

"Goddammit," Roy breathed, he would never get used to the sight of a Tear. Beauty... mystique... home... it was all there, in its golden glory, only twenty paces ahead.

As Roy stood dumbstruck by the Tear's wash, Zhu shuffled to a pallet at the base of the ramp. Moving Loretta and Roy to the side, Jersey began stacking boxes by the clearing entrance.

Roy's feet began to carry him forward. "Doctor, did you not hear me...?"

On the pallet, at waist-height, was a large matt-black cylinder, about the size of pick-up truck's gas cylinder. Even without knowing, Roy could tell it was the Detachment-Array. It looked ominous, weaponised... the kind of thing that would require a two-wire choice at the end of a movie. "I said countless people have been murdered."

"Yes, yes, sorry, I heard you." But Zhu hadn't, he was busy scratching his claw-like fingers on an iPad attached to the side of the Array. "Hmm, hmm, very hard. I understand it must have been shocking for you."

"This is not about me." Roy, over him now, put a hand across the screen, drawing Zhu's eyes up. "Doctor, this is about the people in this world. Not just those that have died, but those still living. This is about what this thing, this Detachment-Array, is going to do to them."

Zhu's face softened; he looked like a parent about to tell a child the lie of Christmas. "Professor, you're a smart man... surely you can appreciate that there is no 'them'. If you need it said, then yes, you're right... this Array does not 'detach' their world."

It can't be... but it was the truth he knew.

As Zhu continued, his voice was muffled in Roy's ears, drowned by the thundering of his own heartbeat. "Only by 'collapsing' this world will ours be guaranteed safe."

A lock of rain-soaked hair fell across Roy's face.

Zhu placed a hand on his shoulder. "This will be the fourth, Professor, deleted so far, so do not feel bad."

"Deleted?" Roy's voice was a whisper. "How can you even say that?"

"Have you never deleted a duplicate file from your computer? That is all we are doing. A duplicate file, or a duplicate world, either way they are taking up space, power, memory, jeopardising the security of the legitimate versions of themselves."

"I can't... be a part of this," Roy stammered, taking a step backward.

"An attitude of ignorance, is that what you said before, Professor?" Zhu's smile was more pitiful now; his eyes were so thin they had to be closed. "You should be careful maybe, what you wish for."

Roy was suddenly cold all over, the blood drained from his face. *Was everyone on this mission a monster?*

He took another step back...

And that was when he heard a muffled cry behind him... and then a scream... Loretta's scream.

Roy spun and felt his breath leave him.

Oh... this was not possible.

David stood at the edge of the tree line, one step in from absolute darkness. Holding Loretta by the waist with one arm, his other was pressing a switchblade into the soft skin of her throat.

In front of both of them, Jersey was on his knees, his eyes locked wide in shock. Balancing somehow, upright in the mud, the soldier's arms were resting slack by his side.

Ear-to-ear a perfect slice of blood shadowed his throat. As his body slowly overbalanced and slumped forward, the slice at his neck opened like the mouth of a festival clown.

Loretta stifled a cry. Shaking, she looked from Jersey to Roy, her silent pleading tears mixing with the rain as they cascaded down her blood-splattered cheeks.

David wrestled with Loretta's waist as her knees weakened. Flush as he was with the glow of the Tear, Roy could see that he still looked pale. A cold desperation clung to him like a drug-addled junkie. His eyes were sunken and the hollows of his cheeks depressed as he spoke. "Step away from the machine. Hands where I can see them."

He was grimacing too with every movement. The shoulder of his knife-hand sagged. Lacking control, the razor sharp metal pushed dangerously into Loretta's throat.

"I said step away, now!"

Neither Zhu nor Roy had anything in their hands, but they obliged, fanning backward from the Array in a V.

As he did so, the bulge at Roy's lower back flared, radiating warmth up his spine. Deryk's Luger was still hidden, tucked in his belt. It was screaming like a silent alarm for attention, for a shot, literally, at intervention.

To Roy's right, Zhu's eyes were alight, wider than he had ever seen them. "You came…"

But David silenced Zhu with just his focus, as if he didn't even hear the doctor; his eyes burned only for Roy.

Roy looked to the campsite pathway, a million variables running through his brain. "Please David…" he started, his words urgent now. "You are playing right into their hands being here. This is what they want. Let her go and…"

"How far…?" David cut him off.

"Wha…?" Roy's head snapped back.

"Tell me…" David slowed his words. "From how far ahead… have you come?"

Roy was gobsmacked, his pathetic poker face revealed as much.

"How far...?" *Oh God.* His mind screamed, *don't say it, don't say it, don't say it,* but without really thinking he found his words forming themselves. "Far enough David... to know who you are."

Fuck.

But behind David's washed-out blues Roy caught the slightest quiver of confliction, a name in there, it caught where it shouldn't have.

"Who I am...?" David's smile quickly masked his slip. "Are you really going to try and bluff me, Professor?"

But for once Roy wasn't bluffing.

Wait... Roy's mind was working with a lag of exhaustion so it took him a second... *Does he not know?*

As a silence filled the expanse between them, only the patter of rain falling thick through the canopy could be heard.

"David... did Abner...?"

"Enough of Abner!" David screamed.

He shook his head, as if physically pushing away his growing confusion. Resetting himself, his voice was angrier now, less in control.

"Why are you here?"

"Our world David, it is in danger."

"And yours is worth the destruction of ours?"

Oh shit, Roy gulped, *of course he had been listening.*

Zhu couldn't help himself then, interjecting into the pause. "You can come with us... in fact you must come with us. It is your only hope. This world, your universe, it cannot be sustained." He was going hard while he had the floor. "Only you are special, only you can save yourself."

David's eyes conveyed no emotion at Zhu's revelation. He harboured no shock, no doubt, just a new unsettling focus.

Don't... But again, even as he thought it, Roy couldn't help himself, he needed to finish his question. "Did Abner not tell you who you are, David? Did he not tell you who you would have grown to become? Why they..." Roy pointed to Zhu, "...would want you?"

"Who can one be, other than who he is?" A rumble of thunder shook the ground, hammering home the poignancy of his point. David could not help a laugh, a heavy, weary laugh. He blinked slowly as he adjusted the knife he was holding. Jumping across Loretta's throat and into the contour of her windpipe, a small drop of blood ran down to her collarbone.

Shit... Loretta, hold on. Through no fault of her own, she had somehow become a sideshow to the tension drowning them both.

As David's smile faded, Roy tried to remain calm. He had an idea, a crazy stupid idea, but still it was an idea. "What did he tell you then, your father, about Himmler and Ferdinand?"

The mention of Ferdinand struck a nerve.

"We were in Sarajevo to prevent a war!" David flashed. "Unlike... you!"

Roy could feel the air alive with electricity. *Oh God, what am I doing?*

"So you know about the wars to come?"

"A war..." David mistakenly corrected the plural, "...that sits on your conscience now."

"David, what if I told you you were in Sarajevo to save the lives of those that would be forever in jeopardy as long as you lived?"

"No...!" David flashed again, but something within his voice cracked.

"Don't you realise?" Roy pushed. "You're the answer to all your own questions, David. We are here because of Abner, and Abner was here because of... you, because of who you had the potential to become."

David's lips were blue; his sunken eyes took in Roy's words without resistance. Like on roller coasters both men were cycling at speed through calm, anger, denial and realisation.

Roy paused. It was time for the truth... the whole truth. He stole another glance at the campsite path... *But is that what he wanted? Did he want now to be found?*

"David... in my world..."

"Roy, what are you doing...?" Zhu interrupted him. "He is..."

"Is he?" Roy turned to Zhu, his point not at all argumentative.

"What you're proposing..."

"I know..." And he did.

"But... he is evil, pure evil."

"In our world, yes. But is a man, any man, just his genetics? Can he be judged without considering the accumulation of his actions?" Roy turned back to David, pleading now. "Taken as a newborn, David... you have lived not a single day on the path that our universe laid before you." Just saying the words, Roy felt his stomach lurch. Was he really suggesting what he was suggesting? "To condemn you, no matter how evil, to the punishment meant for another... it is not something any of us should have the right to decide."

Forgive me...

"Because in my world, David, you as the leader of the German Nazi party will bring about the greatest conflict the human race has ever witnessed. As the single greatest mass murderer in history, you will be responsible for a genocidal regime that will displace, persecute and ultimately execute over six million of the world's most vulnerable civilians. Before your final breath in 1945, a further fifty million will die in a conflict that spreads to all corners of the globe..."

Roy felt sick just saying it.

"In my world, David... your name is Adolf Hitler."

Disbelief, denial, anger, Roy was waiting for something to explode from David.

But nothing came.

Watching the boy, and that was exactly what he looked like, a boy, it was Roy who felt a stab, a stab that flooded his insides with sadness. He stood straight, turned his palms and opened his body. "But you are not that man, David... don't become him."

David lowered his eyes to the pool of mud at his feet.

"Show them that the evil they want you for is not destined," Roy said.

David looked up. His face was empty. His eyes were bloodshot. In that moment Roy realised that deep down he knew it was true.

From Loretta's neck David pointed the knife at Roy. Its tip wobbled on the end of his shaking hand. "I came here for you! For vengeance for my father!" His voice cracked. "Instead I had to listen to you argue for the existence of my world." His arm fell to his side, the breath sucked from it. "What you're saying..."

"You feel it..." Roy nodded.

Roy watched as waves rolled through David. Up then down he looked, the knife in his hand swinging back and forth from the ground to his chest, riding the confliction of his will.

"But David, those feelings, they don't control you."

"Aaaargh!" It was anger that flashed over David as his knife shot up one last time. Through the air, end-over-end, his knife rocketed toward Roy before SPLAT... it sank, handle deep, into the mud at Roy's feet.

Releasing Loretta, David took a step back. As she collapsed to the floor, his words fell away with her. "You...!"

With David now completely exposed, Roy felt the Luger at his back burn hot. Ever so slowly he brought a hand around his back, but as his fingers found the handle, he stopped...

No... Roy pulled his hand back around *...he was not one of them.*

As if he knew what Roy was doing, or not doing, David deflated slightly as Roy brought his empty hand back around.

Two words, Roy felt them weigh down on him heavier than any weight ever could. Caught on the tip of his tongue, so much more than just his humanity hung on so few letters.

Spike, I'm sorry... To so many back home, I'm sorry.

Roy's eyes closed on his breath.

"David... Go..."

David stepped backward, one step, then another until he was on the edge of the forest. When he spoke, his words were soft, no longer angry, no longer for himself. "Good and evil, they can co-exist closer than we care to believe... but something tells me you've realised that, Professor. Be careful, because soon a bigger choice will be yours... and you may find yourself on a side you never expected."

The prophecy chilled Roy colder than the wind through his saturated shirt. On those words, David took two more steps, and immersed himself completely behind the veil of the forest's darkness.

Zhu and Roy stood frozen in position, breathless.

It was not until Loretta let out a sob that their trance was broken.

"Loretta..." Roy started towards her when...

"What the fuck is going on here?"

Clarke emerged from the campsite pathway.

The trio's silence was as deafening as it was incriminating. The rain was all that could be heard between them. It hammered down with a seemingly incensed ferocity as Clarke read each of their faces one after another.

"Adolf..." Zhu tried to get in first.

But Roy cut him off. "I let David go."

"What?"

Her tone, days ago it would have sliced through him, but now, he felt nothing.

"I said David, he was here..."

"And..." Clarke turned to Zhu, who nodded silently. She snapped back to Roy and seethed through clenched teeth. "You let him go?"

"Yes..." Roy let out a slow breath.

He watched one of her eyes twitch.

"Who the fuck do you think you are?"

"I think I am not like you..." Roy looked to Loretta. "I think that we are not like you."

"You think...?" Her chin pushed to her chest as her eyes narrowed. "You haven't fucking thought of anything! You're leaving him here to die, you realise that you fucking idiot!"

"No." Roy flashed. "I'm leaving him here to live. You are going to shut down this Tear, and his life here will mean nothing. If anything could be salvaged from this world, then he, deserving or not, needs to be saved... from you... from us!"

"Aaaaagh!" Clarke, without hesitation marched straight at Roy, her eyes burning.

Roy turned himself towards her; he knew what was coming and he was fine with it, happy even.

She was only a metre away when she threw a right hook into his chin.

CRACK, rain snapped off his face and whipped off his hair.

He stumbled backward into the mud.

But, quick as a flash, she was over him again. Picking him up by the collar, she hoisted him off the ground as her fist cocked back for another blow.

Roy could hear Loretta's scream as Clarke's fist paused at the top of its draw.

"You think you're so fucking smart, hey?"

Roy smiled a bloodied smile. "Yep..." He didn't, but God it felt good to say. Drops of blood splattered up onto his face from a split lip, but he didn't care. He leant his head back and inhaled deeply, a feeling of peace washing over him. They could take this world, but they were going to get nothing more from him.

"Clarke!" Suddenly Mason's voice boomed from over Clarke's shoulder. "What the hell is going on here?"

Clarke's fist teetered at its peak. Her breath was thick on Roy's face. Her stare did not move an inch.

"Clarke!" Mason's voice boomed again.

Roy's head, still a foot off the ground, tilted up to hers. "I think we're done, Major."

Clarke eyed him, his rebellion burning her face red. But as if flicking some sadistic switch, a thin smile suddenly split her lips. She pulled him up a foot or so further and spoke so only the two of them could hear. "Sure we are, Roy... Except you have no idea just how fucking not done you are. See, this whole fucking thing, this Tear, it was just a warm-up for you... your real work only starts on the next one." She almost laughed. "And if you think I can be cruel here... just you fucking wait." Pulling a piece of paper from her back pocket she jammed it into the open collar of his shirt. "Have a look for yourself."

And with that she dropped him, flat on his back into the mud.

"Goddammit!" Mason had noticed the body of Jersey slumped on the floor. "What the fuck is going on here, Clarke?"

"Forget him." She was already off, towards the clearings edge. "Get me a search party. David is here."

"David?" Mason did a double take.

"That's what I said."

"Lane, it doesn't matter anymore." Mason had made his way over to Roy. He held out a hand for him as he spoke. "We got bigger problems, isn't that right Dr Zhu?"

All eyes turned to the doctor. "Ah..." Zhu looked up nervously from the Detachment-Array's iPad screen. "I'm afraid the Captain is right. According to this, we have less than six minutes, before the only welcome we'll have to return to... is a nuclear barbecue."

Chapter 47

Location: .... 51.4613° N, 0.1156° W
Present day name: .... Brixton, London, England
IDTF Classification: . Ridge/Tear Five
Time: .... April 25th 2017/December 21st 2014

Magnus Thorn stared down the lens of his SLR. Today, he'd hung up his track-suited tourist boots and was rolling with something a little more theatrical, something a little more appropriate for the circus he was watching.

"For Christ's sake get out of my shot, I'm working here." The foot-long zoom on his camera, he figured, was his licence to be a knob. He muscled aside a bulimic-looking Channel Five brunette and stepped up to the press paddock entrance. "A cheeseburger love, it'll change your life."

A lanyard was all that was required to pass the village idiot rent-a-guard. Busy drooling, the balding meatball offered only a, "Yeah, yeah, yeah," as he slurped at the reporter behind.

Thorn shook his head. *I put hours into this fucking get-up.*

According to his laminated headshot, today he was 'Mr Lucius 'Nat-Geo' Thorn', a proper flog rolling back from shooting snow leopards in Whereeverthefuck-istan.

Under a fedora, above a salt and pepper beard, his eyes – looking as icy as the imaginary landscape from which he had supposedly returned – glowed bright in the reflection of his dormant SLR screen.

Snap, snap, snapapapapapapapap. The motor drive of his camera blurred his shots into one stop motion film. *Fuck me. It is a circus, a fucking well-oiled circus.* He panned from the Tesco sign to a series of white inflatable tents, and then onto the crest of larger dome-shaped structure behind. Thorn lowered the camera just far enough for his eyes to take in the big top for real. The glow was subtle enough; the way it spilled down from the tent's peak reminded him of the first rays of dawn hitting a snowcapped mountain summit. *Except in this case the light is inside.*

"As you can see John..." The skinny Channel Five bitch next to him was in the middle of a live cross. She was nodding incessantly into a lens. "The place has been sealed tight, John. We have no word as yet what lies inside, John."

Thorn couldn't help a smile, *John, you wouldn't believe her if she did.*

Two nights ago, the Tear had garnered attention almost immediately. With the fucking New Years Eve light show the thing had given off, its exposure was inescapable. Slinking into the shadows Thorn could only watch on as, like flies to a luminescent shit, the thing had attracted local vagrants first, police second and news crews third.

As much as it seemed everyone – even the homeless – were amateur photographers, the ruthlessness of the Tesco lockdown had been crazy effective. Borderline too effective. Aside from some questionably *Cloverfield* cine-matography, somehow, come dawn, not a single clear image of the Tear had made its way onto a major network.

While the media blackout had been impressive, for Thorn it was in the subsequent speed with which the plastic metropolis materialised that his suspicions were rallied. As he had watched the tent city sprout from the Earth, an idea within him had cultivated with it. With each passing hour, new piece of scientific kit and extra American military attaché arrival, his suspicion had solidified to sentiment...

These people, they have done this before.

Inside his jacket pocket Thorn felt the weight of his ever-present TSL tug at his chest, begging for him to draw a correlation.

Of course they fucking had, THREE times and counting.

He pulled the stainless steel block from his pocket and flipped the TSL over in his hand. Fuck, he was sick of the thing.

"What's that?" The Channel Five Victoria Beckham lookalike was next to him again. She was making a habit of interrupting his introspection.

"A block of calories..." his words rolled out distracted, "...nothing you'd like."

"Hu..." The reporter's bony hand couldn't cover her mouth quick enough, but Thorn didn't hear her uptake of breath; his mind was elsewhere, zeroed in on the TSL.

Goddamn, the contradiction of the thing. What it represented to the man he had been, that sentiment, it couldn't have differed more from that that he felt today.

He paused on the device. *How could such love give way to... whatever the hell he was feeling now?*

Lost in the blur of his own reflection, Thorn's eyes glazed over, years flashed by the front of his skull.

"You know I wasn't always like this." His words were soft. He tried to smile, like usual, but the reporter was gone. He was talking to no one but himself. *How many times had he said those words? How many times had he defaulted to that very phrase?*

His eyes were locked on the TSL. *You know I wasn't always like this...* It wasn't until now, when no one was around to hear the words, that their literal meaning hammered true. The words... they had never really been for anybody else.

Intently trained, but lacking all focus, he closed his eyes and let the blackness bring forth a ghost...

He would never forget the moment – in a basement CERN laboratory – that Tabatha pushed the TSL into his hands. Thirty-one years ago... but still seven from now, the day was as glorious as anyone could have chosen to have as their last.

Tee, God she was beautiful. That pink hair of hers, she owned it like no other woman could. She was thirty-two. He was thirty-four. She was lead mission physicist, the genius behind a machine. He was to be her first test subject, Earth's first ambassador.

"Take this." From the slow forming hologram of their embrace, her hazel eyes looked up into his. A solitary tear rolled from one.

"What is it?"

"Call it what you want. It's something I've been working on, a link. It's got everything on it, all my working. It could help..."

"...Help me come back?"

"Don't say that..." She pressed herself into him and they kissed. "You are coming back... you promised me."

His hug encapsulated her, but he said nothing, he didn't need to.

His memory was a crisp as ever. Looking over her shoulder, down at the light on her desk, the hologram was stamped June 21st. A world-altering day, the type you're supposed to remember where you were, it was the summer solstice... of 2024... and it was both the final day he would ever see her, and the last he would spend in his own universe.

A vibration in Thorn's hand jolted him back to reality. His head snapped side to side, shaking away the image of his younger self. That man was a scientist, an idealist, a patsy... and he was long since dead.

Thorn's eyes narrowed on the shaking TSL in his palm. A smile split his lips and a heavy breath chuckled from his throat. "You've got to be fucking kidding me..."

The timing, it could not have been more laughable. As if the Tesco Tear was not enough, Tee's TSL was choosing now to take a steaming hot dump right on top of the situation. Thorn looked up and around for the cheer, for the balloons, streamers and D-grade presenter on the end of a microphone, but he was alone.

No, this was actually happening.

The TSL buzzed away incessantly unaware – as only technology could – of the pit it was creating in his stomach. Its activation could mean only one thing... another universe of his had bitten the dust.

A lesser man would have screamed, but strangely Thorn felt a sudden calmness wash over him. As ironic as it was, while his worlds were literally collapsing, they seemed to be figuratively aligning.

It all made sense.

These people in front of him, inside their plastic Tesco fortress, *they had to be the reason the TSL had activated.* He could see it now that he allowed himself to... *They had to be the reason the TSL had activated EVERY time thus far.*

This final activation meant that four out of four of his originals were dead, that the four worlds he had created for them had all collapsed. Staring once more at the blue digitised TSL screen, Thorn wondered which sod had been the latest, which one had lasted the longest?

The Brooklyn Jew sprung to mind. He was as safe a bet as any. Even though he was first, Thorn was almost certain he also would have been the last.

So are these the people that took you down, Abner?

Thorn raised his camera to his eye, a breath swelling his chest... *these clueless cunts, they had no idea of their hypocrisy.*

Again he started to snap away, a new question surpassing all others in significance...

Show me then, how you did it?

For if he was going to return home, to his real home, he was going to have his vengeance on the way out.

Eden Roy was standing on the exact same patch of pavement as Thorn – close enough to be in his shadow if he had one – watching with his own sense of wonder an almost identical scene play out. The car park, the tents, the guards, fuck... the air, the sun, the pavement, it was all identical... except for the fact that the big Swede was nowhere to be seen.

Maybe he was losing it, but he could almost feel the wake of Thorn's wash drawing him closer, into a shadow across time, until he was standing in the very footprints of the big bastard himself.

Are you still there? Are you seeing what I'm seeing?

Eden's quarantine zone – established almost immediately after his mid-morning arrival – was more a product of his specific time, even if that time was only three years ago. Slinking into the darkness to watch, the wonder, panic and lockdown of the Tesco lot had all the trademarks of a 'terrorism terrorism' operation, rather than the 'close encounters of the third' kind, he knew it to be.

A beacon of Caucasian privilege, Eden's chinos and navy sweater had at least afforded him an easy getaway. Hustled out of the car park by a fireman yelling "get this (white) man to safety", he couldn't help but wonder if the Pakistani shopkeeper manning Farouk's discount tobacco stand was faring as well.

Don't worry Farouk, it gets better... well, kind of.

It was only now, in full sun, a day and a half later, that Eden could sense the shift from 'ISIS' to 'I... don't know' on the other side of the fence. Traffic, especially the black SUV variety, had doubled – a line of midnight-tinted Range Rovers sat in a row, nose-to-tail, like a long line of Uber black drivers – and the beat cops looked to have been replaced by the wraparound sunglasses-wearing type.

Eden bristled as the cyclone fence across from him opened, this time to let a flatbed-truck depart. On the back of the truck was the black plastic-wrapped, half-van-shaped carcass of the 'Vanpod'.

He shook his head. *Seriously... what the hell was he thinking?*

Three measly steps, *disorientated as all hell*, that was what the difference had been. The difference between him standing where he was right now, and him still being in the exclusion zone, crushed under the weight of the ton or so of molten metal van that had followed him through.

Eden made a mental note. *Did Thorn say Grenada?* He envisaged the email. *Dear Mr Thorn. You don't know me, but in regards to your new idea, feedback suggests... it's shit. Kind regards – maybe it was better if he left his name off – Future end user.*

Lost in his thoughts of passive-aggressive retribution, he stared absently at the guard holding the end of the rolling cyclone fence. The soldier glanced in his direction as he closed the gate behind the flatbed.

Shit. Snapping too, he threw his newspaper up in front of his face and shuffled on the spot, as if that was how serious newspaper readers read. *Fuck.* He may as well have cut two eyeholes out in the thing, he looked that stupid. This served him right. He knew he shouldn't have been there. Thorn had been explicit with his instructions... *Emerge and get the fuck out of Brixton.*

Lost in the blur of words at the end of his nose, he waited for a whistle, a siren, a call to arms, anything from beyond the fence. He felt his spine tingle. His body was telling him to drop everything and run, but he couldn't help himself, he had to... see.

He crumpled the paper, the top right hand corner folding down between his lips. The soldier was... *shit* ... still staring at him from behind the fence!

Releasing the saliva-soaked corner from his teeth like an awkward teen, his eyes fell down upon the spit-smudged date printed on the corner of the paper...

Sunday. December 21st 2014.

Shit! Double shit!

The bead of sweat already on his brow dropped to the side of his ear.

Three days.

The deadline, it was ever-present, poised over him like the Sword of Damocles, a constant reminder of both the frailty and power he possessed. Over the beating of his heart Thorn's voice resonated again, a voice of reason, but a source of contradiction. *Delay your action as long as possible... Allow as little deviation as possible until you absolutely need it.*

Eden pushed the advice aside. He had waited long enough. He folded the paper and used it to give a short wave to the soldier, "Keep up the good work... you guys are heroes."

His back was stiff as he powerwalked. He had three days until Christmas Eve. Three days to find a man whom he knew better than any other, but had never actually met.

Lamar Tobin... A scrotum of society, if there ever was one. Serial drink driver, serial unlicensed driver, and serial maniac behind the wheel, he was sole reason Eden was here.

Lamar Tobin... Eden had said the name so many times now he heard only a collection of letters.

But he would be all too real, all too soon.

Because Lamar Tobin... was the man who needed to die if Eden was going to start his life over from where it had been snatched from him.

"This way ma'am."

A fresh faced police officer in an oversized utility vest held apart the tent for her to duck under. He stopped, not following her through. "This is me done, as far as my clearance extends. Continue on ahead, it should be pretty obvious, your designated chaperone will meet you there."

Chaperone? It was another bizarre term to add to the lump of jumbled clues caught in the sieve of her confusion. She nodded a bewildered nod and proceeded on, unac-companied down the white plastic corridor.

She was the best in her field of study, but what that field – Applied History – had to do with a Tesco car park in the middle of Brixton had yet to be explained to her.

"A discovery... like a giant... 'split' in the atmosphere." That was all her constable had mentioned on the drive over. Apparently, among the rank and file, the real description was not as PC – something about a floating lady-part – but her constable made sure to stress that that part of what he'd heard had been third-hand.

She could hear a hive of activity ahead. Men in lab coats hustled both ways across the T-intersection at the end of her corridor, the vast majority of them heading left, in the direction of a soft golden glow. She was almost at the junction when a voice called from her right. A man in fatigues emerged from a room she didn't realise she was passing. He looked young and had a blond head of hair that had been shaved close into a Mohawk.

"Professor Susan Ashbury?" The man extended a hand.

"Yes."

"Names Sergeant Stanley Doran, I'm your designated military chaperone. But you can call me Spike, ev'body else does."

"Spike...?" She looked from him, to the end of the corridor, and back again.

"Guess you got a lot o' questions, huh?" Spike rocked up and down on his heels. "Don't answer that, course you do." His smile was all gums. "Plenty o' time for all o' them, trust me, but first I gotta start by formally welcoming you Mrs Ashbury... to a Tear to another world."

Chapter 48

Location: ....48.1351 N, 11.5820 E
Present day name: ....Perlacher Forrest, Munich, Germany
IDTF Classification: .Ridge
Date: ....April 25th 2017

Roy sat in a cloud of what he hoped was only steam. Vapour soaked his throat like he was dragging down a bathhouse cigarette. Alone on a long wooden bench he sat with his head down, shoulders stooped over his knees. His elbows had cut the circulation to his legs long ago.

For fourteen hours now Roy had sat like this, isolated in his own decontamination chamber. It was protocol apparently, a protocol that no one had thought important enough to explain before he left.

Maybe they had never expected him to return.

In his hands Roy held the piece of paper that Clarke had shoved down his shirt. He flicked the page open, again. He had done so so many times now the moisture-laden folds were beginning to break along the seams.

Roy read the single paragraph again. Clarke's words echoed through the chamber like a haunting as he did... *"You have no idea how mean I can be"*.

Tear Five Traveller – Probability 94 percent – Eden P Roy.

- **Eden P Roy.** 38 years old. Husband to one Florence E Roy – deceased. Father to one Henry P Roy – deceased. Brother to one Jacob A Roy – person of interest.
- **Jacob A Roy,** Associate History Professor. Husband to one Georgina L Roy – deceased... **Possible exploitation opportunity.**

Roy smiled. He couldn't help it. Butterflies smashed at his stomach. His head tilted up to the ceiling as cracks rippled the length of his spine. His eyes watered.

Hope was what he was feeling... unbridled, glorious, hope.

Clarke was right, sure, but her anger had got the better of her and she had played her cards early. If she believed this piece of paper was going to make him roll over, then she was sorely mistaken.

Roy folded the sheet closed. The image of one woman flooded his mind.

It was true he was not done.

There was no fucking way he would give up, not now.

Because the Fifth Tear would be his, not theirs.

He was going to use it to find Georgina...

And he was going to bring her home.

Epilogue

Location: .... 46.2044° N, 6.1432° E
Present day name: .... CERN, Geneva, Switzerland
IDTF Classification: . Ridge
Time: .... April 25th 2017

The landing pad was empty, open, barren, buffeted by wind. Staging, decon, pre-pod, post-pod... none of it was built... not yet.

Weeds owned every crack of the rain-soaked concrete. Pools of standing water, like sinkholes into hell itself, burned red with the reflection of the Tear that had just split the night sky.

Red not gold.

One after another, six pairs of boots, silhouetted black, splashed down to the ground.

The lead soldier of the group extended a hand to catch the rain. Electricity crackled from the Tear behind her. She tilted her head as the rain spattered her glove. The phenomenon of instant change, the jump from day to night, from dry to wet, it always amazed her.

Black clad, in head to toe body armour, she looked beyond this world. A line of neon split the smooth ceramic of her full-face hockey mask. Red like the Tear behind her it ran like a scar from the devil himself under her eyes.

With a hand to her chin the lead soldier pushed her mask up onto her black bob. Awash from above with the glow of her internal readout, her eyes narrowed as she stared out into the night. Those eyes were sunken, buried in blackness, but her skin was tight, pulled sharp across her razor-sharp cheekbones.

She was older, sure, but she had resisted the years, unnaturally so, as if Father Time himself was scared of her... *Cunt had every right to be.*

Her call sign was 'The Raven' – a maxim of her intelligence, of her efficiency, and of the ice that ran through her veins. Her real name though was Colonel Lane Clarke, and she was of the United States Interdimensional Task Force... 2055.

Clarke whispered to herself the name on the tip of her tongue. "Magnus... so this is where you've been hiding."

Magnus Thorn, he was her target.

The first human to travel through time, he was the last left now, jeopardising her world.

Magnus Thorn... She cocked her rifle... He needed to die if she was to save her future... the real future.

END BOOK 1

DAVID VALSORDA, 
is an Australian author local to the
inner north of Melbourne Victoria.

After attending LaTrobe University,
he worked as both an electrician and
firefighter before completing his first
novel. Somewhat slow to adopt writing
as a serious endeavour, it would be a
misspent youth – buried in books,
video games, and cinema (specifically an eye-opening
screening of *Event Horizon*) – that would foster his love
of space and space-time, and thus plant within him the
initial quandary of his first novel – What if there was a way
to travel back in time?

David lives with his wife Georgina and their newborn son
Roy, and still serves his community via the Metropolitan
Fire Brigade.

Further details and contact information can be found at:

http://davidvalsorda.com

Instagram: @DavidValsorda

www.ingramcontent.com/pod-product-compliance
Lightning Source LLC
Chambersburg PA
CBHW030354200726

48286CB00014B/1378